JB MCLAURIN

Black Echoes

First published by Sley House Publishing 2023

Copyright © 2023 by JB McLaurin

This novel is entirely a work of fiction. The names, characters and incidents portrayed in it are the work of the author's imagination. Any resemblance to actual persons, living or dead, events or localities is entirely coincidental.

First edition

ISBN: 978-1-957941-88-2

Cover art by Kristina Osborn Truborn Design

This book was professionally typeset on Reedsy.
Find out more at reedsy.com

For every person that heard a metal band and was never the same.

Acknowledgement

This book never makes it into your hands (or on your screen) if not for the awesome folks at Sley House. A special thanks to the lead editor, Jeremy Billingsley, for giving this book a chance and for being so supportive and easy to work with. Also, he's a Pearl Jam fan which makes him aces in my book. Many thanks to my editor Karen Hough, who taught me more about the craft than I can ever repay. This book is no doubt better because of her work. And it's hard not to like an editor that gives your creative advice by quoting movies like *Airplane!*.

Like Hank, I am a drummer. I started playing when I was twelve and as I write this, I am thirty-seven, so I've been playing for (you do the math). For a few weeks early on, I took lessons and hated it. My mom was kind enough to let me quit. From there on, I taught myself how to play, which was a rocky road to say the least. Somewhere in college, when I was playing in a rock band with some buddies, I had a breakthrough and really started figuring out how to be a drummer. Something I'm still trying to figure out to this day in my band Impossible Machine. But the only way I knew how to teach myself was by obsessively listening to music. That being the state of affairs, it's only right that I list the drummers who were my teachers. Without them, I wouldn't have kept playing and this story wouldn't have materialized. I know the second I see this in print I will realize I left someone out, but hey, it's worth a shot. So here we go:

Abe Cunningham (Deftones), Brann Dailor (Mastodon), Danny Carey (Tool), Tomas Haake (Meshuggah), Chad Smith (Red Hot Chili Peppers), Jon Bonham (Led Zepplin), Neil Peart (Rush), Matt Cameron (Pearl Jam, Soundgarden), Dave Grohl (if you don't know, then I can't help you), Taylor Hawkins (Foo Fighters), Vinnie Amico (Moe.), Sam Fogarino (Interpol),

i

Jimmy "The Rev" Sullivan (Avenged Sevenfold), Morgan Rose (Sevendust), Ben Koller (Converge, Mutoid Man, Killer be Killed), Vinnie Paul (Pantera), Blake Richardson (Between the Buried and Me), Alan Cassidy (The Black Dahlia Murder), Josh Eppard (Coheed and Cambria), Billy Rymer (The Dillinger Escape Plan), Clayton "Goose" Holyoak (Every Time I Die), Josean Orta (Fit for an Autopsy), Jay Weinberg (Slipknot), Art Cruz (Lamb of God), Chris Adler (Lamb of God), Mario Duplantier (Gojira), Des Kensel (High on Fire), Lars Ulrich (Metallica), Dave Lombardo (Slayer, Dead Cross, Testament), Tim Alexander (Primus), Cody Dickinson (The North Mississippi Allstars), Jimmy Chamberlin (The Smashing Pumpkins), John Tempesta (White Zombie), J.R. Conners (Cave In), Jon Theodore (The Mars Volta, Queens of the Stone Age), and Nick Yacyshyn (Sumac, Baptists).

Thanks to my mom for reading I don't know how many drafts. Also to my bandmate and best bud Daniel Kynard for reading an early draft and giving me great advice.

Despite being a knucklehead in my youth, I've been lucky in life. My wife, Katie, who is my best friend, is living proof of that. We have two wonderful kids, Jack and Bay, and their spirit and hers echoes through these pages.

Katie read a draft of a novel I have long since shelved. She was not a fan. To her credit, she let me down easy. Because of that experience, she was terrified to read a draft of *Black Echoes* and refused to for quite some time, despite my begging. Eventually she surrendered. Then she came in quietly one day and told me that she was sorry she hadn't read it sooner. I'll always carry that memory with me. Love you babe and thank you.

Prologue

The First Echo

2017: The Florida Everglades

"Some murder for money. Other vile creatures murder for sexual gratification, which I find disgusting beyond measure. Me, I murder people because I see the *art* in it. It's that look they give me when they know they have reached the end. Can you imagine something more intimate? It's a connection that transcends time and space."

Talking with the polish of an academic, the man walked a slow circle around his captive.

"God saw fit to give me a soul as black as the bottom of the ocean, and each time I take a life, my soul speaks back to me, in echoes, thanking me for the offering."

The man took a breath, his face betraying no feeling. "You may be wondering, aren't I concerned about a reckoning in the afterlife? Don't I fear an eternity where there will be endless weeping and gnashing of teeth?"

He bent down and lifted the other man's chin. He wanted to make sure they were eye to eye before he spoke the last of his mission statement.

"No, because when I enter Hell, I will be home."

Part I

Hermitage, Al
1985

Chapter 1

By any measure, the plan was malformed. The drug-addled minds surrounding the table struggled with every detail. Their thoughts were like driftwood colliding in a turbulent river.

Everett Grant was the de facto leader of the group. His beard draped down like a waterfall, touching the table as he spoke. His eyes were the size of half-dollars, courtesy of the cocaine pumping through his veins. The sleepless nights—staying up to snort coke, taking more uppers to avoid the come down, being coaxed into shooting heroin by fellow addicts—were taking a toll. He had stayed high for days at a time, weeks even, because of what waited for him if he stopped using. He knew what that valley felt like: the odd feeling of homesickness, the depression, the feeling of a ghost hiding behind every corner. The drugs and the booze kept him from that dark valley. And he had no intention of getting lost there tonight. Because tonight they needed what was hidden in the back of Booth Sheridan's house.

Everyone at the table wore the same haggard look as Everett. Though they differed in the sharpness of their wit and the proportion of their addiction, there was a common thread running through everyone at the table: they were all worse for wear.

"I know he has a stack of cash piled as high as fucking Everest in the master bedroom closet. Has it plastic-wrapped to keep from spoiling. He's just beggin' for someone to come along and take it."

Thunder rumbled in the distance. They looked up, reacting to the machine-gun symphony above as rain pelted the metal roof.

Everett continued to lay out the plan, stopping to ask a question. "Kyle, were you able to steal the vests?"

Kyle worked as a custodian for the county. For years he had been assigned to the high school, but recently got moved to the Hermitage County Sheriff's Department. Despite years of committing petty crimes, Kyle had no arrests or convictions. His burgeoning interest in crime grew in league with his heroin habit. The drug he had found after alcohol had lost its shine. Kyle's task was simple: after hours, go into the room with the tactical gear and steal four bulletproof vests. The one thing Kyle needed to accomplish. As with most things in young Kyle's life, he screwed it up.

More driftwood colliding in the river.

Kyle's front teeth crested his lip as he spoke. "Well, ran into a bit of a jam on that one there, boss." As Kyle spoke, Everett did his level best to ignore the sores littering his co-conspirator's face.

"What the hell do you mean?"

"Well, I went in, and it made me a little jittery when I went back there. Damn near had a heart attack when you had me steal that heroin out of the evidence locker the other week."

"And..."

"When I got back there and started poking around, I found the vests. But when I reached up to get them, I knocked a bunch of semi-auto clips off the shelves. Made a helluva racket and I had to get outta there fast."

"I hope you're going to get to the fucking point soon."

"I was only able to get two vests."

"One thing. I asked you to do one fucking thing."

"*I know. I know.* I'm sorry boss."

"Well, you're going to prove it to me."

"Huh?"

"What, you think *I'm* going in without a vest?"

Kyle's shoulders sank.

#

As the storm continued, they started to load the gear in the truck, reserving the heavy lifting for John Hampton. Every group needed a man of few words:

such was John's role in Everett's crew. He was a hulking man with the beard of a Viking. Though he was in his early thirties, the top of his skull had surrendered most of its naturally thin hair. But even with the light shining off his pate, he cut a formidable figure— his eyes screamed this man is not to be fucked with.

After the gear was loaded up, John resumed his seat at the table.

"Alright, listen up." As Everett said this, Kyle stubbed out his cigarette on the table and threw it in the ashtray. Everett shook his head in disgust. *Dumbass. Why not just use the ashtray?*

John cracked open a new tallboy and perked up.

Leslie had just returned from the bathroom. She might be out of heroin, but a little bump of cocaine had just righted the ship. Like Kyle's face, her arms bore the picked-at sores and scars of an addict.

"I'm going in first and Leslie will be right behind me. Then Kyle and John, you bring up the rear and stay at the door. They won't challenge John. And make sure nobody gets out the front. Y'all don't worry about the back. It's hemmed in by a rock wall. Have to go out through the front or jump out a window." He took a quick swig of beer. "So John, you just make sure no one in the house leaves out the front. Don't want them runnin' off and gettin' more of Booth's goons. Got it?"

John gave a solemn nod of approval.

Leslie chimed in, still hazy despite the jolt of the cocaine. "What about a search warrant? Wouldn't they have a search warrant with them?"

"Leslie, we dropped the cop idea. We are just going to keep our heads down and rob the joint. In and out." He rubbed her shoulder as he said the last few words. Where he felt contempt for Kyle, he felt sympathy for her. He didn't begrudge her for her shortcomings. Leslie was kind. And in his time on Earth, he hadn't known many kind people.

Everett lit a cigarette and tensely ran his right hand down his long brown hair.

As the smoke billowed out, Kyle broke Everett's line of thought. "So, who's going to be the one that goes into Booth's room and gets the cash? I'm up for it, if that's good with you?"

"No, it is most certainly not fucking good with me, Kyle. You think I'd trust your dumb ass with that? Your job is to help John herd everyone into the den and keep them there on the couch. That's it. Don't touch anything. Don't say anything. Got it?"

Kyle nodded as he scratched the pockmarked fields of sores and blisters that lined both of his arms. The scabs blended with the ink covering his arms; his tattoos looked like they were cracking and seeping.

Leslie waded back in. "How much you think he's got back there, Ev?"

"Booth has been moving a monumental amount of cocaine over the last month. I'd say he's got at least 100K back there, maybe more. Well worth it. Don't y'all agree?"

They all shrugged, then took a gulp from their beer cans and a drag from their cigarettes.

"Whatever the take, we split it four ways. Then, and this is the most important part, we go back to the normal shit people expect of us. Kyle, you show up for work, and I don't give a shit how strung out you are, you get your ass down there. Leslie, you make your shift at the Hermitage Diner. And John and I will make our shift at the kitchen." Despite his addiction, Everett held it together enough to be a line cook at a restaurant about an hour away close to Birmingham. John worked at the same restaurant as a grill cook.

"No one leaves for at least a month. After that, you can do whatever you want with your take. But if I catch wind that any of you are out blowing your wad around town, it will be the end of you."

With that, they snubbed out their smokes, grabbed their beers, and went out into the storm.

Chapter 2

Booth Sheridan had been the drug kingpin in Hermitage County for about five years. He was shrewd, quick-tempered, and feared by all of Hermitage's criminal underbelly. Even so, Everett was desperate to get out of the shithole that had trapped him all his life. He needed a change, and Booth was going to foot the bill. Consequences be damned.

He had spent many long nights at Booth's house, partying. Booth had an unrivaled record collection, courtesy of some hippie that frequently bought weed from him and usually paid with records instead of cash. On several occasions, Everett and Booth had thrown on record after record, gotten high, and drank every last drop of liquor in the house. One night, as heavy metal music blared, he stumbled into Booth's room on his way to the bathroom. As he did, he noticed a helter-skelter pile of clothes, thrown together as if someone was trying to hide something.

That's when Everett found his way out.

But that's not all Everett had found over at Booth's. There had been women. More than he cared to remember. And one he wasn't ever going to be able to forget, named April. She had seemed nice, sweet, different than the hard-partying, chain-smoking women he had hooked up with over there. But she had a devil in her just like everyone else that darkened Booth's door. During an alcohol and drug-fueled night, he and April had started by talking on Booth's back porch, which led to her inviting him over to her place just a few houses down. She said she would let him partake in her stash if he kept it quiet. Everett was happy to oblige. Free dope didn't come around often.

After they snorted some heroin off her kitchen counter, and then took more bourbon shots than he could remember, they ended up down on the floor, rolling around, claiming each other with abandon. His memory of the sex was spotty, just that it was short and sloppy. Three weeks later Everett got a call at his father's old auto shop, the place where they had just met to discuss the robbery. April said she had missed her period. She was pregnant.

Like the cowardly drug-addicted asshole that he was, he panicked. Hung up the phone. Swore off picking up that same phone for the foreseeable future, which eventually led to him ripping the cord out of the wall. Then he had made himself scarce around Booth's house. With his lifestyle, he was in no position to be anyone's father. And who's to say the baby was his? April frequented Booth's house. No telling how many men she had slept with over there, Booth included. Best to avoid it. Act like it didn't exist. A ghost from a night that would soon fade in his memory.

Except it hadn't. He thought of April every day. And by happenstance, one night as he was pressed against the bar at The Last Stop, one of Hermitage's few watering holes, he overheard the bartender, who somehow knew April (probably from Booth's house) responding to a patron that April had just had a kid. A boy. Which meant that if she had been telling Everett the truth, he had a son.

Since that night, however, he hadn't seen nor spoken to her. Maybe one day he would get up the nerve to call her. Or hell, maybe he could send her some money.

He pulled past Booth's place and kept going. Everett was currently regretting his choice to get the four-door model: all of them could fit inside the extended cab. Kyle wouldn't shut up about the stripper that had said he was different than her other customers. That she had said all these sweet nothings into Kyle's ear while she was separating him from his money seemed to make no difference to Kyle. Everett did his level best to tune him out and focus on the plan.

Booth's house was the last one on Mountainview Road, just before it dropped off to go downhill and meet up with Highway 17. It was a small Craftsman, with its back nestled against an outcropping of rocks. Like Everett said, you could go out the front, you could go out the side windows, but if you ran out the back, all that would greet you was a ten-foot-high wall of rocks.

From his time wandering in the woods as a boy, Everett knew an old overgrown trail that ran behind Booth's house. After they got the money, they could run out the front, sneak into the woods under the cover of night, and run back to the truck undetected, or so the plan went in his mind.

He pulled off the road under a canopy of dark trees that hid the brown truck from view. The rain had stopped.

As addiction had taken a deeper hold of Everett, he went hunting less and less, but he still kept some of the gear in the back of his truck. John hopped out with a camouflage tarp clasped in his hand. Everett and John were hunters: mostly deer and duck, and occasionally, to blow off steam, they hunted dove. John threw the tarp over the truck to hide it. They were far enough off the road and the weather had been horrible. Small chance a hiker would happen upon the truck.

They were all out of the truck now, congregated at the front, ready to go over the details one last time. With Kyle in tow, there was no harm in running through it again. Owing to Kyle's incompetence, instead of the black bulletproof vests that Everett and Leslie had on, John and Kyle wore plain black t-shirts.

As Everett was rolling the plan out again, he looked to Kyle and exploded, "What the fuck? Where is your long-sleeved shirt?"

"Huh?"

"Your long-sleeved shirt, where is it?"

"Shit. I guess I left it back yonder at the warehouse."

"You idiot. Booth knows you, man. You have to cover up."

Everett ran back over to the truck and rummaged through it. He knew that there was no risk Booth or Barry would recognize John or Leslie. Neither of them had ever been over there. But he and Kyle had to be cautious—wear masks, alter their voices, say as little as possible. Luckily, he found an old flannel shirt wadded up under the seat. He went back over and handed it to Kyle.

"Alright, numbnuts, whatever you do, don't take it off. Got it?"

"Yeah, man. Right as fucking rain. Let's do this thing."

They pulled down their masks and became a rolling cluster of shadows as they climbed the hill to Booth's house.

Chapter 3

Everett took a breath, then kicked in the door.

"Everyone get on the fucking ground. Right now!"

The walls of the den were orange and tan, like mesas in the deserts of Arizona, and despite all the debauchery that took place in the house, it was well kept. Everett saw Booth and a young, skinny blonde on a couch perpendicular to the fireplace, facing the door. Everett thought he recognized the blonde but couldn't quite place her.

"Hands in the fucking air. Right now."

Booth and the attractive woman complied. She had one of those short pixie cuts and was wearing a bathing suit as a bra under a white tank top and short-shorts.

"Is there anyone else here?"

"Fuck you," Booth said. Booth had John's height and high shoulders. But where John was meaty, Booth was trim.

The blonde girl spoke: "Barry is back in the—"

Before she could finish, Booth slapped her across the face, causing blood to spill from her mouth.

Wasting no time, Everett lunged at Booth and brought the butt-end of his gun down on his face. Hard. Booth's large nose cracked open, spewing blood that tattooed his chin red. The blow would have knocked out most men. Not Booth. He never showed the slightest hint of pain. Quickly recovering, he cupped his nose and said, "I won't soon forget that."

Everett didn't question his sincerity. Booth's temper was legendary. "Keep your ass on the couch and stay still while we handle our business." As he spoke, Everett concealed his voice in a gravelly caricature.

Reluctantly, Booth complied.

The girl sat next to him, hugging her chin, a look of terror on her face. Again, Everett had that feeling that he knew her. Maybe that he knew the face. But the hair—something was off about the hair.

Everett signaled to Leslie to fan out to the other rooms. As planned, John stayed hunkered down by the door. Kyle walked around the couch and perched on the fraying rug in front of the fireplace. As Everett moved into the kitchen, Booth stared at him with a look of barely-restrained wrath.

While Leslie was gone, Kyle stole a moment to ogle the blonde on the couch. Her bathing suit did little to disguise the outline of her nipples, and her shorts did even less to hide the soft flesh of her inner thighs. The more he surveyed her body, the more he felt his blood redistribute to his dick. Suddenly, being the one that had to stay in the den with big John didn't seem so bad. Within moments, Leslie returned with Barry in tow, her gun nestled against the scruff of his neck. He had been in the bathroom on the toilet, lost in a magazine, when she burst in.

Like Booth, his face was contorted in anger, not surrender. These guys were thinking of any and every way to turn the tide. *That's why we need to get the cash and get out fast*, Everett thought.

Leslie sat Barry down on the recliner cattycorner to the fireplace and crossed the room to Everett. She whispered, "Alright, let's go get it."

They went into the master bedroom, only a few feet from the den. After cutting through the plastic wrap, they got to work and started loading the duffel bags. That is when the house built on sand began to slide into the sea. While Everett and Leslie were gone, Booth saw an opportunity.

"Hey, big fella, how much you and the twig here want, to sell those two out?"

True to form, John responded, "Shut up."

"Oh fuck off, big'un. Only thing keepin' me from putting you and your skinny boyfriend here through that door is those guns. Put them down and we'll see who's got the bigger dick."

John pointed the gun straight at Booth's chest. Booth could see John's eyes peering through the small slits in the black ski mask—they were maniacal. Booth decided to leave John alone and move to the low hanging fruit.

"What about you? What's your price? Your man must not give a shit about you. Saw he and his girlfriend had a vest. Where's yours?"

"Shut your mouth and sit still," Kyle responded.

The thin blonde followed every word of the parry, jerking her head back and forth. She looked terrified, and her cheeks had a filmy gleam from a steady flow of tears. She must have been 23 years old, but right now, she looked like a kid, scared and ready to go home.

"Come on. Name your price. Man like you has needs. What do you want? Dope? Women? Money? I take care of people that are loyal to me." Booth spoke at a low level, trying to keep it from the behemoth manning the door.

Kyle responded in a ridiculous falsetto, an ill-conceived attempt to mask his voice. "Alright. You got my attention. But first, I'm going to need you to jerk off your friend over there to completion. Barry, is it? He looks like he's probably hidin' a dragon. Hope your forearms are ready."

Booth's eyes caught fire.

Lost in the moment, Kyle started to pace in circles, forgetting to keep his gun trained on Booth. "Yes indeedy, get to strokin' and then I'm your man."

"You should watch your tongue."

Kyle pivoted, refocusing his attention on the blonde. "Ma'am. Are you okay? Surely you don't have anything to do with these two?"

"Well—"

Booth interrupted, "Don't talk to her, shithead."

"You're not callin' the shots. We are. So keep that big mouth of yours shut or I'm gonna put one in your leg."

Kyle kept pacing; his nerves were getting the better of him. Switching the gun to his left hand, he mindlessly used his right hand to roll up the sleeve on his left arm.

A band of skulls. It started at his elbow, where the Grim Reaper hurled a fireball of skulls that ended at his wrist. Booth saw the bulb of the fireball, chock-full of skulls with hollow black eyes and grins, screaming that they welcomed death.

He knew who it was.

"Hey are y'all dopeheads? Must be. Have to be strung out to be this stupid. You hear what happened to the last group of sad assholes that tried to rob me?"

"I told you. Shut the fuck up." Kyle walked over and pressed the revolver against the supple flesh of Booth's forehead. "Say one more word. Give me a reason." Booth stared back at him with a look of resolve that made goosepimples overtake Kyle's flesh.

Kyle walked back to the front of the fireplace. He stopped pacing, looked to the kitchen, and when he glanced back, he saw that Booth looked at peace. What happened to the lion trapped in a cage, thrashing around?

Booth met eyes with Barry—a look of recognition—and by then, it was too late.

Neither Kyle nor John had seen either of them nudge out small revolvers. Booth got his from under the couch cushion, and Barry's came from under the cushion of the recliner—all while Kyle was running his mouth. In seconds, Kyle would feel the full weight of not grabbing two more vests; he'd also feel the agonizing burn as three bullets pierced his chest and rib cage, one collapsing his lung and sending a deluge of blood up his throat.

"Hey Kyle. How you been man?"

"Huh. Oh sh—"

With his six-shot revolver, Booth quickly pressed out three rounds—all hitting Kyle center-mass. Kyle yelped like a dog that has just been knocked in a circle by a car, and clutched his left hand to his chest.

Barry's right arm swung and he pressed off two rounds—one hit John in the side and clipped his carotid artery, spurting blood from his neck. The next bullet caught him square in the throat. Blood shot out in a fountain.

John grabbed his throat with his left hand, a feeble attempt to staunch the unrelenting flow. His hand and sleeve were soon drenched with red. Fading, he summoned what his faculties had left to give him, raised his right arm, and fired at Barry.

Amazed, Barry felt himself in disbelief, because he couldn't find the hole that should have been in his flesh. The bullet had strayed.

The blonde—who, moments before, had her hands over her ears and was rocking back and forth like a frightened child—felt a warm sensation in her stomach. Blood blossomed across her torso.

Like a sequoia crashing to Earth, John collapsed forward, still clutching his throat. Despite the first bullet clipping his artery, his circulatory system continued to pulse, trying to pump blood to all outposts of his body. Like a flood breaking a levee, the blood rushed out on the floor in a giant lake of red.

Booth got up from the couch.

Kyle was still standing, holding his chest and praying that the bullets missed all his vital organs. The burn was more than he could bear. It felt like someone had lit a brushfire within him.

But he wasn't on fire. He was shot. And the bastard that did it was still standing. Kyle settled on his last act: he'd shoot Booth and send him to Hell where the devil waited for him. In his head, he saw himself raise the gun and catch Booth unawares, right between the eyes.

As with all endeavors Kyle undertook, it was not to be.

Right when *he* raised the gun, Booth fired again: the bullet rocketed into Kyle's chest, spinning him around and erasing his thoughts.

That left Booth, Barry, and the young woman, who was in a bad way.

The blood just kept coming, soaking her hands with a maroon sheen. To Booth, she had been a walking-talking quid pro quo—she'd needed dope and he needed sex. He turned from where she lay on the couch and signaled Barry with his eyes. He left her on the couch to bleed out, Barry in front as they walked into the small hallway that led to the bedrooms.

#

Everett kept throwing cash into the duffel bags. When they'd come into the room, he had told Leslie to stand watch and make sure that no one came back to the room.

It was taking longer than expected. The money was all in twenties and fifties, and it was hard to keep count with the adrenaline attacking his veins.

They were seconds away; they just needed Kyle and John to keep the tower of cards from collapsing for a few more seconds.

If only it were that easy.

"Dammit, Everett, hurry up. Booth looks like he's getting antsy on the couch, and Kyle won't stop running his mouth."

"I hear ya. I hear ya. But we are already in this thing knee-deep. Might as well grab everything. We're almost th—"

And just as he said this, successive loud claps rang out in the other room. There was a break, followed by more shots, and a giant something crashing to the floor.

For the moment, silence descended.

Everett could smell the blood and acrid smoke from down the hall. He thought of yelling out, but decided against it; he didn't know who had come out on the winning side of the gunfight.

Leslie looked to him. Despite the ski mask, Everett could see the panic in her eyes. Out of curiosity, or maybe shock, she stepped out in the hall.

He yelled for her not to go. Gunshots drowned out his voice.

Her body came careening back through the door, feet horizontal, her 110-pound frame propelled by the slugs that collided with her vest. As if a speeding car had just smashed into her.

He shrank back into the closet and tore his mask off. He looked at her still body, hoping the vest had worked. His answer came in a meridian of blood that trickled from her armpit. He cautiously stuck his head out of the closet, trying to see her eyes. When he did, there was no life left in them—cold greenish-blue stones, freeze-framed.

As his mind spiraled, he saw two bullets hit the wall and kick out plumes of dust; he scampered further into the closet.

He pulled the revolver from his jeans and waited.

Two sets of footsteps were coming toward the room. Then one set broke off, maybe going toward the kitchen. Panic gripped him. *What the hell should I do?*

He could shoot his way out. Six shots in the gun; he hadn't thought to bring extra ammo.

He'd have three shots to kill whoever came through the door. Then, God willing, the next one followed suit. Three shots for him too, then back to the truck and straight to Florida. *Fuck sticking around.* Things had changed.

The patter of footsteps was almost there. Then, abruptly, the footsteps stopped.

Chapter 4

verett heard sirens in the distance. A neighbor must have called the cops. It stood to reason: only so much shooting could happen before Hermitage's finest got involved.

He still didn't hear anyone coming toward the door. This was his chance.

He barreled out of the closet, through the room and out into the hall, gun at the ready.

Caught turning to yell something at Booth, Barry's neck was craned, his back to Everett. The squeak of the hardwood under Everett's feet caused Barry to turn and just as he did, he saw a flash—and then, nothing.

A single bullet caught Barry in the cheek, right through his jawbone, then ricocheted up to nestle in Barry's brain. He fell sideways; there wasn't enough room for his full frame to fall to the floor, so as he came to rest, his face and shoulder smooshed against the wall, leaving his legs splayed out at an odd angle. Years of motor control reduced to a sack of flesh, collapsed slipshod against a wall.

That left Booth.

The sirens were getting closer.

Everett knew that Booth wouldn't make the same mistake as his partner. Everett would have to leave the room. *But how?* The window in Booth's room was bolted shut, a little tidbit Everett had picked up the one of the times he got high here. He had to go out there, take care of Booth as quickly as possible, then come back in and grab the cash; and then if by some divine miracle he wasn't dead yet, he would jump out the bathroom window, escape arrest, and then avoid capture during a high-speed pursuit. *Easy.*

He crept down the hallway, knowing he only had seconds before Booth was on him.

When he looked into the den, he saw the top of John's head and the craggy puddle of blood surrounding it. He also saw Kyle, laid over the coffee table. The blonde dome of the girl from earlier crested the edge of the couch. She wasn't moving.

He crept out. No sign of Booth.

He turned his back to the front door, believing Booth to be in the kitchen. He approached the doorway to the kitchen carefully, trying to keep his breathing in check and ignore the maniacal jackhammering of his heart. All the while, he hadn't the slightest clue that Booth's eyes were trailing him with every step. And he was just as ignorant of Booth aiming his gun right at him.

Booth had hidden behind the wall near the front door, and Everett now had his back to him. Booth could see a sliver of Everett's left arm. In a second, his head would crest the edge of the wood, and then he would deliver Everett to his last stop.

Booth braced himself and moved his finger to the trigger.

Then, just before Booth could squeeze the trigger and send Everett sailing into the hereafter, someone shouted over a loudspeaker, "Police! Drop any weapons and come out of the home with your hands in the air!"

Reflexively, Booth turned at the sound of the shout.

Everett heard the creak of the hardwood floors, and without a second's thought, he spun around and fired.

The bullet flew through Booth's chest, knocking him back with the blunt force of a sledgehammer. Like Barry before him, Booth collapsed with the thud of a body that no longer had a master.

#

Where in the hell where the cops? Why hadn't they come in yet? It was a miracle they were still outside. But his luck could only last so long; the cops had to be coming in soon. Everett had failed to notice that during the chaos of the gunfight, the storm had started again. The cacophony of thunder and lightning made a gunshot hard to distinguish from the cries of Mother Nature. Everett thought he heard one of them say over the megaphone, inadvertently, "Was that a shot? Shots fired?" The voice didn't have the same assertive, don't-screw-around tone from earlier.

How can I get out? The front door was out of the question. And if he went out the bathroom window, they would see him. He had to try the back: a place cordoned in by a natural rockface. A God-made prison wall. The same fucking wall he had warned everyone about. But right now, he didn't have the luxury of good options. The back was his only chance.

He scrambled back to Booth's room and grabbed one of the duffel bags of cash. He couldn't believe he was doing it, but he threw some of the cash out to make the duffel light enough to run with. Getting the other bag out was a bridge too far.

Out of the corner of his eye he could see the blonde on the couch, squirming in mortal discomfort. Softly moving her head to meet his eyes, she beckoned him over. He was overrun with anxiety, and dithered about what to do, but she looked so helpless; he couldn't just ignore her.

Her hands were damp and sticky with blood. She writhed up and down on the couch, pushing down on the ground with her tiptoes as if frustrated. Her tiny hands clutched her stomach but were a poor barrier—the blood just kept coming. She was so petite. How could someone that small spill that much blood?

Her eyes were wide with fear. "You don't remember me, do you?"

Stunned, Everett responded, "No, I—" *It was her*, with different colored hair, but it was *her*. *April*. That night, she had had long black hair. Which made sense; her black eyebrows betrayed that she wasn't a natural blonde.

April, the mother of his child, was bleeding out in front of him.

Everett knelt next to her, his hands hovering just above her legs and stomach, as if he wanted to help, but hadn't a clue what to do.

"I remember," was all he could think to say.

She was so small and broken, bathed in her own blood. For a moment, he locked eyes with her and the naked fear he saw looking back made him weep. She had been so sweet to him that night, even gentle. And now he

20

was the reason she was bleeding out. He started replaying their encounter in his head: dancing in Booth's den, taking shots of bourbon, retiring to the bathroom to blow a few lines, and then in the wee hours, sneaking off to her place, just a couple of houses down the street, and then...

"Well, I remember pieces of it. Long night." He spoke soothingly as a priest would when giving last rites.

She began to mewl and weep, her mouth wide open in grief. "I'm sorry... I didn't know what to do. I didn't even know you. And I could have tracked you down... I know I could've. I was just so scared. I could have done more than just call. I—"

"No. You don't need to say you're sorry." *Hell, I'm the one that should be apologizing.*

"You have five minutes to make contact, or we are coming in the house." The cops again, over the loudspeaker. They both heard it, impossible not to.

He was distracted by the cop yelling over the megaphone, but she ripped him back to Earth. "You have a son, Everett."

Time was short. This was her chance to tell him the truth.

It was his baby. Of that, she was certain, she said.

At the time, the only other man she was sleeping with was Booth, and he always wore a condom. Straight to her face, he had told her: *He would never bang one of his whores without a rubber, 'cause he didn't want a dirty dick and he didn't want to pay child support.*

Everett's mind darted from her to the front of the house, a pinball bouncing off a spring and a rail.

"Is he... where is—"

"He's asleep, two houses down. He's a fat little sucker. Sleeps a good twelve hours every night." Which left her time to leave and come to Booth's to get her medicine. "He needs you. You need to go be a father now. You're all he's got."

He decided to comfort her and lie: "Wait, what? No. You're going to be—"

There was a loud pop, like a bottle rocket going off, and a dense spray coated his face. He fell back on his haunches.

Her head rolled back against the couch, a gaping hole blown in it. Everett

21

could see right through to her brain.

Fumbling the gun in his hands, he turned to shoot at Booth.

Booth was lying still against the floor, mouth open, eyes now lifeless. His final act on Earth, miserable son of a bitch that he was, had been a failure. His shot had been intended for Everett, but the bullet had missed and hit April square in the forehead. Everett wiped away the bits of her flesh and blood that hung from his face with shaking hands.

He stared at the quarter-sized hole in her head and thought: *A son. I have a son.*

Chapter 5

A *son.* The phrase swirled in his head, over and over, hypnotizing. *A son without a mother. A son who is all alone.*

He looked at April one last time. At least the blood had stopped pumping from her stomach. Now she could rest.

An officer yelled over the bullhorn that it was the last chance to surrender, they were coming into the house in sixty seconds.

Everett ran through the kitchen to the back door, then out onto the back porch, imprisoned by the rockface. The trees seemed to stare down at Everett, mocking him from atop the rocks that trapped him in.

He spun in circles. He knew he was too strung out to try to scale the rocks. Not to mention, even on his best day (in high school he started for the baseball team—some dormant athleticism abided in him) there was no way he could climb up the wet, craggy rocks.

After turning countless circles, crestfallen, he collapsed to his knees. A small awning on the back of the house prevented the rain from soaking him.

A son.

In defeat, he stared at the rockface: the heavy rain came down from the trees, ran down a slope that connected with the rocks, and then came down in several small waterfalls. He stayed on his knees watching the water cascade down the rocks. Even though the rockface enveloped the house in a half-circle, the water wasn't pooling up in the small backyard. *How?*

He saw a hole, in a low section of the rock-wall right near the ground with water flowing through it. The small waterfall made for a sight, but its natural flow was cannibalizing a portion of its right side and seemed to be allowing water to escape through a small, muddy tunnel.

It was his only chance.

He put the duffel bag on like a backpack, pulling one small strap over each shoulder. Soaked through in seconds after leaving the shelter of the small porch, he splashed over to the hole and dropped to the ground in front of the small hole. He took a breath, and drove his hand forward.

The rock here was soggy, a collection of mud and sediment. He clawed at it, pulling as much of it away as he could. When there was enough gone, he crawled through the hole like a soldier avoiding barbed wire.

He couldn't believe it: he was out. Covered in mud head to toe, but he was out! He couldn't believe it. Even better, the rock wall formed a natural barricade that separated him from the police. Wherever the cops were right now, he was pretty confident they couldn't see him.

Panting, he stood up and placed his hands on his knees. What now?

Two houses down.

#

Everett made himself into a ball against a dark nook of the house. The storm continued to give him a natural shield of sight and sound from the officers that were just down the way, raiding Booth's house. Though he had been drunk and high that night, he still remembered what April's house had looked like. Booth's house was no palace, but it was leagues beyond this one-bedroom clapboard house.

The back door was unlocked. He had already tried it, but had been too chickenshit to go in. Dithering about what to do, he stared at the knob. *What am I doing? Can I trust her? I hardly knew her.* There had been sincerity in her eyes, though. His head might be running a million miles an hour, but Everett felt, in his heart of hearts, that April had been telling him the truth.

Unbidden, something his father had told him sprang into his mind. Everett's father had been ill-suited for the task of raising his son alone, or at all, really. After Everett's mother died of leukemia, just a year after his birth, his father took up the mantle. The man cussed with abandon, drank, never met a person he couldn't insult, and had no mind for diplomacy. Every dispute — whether it be with his son or a stranger — ended with violence. Cancer had gotten him two years ago. Everett had been as high as a satellite at the funeral, but even sober, he couldn't be sure he would have felt much grief for a man that punched him if put his elbows on the dinner table. But every now and then, his old man had passed along a goddamn golden nugget. Some roughhewn piece of knowledge he had picked up along the way. *Trust your instincts, son. All a man has in this life, is his instincts.*

Every instinct told Everett that April had told him truth. And that the baby on the other side of the door was his blood.

He opened the door and went in.

#

The home was ill-kept. Booth had been one evil bastard, but, he had to admit, he kept an immaculate house. What he beheld now was at the opposite end of the spectrum. He retched at the smell of spoiled milk; it had formed a tiny white hill of curds in the sink amongst the pile of dirty dishes. An overdue bill on the counter was addressed to April Wolfe; he realized he hadn't known her surname until now.

Place was tiny. Everything was caked in dust, all except the record player in the den. There was a large box of records under the player, all clean, neatly in their cases, the only things properly nurtured and cared for in the decrepit home. He quickly flipped through them and noticed it was good stuff—everything from Fleetwood Mac to Rush. None of that phony hair metal. A picture of April with long black hair was next to the record player. She looked younger, happier. No sores or scars. Nothing like the shriveled addict with short blonde hair he had seen tonight. Might have been taken before she started using. As he looked at her image, he heard her voice: *You need to go be a father now. You're all he's got.*

Steeling himself, he walked into the bedroom, hands trembling, beads of sweat lining his arms. He saw a small lamp on the floor in the corner—there was no other furniture in the room, except the crib—and turned it on. The light was faint. Same dirt-strewn floors, same collections of bugs and dust, and in the corner, a small crib. He walked over to the weathered crib and looked down. With every step, he felt that same jackhammering in his heart he had felt back at Booth's house. This time though, it didn't last long. Because when he looked over the lip of the crib, his heart steadied for a moment, and then it sparked alive.

A chubby baby grinned back at him, kicking and clawing at the air in robotic, jerky bursts. The baby looked well-cared for. Happy and healthy despite April's lifestyle. His eyes were hypnotic, an airy, light blue, the color of the sky in spring. He soon realized the baby wasn't grinning, rather he was tensing his lips, as if he needed to suck on something.

Everett bent down to pick him up. He had never held a baby. Like all first-timers, his shoulders and arms tensed up, as if the little creature in his arms was an irreplaceable museum artifact. He looked into his son's eyes and the rest of the world ceased to matter. He could have looked at those eyes for eternity.

"Well, look at you..." He went to say the baby's name and realized he didn't know it. There hadn't been enough time to ask April. He scanned the room for traces of the baby's name. Before had come into the room, he had rifled through every drawer in the house and came up with nothing.

The baby was still tensing his lips. He was hungry. Everett went back to the drawer of the nightstand and grabbed the container of formula out of it. As best he could in the dim light, he read the instructions. He didn't want to turn more lights on and draw attention to the home. Then he found a lone bottle in the kitchen that had some crud stuck to the bottom. He rinsed it, shook it up like a Manhattan, and pressed the bottle against the baby's lips. Without even opening his eyes, the baby sucked the tip of the bottle into his mouth like a magnet.

He paced, sweating and talking to himself, trying to ignore the birth pangs of withdrawal. His body had started to ache; it wouldn't be long before it would beg him for a fix. Fortunately, No-Name, his belly full for the time being, stayed asleep in Everett's arms.

#

Using the storm and woods as cover, Everett and No-Name made it back to his truck with no one else the wiser. It had been a haul. Everett had to make the hike with bags over each arm; one filled with cash and the other with some baby clothes and April's record collection. He had grabbed that picture of her too, and stuffed it in the bag. Maybe the picture and the records would help explain things later on. No-Name would have questions, Everett thought.

He sandwiched No-Name between the dash and the seat. Before he went to turn the car on, he looked at his son.

Am I really doing this?

He could still take him to the Department of Human Resources, sign him up for a life of foster homes, followed by run-ins with the law. Or he could do what he had seen others do in the movies and drop him off outside the firehouse.

All that seemed wrong to him.

While he was lost in his thoughts, the baby woke up.

Those blue eyes drew him in again. Shimmering like the ocean's surface reflecting sunlight. Untamed and unblemished by the world. A beautiful reason to start a new life.

"You need a name." The baby cawed in agreement, jerking his hands and feet in a flurry.

As he brushed the baby's tummy to elicit a giggle, a name dropped from the ether of his mind. His muse had brought him a fine name, as good as any.

It was 1985. Everett Grant was 32. He had lived in Hermitage all his life. Growing up, he'd made mediocre grades, barely scraping by to finish high school. He had been a star second baseman in high school; the only accolade worth mentioning in a charmless life. Then, foregoing college, he stayed behind to work odd jobs, eventually becoming a line cook at a restaurant. He had no family left. No friends to speak of. Everyone he had ties to was buried in Hermitage Cemetery or would soon go to ground in the potter's field owned by the County.

Time to shed his skin.

"Alright, Hank. Here we go."

PART II

The Second Echo

2017: The Florida Everglades

"I used to think we were alone. I thought that God had cut the string and let our world fall into the abyss."

When the captive looked up, he saw the bald man's eyes were entirely black: no sclera, no pupil, no iris, just two solid black orbs. This man spoke of the abyss and when the captive looked into his eyes, he saw a world turned to black.

"It's my eyes, isn't it? Don't let them scare you. I assure you there is a soul behind the black. One still very much tied to God.

"Though I don't think we're alone anymore. I've come to believe that God is like a clockmaker that constructs but refuses to fix. She built a grand clock with iron hands and bells. Then, after making this shaky, unpredictable clock, the first of its kind, God left it to tick, tick, tick on its own. She is content to sit back and watch the clock rust and tick out of time, doing nothing if it fails to chime."

The captive struggled to grasp the point because his thoughts were lost in a narco-haze. He watched the man's hand run over the ropes of puckered flesh that covered his bald head.

"Don't you see? God is a voyeur." The man grinned. "And I'm glad *She* is still there, or *He*, or whatever sad brand of divinity watches us from the sky. Because I aim to give *It* a good show."

28

Chapter 6

Whe fucking metronome. The bile gathering to upturn every drummer's stomach. A drummer would rather drink a glass of hydrochloric acid than hear that click—always in time, always perfect. None of those nasty little human imperfections. It'll have you playing like a machine by dinner time.

There is a beat to everything in life—the mechanical flashing of a turn signal, the rhythm of the wind pushing a tree limb back and forth, the pounding of a chef beating a spoon against a skillet. A drummer harnesses it, warts and all, to create the pulse of the song. Telling a drummer the pulse is off, that they have missed the beat, is like telling a priest that God isn't real, or a chef that salt is useless. When you challenge a drummer's *sense* of the beat, it is as if you are saying fuck you to the laws of the universe. You are stomping on their heart. You would have done better to hand over that glass of hydrochloric acid.

And thus, when someone behind the smudgy studio window comes through the headphones and suggests, "Hey, do you want to play to a click?", a mushroom cloud in the desert comes to mind.

Or maybe those are just the feelings of an insecure drummer like Hank Grant.

The other members of Dead Children's Playground wanted him to play to a metronome. They had started insisting on it, in fact. In the halcyon days of the band, they had politely asked him to try it. These days, when things went awry, they demanded it. In Hank's mind, he *was* the metronome. When they told him he was speeding up, he felt as if they were challenging his very biology. *How come they don't hear it like I do? And since when did we become a progressive rock band?* Their new songs were all complex pieces, clean, perfect, unhuman. Dead Children's Playground had started out with a darker, sludgier sound, swamp water in musical form. The old songs had transitions hard for any musician to accomplish, but they still felt *human*. As time wore on, and the bandmembers became better players, they drained the swamp; the sound got cleaner and cleaner, like using bleach to rub mud from white tile.

The music still had an edge to it. The lead singer, Charlie, had a vocal range that rivaled Greg Puciato of The Dillinger Escape Plan. He had a blood-boiling scream, able to enunciate every word as he shredded his vocal cords, but on the turn of a dime he could shift to a voice that was soft and dreamlike. Charlie's voice still set them apart, but the new music felt over-sanitized. Too much bleach. Too much wiping. Worse, Hank feared, they were making forgettable music.

Hank's distaste had started to show. And his inability to play the complex pieces demanded by his bandmates started to surface as well. Charlie, ever the diplomat, tried to bridge the gap for Hank. "Look man, you'll get it. A few more takes tomorrow and it'll be in the bag." With the sure hand of a politician, Charlie slapped him on the knee as he said it.

They were in the soundboard room of Bell Witch Studios. The producer had already completed rough mixes of the first three tracks. Now, he was working on a fourth, but the two men perched on each side of him were pressuring him to scrap it and start over.

Enter Hank's Achilles heel.

They wanted to start over because they believed Hank was speeding up during the chorus and during the bridge and again during some complex section the song meandered into, and on and on.

Though he hadn't said as much to Hank, Charlie was worried. Simon and Bruce had always bitched quietly about Hank's playing, even before they started upping the difficulty of the songs. *Why* they did was lost on Charlie.

Hank was a fine drummer—competent, solid, happy to complement the band rather than try to steal center stage. Not to mention, drummers that could play the double bass as fast as Hank were hard to find. If they hit it big, he wasn't likely to join the ranks of guys like Danny Carey or Thomas Haake, but he was solid, and as far as Charlie was concerned, an irreplaceable part of the band.

Hank looked at Charlie. "God. I can only see their backs, but I can still tell they hate it. Can't even see their fucking faces and I know they hate it." He had made it through three tracks without that lifeless little click in his ears, but it was coming, as inevitable as nightfall.

"Dude, it's fine. If we have to redo the track, then so be it. We knocked the first three out ahead of schedule. I've still got to do my vocals, but the lyrics and harmonies are ready. I think I can knock it out in two days. The budget is intact. We can redo the track if we need to."

"I know, man. I just don't know how much longer I want to put up with this bullshit. They're hardly talking to me. We used to be fucking friends. Now they barely speak to me unless it's about the band. And even then, they don't want to hear anything from me. They just want to tell me *how* to play. When we started, they asked me if I'd do it a certain way. Now it's 'No, play it like this.' They're tyrants, man. I know they write the songs, but fuck."

Simon and Bruce were the songwriting core of the band. Simon on guitar and Bruce on bass. They were incredible players—their fingers moved in ways that seemed alien.

The band had been together for roughly five years; as their skill and popularity in the metal community grew, so did Simon and Bruce's egos. Neither Hank nor Charlie could dispute that Simon and Bruce were indispensable to the group. But did they have to be such dicks about it?

"Look, dude. You know they're perfectionists. If they want to redo the track, you just go back in there and lay it down again. We both know there won't be a damn bit of difference between the two. But it will make them feel better and we'll move on."

Calmed by Charlie's words, Hank let it go for the moment. "You're right, man... Well, at least, we're ahead of schedule."

31

Taking another sip of coffee, his thoughts moved to the upcoming tour over the summer; it was their biggest yet. They were going to open for Between the Buried and Me at a slate of small theater shows. And then go on their own run of small venues. The album would be released right as they went on the tour.

Simon and Bruce turned to give the post-mortem to Hank. Charlie braced himself, readying his reserves of cheer-up speeches. Hank sipped his coffee, knowing he'd soon have that ever-hateful click in his ear. The earworm for which there was no cure.

While Simon did the speaking, Bruce played the role of the nodding lieutenant. "Man, there's just no way around it. You've got to play to the click. You keep speeding up during the chorus. I hear it, Bruce hears it."

"So, what do you think, Hank?"

"Look, man, I don't think I'm speeding up. We rehearsed these a million times. I have it down pat. I mean, shit, guys, I did thirty-six takes in there of a seven-minute-long song. There's not one that you guys think is worth keeping?"

"To be perfectly honest, no. You're out of time. And once it catches, it's like a damn virus. I've let it pass on the last albums, but this one could get us signed to a better label. It's got to be perfect. So what's it gonna be, man? You in or out? Or do we need to get someone else in to do it?"

Hank looked up in shock, like someone just told him a loved one unexpectedly passed away. Before he could respond, Charlie intervened. "What the fuck, Simon? Don't threaten him. He's as much a part of this band as any of us."

This fight had been brewing ever since they got off the last tour. Simon pushing and pushing Hank to tighten up his performances. During the practices, anytime Simon perceived Hank was drifting out of time, he stopped the song and chastised him, Bruce nodding along like a droid. And the pencil-whipping continued until Charlie came to Hank's rescue. But Simon cowed every time Charlie took up for Hank. Had to; many people aspired to sing, and then there were those that could actually do it. And even in that select group, being able to hit the notes wasn't always enough. There had to be something, the x-factor, that climbed into the listener's brain and made a permanent home. Charlie had a voice that never left your mind once you heard it.

"You're right. Sorry Hank, but I still think you need to give the click a try."

Hank responded with a solemn nod, like a mourning relative nodding to the salesperson at the funeral home. *That coffin will do.* And then he got up and headed back into the studio.

He looked at his drum-set as he walked back in. It was a Tama *Rockstar* with a green finish. He stole a quick glance at his Chinese cymbal, his favorite. It emitted a sound like a stick hitting the top of an aluminum trashcan. After gazing adoringly at his darling, he sat down behind it and put his headphones on.

He waited for the producer's voice to come through and cue him; instead, Simon came over the headphones. "The click is ready to go. And if this one goes well, since we're ahead of schedule, Bruce and I think you should redo the other three tracks too."

Hank showed no reaction. This had become the price of being in the band he loved, or he thought he still loved. Was he staying out of habit? Out of routine? He didn't know anymore. In the end, the only thing he knew for certain was that he loved music. And she was a cruel mistress.

He refused to look up, lest he see Simon's exacting stare. He looked down at his cutoff camouflage shorts and his black and white checkered Vans, waiting for his robotic enemy to start repeating in his ear.

And then like a plague, it came: click... click... click.

Always perfect. Always in time. Always everything Hank could not be.

Chapter 7

Hank tried not to wake Lisa. Their apartment was a shoebox. One bedroom. One bath. There were no blinds on the windows; Hank loved the way the sunlight washed through in the morning. They lived in Del Ray Beach, on the third floor of a small apartment building, a quarter mile from the Atlantic. If he craned his neck just so in the morning, he could catch a glimpse of the sun glinting of the water, like the ocean was made of gold.

As he moved about, trying to muffle the clatter and clank of retrieving his favorite coffee mug from the cabinet, he heard Lisa stir. He saw her come around the corner, rubbing her eyes.

She was tall, with fair skin and onyx hair cut into layers, short near her face, then draping down to touch her shoulders. She had on a tattered Lamb of God t-shirt she'd filched from Hank—she always seemed to take his favorite ones. But he had no qualms with how she wore them: t-shirt and panties, nothing else. He watched her long, muscular legs as she walked to the bar and sat. He marveled at her, a beguiling mix of beauty and brutality. On first approach, she appeared graceful: green eyes and fair skin, an elegant dark-haired woman that was likely well-read, but Lisa had no interest in grace and propriety. Pretty enough to be envied by the girls. Hard enough to hang with the boys. That was Lisa.

"Sorry I woke you up, babe."

She didn't respond. She waved him off and pointed to the French press.

"It needs to steep for a couple more minutes."

She gave him the finger. Then she rested her head on the bar as Hank moved about the kitchen. She didn't move.

At the splash of coffee into her cup, her head perked up. "There. Now I'm ready. What time do you have to meet your dad?"

"In thirty minutes."

"You better get going."

"Yeah. Yeah."

"Seriously. You riding your little cycle?"

"Have to. Only way I can keep my legs healthy enough to play these insane parts Simon and Bruce keep writing. I think they're trying to kill me."

She had a way of cutting through the bullshit and ferreting out exactly what Hank wanted to talk about. "You still worried they're trying to kick you out?"

"No, I mean, I don't know. What made you ask?"

"Oh Hank, come on. I'm inside there." She pointed at his head.

"If it wasn't for Charlie, they already would have."

"Don't let the bastards get you down, babe. You're a great drummer. They need you. Whether they realize it or not. And fuck them if they don't."

"I think they're serious this time. Simon kind of threatened me last night."

"Really?"

"Yeah."

"He's such a douchebag."

Unlike Hank's bandmates, Lisa was in the professional world. She had finished college with a degree in accounting. The first time she told him she was an accountant, Hank had accused her of being a liar. Mostly because she told him right after a barrage of dick jokes. She worked for a construction company. Her time as an accountant did nothing for her decorum: she had the mouth of sailor and the demeanor of a metal-head. Outside of work, that is. At work, she hid the colorful parts of her personality. But her love of Hank's music was no put-on. Three years prior, they had met at a Deftones show in Miami through mutual friends.

"He wasn't always like this."

"Fuck him and his squinty eyes and beaky nose. He thinks he's the next

Adam Jones. He's not. Y'all are great. But keep it in perspective, for fuck's sake."

"It's like I told Charlie last night. I'm just not sure about this new music."

"Why not? Not enough drum-fills to perk up that sad little wiener of yours?" She grinned as she said it. Even her insults were sexy.

"No, it's not that. The stuff is so complex. It just feels forced."

"Well, I'll be the judge of that. When do I get to hear it?"

"In a couple of weeks, maybe. Simon and Bruce have the next few days to put down their parts. And then Charlie is knocking out vocals over the weekend. We rehearsed everything into the ground to save money on studio time. We should come out ahead."

She took a sip of the rich coffee. "What are y'all going to use the extra for?" The question had an air of hope. But she knew what he'd say.

"The tour. New gear. Whatever."

"Well, I plan to see you and your little tattooed group of wannabes as many times as I can. My shithead boss said I could keep working from home. He knows no one else would put up with his shit, so he gave me what I wanted. I hate that motherfucker. But, God, he pays me well." Even Hank, a tattooed, pierced, swashbuckling member of a metal band, still winced at her cussing. *Did she have to do it in the morning?* Something about the word *motherfucker* in the morning seemed wrong, unholy.

"Why do you keep putting up with that guy?"

In response, she gave a surveying look around the apartment. And he understood. "Everybody has bills to pay. And he lets me come and go as I please."

Hank tidied up the counter, then moved toward his backpack. As he did, Lisa was chewing her bottom lip, staring down into the coal-black coffee in her cup. Hank didn't see it. His mind was elsewhere, as it so often was.

"Hey babe, Danny called a couple of days ago..." Hank nodded along—nothing unusual about Danny calling. He called his older sister all the time. Lisa was Danny's guiding light. But they had plenty of time to talk about him later. Discussing Danny at night over a few beers had become one of their rituals. So why, as he was trying to get out the door?— "...and he asked about coming to live with us. He told me the doctor said he is ready. I think—"

Hank looked around at their tiny apartment. "How would all three of us live in here?"

"Well, that brings me to my next point...."—she spoke delicately; for the moment, the sailor that lacked a filter had left the room, and she spoke the way she did at work—"We would need to get a new place. I've been saving up, and I have enough for a down payment on a townhouse."

"You've been saving?"

"Yeah."

"Why didn't you tell me about it?"

"What? I don't have to report to you. It's my money. It's not like we're married. You've made sure of that."

Ouch. Stumbling like a gut-punched boxer, Hank mumbled, "Baby."

"Save your fucking *baby*." She bit her lip and took a breath. She wanted him on board here, and it called for a little diplomacy. "Sorry, I don't want to get into that right now. But, *really*, what do you think? I think Danny would be happy with us. And it would give me someone to spend time with when you're on the road. Not to mention, he gets a disability check. So we'd have some help with the money from good ol' fat, misogynistic Uncle Sam. What do you think?"

Hank liked Danny. And best of all, Danny loved listening to Dead Children's Playground. But living with them? *Would having Danny here be like having a child?*

In the end, he knew what he had to say.

"I think that he's your brother and if he needs to be with you, then I'm in. And if that means we have to move, then that's fine too." She gave a silent thank you by blinking and pursing her lips; the threat of a storm had passed for now.

"I've already found a place for us with two bedrooms. I paid first and last month and paid the penalty for us leaving our lease early." She said all of this over her shoulder, coffee cup in hand as she walked to the bedroom. "We move next Friday. I already paid the movers."

He yelled out, "What if I had said no?"

She closed the door and got back in bed to read.

Chapter 8

Hank straddled his bike, then reached into his pocket for the photo of his mother. He rubbed his thumb over it to help staunch his anxiety—about Danny, about the band, about marriage, about everything. He had made hundreds of copies over the years. The original was stowed under his bed in a locked box, and only he knew the combination. He allowed no one else to see it or touch it, as if contact by another human would rid it of its mystical power.

He knew little about her, other than what Everett had told him. Her parents were German immigrants that had come to Huntsville. Her father had worked on the Saturn 5 missile with a German scientist named Warner Von Braun, and that is how they ended up in Alabama. She'd left Huntsville after high school and her parents died soon after—killed in a car accident by a drunk driver.

Everett had given the photo to him when he was eight years old. It was the only tangible link he had to his mother, connecting them between the worlds of the living and the dead. He believed that losing it would be like having her die all over again. Over the years, he had invented an entire lifetime of conversations, laughs, and fights from that one image. At times, looking at it was the only thing that made him feel better.

He pulled it out of his pocket now to look at it. This copy was torn and crumpled from having spent the last few weeks in Hank's pocket. He'd have to trade it out soon.

Studying her, he rubbed the photo: her hair was jet black just like his.

Her eyes the same ocean blue, skin milk-white, just like Hank's. Hank still didn't know where he got his height—she was even shorter than Everett. He thought often about how nice it would have been to bend down and let his mom kiss him on the cheek.

From the corner of his eye, he saw the time on his watch, breaking him from his trance. He had to be at his dad's restaurant in twenty minutes.

He crumpled up his mom and put her in his pocket. Then he pedaled as fast as he could.

Chapter 9

From the front parking lot, Hank saw the smoke billowing out like plumes from a factory. He went through the door, grabbed his apron off the wall, and then walked out to the smokehouse. The yard behind The Hickory stretched out in a half-acre of lush green grass. At the back of the property, cinderblock pits, which were nothing more than squat rectangles with expanded metal as a grate for the meat, were hidden away in small brick buildings. When the place first opened, the pits rested under A-frame roofs made of corrugated metal. Meaning Everett had to scramble out in bad weather and hang up tarps to protect the meat already on the smoker. As time passed and money rolled in, he had brick walls put up around the pits and new roofs installed. Now, each pit looked like a tiny brick house. Behind the smokehouses, a thick line of trees closed the backyard in, forming a natural fence. Hank could see Everett inside Pit Two, tossing hickory logs on the fire. For reasons beyond comprehension, this one gave the butts a taste that surpassed the other two pits—same design, same length of time in use, same cooking method, yet the barbeque that came off 'The Deuce,' as the employees called it, was unmatched.

"Hey Dad."

"Hey bud." Everett stood up and dusted himself off. He gave Hank a bearhug around his chest, a funny sight because Hank towered over Everett. And then there was the contrast in dress: Everett in his favorite trucker hat, cargo shorts, and running shoes, Hank with a kaleidoscopic sleeve of tattoos on his right arm and left leg, his obligatory metal shirt, and checkered Vans.

"Alright, man. You ready to get to it?" Everett said.

"Yeah. Which one you want me on?"

"Get over there on Pit Three and check the butts. We're on hour twelve over there. I've got it timed just right to hit eighteen hours before we open. Give us enough time to help Alice and Maria pull it. Seems like more air is getting in over at that side of the house, keeps causing flareups. Don't want to lose any meat."

"I would never let such a thing happen." Hank, jokingly, looked to an invisible audience and gave a hammy speech: "As your leader, I will give nothing back to the community, but I will always make sure your meat doesn't burn."

"Alright, alright, just get over to the pit. And hopefully you do this better than you play drums." Everett socked him in the arm and grinned.

"You an AARP member yet? Also, I hear they give people your age free coffee at the McDonald's. There's movie discounts too."

Grinning ear to ear, Everett kicked some gravel at his son.

#

Everett's escape south with Hank had ended in Belle Glade, Florida. He'd found work there as a cook. It was a simple life: no thrills, no bullshit. But there was always an undercurrent of anxiety and a deluge of panic every time a cop car passed by. He went to meetings when he could. Hank had made that part hard. Can't really plop the baby in a papoose and roll into a meeting. Everett preferred the AA meetings at the old Methodist church in town to the NA meetings. The crowd wasn't as rough. And after all, he was an alcoholic and a drug addict. *One was as good as the other*, he thought, and so he attended whenever he could, a habit that abided to this day.

The specter of law enforcement finally bringing him to account for the gruesome scene at Booth's house, plagued him in the early years. At night, the anxiety of being on the run would overwhelm him and he'd wake up drenched in sweat. All he could think about was how bad he wanted a drink. One drop to ease the pain. In those moments, while baby Hank dozed in their small apartment, he paced the meager square footage until dawn.

For the most part, over the years, Everett held fast. No booze. No drugs.

The only relapse to report had happened when Hank was a teenager. Hank wasn't even aware of it; it had happened when he was away at camp. Other than that misstep—which ended in a ferocious hangover, a flood of tears, and a generous helping of self-pity—with Hank as his anchor, Everett had toed the line.

And the day of reckoning had never come.

#

Hank watched his Dad walk into the restaurant, and he couldn't help but notice the slouch in his back. Everett was slight of build but thick-shouldered, and stout through the chest. He was not frail, or at least, he had never appeared frail to Hank—until now. This hunched man in his sixties, wearing horn-rimmed glasses attached to strings as if he were a librarian or a museum curator giving a tour, was a far cry from the addict plotting a robbery.

They continued to go back and forth until each butt, rack of ribs, sausage, and brisket made it onto the massive cutting table in the kitchen. Three Latina women had their heads down, focused intently on their work—chopping, dicing, pulling.

Maria smiled at Hank and told him good morning. In his early twenties, Hank had had a crush on her. And she, when her husband Hector wasn't working a shift in the kitchen, had flirted with Hank right back. All it ever amounted to was a little harmless banter, though she still winked at him every now and then.

Waiting for Everett to return with the last of the haul, Hank now found himself unable to look away from Hector over at the dishwasher. By any standard, Hector was a handsome man: sharp-lined jaw, stern forehead, large brown eyes that commanded attention, but his arresting visage was withering. Being replaced by dark crescents under his eyes and sunken cheeks. From his time touring, Hank knew a drug problem when he saw it.

Hector abruptly stopped his work and went to his pocket, the same pocket he had nervously tapped umpteen times while Hank watched. Hank used the door jamb to shield himself from view. Hector pulled out a wad of cash, much more than he could ever squeeze into a wallet. *Certainly didn't pull down that much washing dishes.* And from Hank's view, they all looked like twenties. *What was Hector into?*

Hank wondered if Maria had caught on yet. Wives always knew such things, according to Lisa. Whether they wanted to admit it to themselves was another question.

Everett gave Hank a rap on the shoulder: "Well, phase one complete. Take five and hang back here for a minute. I'm going to go see how Alice is doing with prepping the sides."

Hank hadn't seen Alice yet this morning, which was odd. She was usually back here helping Maria with the prep. A few minutes later, as he sucked back some water—the fourth beer last night with Charlie had been ill-advised—he saw Alice's portly frame, tilting on her worn legs, come through the swinging kitchen door.

At seventy-three years old, she walked with a limp, but she still kept pace with the young employees she managed. The only evidence that her aging limbs bothered her was a slight wince every now and then; like all hardworking women, she never complained. Her hair had thinned so that you could see patches of her brown scalp. She didn't seem to mind; in fact, nothing seemed to frazzle Alice. Without her, The Hickory never would have been a success. Everett had started barbequing in his backyard out in Belle Glade as a way to soak up his free time and keep him from drinking and drugging. He soon found that it was more than a hobby: losing himself in the slow craft of smoking meat helped him reckon with the man he had been and the one he wanted to become. The long hours, smelling the smoke, watching the temperature like a hawk, helped him mend. Soon his neighbors, drawn by the savory aroma of the hickory, started to ask him for samples. Before he knew it, he was selling more than he could make on his own. He hung some signs up downtown and Alice knocked on his door soon after; none of their lives had been the same since. Alice may not have been blood, but she was family. And over the years, her role grew until she became a full-fledged partner, not just a manager. The least Everett could offer, after so many years of unflinching reliability.

When she reached Hank, she wrapped him in a tender hug. She could be terrifying when commanding her troops during the shift, but the moment she turned away from work, she was a mother to all in proximity.

"Hola mi'jo. Como estás."

"Bien."

"Y Tu' novia?"

"Ella es bien." And with that, Hank exhausted his Spanish. Alice always kindly transitioned to English to put him out of his misery.

"How's Dad been doing?"

"Moving slower lately, but he won't admit it. Stubborn as a mule, your father." Hank laughed. "But he is getting on. And business has never been better. We are standing room only most days. That damn line starts at 10:30 and goes to the end of the parking lot every day. *Every day.* We need all the help we can get. People are nuts for all that Asian stuff your father uses." For the rub, Everett used Chinese Five Spice Powder as his secret ingredient. There were traditional southern spices in the rub, but the Five Spice powder gave the ribs a rich licorice taste that was new to customers.

"Well, I wish I could help more. But we're hitting the road soon. Have to promote the new album. You ever going to come see us again?"

"Mi'jo, I love you. And that's the only reason I came last time. But all that screaming and pushing makes no sense to me. I'll leave the headbanging to you. I'm good here." Then came the question he always got from Alice. "And when are you two getting married?"

"Well, I think I have to ask her first, don't I?"

"She is crazy for you. Stop screwing around and get it done, or you'll find yourself eating a lot of meals alone. Just ask your papa; he had his chance." For years, Everett dated a plain-looking woman named Diana; she wore no makeup and put on no airs. Calm in all things, equipped with iron grit, she was perfect for Everett. After five years of dating and three of living together, she asked for one thing—marriage—and Everett balked. And that was the end of it. Hank hadn't seen her since.

"Even if she does love you, pretty girls like her don't wait around forever."

"I hear you." He held his hands up, signaling *I surrender.*

Saving him from more time-to-grow-up questions, Everett came barreling through the door. "Alright, beans and potato salad are good, where we at with the meat?"

Alice yelled out some Spanish at the speed of light. "The ladies say five more minutes."

A black sheen on Hank's leg caught Everett's eye. "Damn, son. Is that another tattoo? God bless, how many is that? Do you even know?" The image crept up Hank's leg in waves of shadows and smoke, revealing a woman, whose black eyes wept. She stared out at the world, sad and lost.

"Yes. And this one was actually inspired by the stories Alice told me when I was a teenager. La Llorona, The Weeping Woman." Dark story to tell a kid, but Hank remembered every word. It was about a lady who threw her kids into the lake trying to get a rise out of their father. When she realized it was a great mistake, she jumped in to save them, but it was too late. And from then on, she haunted all of the children in Mexico. "God, it freaked me out when I was a kid. But the images of the ghost I found online were beautiful. Just like Alice."

"Ohhhh mi'jo, give me a hug."

"Alright. Alright. I get it, an ode to Alice. I suppose there are worse reasons to get a tattoo."

Alice walked over to help with the prep.

Everett leaned in to talk to Hank. "Hey bud, you got a minute after work to talk?"

Hank looked back at him nonplussed. "Sure. What about?"

"Not the time right now. But we need to talk."

#

"Alice has cancer, bud."

Instantly, Hank felt hollowed out. Bereft of his biology. His hand went searching for his talisman. Anxiety mounting, he rubbed the photo.

"How bad?"

"Bad."

"But she still has her hair. People with cancer are usually missing their hair or wearing a scarf or something."

"She is a proud woman, son. She refused the treatment. She said God

46

would let her know when it was her time to go."

"But people live longer now. She should fight."

"She's tired, bud. Alice has had a rough life. She's seen things you can't even imagine. She told me she is ready to go home."

A devout Catholic, Alice always left things to God. And managed to love God even though the Almighty had taken her husband and son when she was a young woman.

She often told Hank and Everett that when she died, her husband and her son would be waiting for her. She and her husband would be young again too. The table would already be set, an overflowing bounty covering every inch, and then they would eat together and talk, for eternity.

"How much time?"

"Doc said if she would do the treatment, it might buy her a year, maybe two."

"And without it?"

"Three months, maybe six."

After using his shirt to wipe away the tears, Hank spoke again, "Does she talk about it? Has she made arrangements, you know, for her things?"

"She has a will. I was a witness for it five or six years ago. But I can't remember the terms. Doesn't matter right now."

"Does she have any family left?" He continued to nervously rub the photo of his mother, hoping its power would erase the pain.

"You're looking at it. Us, and the people in that kitchen." He pointed to the restaurant. The Hickory itself was a small structure just off the highway, with a gravel parking lot in front and a screened-in-porch on the back that led to the kitchen. The bones of the place were made of cedar, as was the outside that Everett had painted a dull red. On approach, people saw the place and it looked like something straight out of the South, as if it was on the side of an oak-tree lined Alabama highway.

"I just can't believe this. She still works every day, right? She's still in good spirits?"

"She is. I couldn't believe it either when she told me. You know she's never missed a day sick. *Never*. And then all the sudden a few weeks ago, she

47

dropped the bomb on me."

"Should I talk to her about it or just act like nothing is wrong?"

"Don't talk to her about it. It will only upset her. Can you just work every day until you head out on tour? I know y'all can't postpone it, but can you at least do that?"

"Yeah, Dad."

Everett nodded toward the screen door. "You coming?"

"I'll be there in a second. I just need a minute."

Everett went in.

Hank took the photo of mother out and stared it. His ritual. Rubbing and rubbing, like he always did. He still held on to his boyhood dream of rubbing her back to life within the photo. But no matter how long he did it, his mom stayed still. He couldn't bring her back to life, just as he couldn't do anything to stop Alice's cancer.

Chapter 10

Three weeks had passed since Everett delivered the news about Alice. In the meantime, Hank had been working at the restaurant every day as promised, only taking breaks to go to band practice and then having to leave early, which wore on Simon to no end. The band was set to embark on tour in two weeks. And adding to Hank's schedule, already bursting at the seams, was *the move*. He took today, a Sunday, to do it. He had convinced Lisa not to hire movers after all, to save cash. They'd be sweating it out themselves in the Florida heat, one piece of furniture at a time.

Lisa and Danny arrived. As he looked at Lisa, Alice's advice swirled in his head: *Pretty girls like her don't wait around forever.* Somehow, she had covertly swiped another of his Lamb of God t-shirts. She always told him she liked taking them because they smelled like him. Though she would never admit that in public, not even at gunpoint.

Danny got out slowly. His walk, like all his movements, was sleepy. The same carried for his voice. He spoke in a constant monotone, like a sludgy pond. Hank was happy to see him wearing a Dead Children's Playground shirt. When Danny talked about DCP, Hank thought he could see the slight crack of a smile. Hank struggled to remember if he had ever seen Danny smile, *really* smile.

Hank stepped off the curb and wrapped Lisa in his arms, one covered with ink, the other as white as moonlight.

Hank moved to give Danny a hug and Danny submitted, keeping his arms limply at his sides. Danny wasn't a hugger or a handshaker. Social cues were lost on him.

"Danny, buddy. How've you been?"

"Good."

"You found any new bands lately?" Lisa, at Hank's urging, had gotten Danny a Spotify account. Gone were the days of standing at the record store, agonizing over what album to pick.

"I've been listening to High on Fire. Do you like them?" Danny stood stock-still when he spoke. No hand gestures. Not the slightest muscle movement.

"Love them. I saw them in Nashville a few years ago when we stopped there for a show. God, they were loud. I thought the reverb from the amps was going to shake my teeth out of my head. It was awesome."

Lisa rolled her eyes. "Boys. Always content to light something on fire, giggle at a fart, and think it's cool to let a rock band destroy your eardrums. Dumbasses, the lot of you." She turned to Danny. "Hey, I've got the iPad charged up and ready to go. Hank will pull one of the chairs off the moving truck and you can watch some videos while we unload."

Lisa walked back over to Hank after letting her brother in.

"He looks good, doesn't he?" Hank said.

"For a twenty-four year old that exists in a parallel universe and ages faster than the rest of us, yeah, he looks pretty good."

Hank shuffled some miscellaneous boxes to find a chair for Danny. Something occurred to him. "Hey, what is he going to do during the day while you're at work?"

"What? You don't think I already thought of that, you little cunt-burger?" Cunt-burger? Really? "And...?"

"Well, my little man-slave, I already work from home three days a week..."

"That still leaves two days."

Her demeanor changed, and she nestled up against him, assuming that cute look she always did when she was about to ask a favor. "You're right. So, I was thinking..."

"Uh huh..."

"That maybe he could be with your dad at The Hickory. Could you ask him?"

"Why don't you? He loves you." It was true. Everett wrapped her in a bear hug every time she came through the door. And then fired off a dry joke about his son being a world-class dumbass for not asking her to marry him.

"Well, I know. And he's right about one thing."

"What?"

"You're an idiot. And you know *why*. And this should come from you. It's your family's place and technically, *I'm not family yet*, so I think you should ask." And there it was again.

A grandmotherly voice creeped back into his head, "Pretty girls like her don't wait around forever, you self-obsessed dipshit."

Well, it wasn't just Alice's voice up there; Lisa's voice was in his head too.

Chapter 11

Hank looked up to see the black shadow of a man standing still in the doorway. No features, only an outline. A monotone voice broke the wave of anxiety holding him captive. "Hey Hank. Would you come listen to music with me?"

Only Danny, not an intruder.

The shot of adrenaline faded fast. His mind returned to the fugue between sleeping and waking.

Lisa slept like the dead, and short of a shot of pure adrenaline to the heart, *Pulp Fiction* style, there was no waking her.

"Sure, bud."

Hank went across the hall to Danny's small room. Earlier that day, Hank had set up Danny's record player—a must. It had two speakers, the type with wood paneling on the side.

Danny asked Hank to make a pick. After searching for a few minutes, he found the perfect album to match the moment. The right pick could never be made in haste; there was a song to match every moment in time, all the way up until this whole Earth blinks out of existence, and even beyond. There will always be the right song.

Hank placed the record on the turntable and moved the needle over. The opening sounds forced an infinitesimal smile to appear on Danny's face; or, at least, it looked that way to Hank.

"Have you ever seen Tool?" Danny asked.

"I have. Three times."

"I want to go see them. I haven't gotten to go to a lot of concerts."

"And we're going to change that. You and your sister are going to come see us in Philadelphia. We're playing at a theater there. Theaters are the best place to see a band. Big enough to have a good crowd. Small enough the sound doesn't go to shit."

"I have never seen your band."

"I know, man. That's why I told Lisa to bring you along. You'll love it."

After he flipped the record, Hank lay down on the carpet. Danny did the same. Neither spoke during the song. It was an epic, clocking in at over nine minutes.

When it came to the daily stuff of life—paying the utility bill, taking out the trash— Danny was in the dark. Same thing with social cues, still wandering in the black looking for the light switch. But no one had to explain music to him.

When the song ended, Hank looked over and saw Danny had fallen asleep.

Lisa had told Hank that Danny had trouble sleeping after the accident. Sometimes, he'd stay up for days on end, an odd form of insomnia induced by such a hard blow to his head.

Danny's chest moved up and down, like a wave rolling over the sand in the still of night. It seemed Danny only needed the right song to find rest.

Chapter 12

Watching the smoke billowing out of the smokehouse always comforted Hank. Though he had grown up in Belle Glade and Boynton Beach, The Hickory was *home*, and the smoke that poured out of its heart was the signal guiding him back. Today, he had Danny in tow, so he borrowed Lisa's car. It had been years since he'd owned a car. He left his drums at the practice space, and if they needed to be moved, the band had a van they'd bought two years ago with extra money from a European tour. He was rusty. Driving felt awkward.

Hank kept letting the car drift to the curb, lost in his drum parts from the new album (*Astral Curse* is the name they settled on, after some heated back and forth. Simon and Bruce ended up ignoring how much Hank hated the title). They were due to leave for the tour in two days. After work each day, Hank went to the practice space, and they hammered through the set list. They planned to play *Astral Curse* from beginning to end, no interruptions. The last track was an epic, as complex as it was long. Hank was tapping it out at the wheel. *I have to syncopate my feet right after—*

"Hank, the car is riding on the curb."

"Oh shit." After a honk and the finger from another motorist, Hank jerked the car back on the road. "Sorry, Danny. It's been a while since I drove."

His phone buzzed. A text from Lisa. "Well, what did your dad say?"

I'm about to find out.

#

"Hey, Dad."

Everett had left the door open to the smokehouse. He pressed against the pork butts with his fingers, going down the line, checking to see if they were done. He never used a thermometer. Everything he did, when it came to cooking, was by instinct.

Hank walked up slowly and tapped him on the shoulder.

Everett removed his befogged glasses, letting them dangle on their lanyard, and grinned ear-to-ear. The same smile every time he saw his son. "Hey bud, I didn't think you were working today."

"I know. I'm headed over to practice in a minute."

"So, what's up?"

"Well, I have a favor to ask. Well, actually, Lisa and I have a favor to ask."

"And..." Everett couldn't help but wonder if this was about money.

"You know Lisa's brother, Danny?"

"Well, I've never met him. The one that had the accident, right?"

"Yeah, him."

"And..."

"Well, I'm gone for the next six months. Lisa's boss lets her work from home three days a week, but that leaves two days where she doesn't have anyone to take care of Danny."

"And you want him to be able to come here, is that it?"

"Yeah Dad. Can he?"

"Well Hank, is he okay, you know, in the head? Do I have to keep him by me every second? I mean, is he going to pick up a knife and not know it's dangerous?"

"No, it's not like that dad. He's not—"

"Retarded?"

"No. It's something different. And you can't say that anymore."

"You can't?"

"No."

"World is getting pretty damn sensitive. The other day a customer was talking about how you can't say sitting Indian style in school anymore. You have to say something like crisscross applesauce, or some bullshit. But whatever..." Everett threw up his arms in mock surrender.

"Look, he's just forgetful. Sometimes he doesn't remember to eat, or he'll wander off to a place and have no idea how he got there. That's why Lisa had him put in the home."

"He sounds like an Alzheimer's patient."

"Sometimes he's like one."

"Well, what if he wanders off here, or he hurts himself, I'd be on the hook then. You said yourself, he can't take care of himself. And we have to work around here. Things have to get done."

"He'll be fine. Let him help with the prep and just keep an eye on him. He just wants to be included. And he won't say much. Oh, and make sure to give him lunch when he's here."

"You're speaking as if I've agreed to this."

"Dad, it would help Lisa out. Her boss is a dickhead, and he won't let her have the other two days at home."

"It is just the liability, son. If something happens, who knows what could happen to this place."

Just then, Hank saw Alice and Danny walking out of the back of the kitchen. Alice had her arm loosely draped around his shoulder. She grinned, as her and Danny walked over.

Everett looked at them with a cock-eyed stare.

"So, Everett, have you met our new friend here." Alice spoke with a chipper tone, one belying the fate that awaited her.

"I have not. Name is Everett. And you?" Everett stuck his hand out; Danny spoke, but kept his hands at his sides.

"Danny."

Everett drew his hand back.

Alice spoke, "We need more help around here. You and I both know it. This young man looks like just the person to mix the potato salad and the beans. Not to mention, he could sweep out the kitchen." Before Everett could respond, she gave him a steely look. Her deep brown eyes—wrinkled skin crowding each socket—gave him a look he had seen many times. She had made up her mind. And there was no changing it.

"Alright, young man. You're hired, two days a week. You'll work under

Alice here. Just do whatever she tells you."

"Okay." Danny also responded with a few hearty nods that, as usual, didn't match the social tenor of the moment. But that was Danny.

"Danny, why don't you head in and ask Maria to get you an apron. I'll be there in just a minute." Like everyone else at The Hickory, Danny did as Alice said.

Everett shrugged, put his glasses back on, and went back to his ritual of checking the meat.

Hank looked to Alice, who gave him a wink. "When I saw him standing still in the kitchen—and I'm talking absolutely still—I figured it was Danny. We started talking, and you know what he said?"

"That his sister wanted him to work here?"

"That came later."

"Well, what did he say?"

"That you were his best friend and you two listen to music together." A sharp, piercing feeling cut a pinhole through Hank's heart. "I'm not sure what happened to that boy. But whether you asked for it or not, mi'jo, he idolizes you. Don't let him down."

Alice smiled at him and gave him a hug. He squeezed her a second time as they hugged; he wanted to make sure she was still there.

Chapter 13

"So, what's wrong with him?" Charlie asked Hank. They were sipping beers backstage in Philadelphia. Soundcheck had gone well, and the shows in Atlanta had gone off without a hitch. Simon and Bruce chalked it up to the metronome playing into Hank's headphones. Unbeknownst to them, at both shows, Hank had the sound guy cut it off as soon as they walked away. After the shows, Hank felt a warm glow of satisfaction—*There is justice in this world.*

"They're not really sure, actually. Lisa said the doctor told her parents a bunch of medical babble that really just showed they didn't know what the hell happened."

"How did it happen?"

Suddenly, it occurred to Hank he had never told this story to anyone else. Sure, he and Lisa had discussed it. But it had never left their small circle. Was he allowed to share this with others?

But Charlie was family.

"Lisa and Danny grew up in Tennessee, up in the Smokey Mountains. Her and Danny were throwing the frisbee to each other on the back deck. The cabin was built against the hill. So, the deck was about forty feet up from the ground covered with rocks. Lisa threw Danny the frisbee and he ran for it instead of letting it go. And when he jumped for it, he tumbled over the side."

"Holy shit, man."

"Yeah. One of the rocks cracked his head open. He still has a scar, but his hair covers it. I've never actually seen it. Pretty gnarly, Lisa says."

"God, man. Lisa, she must have thought it was her fault, right?"

"She still does, I think. Her parents made her go see a counselor for years. She quit going a few years ago. Said she didn't need it anymore. It's been a long time since we talked about it." They each took a liberal pull from their respective beers.

"What time do we go on?" Charlie asked.

"Eight."

"What time are Lisa and Danny getting here?"

"She said probably right as we go on. I told the security guys to just let them in the back."

"And you sir, are you warmed up yet?"

"Who are you, my father?"

"No. I'm just a concerned friend that wants to see you do your best, sport." Charlie ruffled Hank's hair and then said, "Go get 'em, buddy."

"Thanks, Dad."

With a subdued grin, Charlie pointed to the drum set with practice pads set up in the corner. Hank went over, put his headphones on, and started sparking the wires in his legs to life.

#

Over the speakers, he heard water cascading down the rocks of a creek—his cue to walk on stage and get ready. The sound of the water was real. Simon, being the diehard perfectionist that he was, actually drove to Maine and recorded an overflowing creek just after the spring thaw. The sound takes the listener to the secluded cabin where the protagonist sits ready to start his out-of-body experience.

Hank waited for his first hit. Simon was stage left, picking away; Hank watched the rainbow of lights wash over the crowd, psychedelic colors imbuing the upturned faces with a glow. The colors would fade as the man started his astral travel. He would shoot out of his body like a rocket. The music changed, matching the story, from aw-that's-so-pretty picking, to a lightning-fast death metal riff. Those that had bought the album were ready for it; those that hadn't were in for a beer-spilling surprise.

He put his feet on his bass pedals. Simon looked back at him and mouthed: *Click.* Hank gave him a deceitful nod, bobbing his head along as if the click was in his ear.

In the last seconds of the peaceful guitar part, just before chaos ensued, he looked out at the crowd and saw a young girl in her twenties. It froze him; the girl was the spitting image of his... *of my mother.* The girl stood there, stone-faced. He stared at her, wondering if *she* had loved music the way he did. He lost track of time, his feet relaxed, and he stared at his mother's face. She was out there, looking back at him, finally getting to watch him do what he loved. His mother started to say something to him—

"Hank! Hank! Dude, you have to start playing." He looked over to see Charlie had come up on the drummer riser.

Simon and Bruce were both giving him the *What the fuck?* look.

He counted off with the sticks.

The lights dropped.

Charlie jumped from the high stacks of the speakers, and when he was in midair, the band took off.

#

"Alright. What the fuck happened out there, man?"

Hank knew this was inevitable. Simon couldn't let anything slide.

Before Hank could answer, his perpetual defender spoke up, "Dude. The rest of the show was fine. And the crowd didn't know any better."

"Yeah, well I did. That's not the way the song is played. So I want to know why Hank missed his cue."

The fight was always about him.

In better days, he fought against the undertow. Maybe it was time to surrender and let it take him. Defeated, he told them the truth, "I thought I saw my mom in the crowd. I saw a girl that looked just like her. And I got distracted. *Sorry.*"

They all knew the story, *not the real one*, but that Hank never knew his mother.

To Charlie's surprise, Simon kept staring at Hank, his face contorted in anger. He wasn't done. Simon went to speak, but before he could, Charlie

60

grabbed his arm. "Let it go. Let it go, right the fuck now. You still have your mom. He never had his. Hank hasn't made a single mistake all tour. Let it go." Charlie looked him dead in the eye. The look said everything; it said if you press this right now, *I'm gone.*

Simon knew better. He would bide his time.

Chapter 14

"Look I just need a minute," Hank said.

"You sure about this?"

"Yeah, I need to take a break from Simon and Bruce."

"They will get past it."

"No, they won't."

"Well, if you go, then I go." Even as Charlie said it, he knew it was a lie. But one you told for a friend.

Over the last few months, he and Charlie had had this discussion many times. One he'd never thought they'd have. In the beginning, everything had been fun. Show after show. Creating and creating. No boundaries. No limits. And they had all been friends. Naively, Hank thought that's how it would be forever.

"Don't say that. We aren't kids anymore. You have to make a living. If they want me gone, then maybe after this tour, it's better if I leave. Before they fire me."

"No fucking way. I'm not changing my mind on this."

"Look, let's talk about it when I get to Boston."

They hugged and Charlie shut the driver's side door to Hank's rental car. Thankfully, before the tour, Lisa had convinced Hank to get a credit card. Though he rarely used it, he wouldn't have been able to rent the car without it.

He already missed Lisa and Danny. It had been nice to see them, even nicer to watch Danny enjoy the show. Her presence had soothed him, but the second she left, he felt hollow and defeated again, as Simon's comments gnawed at the fibers in his brain. Fat slug-like monsters that ate and ate, pausing for the occasional belch.

He needed some time away from his bandmates to get his mind back. His medication was doing little to stem his anxiety. He had hardly slept in the two days since the show.

The only question left now was the playlist. He planned to listen to music nonstop on the way there. Between renting the car and seeing Danny and Lisa off, he hadn't had time to make it. So, he was doing it helter-skelter, improvising as he drove. He couldn't settle on an album. He kept flipping through the Artists tab in his account.

Looking down and then up. Down and then up. He merged on to Interstate 95 and headed north. The next exit was two miles ahead. He was already gassed up, no need to stop for miles.

Converge came blasting through the speakers and he put the phone down. Moments later, he noticed an entry ramp. Just ahead cars were merging onto the interstate. Looking down, Hank failed to see the cars speeding up the ramp.

He kept his speed the same: ten over the limit, right at 80 mph. Looking down to flip with his thumb and then looking up.

Down and up.

Down and up.

While Hank's head was down, the driver of a black SUV got tired of the three cars in front of him being gun-shy, and decided to merge. As he did it, he screamed out, "Time to shit or get off the pot, people." The tall, overweight man jerked his hulking SUV over into Hank's lane. Hank's head was still down.

The back of SUV rocketed into the front passenger side of Hank's car.

When Hank looked up, the world was spinning.

Chapter 15

Flashes of light. Sparks glittered. Like fireworks right next to him, within his reach. His eyes fluttered open; he saw thick streamers of light shooting out from his car. And the sound. He knew that sound. It was a table saw, but more powerful: a table saw on steroids. The sound of metal on metal made his teeth clench.

What is this? Where am I?

His hands were caked in blood and black cuts lined his forearm. Dazed, he looked to the smashed window and quickly made the deduction: the glass had shattered inward. But he could move his upper body and he could move his arms. He chose to look around, rather than look down.

He had wrecked his car. So much blood, but no pain?

Then he tried to move his right leg, and the world went white.

"Oh my God, oh my God, Ahh, ahhh!" His hands shot out, but he knew better than to touch his leg. The sound he made, which rang out louder than the scream of the saw, reminded him of a horror movie he had seen, a character that got his leg caught in a bear trap. The metal jaws had clamped shut, turning the flesh into red-stained tendrils that swayed like a curtain. The character made a guttural sound over and over, teeth clenched, jaw jutting out, as saliva spilled out over his chin.

That was Hank now. He tried to move his leg again; the pain shot to every corner of him. In seconds, he became a slave to the pain. Exquisite in its awfulness. His body and mind at war.

He was terrified to look down at his leg. What if it was mush? Or worse, flayed skin dangling off like dark meat from a chicken bone? The thought of seeing his leg covered in red and splotched with ichor was almost worse than the pain.

But even now that wasn't his only thought. There was another fat slug crawling around in his mind amidst the agony: *How can I play?*

The saw stopped for a moment. "Son, we've got you, alright? Just hang in there and we'll have you out as soon as we can."

He would just have to stay still. That was the only way to keep the pain in his leg at bay. Stay still and don't look down.

The saw started again, followed by another fountain of sparks, shooting out in long arcs.

Somewhere in the halo of sparks, the door gave, and a rush of air came in. At first, he grinned, then as the wind shot in, his smile disappeared as the fresh air overwhelmed the wound on his right leg.

Another blast of white consumed his world.

Another chorus of the guttural sound from the horror movie.

"Son, we are going to pull you out in a minute and get you on the gurney. Can you hear me?"

"Yes, yes, I can hear, just please, my leg, oh my God, my leg."

The fireman looked down and saw the shredded leg. Years of work had taught him to hide any reaction. "I know. But we can't do anything about the leg until we get you pulled out, alright? I need to ask you a few questions." The fireman rattled off the script to make sure Hank had no signs of brain injury. Hank passed. No cognitive damage. "Son, I need to feel around and take a look at you to make sure there are no other injuries. I'm going to pull up your shirt, alright?"

"Ahh. Ahhh. Just do whatever you need to. It's just my leg. It hurts so bad. Please take care of it. I play drums. I need my leg. Please."

The fireman ignored his pleading, said something polite, and lifted Hank's shirt. Hank was bruised to hell and back from the seatbelt. His torso was a canvas of blue and black, splattered with red.

The fireman released the seatbelt. In his periphery, Hank saw another medic wheel up a yellow gurney. "Alright, bud"—the other medic was speaking now, a young bearded man with blue eyes— "we are going to pull you out now. It's going to hurt like hell for a minute, but once we get you out, we'll get that leg stabilized and then we can give you something for the pain."

The fireman cut back in, "You'll be fine. But this is going to hurt like a son of a bitch. You ready?"

Absolutely fucking not. *But what choice do I have?*

The medic bent down to cradle Hank's legs, as the fireman wrapped his arms around his torso. "Alright, we are going on three. One, two, three."

When the fireman lifted him, he arced Hank forward, and for the first time since the wreck, Hank saw the ruin of his leg.

The sight of it made him gag.

He would remember the pain that came next for the rest of his life. As they moved him, he heard his bone scraping against the dash—nails on a chalkboard—and felt the jagged edge of it get wedged in a hole. The medic wriggled Hank's leg but couldn't get the bone free. As the medic pulled, the fireman reached in to wrestle it out.

By then, Hank had passed out.

PART III

"Do you think that one creature could make God regret creating the whole of humanity?"

The captive saw a pile of jagged rocks in the corner. *What were they for?* Stacked neatly, like a pyramid, they must have a purpose. He also noticed he was in some kind of shed. Steel walls, wooden shelves, tools, like you'd see in someone's backyard, except longer, and there was a horrible, putrid smell. The scent of death.

"Sure, there have been many before me do awful things. Things that people avoid in conversation. But they were doing it for their own selfish reasons. Or because they had no control over their mind. Not me. My craft speaks directly to God. My *art* shows Her She faltered when creating us.

"Don't you agree? We stink. We lie. We steal. We murder. We push our foot down on the heads of those asking for help and plunge them right back in the water. We are no better than animals. People can surrender in war, but can they in everyday life? There is no real compassion within us. That is why I aim to beat God over the head with Her mistakes until She finally gets up the courage to wipe us out and begin anew."

The man with the black eyes stood and began to pace the room in frustration.

How long had he been speaking?

The captive couldn't tell. They had given him a pill. Something that made time disappear. In a way, he was thankful too, because the pill kept withdraw at bay.

The captive blinked, trying to focus. The back of the Black-Eyed Man's head was a network of scar tissue. Like the pink sundried seams of a baseball had been melted across it.

"My scars, they are monstrous, are they not? But that's only if you choose to look at them that way. Do you want me to tell you why that is?"

As if I have a choice?

"When I was 21 years old, I lived with my older sister. She had a boyfriend. He was tall, hulking, the type of man that instills fear just by walking in the room. His size made people respect him. But the man was of little substance. Making matters worse, he was thin-skinned, and my sister had a sharp wit: two things that cannot coexist.

"He dulled her wit with his fists. At first, she gave me the hackneyed excuses you hear about: falling down the stairs, tripping, colliding with random objects, and so on. I never believed anything she said about her bruises. I knew that half-wit was pummeling her. But, alas, I was just a lanky kid, light as a feather, only my wits to guide me.

"This went on for months and months. She had stopped saying much of anything to him out of fear. Over time, his pride grew, and he started beating her in front of me. He'd beat her until her eyes swelled shut. She started getting fired from any job she could hold down because she couldn't go in after he left her in tatters.

"When it would happen, I'd stare, paralyzed, afraid to get beaten like her. I was no match for the man. What was I to do?

"But one day, I had had enough. I was no stranger to crime. I had been stealing from a young age to help provide. My sister never asked where things came from, and I never told.

"We were all watching television, and my sister dozed off. He told her to go get him another beer. When he looked over and realized she was asleep, he yelled at her to get up and fetch him a beer. Groggily, she sat up and told him to go fuck himself. So, he got up, held her down, and alternated between punching her stomach and face. I grabbed the only thing in sight, a fire poker, and I went for him.

"The first blow knocked him to the ground. I got another in. And another. I felt the high of winning the fight. But my bliss didn't last long. He took my legs out from under me and when I fell, I dropped the fire poker." The Black-Eyed Man shook his head in disappointment, still troubled by his error. "And then that beast went to work on my head. My sister tried to help me, but he swatted her away like a fly.

"She got me to the hospital. We lied to the staff. I was old enough to be in a bar, so we told them in a melee, someone broke bottles over my head. They had to shave my head, so they could stich me up. And after they removed the stiches, this is what remained, puckered flesh fighting for space. My hair never grew back."

The captive man thought he saw hate in his captor's eyes. But what he saw was worse than hate. He saw the absence of light.

"One morning, as I stood in front of my bathroom mirror, I looked at my scars for hours. But really, in that span of time, I did much more than that. For the first time, I studied them. I admired the bulbs and the wormy curves, no longer thinking they were hideous, but that maybe they had a purpose. I made a decision. I had always felt the darkness from within. The thoughts had abided for years; the thoughts *the weak Puppeteer* in the sky made me think. They were there, churning within, but I had never acted on them. Perhaps, the dark things I thought and felt were the right way to navigate the world. Perhaps, the only way.

"So I waited for him. He worked as a bouncer at a bar in the neighborhood. He got off work in the middle of the night, and when he came out, I made short work of getting him down on his knees. I stabbed him repeatedly in the back. Quick, short strokes, like the needle of a sewing machine applying the stich. He was caught completely unaware. I can still see his face as he dropped to his knees and reached his hand back to feel of his wounds. I remember the look in his eyes when he realized it was me, skinny-weak me, that was grabbing him by the back of the head, and made him look me in the eye as I opened his throat from end to end. Blood rained down onto my shoes. He gasped and gulped and writhed. I held him still. I made sure he looked at me as he fought for air.

"I took the cash he made that night to cover my tracks. As a result, the media painted it as a vicious robbery. The police never solved the crime. My sister found peace. I still send her money. She doesn't ask where it comes from, and I don't tell."

The tall man with the black eyes resumed his seat and lifted the other man's chin, forcing him to look into his eyes, a thing he did repeatedly to make sure he was heard; he needed an audience. People needed to hear his poison gospel. "You know, my eyes had begun to turn about a month before he attacked me. At first it looked like someone had spilled black ink into them. Over time, the black consumed my eyes. I never sought a medical opinion. I didn't want to know the answer behind what was happening to me. I welcomed the transformation.

"When I got home that night, after dispatching that coward, I looked in the mirror and saw that my metamorphosis was complete. My eyes were entirely black."

A satisfied grin came over the Black-Eyed Man's face. "After all, they say the eyes are the window to the soul."

Chapter 16

When Hank came to in the hospital, it was different from when the spray of sparks awoke him in the wrecked car: this time he felt no pain. The doctors had ordered the nurses to keep him on a steady IV drip of one of the opiates he had heard of (Oxycodone? Oxycontin? Hydrocodone?)—he couldn't remember which one the doctor said. His leg was quiet. So, he was quiet.

They planned to release him tomorrow. Lisa and Danny made the trip up as soon as Charlie gave them the news. Charlie had stayed as long as he could but then departed for the next gig. Their record company had already booked a fill-in drummer for the rest of the tour, even though Charlie pleaded with the guys to cancel or postpone the shows. They didn't budge.

Hank looked down at the formidable cast that went up to his knee. In the initial days, before the doctors put the cast on his leg, he could still see his gnarly scar. He had a vague memory of the doctor saying it didn't take too many stiches to sew him up (thirty or so, or was it forty?). All the facts from the doc were hard to recall. Fallout from the accident? Or this medical-grade dope pumping through his veins? Hard to tell.

The doctor, a tall, gangly cut of a man, said the stiches would dissolve. Like a pill in his stomach, the string would eventually cease to be. They just wanted to monitor the wound for a few days and make sure things progressed as planned.

The anxiety he normally felt was an afterthought. A specter that was there, yet not there. And the worry of not playing drums—a thought that normally made his heart palpitate and his breathing speed up—was somewhere lost in the clouds. In fact, he felt like he was walking on clouds. *Was that a song lyric?* Right now, he didn't care. He was happy. And he was whole.

Right as rain.

Danny and Lisa came through the door and strolled by the TV, turned to CNN. The first day, the TV had displayed Fox news, but as soon as Lisa got there, she set that to rights. "No way we are watching this bullshit. Fucking propaganda machine. Tune in and turn off your brain. We'll have you scared shitless before the sun goes down." Lisa turned to the nurse. "Do the rest of us a favor, make sure this shit isn't hurting anyone else on your rotation. Don't you guys take an oath too? Do no harm? You'll feel better. Trust me."

The young, pale-skinned nurse stared at Lisa, astonished, as she handed over the remote. "Sure."

"Excellent. Glad to have your support. We'll be watching."

A steady flow of nurses and nurse practitioners came through over the intervening days. Hank grew somewhat accustomed to the meds and started peppering the staff with the same question: How long will it take for my leg to heal? The nurses dodged it, referring him to the doc. And the doc would make no guarantees.

"I'm sorry, son, I can't say. Six months before you're back behind the set? Maybe a year? I'm confident the bone will heal, because it was a clean break. But you'll still have to go through physical therapy. And when it comes to that, everyone's progress is different. Bones can heal, but that doesn't mean they heal in the same way."

"What do you mean?"

"You'll be able to walk. After the therapy, I'm confident you'll be able to run. But coordination, I can't speak for. I also can't guarantee you'll be able to do the same exact things as before. This was a bad break, son." Hank looked defeated. "This is just going to take time. Which I know is not what you want to hear, but it's the truth."

Everett called several times to check in. Each time he offered to come up and leave Alice to run things, and each time Hank declined. When Hank was asleep, or too far gone on the pain-med superhighway, Lisa took over and let Everett know things were fine, and they'd be home soon.

And so it went until they discharged him.

"Hank, I'm going to give you a prescription for oxycontin. This won't last you long, but it should get you to the next stop. Oh, and when you transition from your chair to your crutches, you may need some more pain meds. The first time you put weight on that leg, it's going to hurt."

"How bad?"

He leaned down to whisper. "Like hell, son. Like hell." He stepped back and started speaking normally again. "Good luck, and I hope to see you behind the drum set again soon on—what is it?"

"YouTube."

"Yeah that. I read mostly. Not big on TV."

"It's the internet, but whatever."

"And what is your band's name again?"

"Dead Children's Playground."

Wide-eyed, the doctor spoke, "Well, that's some name. I take it I won't be seeing you guys on Good Morning America any time soon."

Hank laughed. "No. No you won't."

"Good luck."

"Thanks."

And with that, Lisa pushed him out of the hospital. They were due to fly out in four hours; the airport had a handicapped shuttle coming to get them. They sat out front of the hospital and waited.

His band was touring without him. And he wasn't sure if he could even play anymore. *Whatever.* He felt good.

Right as rain.

What was that drug the doctor prescribed me?

Chapter 17

Five months passed; Hank transitioned to crutches. And true to the doctor's word, it had hurt like hell. But he had something to ferry him through the pain, something to keep his nerves from catching fire. The first script the doctor in Philadelphia had given him ran out after a month. A local doctor Lisa recommended bridged the next gap. When Hank went back for more, the doctor declined, saying that Hank was far enough removed from his surgery and it was time to learn to get along on his own.

Hank scoffed. "I'm still in pain."

"Well, pain is a part of healing. I'm not writing you another prescription. Have a good day."

After leaving the clinic, Hank consulted Uncle Internet and found a pain clinic nearby. Still in his cast, the sight of it quelled any of the staff's concerns. After a few perfunctory questions, he was rated a low risk for abuse, and then, poof: more magic pills.

The months had slid by easily enough. Hank spent his time working at the restaurant. Everett gave him a day off each week to let his armpits and shoulders rest; the constant clambering on crutches caused bruising and a weird, subdued pain, deep in his muscles.

Leaning against the silver prep table, Hank chopped cooked bacon to transfer over to the giant pot of beans simmering on the stove. It was Sunday. Hank had taken his day off yesterday, so he had to be here. For now, it was just he and Alice in the kitchen. The other girls that helped Alice worked to the bone every day. As was her nature, Alice pitied them and let them come in right before opening time on Sundays; it also gave them time to go to mass. Save for losing a few pounds, Alice looked the same. Her appetite had changed, however. She used to take a sandwich, beans, and a dollop of potato salad every day before the lunch rush. Now she settled for a small bowl of the beans. She wouldn't say it, but it was the only thing that didn't send her stomach into a tailspin.

"Where did Danny go?" Hank asked.

"He went out back with your Dad."

"What's up with those two?"

"Those first weeks, we were having trouble getting Danny to listen to us. He wasn't doing anything disrespectful. But we couldn't get him to help. He would just go sit out back on one of the tree stumps"—years ago, Everett had brought in large tree stumps and arranged them in a circle around a fire pit next to the smokehouse— "and not move for hours."

"So, what did Dad do?"

"He just started saying: 'You know Danny, Hank always helps me in the smokehouse, it's one of his favorite things to do while he's here.' And then Danny was in. Now, he trusts your dad, and follows him around. He even got comfortable enough to ask if he could change the playlist in the kitchen. Everett let him one day. Ohh, you should have seen the girls' faces when that death metal you guys love started blaring. They looked like they just saw the devil. I laughed until I cried."

Hank laughed with her.

"Well, your dad said the metal music was after hours only. And told him during work he'd have to wear his headphones if he wanted to head bang."

Silence fell between them. Hank stirred the beans.

Alice saw an opening. She hadn't had the heart to have the conversation in front of Everett. She had yet to cry in front of Everett Grant, the man that gave her a life after losing her family, and she planned to enter the grave with dry eyes. But there were some things that needed to be said. Giving unsolicited advice to Hank was her stock and trade. And time was in short supply.

"Mi'jo, I'm not going to be here forever."

"I know." He couldn't look her in the eye as he said it.

"Just listen. Your father is going to need you when I'm gone. He can't run this place by himself. Restaurants are tough. They fail all the time. This one has been successful, but it's because we are up here every day busting our butts. And there is too much work for him on his own. But I know your daddy. As stubborn as a mule, he will think he can handle it all on his own. He can't. He needs you here."

"But Alice, what about my band? I'm going to heal up."

"I know you will heal, mi'jo. And I know how much you love your band. But you can love music *and* honor your family. And when I'm gone, your family is going to need you."

"What about him hiring somebody else? Someone like a manager, which is basically what you've done all these years. Couldn't he find someone like you to help?" Hank realized how stupid he sounded. There was no replacing Alice.

"Maybe. But what he needs is *you*. Just like I won't be here forever, your father won't be around forever either. He could hire somebody else, but he wants *you* here. He's just doesn't want to get between you and the thing you love."

"Okay." That's all Hank could muster. He didn't want to lie to her. He still planned to go to physical therapy, which would start in roughly two months, when the cast came off, and then get back to DCP. Everett could find someone. And, in the meantime, Hank would help as much as he could.

"You'll find your way. But remember, sometimes the thing you're out there chasing for has been right in front of you the whole time." She shifted her weight, girding herself. "Now, there's one more thing. I tried to talk to your father about it and he shooed me off. I had a will made. Nothing complicated, because I don't have all that much. But you and Ev, make sure that my house goes to Maria. She has three kids to look after, and with everything Hector's into, she could end up on her own. You understand? There is also a little something in there for you and Lisa too." Alice paused and laughed. "You know, your future wife, if you would ever get your head out of your ass long enough to ask her to marry you."

"We back to that again?"

"No. No. Everyone has the right to screw things up on their own. Do what you want." She winked at him as she said it.

Then, as they laughed together, the moment got the better of her.

Hank couldn't see her face; her shoulders slumped, her head down, the weight of the cancer pushing her closer to the soil.

He dropped the spoon and walked over, wrapping her in a hug. She embraced him from her stool. Hank bent down to rest his head on top of hers. He could feel the hard skin of her head through her remaining wisps of gray hair.

Against everything in her nature, Alice cried.

She cried for the family she lost so many years ago. She cried for this place she loved so much.

The tears were not all bitter. Beneath the pain, she felt an undercurrent of happiness. She knew that as bitter as it was to leave this life, a life where God had given her a second chance at happiness, she would soon see her husband and her son and they would all sit down for dinner, the setting sun the only other witness to their reunion.

For now, she cried.

So much for shedding her mortal coil with dry eyes.

Chapter 18

"What is that divine smell?"

The teenager Everett had hired as a cashier hadn't bothered to show up, forcing Everett to work the front counter. He had his back turned to check tickets at the expo window, making sure the to-go orders weren't too far behind, when the man walked in.

Turning around, Everett said, "I'm sorry, I missed what you said." For a moment, the rest of Everett's world faded away—there was only the man before him and nothing else. Some advice one of his grade-school teachers had given him came into his head. She had admonished Everett again and again about staring at people that looked different, that it was impolite, rude, even hurtful. Good advice for anyone that wanted to be a functioning member of society as they grew up. But his teacher had never seen this man. Her advice wasn't fit for this moment. Everett had only heard this man's voice, had just now seen him for the first time. Yet, the mere sight of him, his mere presence, sent an electric jolt through Everett's body; Everett's reptilian brain was telling him to run, to hide, that a predator was about to rip him open stem to stern.

"What is that heavenly smell coming from the back?" The man's voice came out like sludge, thick and black. Yet, somehow, he was still able to overlay an academic lilt on top of every syllable, his tone at once disturbing and elitist.

An electric hum in his bones and veins made him slightly nauseous. Everett stammered, "Hickory—"

"Ahh. Hence the name. How silly of me. I suppose we are all entitled to a misstep every now and then. Don't you agree?"

Everett nodded and without meaning to, cocked his head at an odd angle, continuing to study the physical oddity of the man: taller than Hank, maybe as much as 6'5", clad in all black, with a bald head and rimless glasses with dark black shades. *Who wore all black in the Florida sun?* The man's bald head was covered in scars that rose from his skin like welts. As if someone had melted peach-colored wax on his head.

His teacher's voice spoke again and then faded. Ms. Conners never dreamed a person like this existed. The man was a monster, one that Everett couldn't help but keep staring at.

In a faint and distant way, Everett felt some remorse for having such a visceral reaction to a perfect stranger, but every cell in his body told him there was something wrong with this man. And it didn't inspire Everett to pity him for his deformities. To the contrary, all he felt was fear and disgust.

To bridge the gap, Everett spoke again. "You a fan of pork?"

"I do enjoy a good cut of pig now and again. But truth be told, I prefer a nice steak."

"Why is that?"

"Because I can eat it rare. Pork has to be cooked to at least mid-rare to rid it of all impurities. Steak comes ready to devour." The man smiled. "Where is the fun if you can't see a little blood run down the fibers of the meat? Seeing that blood awakens my animal instinct. Takes me back to my ancestors running and chanting around the fire. A simpler time, you could say."

Who the hell is this guy?

"Sorry, please excuse my digression. I'm sure you sell a fine product here. But other business brings me here today." He spoke with purpose, the tone of a supervisor marshaling a board meeting.

The man shifted his weight and placed his phone on the counter. He then removed his glasses and set them on the counter, unmasking his pitch-black eyes—no sclera, no iris, no pupil, only black. In a small way, Everett felt vindicated: the man really was a monster.

"Now, to the reason I have darkened your door: I need to speak to Hector."

The pointed question shook Everett from the spell cast by the man's eyes. "Hector hasn't been around for weeks. Word is that he got deported." A lie. No one around here really knew what happened to Hector.

"Is that so?"

"Yeah, so do you want something to eat? If not, you need to move on. We have a lot of work to do. And the rush will start soon."

"A man with a purpose. I respect that. But you see, I have a purpose, too. I do hope our ends aren't at odds. I hate when that happens. But there is a ready-made solution. Though it is one I fear you wouldn't like."

Clenching his teeth, Everett snarled, "I asked you nicely. Now I'm telling you: Get out."

"But you haven't even heard why I need to speak to him." A bearded man, his brown hair slicked back from his forehead came through the door and rested his back against the wall. The man had beady, intent eyes, and the gun attached to his hip, poking out from his coat, was the means to inflict the harm his eyes longed for.

"Oh, I see you've noticed my familiar, Melvin. Don't let him frighten you. Now, back to the subject at hand, it seems no one has a line on our dear friend Hector, a shame really. But I would still like to speak to his wife Maria. Is she in?"

For a moment Everett wondered what in the hell a *familiar* was, and then said, "She's not here, and I don't know where she is."

The man stepped forward, tensing his jaw, pressed his weight against the counter as he leaned over it. He had to crane his neck down for them to make eye contact. Everett saw his black eyes moving back and forth and thought of pitch-black eels, slithering over one another, fighting for purchase.

Towering over Everett, the man said, "Perhaps you could tell me where she lives. An address?" Decorum had faded. His last words were drenched in acid.

"Not sure. Never been to her house."

The man leaned his head down even further—close enough for Everett to smell his breath, which stank of stale coffee. "Well, Melvin and I are quite motivated. We will find her in time."

Everett knew a threat when he heard it. Riding on shot of adrenaline, he screamed, "If you lay a hand on her, I'll kill you."

"Oh, Mr.—"

"Grant."

Everett could tell his words had fallen flat. Nothing he had said had scared this man in the slightest. In fact, the monster was grinning: a knowing grin, as if he knew all the secrets the cosmos had in store. In a way Everett couldn't quite describe, there was something godly about him. A dark divinity that emanated out from him.

With a tone equal parts oil and acid, the man said, "Trust me, I'd love nothing more than to bleed you like one of your pigs out back. But you are not the target of my ire—Hector is. So stop being a child and tell me what I want to know."

With a grumble Sam Elliot would be proud of, Everett spat out: "Go fuck yourself."

Exasperated, he responded, "Again with the petulance. Why do you try my patience? Worse, why do you try Melvin's?"

"Leave!"

"Do you not agree that people should pay their debts?" Everett didn't answer; he was done talking to this man. "Your friend Hector stole from me. Am I supposed to just overlook that? Those faded tattoos on your forearms tell me that you know something of my world." Everett glanced down in spite of himself; on his forearms and across his elbows were the remnants of the ill-advised tattoos he had gotten years ago, after he reached Florida, to hide the scars. A trained eye knew their former purpose, though they hadn't served that purpose in decades. "A few pictures on your arms to hide bad habits, I imagine. So you know the types of transgressions I speak of. Thus, I ask you again, do you not believe people should pay their debts? Does God Himself not ask us all to settle our accounts when we come to the hereafter?"

"You need to—" And as Everett said it, his saving grace came through the door: a gaggle of customers on their lunch break.

The bald man turned, and he and Melvin met eyes. A signal passed between them that it was time to go.

The room was still electric with tension. Everett noticed the group of men (engineers, judging by their off-brand golf-shirts and lanyards with company IDs) that had just come through the door could sense something was off. They gave the tall man and the one behind him a wide berth.

"Crowds make me nervous. Please do tell Maria we stopped by." His last words came out polite, like he was saying goodbye to someone at a dinner party. He was toying with Everett. Watching him squirm.

"Get the hell out of my store." Everett meant to whisper it, so the gaggle of engineers couldn't hear. But he gritted his teeth and growled the words.

"Nice place you have here, Mr. Grant—we will be in touch."

Right as they went through the door, Hank clambered through on crutches, almost colliding with the two men. The bald man held the door for him; he had his glasses back on now, preventing Hank from seeing his eyes. The man displayed his pearly whites as Hank came through and even nodded as if to say hello.

Hank awkwardly made his way around the counter as Everett took the orders, having to redundantly ask each man what they wanted because he kept forgetting and fumbling his pen; when he finished sending the tickets back to the kitchen, Everett stepped back from the counter. They had about fifteen minutes before the regulars started pouring in. He turned to his son and said, "His eyes, Hank. That man's eyes were nothing but black."

"Huh? Who are you talking about?"

"The tall one with the glasses that held the door for you. His eyes were pure black."

"Like in horror movies?"

"Worse." *Because this was real. This wasn't fiction.* "He was looking for Hector. He asked where Maria lived. I need to tell Alice to get Maria and the kids to a new place and keep it quiet."

"You really think so? That guy could have been full of shit."

Everett couldn't fully explain himself to Hank, a problem that had existed ever since that fateful day in Booth's house. But it was a problem that, unexpectedly, hadn't cropped up that often over the years. Everett had known many bad men before he got clean. He'd bought drugs from them.

He'd done favors for them—stole things, robbed people, all part of the life of an addict. But this man was something else. Everett had done everything in his power to make sure his son knew nothing of that world. He would be damned if his boy ever came into contact with the predators and fiends that waited—lurking—to corrupt the newest soul that had strayed from the path. Hiding his past from his son was definitely not something he took pride in, and at times, the guilt from it was overwhelming him: made him anxious, restless, pins and needles poking and prodding him to confess his sins. Then he reminded himself he was doing it to protect the most precious thing in his life—Hank.

"Something about that guy and the other one with him. He called him his *familiar*. What the hell is that?"

Hank shrugged, letting Everett know he didn't have a clue. Everett also sensed that his son may not believe his story, that he was just humoring his old man.

"You got things up here for a minute? I need to talk to Alice."

"I got it."

Everett turned to walk back and then turned around. "Oh hey, how did the physical therapy go?"

"Hurt like hell."

"But you're making progress."

"Yeah."

"Good. How much longer you got on those things?"

"Two more months if things keep going well."

"You off those pills yet?" There was one thing Everett had learned during his travels on the addiction superhighway: pills were a powerful poison. Quaaludes were one of the demons Everett had shed. More and more young people had started showing up to the meetings—fallout from the opiate epidemic sweeping the country. The stories differed at the fringes, but at the core, they were the same: it started with pills and when that well ran dry, they found heroin on the street—cheaper and easier to get. What worried Everett was although some of these young people fit the bill—broken families, physical or sexual abuse, depression—others didn't. It started with a sports injury, an accident skiing at the lake, or a car wreck. Doc gave them a script, they took it as prescribed, and before they knew it, addiction had them in its clutches.

"Yeah. Don't need them anymore. I'm getting around alright."

"Good. Glad to hear it." Everett looked to a group of business types coming through the door, the signal for Hank to get to work.

As the customers stood and looked over the menu on chalkboards that were mounted above Hank's head, Hank broke a pill in half in his pocket, an oxycontin; he still had sixty of them that he'd bought from a neighbor. He was tired of going to the pain clinic. He knew if he pressed them, he could get more, but this was easier. He quickly put it in his mouth and swallowed. He had downed so many of these little white friends during his recuperation that he didn't even need a sip of water anymore.

His mouth watered at the thought of the escape.

Chapter 19

Melvin, the familiar, looked to his phone and saw a text that confirmed what he and his boss already knew: Hector had never left Florida. It had been four long months since they went to the restaurant searching for Hector, which only fed their longing for what would come at the Portal. A place where time stopped. A place where they were free to torture, mangle, and experiment. A place not of God.

"He was laying low in Belle Glade. One of our guys got a tip about the flophouse he was hiding in and picked him. What now?"

"You know the process. Tell him we will meet in Belle Glade to collect Hector."

"When?"

"Immediately. Are the buckets ready?" Melvin always cleaned the tools, buckets, and other implements. Each tool they used had to be spotless. Pristine. Ready to welcome the next passenger to the Portal.

"Cleaned and in place at the shed."

"It's not a shed, Melvin. You wouldn't call a museum a warehouse, would you?"

#

Hector had been mumbling prayers ever since they picked him up in Belle Glade. He begged that *Thing* in the sky to spare him from what was in the offing.

The Black-Eyed Man intervened. "Who is that you're praying to, Hector?" Hector understood enough English to grasp the meaning of the man's words, but not enough to respond in kind. "Ahh. You do not speak the native tongue. That is of no consequence. Soon we will have you speaking a universal language." Hector grimaced. "Hector, I have a question for you, one you may not understand, but I must ask because of the circumstances that have befallen you: have you ever considered that your God doesn't care about what happens to you? Have you ever thought that maybe He built the machinery, hit the on-button, and then decided to sit back and watch the show?" Hector's mouth contorted in confusion. "I can see that you don't understand me. That is fine. We will understand each other well enough once we reach our destination. There, we won't need words to speak to one another."

Shaking, and mumbling to himself, Hector began to cry.

"Oh Hector, don't cry. No one escapes the end. Say another prayer if it makes you feel better. If your God isn't too busy, maybe He will listen."

Through his whimpering, Hector asked a question: "Cual es tu nombre, senor?" The Black-Eyed Man knew enough Spanish to understand, but not respond in kind.

"Why Hector, not even Melvin here knows my name. Names are so burdensome. They take away from what could be."

#

When Hector came to, he had lost all sense of time and place. His vision was foggy and his head felt like someone had smashed it against a cinderblock. He looked around and saw gritty aluminum walls and a dirt floor. He noticed too that he was in nothing but his underwear. There was enough of a glow from a few dangling lights for him to see the man that had been speaking to him. The scars intersecting across his head looked dirty and red under the dim light. Like they were rotting.

"It seems that the stress was more than your constitution could withstand. You slipped into unconsciousness the moment we arrived. Better really. After all, we come here to leave behind the trappings of time and space. Here, I can teach you to be more than human."

Hector swiveled his head from side to side, scanning the room with pleading eyes. Curious, he looked down: he saw two buckets placed—just so—under his thighs. He realized too that even though he could feel the ground under his feet, he could not move his feet or legs. They had strapped his legs to the thick wrought-iron chair he sat in. And as for his feet, there was some contraption anchoring him the ground.

"What we have here is simple magnetism. We fit you with a pair of steel-toed boots, we strap you in, and our industrial magnets keep you stuck to the floor.

"Now to the point: You took something from me. Don't deny it. I have eyes everywhere. You can tell me where it is, or in a moment I am going to open you up as an offering to God. Call it an act of worship."

Hector thought of Maria and his three daughters, making hope spread through him, like rainfall refilling a lake stricken with drought. Against all the evidence, the light from his loved ones still shined in him—telling him to live, pleading with him to survive. He had to try to see his family again.

Time to confess his sins.

"Alejandro's casa."

"From Alejandro's?"

"Si." The man's eyes made Hector's stomach tense, coil into knots. They reminded him of an insect's eyes—wet and black, no soul behind them, only instinct and appetite.

"How many?"

"Two." So, two bricks was the measure of the take. Thousands of dollars of heroin that he and Melvin were on the hook for. They could pull from their own personal bank and cover up the error.

"Alejandro's. Lo siento. Por favor. Por favor. Mi familia. Yo tengo tres hijas. Por favor. Yo tengo tres hijas."

"Melvin!" Melvin popped his head in. "Alejandro's in Belle Glade. Make the call."

"How do you want me to handle it?"

"They get a pass for now. Too many bodies. Tell them they are on a short leash. Also tell them we will soon have a totem for them."

"A totem?"

"Yes."

Melvin grinned and then stepped out to make the call.

The Black-Eyed Man got up and walked to the other side of the room. The shelves were lined with implements. Tools that changed the meaning of time and space. Tools to make people immortal.

He returned with a long knife. "Hector, forgive me for speculating, but I assume you've never studied human anatomy. I think we both know you are never leaving here. But that contagion called *hope* got the better of your judgment. And then you told me what you stole, anyway, so I can't let you go. Men like me, we don't release a catch. Never. That would be to admit fault. And I see no fault in what I do. In fact, I see a beautiful divinity in it." The man ran his fingers along the edge of the knife. "There has been one constant in all the people I have brought here: That stubborn voice in them saying that somehow, someway, God will save them."

He kneeled down, to make sure Hector could see into his black eyes: "God is a spectator."

Surgically, he cut open Hector's thighs, each slit the length of a hardback book. The blood came in dark torrents.

At first, the pain that shot out from Hector's legs was sharp and searing, so awful and overwhelming all he could manage through rapid breaths was a keening gasp. Then he screamed and bucked against his restraints, trying to free himself from the fire in his thighs. The blood loss soon calmed him, making him feel sleepy. He looked down and saw the blood, glossy and crimson, thudding against the bottom of the buckets and thought he had never been more tired in his whole life.

"Unlike you, Hector, I'm a student of anatomy. I'm particularly fond of the femoral artery. The main blood source for your legs. When damaged, as surely as both of yours are now, well, death follows. Tell your God I'm eager to meet Her."

He put duct tape over Hector's mouth. He didn't want him to speak and ruin his moment of serenity. And he had grown tired of hearing him whimper like a dying animal.

Hector's breaths grew shorter, changing from whole-hearted gasps to tiny puffs of air. The train slowing down to reach its last stop. He gently rubbed Hector's face and stared into his eyes as they lost their sheen.

The dismemberment would come later.

Chapter 20

Hank sat down behind his drum-set. Trying to remember. Trying to reclaim his ability. The practice space was empty. Two weeks ago, while DCP was still on tour, he had started coming here and practicing. After months of walking on crutches, he had left his false appendages behind.

Did he still have it?

Hank had spent the last two weeks trying to find out.

Once he heard from Charlie that the band, due to strong ticket sales, had decided to extend the tour, he knew he could come here and play without oversight. The last thing he needed was Simon and Bruce casting doubtful glares at him.

He put the headphones on and shuffled through the songs on his old iPod. He cued up the same song he had been trying to get right: "Sorcerer's Cave," from their first album. One he had never flubbed live. A perfect tune to help him get back on the saddle. The problem was, he wasn't able play it right. Not even once.

The song opened with a quick shot of double bass rolls, followed by a long section of sixteenth notes, like a train chugging down the tracks. Every time he'd get halfway through the song, his right leg faltered and slipped off the pedal. Also, there was the part he didn't want to admit: every time he played, the pain flared up, magnificently.

With varying success, he had been trying to wean himself off the pills. His goal (really, Lisa's goal for him) had been to get down to one pill a day, then taper down to one-half pill per day, and eventually switch to something over the counter. The problem was, when he played, the pain came, and he did his level best to trick himself into believing it wasn't there; that it was a phantom remnant of his wreck, a psychosomatic ghost that had made a temporary home within him and would soon leave. That with enough willpower, self-discipline, and a shitload of denial, he could overcome it.

The doctor had warned him he may not have the same strength or coordination after the wreck. But over time, maybe, he could recapture it.

He tried the song again. Again, his foot faltered at the halfway point because of the pain.

Time was something he did not have. Charlie and Hank had been speaking every week, and according to Charlie, the studio drummer in the band, Pearson, had been wanting to play in a metal band for years. Hank had seen the YouTube cellphone videos from the crowd; the audio was shit, but he heard enough to know Pearson was killing it. He had not only mastered all of Hank's parts, but he had added new flourishes that had never occurred to Hank. Hank had been too timid to ask Charlie if he played to a click, but Hank knew. The guy made his bones as a studio musician. The robots of the music world—you plugged them in, hit the on-button, and got the desired result.

Hank appreciated his friend shielding him from the truth. But *what if* the mercenary finally decided he had found a home?

Simon and Bruce must be content; they had found the drummer of their dreams. But there was always Charlie, and Charlie wouldn't desert him.

He tried again. This time, he made it past the bridge, and then faltered again during the transition to the chorus. A cocktail of pain and fatigue halted him in his path.

He took out the crumpled picture of his mom and set it on his snare drum. Her body turned into a splotchy lump of pink, green, and purple as the tears hit the photocopy.

#

Two weeks later, he tried again. He played three songs without a mistake.

91

His neighbor had given him a cure.

Chapter 21

"Does Hank seem, I don't know, a little *not there* to you?" Everett asked.

Alice shrugged her shoulders, the universal gesture of *I don't know.*

Cancer had robbed her of her energy, along with her keen skills of observation. In truth, she had noticed little difference in Hank's behavior. Restaurants were stressful places, not for the faint-hearted. Everyone that worked at The Hickory for a long time bore the evidence—another line carved in their face, the shoulders drooping a little further. Everett knew Hank was burning the candle at both ends—practicing before work, working all day, and then going and practicing again. But Everett thought this was different. This wasn't being overworked.

"He looks too thin. That's the only change I see," Alice said.

"He keeps nodding off during his shift in the back. Sometimes he'll do it while he still has a knife in his hand."

"Really?" In the halcyon days of the restaurant, this response would have been full-throated, enough to make the dishwasher drop whatever was in his hand. Now it was wan. A response of obligation. The pressure to keep talking and comforting the living, though her thoughts were with the dead. But she'd be out here giving half-hearted responses until the clock ran out. Because, what else could she do?

"Yeah. *Really.* I've seen Maria shake him awake more than once. Caught him sleeping out back in the smoke pit when I told him to go pull some ribs.

Lost five racks. Which, fine, whatever, we lost a little food. But it's just that this type of stuff has never happened before, you know. Hank's no scholar, we all know that, and shit, neither am I"—Alice and Everett had always freely talked about Hank's shortcomings when it was just the two of them, but they never would have told Hank to his face, never— "but it's just not like him, is all."

"His mind is just on his band, don't you think?"

Everett knew Hank's mind was elsewhere. But he feared something much worse. Everett knew the eyes. He knew the ticks. And he knew the fatigue.

"I'm going to cut his hours back. That way he won't have to spread himself so thin. The band is about done with the tour, and they're about to start working on new music. He wants to be ready. I'll cut his hours back and let just him focus on that."

A flash of energy moved through her. "What do you really think is wrong with him?"

And then Everett did something, by his memory, he had not done since he had relapsed in the nineties: he lied to Alice. "Nothing. I think he's just tired and stressed. He's always worrying that Simon and Bruce are going to give him the boot. And you know with his anxiety... once we get him back playing in the band, he'll be fine."

Everett could tell his response rang hollow.

Alice gave no reaction.

All told, since her diagnosis, she was down forty pounds. Her excess skin, formerly stretched out to accommodate her plump body, hung from her arms like long neglected drapes.

"You got the girls? I'm going to go take a nap." Back in the office, where receipts and invoices were scattered helter-skelter, Everett had set up a cot for Alice to take breaks. She would have preferred to go home and nap, and had stated as much. But he couldn't stand the thought of her being alone at her house, or worse, having a wreck on the way home. Another concession she made to those with ample life left to live.

"Yeah. I got it. Go get some rest."

She turned, standing in the doorway of the office and spoke. "Just talk to him, Ev. He'll talk to you. He always has."

Still worried about his son and trying to hide how much Alice's appearance upset him—she was withering into a husk and all he could do was watch—Everett gave a silent nod of recognition. Then Alice retired to rest.

Chapter 22

"**A**re you sure you want to do this?" Against type, Lisa asked the question meekly. She knew the band was where Hank was most sensitive.

Hank's hand trembled as he ran it through his hair. He was tapping his foot against the floor too, a nervous habit of his. Sometimes he did it because he was working out a drum beat in his head. Other times, it was brought on by nerves. Today, Lisa could tell it was the latter. "No. But what else should I do? The guys are back. No one has kicked me out. So, I don't know." DCP had booked some homecoming gigs to stay sharp while writing the new album.

"Just don't let Simon and Bruce be dicks to you. Stand your ground if they start in with that maybe-it's-just-time-to-move-on bullshit."

"I know, babe. I won't."

"Is that same guy still filling in? Pearson?"

"He's just a mercenary. He'll move on to the next gig as soon as I come back. Those guys are headhunters. They just move from band to band." Charlie's comment bounced around in Hank's head, turning over and over, clothes in a dryer: *He always wanted to be in a metal band.*

Lisa was sitting on a stool across the granite counter, clutching a warm mug of tea. To her knowledge, coffee and tea were the only mind-altering substances in the house. During Hank's rehab from the wreck, Lisa had purged the house of all booze, and even the small stash of marijuana she kept in the nightstand. Long gone were the days of a glass or two of wine (or three or four) before bed, or on the weekends rolling a loose-fitted joint and taking the edge off. Some old habits needed to die.

Without hesitation, to her surprise, Hank agreed to the changes. Ever since they started dating, Hank had always had a beer or two before bed. When he sloughed the habit off, like swatting away a nettlesome fly, she was happy, but skeptical that he had agreed to it so easily. Hank had always been a hawk when it came to his daily habits. Always two cups of black coffee in the morning. Always two hours of practicing drums in the afternoon. Always a sandwich from his father's restaurant for lunch. He always ate the pulled pork; had been doing it ever since she met him. And for the days he didn't work at the Hickory, he had a stockpile wrapped and frozen at the house. She had suggested once that he vary what he eats for lunch, that it wasn't good for him to eat the same things every day. She even joked with him and said that he had the diet of a child. When she had, he had looked back at her sadly, like he was asking her not to take that piece of comfort away from him. And most importantly, always a craft beer with dinner and then another as he watched TV before bed. Hank was a man of ironclad rituals. Her asking him to stop shouldn't have been enough. They should have had an argument or a fight or something. He had given it up without even so much as a sigh in protest.

Something felt off.

"How has the playing been going? Were you able to make it all the way through the new album?"

Had he not told her last week? Surely, he did. He *had* made it through the new album. Twice, in fact. Lately, his memory felt like Swiss cheese. Things just kept dropping through the holes. He was just tired. Too many irons in the fire, as his Dad would say. "Yeah. I made it through twice, actually. If the guys would agree to play a shorter set, then I could be good to go in a week or two."

A glimmer of hope in her eyes, Lisa said, "Well, that's good, right?"

"Yeah, it's great." Hank looked at the clock on the oven. "You about ready to head out?"

She needed to trust him. But she *had* to ask. He wouldn't mind. After all, if he had nothing to hide, then he would just simply answer the question.

"Hank, you're not still taking the pills, right?"

"No, babe. You watched me flush every one of them."

Unbeknownst to Hank, who never passcode-protected his iPhone, she had downloaded an app on both their phones that let her track him. A little over the top, yes. A little on the stalker side? Duly noted. But Lisa had never been known for her modesty. In the end, she had seen too many friends from high school and college fall victim to pills. So what, she trespassed into Hank's business. Love makes you do crazy things. Batshit crazy things.

"I know baby, but I also know how much you love this band and—"

"Babe. I told you. I flushed them. You can even check my pockets."

She balked at the thought of rifling through his pockets. No need to kick the night off on a bad note. But, then again, if he has nothing to hide... "Okay, turn out your pockets." Hank did as commanded. And just as he said, no clickety-clack of a pill falling to the floor.

"Do you mind going and getting Danny? And on the way, I think it'd be best if we talk to him about how you're not playing tonight. I don't want him to get sad."

"Okay, babe. Sounds good." That's the way he always sounded lately. All his responses prepackaged in nice, boring little boxes. In times past, he would have taken over and said, *I'll just talk to him now, we'll do it over a song.*

Her mind raced: *I could drug test him. Nice way to show I trust him.* And she could hear him saying that word, that fucking word: Babe, I'm fine, I think you're just *overreacting.* God, how she hated that word. *Overreacting.* Like she wasn't entitled to her emotions. As if feeling them was a crime. What was so crazy about loving someone so much you didn't want them to harm themselves?

No harm in checking the app again, though. She could just take a peek.

Hank lumbered down the stairs with Danny in tow.

I need to drug test him. No, I need to keep my head and not run him off.

She went back to her app, as Danny and Hank walked out the door.

Hank yelled back, "You coming or staying?"

"Yeah, yeah, I'm coming."

"You and that phone."

"Hey, I'm not on it that much."

"Whatever. Let's go."

"I'll meet you guys at the car."

She looked again at the travel history. Home, work, gas station. Rinse and repeat. No tangents to a shady part of town, where a guy with a nickname like *Murda* waited to sell him heroin.

Chapter 23

Alejandro Mercano lived in a one-story rancher just outside of Belle Glade. The house had red brick, black shutters in dire need of fresh paint, and looked like many of the homes built in the Fifties and Sixties. The street Alejandro lived on was lined with these squat brick homes. Each had a chain link fence hemming in the back yard. Nothing about the home's outside spoke of the things that transpired within it.

A woman named Silvia Heatherford lived there too. To others on the quiet street, she appeared to be his wife, and Alejandro and Silvia did nothing to disabuse their neighbors of that notion. Alejandro spoke English with ease, giving them further cover for their exploits. Nothing to see here. Same as everyone else. Ready to light up the grill and throw back a light beer.

The truth was Alejandro had not immigrated here—he had been sent, conscripted against his will by some of the most violent men on earth. And when given an order, you followed it, or you and your family met an early grave. What choice did he have?

Silvia was different. In the beginning, she had only longed to make money. Her motive was as old as the Bible: she wanted to get rich, and she knew these men would line her pockets. All she saw was what the money would bring her: power, respect, no longer being a poor, pissed-on daughter of a sugarcane farmer. Follow orders. Recruit trustworthy dealers. And help spread the brown disease sweeping America.

As the epidemic spread, spurred along by opioid pills, Melvin had given her more responsibility, which meant more money. Along the way, however, she discovered something about herself: it wasn't just about the money. The power that came with it, the control—she liked that too.

Over time, Melvin had convinced his boss that Silvia deserved their trust. Melvin had watched her for weeks, going from one flophouse to the next, collecting money from underlings, robbing junkies if need be. He saw the black stirring within her—bubbling beneath the surface—and he knew that they could put her to good use.

With horrifying efficiency, the Black-Eyed Man had done the Cartel's bidding for years. Now, the trust for the Black-Eyed Man's ability as an independent contractor was beyond reproach. As long as the money arrived on time, the shadowy men that lived in undisclosed desert-locales asked no questions.

For the past three years, Alejandro's fear and Silvia's greed had made them an efficient pair.

As instructed in the message from Melvin, Silvia walked into the den where Alejandro sat, watching the Cooking channel, which was pretty much all he watched these days. He had told Silvia that it relaxed him to see happy people doing mindless things. Trying to erase her past, Silvia ate everything in sight. She was not obese, nor was she skinny. She existed somewhere in between—thick thighs, a droopy belly that hung like a tear drop over her too-tight denim shorts, and a red tank top revealing arms dimpled with fat. She walked into the room and stood in front of the T.V. Her dark black hair hung down to her shoulders in rich waves.

"You need to check the porch."

"Not now. Out of the way."

"Now."

"Why? I want to finish this show."

She pulled her favorite blade, a long, serrated knife, and rested it against the sag of her belly. "You know that you and me don't make our own decisions. Do it now. Melvin's orders."

He got up, his recliner bobbing back and forth now free of his weight.

She smiled, her tan face covered in cracks, prematurely aged from years in the sun as a kid. "Let me know what you find. And after, I will read you the message from Melvin." She used the calming tone of a mother, but one that spoke to you kindly as she pushed your face under the water in the tub.

A recent victim of middle age, Alejandro's lower back screamed and his knees cracked like walnuts as he bent down to pick up the mahogany box he found on the porch. The box was roughly the size of a hardback book, polished and without blemish. Far too nice looking to be sitting out in the Florida sun on Alejandro and Silvia's weather-stained concrete porch. Alejandro knew that the fine exterior was a clever ruse. He had heard the rumors about the Cartel's contractor, and he had had enough contact with Melvin, the man's enforcer, to know he wanted no part of whatever was in the box. Without looking inside, he brought it back in the house and set it down on the coffee table. And backed away.

"Melvin's text said to open it." She motioned with her knife. "Get to it."

As he looked down at the box, an image of his children, running on the shiny brown square tiles that lined his home in Juarez, flashed through his head. How he wished he could go back there right now, hug his sons, kiss his wife. Fading dreams from another life.

He opened the small jewelry box: a piece of human flesh had been stretched to make a small rucksack for shards of bones. It looked as if the skin had been melded to the bones. Sprinkles of black and red lined the edges of the gnarled flesh, curled and twisted, the beginnings of decomposition halted by chemicals. At the top of the sack, there was a small hole with a key chain hung from it: a papier-mâché of human remains.

In disgust, Alejandro placed his hand over his mouth, making sure his lunch stayed down.

Scratching the bare skin of her stomach that poked out below her shirt, eyes glistening in wonder, Silvia smiled and said:

"Now, listen. From Melvin: 'This is all that remains of that parasite Hector. Silvia, though you recruited him, and bear some blame, you did not attempt to hide anything from me. Alejandro, the same cannot be said for you. You learned of Hector's thieving and said nothing. Think—what will become of your family? I know, and so do you: their rotting carcasses will line the desert. Is that what you want? So here is how we will wipe this blight from your record: you will carry this totem everywhere. If not, then we will take you to our special place in the glades. Put the totem in your pocket. Godspeed.'

"Got it? Every day, everywhere you go. It's in your pocket." She tapped the knife against her stomach as she spoke.

Melvin had not crafted those words. He rarely spoke, and when he did, it was always in clipped phrases. Silvia knew who had written it.

And Alejandro knew who had crafted the words too: the man with the dead eyes.

He put Hector's flesh and bones in his pocket.

Chapter 24

They got to the venue late. The opening band had already gone on—a local Hardcore group called Ocean Black was ripping through a set of short songs, and God, they were loud; there was no hope of any small talk while these guys were on stage. Hank could feel the bass bludgeoning his stomach, the distorted guitars swallowing his ears, and the sludge of the bass drum shaking his heart, and it all felt like coming back home. He, Danny, and Lisa listened to a few songs and then headed backstage.

The venue was a tiny but hallowed spot for local heavy music. The Knot had been around for decades and like St. Vitus bar in New York, playing there was a badge of honor for any heavy band on the rise. Playing at The Knot meant your band mattered, not just to the fans, but to the metal websites that gave your art life on the internet.

They were entombed by the bar's darkness as they walked to the back hall, passing the stage on the way, scuffed and scarred from years of guitar players jumping up and down. The hall they walked through was lined with flyers from past concerts.

Lisa and Danny stayed behind Hank as they walked through the claustrophobic corridor. Danny kept stopping to look at the different band posters decorating the walls. Some he had heard of, like Mastodon; others, he hadn't the foggiest, like Goathead Revival.

Band after band. So many of them trying to become a part of America's grand tapestry of music.

"Danny, man, hurry up. I want to talk to the guys before the show."

Lisa shot Hank an angry look. "Don't be a dick, give him a second."

"Alright. Alright." Hank stopped and looked back with his arms crossed.

Danny's eyes were glued to the wall, as if he was searching for a loved one's name on a list of the dead after a disaster.

"Danny dude, what the hell? Let's go."

"Hank." Lisa's eyes were the size of saucers as she spit out his name.

Brimming with stress, Hank uncrossed his arms and tried to steady his trembling hands. As the seconds slipped away, he reminded himself, *This is just Danny, give him a minute, it's not his fault. It's not his—* "Danny, what the fuck, man? Will you just come on!"

She grabbed his arm, "You can't yell at him like that."

"Oh, stop it. He can handle it. You baby him. He's an adult."

"Don't talk to him like that again, alright?"

"Alright. Alright. Danny, come on."

Danny was already at Hank's side; he had scurried over after Hank yelled at him.

#

"Hank, good to see you."

The room was snug, only a tattered couch (no telling what deeds had been performed on it, judging by the stains) and a coffee table pressed against the wall, covered with candles and take-out food. Charlie wrapped him in a hug.

Simon and Bruce stayed seated. They both offered up their hands and exchanged an awkward embrace with Hank. Simon's aquiline nose jutted out, parting his dark hair, which partially obscured his tiny eyes, the size of kidney beans. Bruce's dark hair was cut in the same style, his rich brown eyes peeking from the draping curtain of hair. Both had baby faces, even though they were pushing thirty, and both looked displeased to see Hank.

The small room couldn't hold them all. Danny and Lisa waited by the door.

Charlie asked, "So, how's the playing been going? You feeling better?"

"I made it through the whole set we were playing on the last tour. The other day I even played it back-to-back. I should be ready in a few weeks."

Smiling ear to ear, Charlie popped him on the shoulder, brimming with energy. "That's great. Can't wait to have you back." Charlie's comment caused Simon and Bruce to shift.

Hank scanned the small room. Where was the fill-in guy, Pearson?

"What about work, man? How's your dad? I stopped in there to eat the other day, but I didn't see you there."

"He's good. Listen, I was thinking that maybe I could play the last two shows with you guys. I looked at the Facebook page and saw the last two gigs are two weeks away. I should be good by then."

Charlie didn't need any time to think. "I'm good with it."

"Hank, I don't know. Don't you think it'd be better to just wait for the next tour?" Nasal and dismissive, Simon's voice had the sound of an elitist professor, frustrated to have to bother with the lesser mortals. "After this one wraps, we can meet at the space and try it out. But I just don't know about interrupting the flow we've got going. Not to mention, you sure your leg's up for it?"

"I can handle it. I've been working for months to get back to you guys."

"Listen, you can come practice with us after the tour and we'll see how it goes. There's no need to rush it."

"There is for me, man. I need to play. I need to—" *I need to still know that I can do this.* "Look, playing in *this* band is the reason I practiced every day for the last three months. For weeks, every time I kicked the bass, I felt pain. Every time. But I played through it. And now you're telling me you won't give me a chance?"

"Look, that's not what I'm saying. What I'm saying is that we have been on the road with Pearson for months. We have the set down pat. And I don't want to change things up for the last two shows. I'm not saying that you can't come play afterward. You can. And we'll see how it goes."

He keeps qualifying it; he wants me to try out for the band, like I'm trying to make the high school baseball team or some shit.

"Simon, man, he's worked for months. He's been in the band since the beginning. He's earned it." Charlie said.

"I still think it's a bad idea," Simon responded.

"Can you imagine having to play through pain like that? What it would take? He deserves to play. I like Pearson, but he's a scab."

"Well, he's a scab that plays every song perfectly."

I bet he plays to a click too, doesn't he? "And where is the scab? He doesn't hang out with you guys before the show?"

Simon glared at Hank, his eyes the size of kernels of corn, "No, we text him fifteen minutes before we go on, and then he comes."

"Nice. Must really like you guys."

"Oh, fuck you, Hank, at least he plays every song right."

"What's that supposed to mean?"

"You know exactly what it means. You fall out of time constantly. I hear it and so does Bruce. And I know Charlie does too, he just won't adm—"

"Hey man, don't lump me into this shit. I want Hank to play with us at those shows. And what's so wrong with him speeding up or slowing down a little here and there. What if that's the mood of the crowd that night? Isn't it more fun to respond to the energy in the room? If they wanted to listen to the record, then they could just stay at home."

In times past, Simon quieted down right about now, terrified to lose his golden goose. But things had changed. "No. Every part of the song serves a purpose. And I wrote them exactly as I wanted them. Those *alterations* you're talking about—they're called *mistakes.* And Hank makes shitloads of them. And I don't care if the scab doesn't hang out with us. When we get out there, he doesn't fuck anything up. So there. That's what I think."

Charlie went to respond but Lisa beat him to it. "Is it like a tiny dick thing or something? Or maybe daddy didn't hug you enough? Oh wait, oh no—Simon, are you still a virgin?"

Simon shrugged her off. He scanned his bandmates, a slight grin on his face, trying to reassure them that Lisa's accusations were baseless.

"He doesn't play with any heart." Before anyone else could chime in, Danny repeated himself. "He doesn't play with any heart." As he said it, he mashed his stubby finger against his chest slowly, as if on a delay.

Simon asked, "How do you know?"

Lisa responded for him. "He begged me to take him to a show for weeks. He had heard you talking about how the band was doing a run of shows in the area for the next two months. He begged and begged. And so, a few weeks ago, I thought, *Fuck it, let's do it.* You were out working at the restaurant. And we just went."

She wasn't looking at the rest of the band when she spoke, only Hank. She didn't give a shit what they heard or thought, except Charlie; she liked Charlie. Everyone did.

"What did Danny think?" Hank asked.

"You just heard it. He said the same thing to me when we left. And what Danny means, is that the scab plays like a robot, like a computer. Does everything perfectly and lulls you to sleep in the process."

"Why didn't you tell me about it?"

"I wanted to try and give Danny a chance to tell you. Danny thinks you're ten times the drummer Pierce or Proctor or whatever the fuck the guy's name is. Don't you get it, Hank? He begged to go because he was worried they were going to kick you out of the band. He wanted to make sure *you* were better."

Danny hadn't heard a word she said. After he poked his chest, he had turned to marvel at the collage of posters that covered every inch of the hallway.

Even though he hadn't been kicked out, there was growing sense of finality to this conversation. Simon had no real intention of letting him play with DCP again.

Mustering what energy he had left, he made his final plea to stay in the band he had given a decade of his life to. "Guys, I went through hell to make it back. The pain in my leg, it was terrible. I can play again. Please—"

"What's up guys? When we going on? I need a minute to go and check my set and make sure the opening band didn't screw with it." A tall, bald man had seemingly materialized out of nowhere.

Pearson.

Lisa turned on him. "Ahh, the illustrious Pearson, I presume." Hank saw him nod back at her. "So. Mr. Robot. You oiled up for the show?" Wide-eyed, the man looked at Bruce as if to ask *Who is this?* Lisa continued on before anyone could save him. "Can I ask you something?" She didn't wait for a response. "How can you have just one name? Cher, Madonna, Beyonce, Slash for God's sake, and let us not forget Prince's sexy ass... they have one name, and you know what they all have in common?" Lisa grinned and stepped closer to Pearson. "They are not unknown studio musicians." She laughed and stepped back, "And do you really think Pearson has the same ring as Slash?" Pearson's eyes scanned the room, hoping someone would interrupt. "So, I guess what I really meant to ask was: Are you bit of a douchebag, my friend?"

Much too late, Simon finally intervened. "Jesus, Lisa."

"No, my name's just Lisa. And Jesus never could have looked this fabulous." Lisa stuck out her hip, raised her hand, and then slowly lowered it, as if she were presenting herself on stage. Pearson looked like he had woken up in alternate reality.

Ignoring Lisa, Simon said. "Sorry dude, just ignore that. And yeah, we'll make sure you have time to check your kit before we get started. You want to come in for a minute, so we can discuss the set?"

Pearson took a quick look at Lisa again, and then Hank, and shook his head. "Nah. I'll see you guys out there. Same set we've been playing for months." He turned to walk away and then a look of recognition came over his face. "Hey you're Hank, right?" Hank nodded. "The one who is terrified of the click?" Hank gritted his teeth and looked to his bandmates, particularly Simon. They had discussed Hank's playing in his absence, no doubt. "Hey man, no worries, they didn't say anything bad. All I have to say is—surrender to the click. It did wonders for me. See you guys out there." And with that, the tall studio drummer from Hell walked into the venue.

Lisa made to shake his hand as he walked by. When he extended his hand to shake hers, she pulled it back and rubbed her hand down her hair. "Too slow, dipshit."

Shaking his head, his face downcast in bewilderment, Pearson left.

"Hank, I just don't see how it's going to work. I just don't see it."

"Hank deserves a shot—"

Danny interrupted Charlie. "Hank plays with heart. You should let him play." Danny had re-inserted himself in the doorway. Lisa had stepped back to allow Danny through and now peeked around his shoulder, doing her best to gore a hole into Simon with her stare.

"Look, I understand that, Danny. But Pearson has been doing a good job and we don't know if Hank's leg can hold up."

"Please Simon, let him play." Danny kept poking his chest. Without the aid of words, he strained to make his point. "Hank's not perfect. Pearson is perfect. But he can't..." Danny struggled to find the word. Seconds passed. And then more. No one dared interrupt him. Everyone, even Simon and Bruce, could see how hard this was for him—the veins rising under his skin, sweat trickling down his cherub cheeks. "He can't... create."

Charlie picked up the baton. "What Danny is saying is the guy can only reproduce. He can play anything he hears perfectly. But how will he be as a creator? What will *his* art sound like?"

"Please let him play." Danny's last words hung in the room as he turned back to the posters in the hall.

Simon could say no to Hank. He had even found the strength to say no to Charlie.

But even he couldn't say no to Danny.

No one could.

Chapter 25

They agreed: Hank would play the last two shows of the mini-tour. Whether Hank would help them write the next album was still up in the air. Hank didn't push his luck—once Simon agreed, and Bruce nodded along like had a real say in the matter, he wished them good luck and left the dressing room.

He, Lisa, and Danny waited amongst the crowd for DCP to come on. In the past, this would have been when he headed to the bar and got two 16 oz. tallboys. Lisa had taken the no-drinking thing to the extreme. The house was booze-free. He didn't miss it. He didn't need it; he still had his little oblong friend there to blanket him in euphoria.

Alcohol was no rival to his pills.

Waiting for the band to come on, Lisa grew impatient. "I'm going to get us some waters. You want one?"

Hank didn't respond; he just kept staring forward, blankly.

"Hank. Yo." She waved her hand in front of his eyes. "Do-you-want-a-water?"

"Sure," he said.

Lisa left to get the waters.

Hank kept his eyes on her until she was swallowed up by the crowd, then turned back to the stage.

And then, the payoff, the moment that dwarfs all others for a concertgoer: things went black.

A voice came over the loudspeaker, the monologue that opened their latest album.

As the words flowed on, a maggot crawled into Hank's brain: when was the last time he took an oxy? Four hours ago? Three? How many had he taken today? He used to be able to keep count, but now the numbers bedeviled him.

He knew the sight of Pearson outplaying him would rankle his nerves, make his hands shake, make his heart beat out of time.

Lisa had checked his pockets, but not the lining of his wallet. He reached down, pulled it out, and surreptitiously brought his hand up to his lips. But as he opened his mouth, he felt a sting on his hand. *What the hell?* The pill went skipping on the grimy floor, lost in the sea of feet around him.

"What the fuck was that, Hank?"

"Huh?"

Lisa dropped the water; the plastic bottles bounced off the floor and collided with a couple standing nearby, who were too lost in the music to care. "Was that a pill? I cannot believe you." She was shaking, she was so mad.

"What are you talking about? It was a piece of gum."

"Oh, really, genius? You think I'm that stupid, then show me the rest of the pack."

"That was the last one... I've already thrown the pack away."

"Whatever, Hank. We're leaving and you're leaving too. And if you want to keep living with me, you're getting some help."

"Help? Like rehab? I'm not an addict. I need it for my leg. Don't you get that?"

"Oh really, Hank, from a broken leg? You haven't had a cast on for months and the wreck was almost a year ago. You don't need—"

"Yes, I fucking do." His voice pealed like lightning. He had never yelled at her like that before. "I need them to help me play. You heard Simon in there. If I can't show them I'm fine, they are going to kick me out."

"I don't care, Hank. You have a problem. And you lied to me. You *lied.* You told me you stopped." Her shoulders drooped. The reality of Hank lying, *He's a liar,* cut into her.

"I don't have a fuc—" The blare of Simon's guitar cut Hank off. The band ripped into the first song. To incite the crowd, right as the drums kicked in, Charlie jumped off the stack of amps in the back and people lost their minds.

Hank's head had pivoted to the stage, instinctually. *God, he's a showman.*

When he turned his head back, Lisa and Danny were gone.

#

He found her in the parking lot, smoking a cigarette. Danny had his headphones on, lost in his music.

Hank spoke first. "Babe, I will stop taking them after things get back on track with the band. If I stop right now, I may not be able to get back in the band."

"You may be able to lie to yourself, but you can't lie to me."

Neither of them noticed Danny remove his headphones.

"I'm not lying."

"You really going to try that right now, Hank? After I just caught you lying. You told me you were done with the pills. And I believed you. *I believed you.* I'm just as stupid as you are." She kicked some gravel after saying it. She looked at the cigarette and threw it down. *There goes two years of not smoking.* She had bummed it off a bouncer as she exited. She thought it would calm her nerves, but it just made her feel worse.

"Babe, I'm sorry. It's just that, you know how much the band means to me. It's my life."

At the sound of those last words, *It's my life,* Lisa felt exhausted. Her eyes grew heavy with tears. "No, you idiot. *We* are your life. The Hickory is your life. Your dad and Alice are your life. That's where you need to be: the restaurant. I know how much you love music, Hank. And I supported it because I love you. But you're obsessed. You're not thinking right."

"You're overreacting. It's a pill."

"I'm what?" The sadness abated, and anger took its place. That fucking word. The one she hated above all others. "I'm what, Hank? Overreacting? Screw you. Don't try and make me feel stupid for caring about you. I'm trying to help you."

"Look, I'm just saying that it's not a big deal. I need to play. And when I don't, I'll just stop."

"Oh, you will? The same person I found passed out the other day in the middle of the afternoon."

"That was a nap."

"Bullshit, Hank. You were pale. I had to put my hand on your chest to make sure your heart was still beating." After an awkward silence, she pivoted. "Well then, just stop now. You said it yourself, you made it through the whole set twice, so why wait? Quit now."

"No."

"What do you mean, *no*. Like, no, you won't try? Or no, you're not stopping?"

"*No,* I won't stop until I feel like I can play without them. And right now, I don't know when that will be."

She was confident that deep down, under the fog the opiates created, enough of Hank was still there to choose her over the pills. "You can't live with me while you're on those pills. You've been snapping at Danny. And you snap at me if I ask you about them. I need to be able to trust you. And I need to know that you're *my* Hank, not some stranger chasing pills. You're a different person when you're on them. And what's worse, is when you're off them, you get angry. I don't want that in my house, and I don't want it around Danny.

Gently, she clasped his hand and lowered her voice. "But I love you and I want to be with you. Please come home with me. We'll take it day by day. Please."

On the defensive, Hank tried to summon his anger to protect his identity, but the words came out weak, desperate, like he was trying to convince himself. "If that's the way you feel, then I'll pick up my stuff. I can stop when I want to. You're overreacting, whether you want to admit it or not."

"Wait. You're not coming home?"

He avoided eye contact with her, nervously shuffling his feet. "I'll wait around for Charlie. He will let me stay with him tonight. I'll come by tomorrow and get my stuff while you're at work." *Was this really happening?* It seemed like the moment was getting away from him.

"You're serious."

Still avoiding eye contact, Hank nodded and offered a barely audible, "Yes."

"You're going to pick those pills over us?" As she pointed to Danny, she realized he didn't have his headphones on. And she saw something she hadn't seen since they were kids: he was crying.

She bounded over to him and gave him a hug.

Hank responded to her question: "That's not the way I see it. I don't have a problem." He had to look closer because at first, he couldn't believe Danny was crying, either. Hank had never seen him do that.

"You're not just leaving me, Hank. You know that, right? Don't do this."

"I'm not doing anything. You gave the... what's the word... you know what I mean, you forced me into a choice."

Pitying him, Lisa said, "Ultimatum is the word."

It was Hank's turn to look defeated. "God, why is that so easy for you and so hard for me." Offloading his frustration, Hank kicked some gravel.

"And I'm asking you to make the right one. Choose us. Come on, let's just go home." She reached out her hand to Hank as she said it.

#

At the same time, Hank felt a faint twinge of pain in his knee: the devil there to remind him that he could take the thing he loved and not feel a second's remorse.

What Lisa and Danny didn't know was that Hank had found that pill she'd knocked out of his hand. Got down on his knees in the floor-grime and found it. And the sight of Pearson playing and Charlie grinning back at him, mixed with Lisa yelling and storming out, was just too much. Hank had taken the one he found on the floor and the other one he had stashed in his wallet.

He didn't know how to see a life for himself without the drums. The pills would get him his life back. What didn't she see that?

Just then, the oxy started sluicing into his blood stream. He felt the chemicals numb out the pain in his knee and blank out his thoughts. In a faint way, a voice in his head told him to respond to Lisa; it was muffled, like someone was yelling through a wall next door. He ignored it. For now, he wanted to stay right here in the beautiful nothingness. Hank turned and walked back into the venue.

Chapter 26

"Alright Hank, we go on in fifteen. Just like we practiced it." Simon said this with the self-righteous tone of an overbearing teacher.

"I got it. Just like practice."

"And you good with the click?"

"I've got all the tempos saved on my drum-pad." All Hank had to do was hit the pad before each song and the pre-saved tempos would repeat in his inner-ear monitors.

"Excellent. Alright, I'll see you guys at stage right." Simon left the room.

"How you feeling? You ready?" Charlie asked.

"Yeah. We practiced these songs to death. I keep hearing them in my sleep. If I wake up in the middle of the night, I still hear them. That ever happen to you?"

"All the time. You missed eight months of the tour. We have played these songs into the ground. I can't wait to work on new stuff."

"Well, hopefully, I'll be a part of the new stuff. You think they'll kick me out if I fuck it up tonight?"

"Yeah, bud. If it goes wrong out there, then Simon is going to kick you out and then give me the ultimatum. He should have given you time to let your leg heal. Time where you knew your spot was guaranteed. Instead, he fell in love with that studio drone Pearson. One name: Pearson. Douchebag."

"Well then, I won't give him a reason to give me the boot."

"I know. You got this."

Charlie got up to do a few sets of push-ups, an abiding pre-show ritual to get the blood flowing. While Charlie got his body into gear, Hank looked down to his phone: two missed calls from Lisa and three from his dad. He'd call them after. For now, the only thing that existed to him was getting the gig right. They could wait. He would call Everett first, and then Lisa. Maybe. The word she called him popped into his head, as big as a skyscraper, looking like the hyper-animated words from a comic book: ADDICT. Did she even deserve a call?

Five minutes until showtime.

His warmup finished, Charlie looked over to Hank and noticed his drooping eyes. They were half-shut, the look of someone fighting to stay awake.

"Hank. Hank."

Hank bolted up.

"You been getting enough sleep, man?"

"Yeah, yeah. I'm good. Don't we need to get out there?"

Charlie nodded and quickly left the room.

Hank stood up from the couch and felt a sharp pain shoot up like an arrow from his lower leg into his thigh. *What pill am I on today? Sixth? Seventh?*

The neighbor at the old complex had introduced him to a different supplier: a man named Vince, who said he got the bulk of his stuff from someone who lived out in Belle Glade. Hank's orders were getting too big—the neighbor was a small retailer, a boutique outfit. Hank needed someone that could handle bulk. On the last round, he got ninety. Cost him a pretty penny too; he had to get the money from Everett on loan. Everett, begrudgingly, handed it over with the understanding that Hank would work it off at The Hickory.

Even with the pills, the pain had been intermittent ever since the wreck, rearing its head unpredictably, reminding him that the crash had forever changed the makeup of his body.

He moved to walk, and his leg seized up.

He reached for the photo of his mom in his pocket. He searched and searched, turning out every pocket on his cargo shorts. Soon after, it hit him, he had never gone back to retrieve the copies.

How did I forget?

The photos were legion; he had them hidden all over the townhouse. Hell, he even had them stashed all over The Hickory. Two places that had drifted to the back of his mind as he swam down the river after his dream. A tangerine river, the same as the color of the poppy.

There was one thing he found when he turned out his pockets, however. His new talisman.

He downed two of his little friends. They would see him through. He had never met his mom anyhow.

#

The venue was bigger than The Knot, but not as well known. It held around a thousand people, and to the band's surprise, they had sold the place out.

They all waited stage right as the monologue from *Astral Curse* played. Charlie and Hank always bumped fists before going on. Simon and Bruce refused to engage in any pre-show send off.

Charlie extended his clenched fist and looked to Hank. Hank's eyes were glazed. "Hank."

"Oh yeah... it's been a while." Hank bumped Charlie's hand.

And with that, the band shuffled out on stage to take their spots.

Hank took his seat. He adjusted the drum throne just so, and checked his reach, making sure he could hit each cymbal. And against everything in his nature, he hit the drum-pad to unleash the metronome in his ear.

And before he knew it, they were already on the third song. He started to remember how time collapsed on itself when he played live, minutes turned into seconds. So far, he hadn't made any mistakes.

Right as rain.

Even better, his leg was holding up. The pain there, but not there. Synapses still firing and finding their receptors. Everything still connected, but with a veil of narcotics numbing the energy shooting through the wires.

Fourth song. Over, and without incident.

There was an interlude between the fourth and fifth song, where he hit one of his electronic pads and some samples played. He dabbed his forehead with a towel, and when he leaned back up, the room spun. He shook his head to get his eyes to focus, but the room remained blurry, like he had opened his eyes underwater. He shook again and to his relief, the world fell back into focus.

Fifth song. Full of twists and turns, and ample helpings of the double bass-pedal. The song demanded everything Hank had from his legs. He snapped his head up to look at the crowd, and again, the world fell out of focus.

The stagehand of sleep started to pull again. This time, he found no resistance because the pills had severed the counterweight. *Show's over, folks, time to go home.*

#

Mid-lyric, Charlie looked back in confusion, Hank was supposed to be playing. In fact, he was supposed to be holding a steady sixteenth note with his double bass. But the bottom had dropped out. Charlie didn't see Hank's face, only the top of his head. Charlie walked over and saw Hank's cheek pressed against his tom-drum.

Hank had passed out.

Charlie lifted his arm and it fell right back down. Deadweight. Charlie thought of Keith Moon, and the footage he had seen of Pete Townsend going back to the drums and realizing his drummer was unconscious. Allegedly, horse tranquilizers had gotten the better of The Who's drummer that night. Maybe like Townsend, he should ask if there were any drummers in the house.

Realizing what had happened, the crowd began to turn on them, demanding their money back and throwing drinks at the stage.

Charlie teared up, knowing what would come next.

He turned to see Simon staring at him, shaking his head, and watched him make a wordless motion: Simon drew his thumb across his neck and pointed at Hank.

Charlie and one of the roadies lifted Hank off his set as the crowd jeered, hurling expletives at the speed of light. They got him to a couch backstage. Charlie looked down at his friend, shook his head, and walked off to get some air.

#

It was 2015 and Hank Grant was 29 years old. He had lived in South Florida all of his life, meandering his way through school, finishing high school in the bottom third of the pack (he knew better than to apply for college). When he was ten, Everett got him his first drum-set for Christmas. Back when classified ads still drew eyes, Everett had found a used Tama drum-set. *No sense in spending lots of money on the first set,* Everett thought. *After all, he might abandon it after a few weeks.* But Hank didn't quit. And month after month, he got better and better.

His drum-set saw him through everything: the only thing aside from the photo of his mother, that could calm him. Whether it was bad grades, insults from kids at school, or anxiety attacks so bad he couldn't catch his breath, through all things, his drum-kit was there. Given to him by a man that adored him and encouraged him to chase his dream.

In their biology, however, there was a common enemy running through Everett and Hank, a demon that paid no mind to race, status, or gender.

Lisa had told him, but he couldn't hear what she had to say. There was no room for her. With the ghost of his mother, his drums, and now the drugs, where was Lisa to fit?

In the end, drugs strip away all the other elements of life, an attention grabber discontent to share the limelight. They take and take and take.

Now, all that remained was the muddy powder that came from grinding together the pod of the poppy, there to lull Hank into eternity.

Hank Grant was an addict.

PART IV

The Fourth Echo

2017: The Florida Everglades

"I think art is mankind's greatest talent. Though, judging by what I see on television, I think modernity would disagree. To them, it seems that sports figures triumphing over the odds, or glossy movie stars, are more deserving of attention. Or following the lives and minutiae of people famous for seemingly no reason at all—*famous for being famous*—the absurdity of it drains me. Same with music. Pop stars, most of them, aren't artists, not in the sense that they are the creator; they are the presenters—a pretty face to sell a product. In most cases, they don't even craft the songs they go on to claim as their own. Someone else, the creator, the person behind the curtain, *they* are the artist. But, I digress. I've done that a lot over the course of our little talks. But you don't seem to mind."

They had moved on from the pills. They now had the captive doped up through an IV running into his forearm. The IV pumped one drug in to keep him awake, so they could continue the beating. In a separate line, another kept him from withdrawal.

The captive man was covered in cuts, blood, and bruises.

When they were beating his leg, that's the first time he had blacked out.

They took turns swinging an axe-handle at his shin. By the time they finished, the flesh was ripped away—now hanging in tatters like shredded leather—the bone exposed to the humid air.

Then, they woke him back up.

The Black-Eyed Man made him watch as he gripped the exposed bone of his leg with large pliers, squeezing and twisting; the ridged teeth of the pliers grinded against his bone, tearing off the enamel.

He passed out again.

And then they woke him up again.

They had done other things to him, things he wished not to think of ever again, in this life or the next.

Shuddering, he looked over to see the man with the beard grab a power drill and walk it over to the man with the hollow eyes. He handed it off and walked back over to the shelves—jars lined the hanging wooden planks jutting out of the wall. Some looked filled with maroon liquid. Others held bits of matter: *Flesh? Skin?* He couldn't tell from this distance, but they were human remains, he could see that much. There were also dark masses hanging on the side walls of the room. The sunlight coming through the door wasn't bright enough to reveal the figures. But several of them were spread out in a grid on each side. *What were they?*

Fear shot through him anew as he peered at the jars and whatever was hanging from the walls, then back to the drill in the man's hand.

Hope had left him long ago.

Now he wished for the mercy of death.

"I've learned that I have a talent for a form of art people overlook, or worse, one they consider a human ill, not a craft. You see, that lout that beat my sister, he taught me something. As that bastard dragged the fire-poker across my head, I didn't appreciate what he was doing at the time. But now I understand. You see, he didn't keep beating me with it. He knew that would kill me. So, he started carving my scalp, instead. He was marking me for life.

"He created his form of art: he needed to control me, and make sure the rest of the world knew what happened when you crossed him. He branded me.

"You too, will be a symbol to all those in our little underworld. They will interpret it as a symbol of fear—what happens to you when you cross the man with ties to Mexico. But it will have another meaning to my associate and I, a deeper one, one that transcends time and space: you will be an everlasting symbol in the war against my creator.

"You see, a lifetime of disappointment and violence has taught me one thing that outstrips all others: bloodshed is *art*."

The next thing the captive man heard was the sound of the drill.

Come now, death. Please come.

Chapter 27

Fall 2016: Near West Palm Beach, Fl.

The plan was simple. Harebrained, but simple. Clyde Brewer would wait at the garden exit with the car running, and when Hank left the store, he would get into the car without fanfare and they would exit the parking lot. No speeding. No sharp turns and screeching tires. No need to draw attention to the misdeed accomplished.

Drugs were not free. And high-power drill sets equaled quick cash at pawn shops, one of the many things Hank had learned about the drug underworld. TVs were too hard to come by. For that, you had to burglarize a home, an offense that scored you prison time in Florida. After spending some time in jail, Hank had also gotten savvier about the sentencing laws. He had yet to be charged with a felony like burglary, but his bunkmates had stories to tell. The experienced guys, the ones that wore their institutionalization like a bad tattoo, they could tell a rising misdemeanant like Hank everything he needed to know about committing petty crime to get more dope. And hopefully enough to avoid prison.

Before the debacle that ended with his face squished against his drums, then his unconscious body being carried away and thrown on the floor of the dressing room by the Knot's sound-guy and a couple of bartenders, Hank had no criminal record, only the usual collection of speeding and parking tickets. After his first two arrests for theft, he took time served the next morning when they brought him down for first appearance. On one of them, they even waived the court costs and restitution because Wal-Mart got the tools back. But on the third, coming only days after his second conviction, they jacked up his bond. He had to call Everett and ask for bail money. That stung.

Everett had bailed him out, but they hadn't spoken since. Hank didn't even see him when he did it. Everett quietly paid the bonding company, and after Hank bonded out, he ignored his calls. That had been three months ago.

Somewhere in his befogged mind, Hank knew that, for the moment—a moment that had turned into a lifestyle—he couldn't bring himself to care. He was still floating atop the tangerine river, staring at a cloudless blood-orange sky, listening to the water lap against his skin. Everett's love, and the consequent disappointment that comes with all love, was lost on Hank. All he could feel was the euphoric water. All he could see was the empty sky. All he yearned for was the blankness in his mind and heart the muddy powder induced.

Things were easier when everything got erased.

Sometimes when the heroin sloughed the hours off, robbing time of its meaning, he would float on the river, staring up at the blazing sun, and feel that his mother was about to float up to him. Somehow, in this dream, they had both ended up in the same parallel world. During the fantasy, she floated up, their faces turned to each other, and they talked, a quiet, simple conversation: the most mundane of things to the living, something taken for granted.

As they talked, Hank finally got to ask her where she came from, her favorite ice cream as a kid, her favorite movie, and whether she liked seafood.

But when the high wore off, as much as he tried, he couldn't remember the things she had said.

Made sense. He couldn't remember much of anything lately.

The automatic doors of the Home Depot opened in front of him and he kept his head down as he glided past the greeter. He knew exactly where the drills were located.

He also knew exactly which brand and model he needed. They used the same pawnshop each time (Bill's Pawn) and the owner liked DeWalt drills—good sellers, is all he ever said in response when he and Clyde asked questions. Bill didn't ask where they came from, and they didn't tell.

He grabbed the drill and kept moving.

Hank had stolen from this Home Depot before, as well as two others further outside of town. As far as he knew, he wasn't in their crosshairs. If you got flagged, then the LPOs had an email network and they would send your photo out to all the other stores in the area.

So far, so good. He moved through the store, undetected.

Hank moved to the lawn equipment and after looking at the weed-eaters for a few seconds, he moved toward the exit.

"How are you doing, sir?" A man in a plaid shirt with a walkie-talkie blocked his path.

"I'm fine, thank you."

"Don't you think you should pay for that, sir?" The sliding doors were only about five feet away. He had been so close. Customers streamed by, heading for the outdoor garden section, casting quick looks at the confrontation between Hank and the mall cop, like it was a car wreck.

"Um, there are registers outside, and I wanted to go look at the flowers."

"Oh, a gardener, are you? Which variety are you interested in? We have many."

Hank had no clue. He had never gardened a day in his life. "I like magnolias. So maybe those." Through the fog, something Everett had mentioned emerged. He said he'd loved to look at magnolias when he was a kid. *Those are flowers, right?*

"Like the tree? I thought you said you were interested in flowers."

"Look, I'm a customer just like everyone else. I can pay where I want to. And I'd like to go look at the flowers. So, could you please get out of my way."

Hank moved to go around the man's flabby girth; the buttons on his plaid shirt were moments from shooting off like bullets. Hank shifted. The blob stepped closer to Hank's sickly frame, cutting off any exit.

Already skinny by nature, Hank had lost weight steadily since the band gave him the axe, roughly a year ago. Every vein of his arms and legs showed through the skin, like rolling, unpredictable hills of a desert seen from above. Sores dotted his body, too: some black, some peeling. Some oozing.

"Sir, like I said, I would prefer for you to pay at one of the indoor registers, and then you can step outside and look at the flowers."

"Isn't the customer always right, asshole? Get out of my way."

"Sir, no need to get testy. Also, can you help me out with something?" The man pulled a crumpled piece of paper from his pocket an email of some sort, with a picture.

Horrified, Hank saw it was him.

"You bear a striking resemblance to the man in this photo. Is that you?"

"Get out of my way, fat ass."

"Ahh. So it *is* you. Let's head back to my office and you can have a seat there." As if to comply, Hank slumped his shoulders in defeat. "Thank you, sir. Now, if you'll hand me that drill and then follow me to my office."

The man reached out for Hank.

Right then, Hank made a decision, one that would leave his misdemeanor days in his rearview.

The man in plaid never saw it coming.

Hank swung the drill box—a rock-hard plastic case filled with pounds of metal—as hard as he could at the man's head.

A string of blood shot out from the man's face—later, as the scene replayed in Hank's mind, he thought the spray of blood looked like a string of beads, a necklace—and splattered messy red splotches onto the kettle grills. The officer tumbled to the ground, face first.

Concerned customers spilled into the aisle, but Hank was already sprinting out to the garden center.

He passed the registers, looking for the rundown Ford Taurus that should have had a skinny man at the wheel, experiencing the same state of decay as Hank; but as Hank scanned the lot, he saw a sea of sedans, mini-vans, and sparkling-new SUVs— but no beaten-down sedan puttering along with a driver in need of a dentist.

Clyde was nowhere to be found.

Without another option, Hank ran out of the parking lot, the drill banging awkwardly against his leg. The house he had been living in with other like-minded addicts was three miles away. He would have to make it on foot, without being seen by the police. He tucked the hard box under his arm, smearing the fat man's blood on his mangy t-shirt, and ran.

\#

Out of habit, when the Home Depot was no longer in sight, he stopped and reached into his pocket for the photo. Panic and adrenaline had deluded him into thinking he still had a copy of it. The truth was, he had never gone back to get his things at the townhouse, nor had he found the courage to stay at The Hickory long enough to grab one of the copies he had hidden there. These days, he rarely stepped foot into the restaurant, unless he had to do something he and Everett hated in equal measure: asking for money.

He had not looked at the image of his mother in over a year. The last copy—one he'd filched from one of his old hiding places at The Hickory—he lost one night; deeply consumed by his high, he'd pulled it out to stare at it. Hours later he woke up on a ratty mattress, the photo nestled against his side, but when he left to go find food, he forgot about it. He and Clyde moved a few days later, and he left it behind. It was probably still there, gathering dust, a sad prop in a room where people went to forget.

Now, all that was in his pocket was dust balls and cheap cigarettes.

He lit one, and then walked on, doing his best not to look like a drug addict that had just committed a theft.

\#

"Clyde, where the fuck where you, man?" The glass door slammed behind him. The hydraulic pump that slowed the door had long since bitten the dust.

Clyde threw his arms up to signal it wasn't his fault. "Hey man, I waited there for ten minutes. We agreed before you went in that if it took longer than that, then you'd been caught. And shit, you could have just texted me."

"Huh?"

"Texted me. You could have told me to swing my shit-wagon back around and pick you up. So don't bitch at me because of your fuckup."

Hank had lost his burner. He and Clyde each changed numbers. He rarely remembered to save Clyde's new number. In truth, he had no clue where the last phone they bought even was.

"That's not the point. You should have stayed. I had to run all the way back here. I'm lucky I didn't get caught."

Clyde scratched his arm, grinning. As he smiled, he ran his untrimmed nails over a sore on his left arm: fresh trickles mushroomed out, spreading new blood over the dried.

"Hank, why don't we skip jawing at each other like teenage bitches and go get some cash."

Chapter 28

They got $250 for the drill set at the pawnshop. With cash in hand, they were headed straight to Vince Smith's house.

A middling drug dealer, Vince lived in West Palm Beach in a small single-family house. Hank found Vince after his old neighbor got tired of seeing him darken his door. That guy—Hank couldn't even remember his name—only liked giving Hank a handful of pills, charging him around $50, and then pretending like they didn't know each other. Once he tired of Hank, he recommended Vince, a dealer that let customers buy wholesale. Vince only let a select few of his customers come to his house. Thanks to Clyde being one of Vince's fanboys, Hank and Clyde had special privileges.

"How much you think $250 will get us?" Clyde threw the question out with a thick layer of desperation drowning his voice.

"Enough to last the week, if we stretch it."

"We're fuckin' up, going from high to high like this. Vince is connected. We should ask for more responsibility—we could ask to sell for him."

"Clyde, I'm not looking to go up the road. You know as well as I do, if we sell, we are looking at min-mans. And I'm not doing mandatory time." Hank argued half-heartedly. He was scared of the crushing minimum mandatories—which increased in proportion to the weight of the dope. But even he had to admit he was tired of the petty thefts and the scrounging.

Maybe Clyde had a point.

"Says the motherfucker that just pounded a rent-a-cop in the face and definitely has a felony warrant."

A scholar, he was not. But guys like Clyde—that cut his teeth in Alabama's Juvenile system (car thefts, assaults, burglaries—the list went on) and then moved to Florida to get far away from his fucked-up family, embarking on a criminal career to support his habit—knew criminal law front to back. Hank had used force to get out of the store: he was no longer in misdemeanor-land.

He just wanted to sink back into the mud and float peacefully on the river, find his mother again. If he had to follow Clyde to do it, then so be it.

"Alright. Alright. Maybe I overdid it. But he was going to have me arrested."

"Well, all I'm sayin' is, if you can do that, then I think you can handle selling some dope."

He was tired of living like a bum, of scheming with Clyde, night after night, to find ways to get petty amounts of dope. It was time to graduate.

#

"Clyde and Hank, my two favorite customers. Come in, gentlemen." Vince was an imposing figure at over six feet. Hank met him at eye level, but rarely said anything to him. Clyde did the talking.

Vince negotiated some deals from his house, but not enough for the extra traffic to draw the attention of neighbors. It was in a decent neighborhood: a few burglaries here and there, the occasional domestic dispute, but quiet, for the most part. And Vince never dealt from the house, never.

Vince had ambition, something Hank lacked. Hank remembered what that had felt like when he played in DCP. He hadn't felt a shred of it since being kicked out of the band, which happened the very next morning after his epic pass-out, via text from Simon. A band he had spent years to help build, and he got the axe in a text. At the time he was furious. Now he couldn't find the will to care.

"Guys. Sit. Sit." Hank and Clyde sat down on a modern couch, built for looks, not comfort. Positioned to give everyone seated a view of the pool through the sliding door, the couch and two matching chairs formed a half circle around a spotless glass coffee table. Vince eased into one of the chairs, rakishly crossed his legs, and said, "So, Hank, Clyde tells me that things went wrong at the Home Depot. Said you fucked that guy up pretty good."

Hank looked to Clyde with an unmistakable what-the-hell-look and then turned back to Vince. "Yeah. Dude got in my way, so I dropped him." He felt like he was outside of himself, hovering, looking down at the person he had become, hearing the type of alpha-male bullshit he used to hate coming from his own mouth.

"You did what you had to do. Anyway, gentlemen you're here, I assume, for the usual?"

"Yes sir. Where's the pickup?" Clyde had left Alabama behind, but not the accent. Part of Hank liked hearing Clyde's drawl; it reminded him of his father.

"I will text you when you leave and give you the location and time. Dump your phone after." Vince didn't keep any contraband in his house, only cash.

With business done, the conversation shifted to lighter fare. "Hey Vince, you still fuckin' that bitch from Jupiter? The one from Russia, legs for days, man. I'd do anything she told me to. I'd even lick her butthole." Clyde playfully socked Hank on the arm after he said it, giving him the shit-eating grin to end all shit-eating grins.

Hank had a vision of Lisa punching Clyde in the face. She'd revel in putting a misogynist like him in his place.

"Nah. She wanted a commitment. Which I avoid in my personal life. In business, however, I'm as loyal as a pitbull." Ever since they had been buying from Vince, Hank had seen the dealer with a steady stream of gorgeous women. Made sense, they guy was as pretty as the girls he regularly sent packing.

"Well, if y'all aren't together anymore, then I hope you don't mind if I think of her when I jerk it."

God, I wish I was high, so I wouldn't have to listen to this shit, Hank thought.

"Have at it, my friend. Tug to your heart's delight." Vince shifted in his seat, folded his hands, and placed them in his lap. A subtle signal that he was ready to get to the point. "You know, fellas, you aren't the only ones I allow the special privilege of coming and placing an order directly with me. When they grace my couch, they tell me things. Amazing what people will reveal after some alcohol. Who they work for, different dope houses they have been in. Stories of houses with dope inside every inch of the walls and stacks of cash hidden in crawl spaces. All there for the taking."

Clyde cracked a grin and lit a cigarette. Vince slid him over an ashtray. "I've had some of these same customers do some reconnaissance for me, and I have three houses in mind. I know when people come and go. The treasure is there, just waiting to make somebody rich. If you guys know anybody with the balls to pull it off, point them in my direction."

A look of disappointment came over Clyde's face. "What about us, Vince? We could handle it."

"Uhh, we're not talking about lawn equipment here. If you mess this up, there are real consequences."

"I hear you, man. But I'm telling you we can take care of it. Shit, you said you know when they're not home. In and out. No problem."

"I don't know, Clyde. There's no question you guys have the big box store thing down to a science. But this is next level stuff. I just don't think you guys are there yet. How 'bout a beer?" Vince walked over to his fridge and retrieved three bottles. When he returned, he passed two to Hank and Clyde, then resumed his seat.

Hank screwed the top off and took a generous swig, wishing he was anywhere but here.

True to form, Clyde used his teeth to unscrew the cap, then spat it in his hand. He took a pull from his beer. "And I'm fuckin' telling you that we can handle it. Give us the first job. If we deliver, then we can handle the other ones too. No more bullshit Home Depot thefts. We're done with those. Let us have this one."

Hank stayed silent. They hadn't quite crossed the Rubicon yet. But they were nestling up against it. Let Clyde voice all the bullshit he wants. Vince was never going to give him the job anyway. And even if he did, Hank could always walk away.

"I'll think about it."

Chapter 29

"When is the last time you talked to him?" Lisa knew she wouldn't like the answer, but she needed to know. She worried about him all the time.

"A month ago. He showed up in a ratty t-shirt and asked for forty bucks. I told him he wasn't welcome here until he admitted he was the one that took cash out of the office. He told me to go fuck myself. *Hank said that.* I didn't respond. He turned and left." Everett continued to work as he spoke. He checked the ribs in his high-tech warming drawer—his new toy, some fancy contraption that kept all the pre-made meat warm but somehow (Everett read the manual but the science was beyond him) didn't dry it out.

Maria squeezed by him as he spoke, prepping the sides. Her thick black hair had grown down to the middle of her back. She still looked young, thanks to her unblemished brown skin, but in the wake of Hector's disappearance, a few lines had emerged on her face, the tattoos the world gives us as it pushes us toward the grave.

Lisa smiled at Maria, and she responded in kind. "Hey Lisa. How is your... job?" Maria looked at Lisa with wide, inquisitive eyes—asking *Did I get the word right?* The words came out slow and choppy, but she was getting better. Lisa grinned and nodded *Yes* to her.

With Alice gone, Maria was now the head of all the prep ladies in the kitchen. She recruited a new one from her neighborhood. Each of them understood enough English to get by, but not enough to converse. Maria needed to be able to command her troops, as Alice had. So, to really be of help to Everett, she needed to learn English. Maria walked away to help with the prep.

"You think he'll ever try and get help?"

"I don't know. You can't make somebody. I'd like to say I know that from experience. There was no one in my life that cared enough about me to make me get clean. I've just heard from other people's stories at my meetings. Person won't quit something until *they* are ready to. It's like telling a smoker to quit. They won't until they're ready..."

"Rock bottom."

"Yep. Rock fucking bottom."

He met her, eye to eye. "I ended up in a darker place than I ever could have imagined. And the scariest part was that I knew I needed to get clean. I hated myself for what I had become. But those short moments of self-hatred, they didn't last. I always ended up high again."

He paused, then he delivered a philosophy earned through surviving addiction. "Treading water. It's the only way I know how to describe it. To stay clean, I had to tread water, use all my energy to stay on the surface. Knowing the whole time it would be easier to just sink. After the things I had done as an addict, the people I hurt, the crimes... I didn't think I was good enough to be clean. I didn't think I deserved to have a good life. I thought I should just let the water take me. Until Hank came along. He changed everything."

Lisa gave him a sympathetic look, one that said she—someone whose only addiction was foul language—was trying to understand his pain. "Do you think that he inherited it from you?"

"Oh, I don't know, sweetie. All the stuff about it being a disease, I'm not sure. But I do know that once it has its teeth in you, it never let's go."

She had tried to move on. There was the bar-hopping stint, with more one-night stands than she cared to remember. Well, if she was being honest with herself, some of it she did care to remember. She had enjoyed the release that came with the sex, that it had made her forget, if for just a few hours, that Hank was still on Earth. It was what came after that she couldn't shake: every time she sank right back down to the pit of the drain where the ghost of Hank was waiting for her.

Eschewing the one-nighters, thinking that was no way to climb out of the hole, she finally agreed to go out on a date after a few months of wandering the bar scene. It was time for something more formal, more responsible. He was one of the construction foremen at the company. Handsome, a body fit for a statue of a Greek god, even polite. He did nothing wrong on the date. In fact, he did everything right. Kept things light and unawkward. Held the door for her. He even told her that he was a Bernie supporter. But she was checked out the whole time—stuck at the bottom of the drain with the ghost.

They never went on that second date.

"I have to get to work." After Hank left, she'd given up on working from home. She preferred to get out of the house—she needed noise, the buzz of other humans.

Everett looked at her, saddened at the sight of what Hank's absence was doing to her—stealing her best years, years of confidence and hope about what the rest of life will bring. Around the eyes, and around her mouth, she had aged since Hank's exile; anyone could see it.

He gave her a hug and told her to keep her head up.

She walked over to Danny, kissed him on the cheek, and pulled out his earbud to whisper she loved him.

Chapter 30

"Alright, Clyde, you and your boy are up."

Clyde hadn't expected the call; he was half in the bag, a half-empty bottle of cheap bourbon the culprit.

"These two guys work nights to keep up appearances. So the home is empty from ten to six every day, except Sunday. Don't go until eleven, at least. You have to give them time to get out of the house."

"I got it, man. I got it."

"There are two stores of money in there: one in a false-bottomed floor in the master bedroom and another in a small bunker out in the shed. When you rip it up it will look just like plain dirt. But trust me, start digging. Don't bring tools. You'll look suspicious. There should be some out there in the shed."

"How much money is there?"

"Enough. But this isn't the big one. These are lower-level guys. Knocking them off won't make waves." Clyde liked the sound of that. He didn't want to rob anyone too high up the food chain.

"And what's our take, chief?"

"Seventy-thirty."

Clyde thought that sounded unfair, but he didn't want to stir the pot. He would negotiate a better rate after a successful job.

"Alright. You can do better than that, but we'll take it."

"Show me that you can pull this off and there might be a bonus in it for you. And Clyde?"

"Yeah."

"Wear masks. Don't bring your wallet with you. These guys will have cameras all over the house. Wear all black. I don't need them seeing Hank's tattoos. But ditch the clothes after. No one cruises around Florida blacked out from head to toe."

"Got it."

"And don't bring the money to my house. After you guys get it, I will text you a place to meet."

"Understood. Anything else?"

"You just do the job tomorrow night. In an hour, go behind the laundromat two blocks down from your house, there will be two guns waiting for you in a black backpack behind the dumpster."

"Guns? What for? They won't be there."

"Nothing is certain in this life, Clyde. Best to plan ahead. You screw this up, and we're done. No more little drop-ins for discounted dope. You understand?"

Chapter 31

Around the same time Hank's dope sickness took hold, Clyde walked in and said they needed to go buy black long-sleeved shirts and pants. Hank followed suit without a question.

Still groggy, Hank said, "I need to fix up soon."

"I know. Me too. We'll take care of that. But first we need to pick something up."

On the way, Clyde parked by a dumpster and jumped out. After grabbing a black backpack, he hopped back in and threw it over to Hank.

Hank put it in the back, then wrapped his arms around his stomach. Hands shaking, stomach feeling like it had been trampled underfoot, he turned to look out the window.

"Here man. Take it. It's my last oxy. It will tide you over while we drive over to see the dope man." Hank knew Clyde was lying to him. Clyde always held back a few of his stash of oxy from Hank. Right now, Hank didn't care. Grateful in the same way a battered wife is happy when her cowardly husband stops beating her, Hank took the pill.

His mouth gushed before it even touched his lips.

#

The next night, they drove out west, past Wellington, into a town Hank had never heard of—Palm Grove. They made short work of finding the house.

They pulled past the house and parked, half the car leaning into a small culvert, darkness enshrouding it. The streetlights were out for some reason, making the area naturally dark, an eerie black seldom seen by a city dweller like Hank.

They pulled their masks down and headed to the back of the house. Per Vince's instructions, there should be a window unlocked in the back that they could shimmy through.

As they ran past the side of the house, Hank noticed a lazy blue light hitting the wall: a TV was on. No cause for alarm. People left their sets on all the time when they left for work.

As promised, the window was open. It gave off a loud creak, as Hank pushed it up. Clyde climbed through the window first. Hank followed suit.

After he hit the ground, he looked around: a plain house, wallpaper with small pink flowers on it, deteriorating linoleum floor with some indiscernible brown design, a carpeted den with the requisite brown recliner and pictures of ocean life hung throughout the house.

They still had to dig out in the shed. But they agreed to sweep the house together first, then Hank would head out back.

Clyde crept through the den, opening the door to look out in the garage—no one there. Clyde moved from the den to foyer and then to the hallway that led back to the two bedrooms.

Hank followed.

As Clyde disappeared into the master at the end of the hall, Hank walked toward the small bedroom to the left. Again, as promised, nary a soul to be found.

Clyde made his way over to the small bathroom and gave it a quick look, not thinking to look behind the shower curtain, nor taking note of the water beads that lined it.

He ripped away the thin rug that covered the aged hardwood floors. He felt for it and pushed down—there it is, the false floor. He pushed and slid the panel out of the way: he saw the black bag that Vince said would be squirreled away here.

"Hey Hank, go ahead and head out to—"

A cold press of metal against the back of his neck silenced him.

"Huh?" Hank couldn't make out what he heard. He was still in the small bedroom off to the left.

With no sign yet of anyone else, Hank nonchalantly walked to the larger bedroom to see what Clyde needed. As he breached the door, he saw a tall, tanned man with a towel wrapped around his waist, pointing a gun at Clyde's head. The man was shaking. His voice was manic as he demanded information from them: "What the fuck are you doing in my house, man?" And then, "Who sent you, motherfucker? Who sent you?" He repeated the questions over and over, pressing the gun deeper into Clyde's temple each time he didn't get an answer.

The man's back was to Hank, so he couldn't see him coming, but the phrase came out before he could stop it: "What the fuck?"

Hank's words startled the black-haired, half-naked man with the gun. When he turned his ample frame toward Hank, the gun was coming with him; it would soon be pointing at Hank's chest.

Hank already had his gun trained on the man. The opportunity was there; he could just take the shot, lay him out.

In the end, Hank just didn't have it in him. Clyde didn't suffer the same scruples.

When the man turned, Clyde pulled his gun, and fired two quick rounds into the man's leg. The tall mass of flesh crashed to the floor; the gun sailed out of his hands during the tumble.

"Hank, get his fucking gun. Grab it."

Hank ran over and grabbed the gun. His legs trembled as he stood up, swaying, now holding a gun in each hand.

Moaning in pain, grabbing at his wounds, the man writhed on the ground near the bathroom.

"Keep your gun on him. And keep your mask down. I'll be right back." Clyde ran out of the room.

Shortly, he returned with a roll of duct tape.

There was little blood. Clyde had shot him two times. *Shouldn't there be more blood?* Hank thought. Not just this limp trickle down his legs. Maybe this was a good thing, he reminded himself—less blood meant the man would live.

Clyde crossed over to the man, pulling a piece of tape from the roll. "You're dead, motherfucker, you're a walking cor—" And then silence.

Clyde went on to tape his wrists together, then his ankles.

He grabbed the bag out of the hidden space.

"You keep an eye on him. I'm headed to the shed."

"What? Let's just get out of here."

Clyde shook his head. Hank couldn't see his face behind the mask, but he could see his eyes—they looked maniacal.

"Vince expects this done, and we're finishing it."

Hank saw Clyde's hand clench around his gun and thought: *What is Clyde capable of?*

"Is this going to be a problem, Hank?" Clyde moved closer as he said it, still with a death-grip on the gun.

This half-witted redneck from Alabama aimed to move up in the drug underworld. Vince was his ticket. How had Hank not seen that?

Inertia. An object will remain at rest until another moves it. And it will remain in motion until another stops it.

It used to be Lisa that moved him from rest—sending him in the right direction, challenging him, the type of insistent prodding only someone who loves you can give.

Lisa was gone. There were the occasional texts between them, a fraying string that kept their relationship on life support, but her power over him had disappeared.

Now, he let Clyde move him from rest. And Clyde wanted what was best for Clyde. But Hank didn't care—Clyde would help Hank get back to the tangerine river to see his mother.

"Alright, man. Hurry up," Hank said.

Addiction has its own inertia.

#

"WOOOOOOoooooooooooo, that's right boy, we got that bastard, didn't we?" Clyde's adrenaline had him sitting bolt upright, gripping the wheel like the edge of a cliff.

"How much was out there in the shed?"

"Twelve thousand." Add the seven thousand from the house: nineteen thousand. They weren't even there twenty minutes, and they walked away with almost twenty grand. Hank couldn't believe it. That kind of money, that fast.

"Damn..."

"I know, boy. Wooh! I told you Vince would take care of us. And the next one will be bigger. He gave us the easy pickins' first. He needed to know he could trust us. He even said he'd throw in a little bonus if we pulled this one off."

Even without a bonus on top, their take was close to six grand. They had been living in one- to two hundred-dollar increments, always barely finding the bridge to the next stop, and then scrounging, stealing, and begging to get more cash. This was different: cash in minutes.

"Do you think that guy is going to be alright?"

"Who gives a shit, Hank? You cash your ticket to join the life, you take the risk. That simple. But if it makes you feel better, yes, I think that bastard will be fine. Shots were to the shins. Didn't hit any arteries."

"What do you think Vince will say? That guy wasn't supposed to be there."

Clyde grinned. "What Vince doesn't know won't hurt him, my boy. We need that next job. And ol' fresh-out-of-the-shower ain't going to let anybody know that he let two guys get the drop on him. We're good."

"But what if Vince gets word of it? He's got all these junkies that answer to him and give him information for money. He's going to ask."

"God, Hank. We just robbed a guy at gunpoint and you're worried about having to lie? We lie to him, you dumbass. We lie our asses off."

Hank shook his head and sighed. Yeah, *lie our asses off* and pray that, at the next house, the people are actually gone.

His next thought was of the tangerine river. He would be there soon.

Chapter 32

I t only took three days for the information to make it to Silvia. They were out nineteen grand; that house fell under their watch, and they'd have to answer for what was missing. She gritted her teeth so hard when she got the call, she thought her incisor cracked. Alejandro gave little reaction, just kept watching television and guzzling his beer. They had moved to a different house in Belle Glade, the shutters and garden a little worse for wear, but otherwise, the home still looked like any other in the neighborhood.

He knew the answer, just as she did. This wasn't the first time they had been ripped off, *Cost of doing business, bruja,* as Alejandro would say to her. She and Alejandro would just have to front the money out of their own personal stashes, so the bald man and Melvin had enough to send back to Mexico. She had to meet her quota, no question. Those that didn't met their end out near the glades, if the rumors were true—and she actually hoped they were. Melvin and his boss, the one with the eyes and the scars, had captured her imagination with their methods.

Since the move to the new home, while Alejandro sank further into depression and lethargy, she had begun to transform herself, as an exercise in proving her worth to Melvin.

First was her body. Running, dieting, planks, and pull ups. She looked nothing like the sweaty, tank-top wearing, countrified girl that Melvin found a few years ago. To be like Melvin, who was in impeccable shape, she needed to be sleek, furtive.

And there was another reason to trim up.

She had a round face, plain, forgettable, one that even looked kind when she wasn't scowling. But men, no matter their age, color, or creed, were slaves to a tight body. With a trim figure she could outpace her prey; she could seduce them, get them into that vulnerable world where a man followed his dick instead of his brain and for all intents and purposes lays himself out on the cutting board. She just needed to be desirable. Not beautiful. And then she could have her way with them in her *room*, one she had designed to serve a special purpose.

Tighter fitting clothes came next. She liked the feel of the tight shirts against her flat stomach, especially the no-wick fabric, skin-tight—the ones that kept the spit and the blood from soaking into the fabric. And every new piece of garb was black.

Tighter.

Trimmer.

Sleeker.

She even started straightening her curly black hair. The bushy curls had made her look clumsy. Her new, smooth strands flowed down in thin tendrils, like blackened tentacles.

All the changes were calculated to make her movements secretive. As quiet as the spider that crawls up your arm to your neck and deposits its poison without detection.

Next came the skills. For that, she read every gun and military magazine she could get her hands on. No small task for someone that hadn't finished high school. This led her to online mercenary groups. Their tactics hypnotized her; one in particular, Los Zetas, held unmatched sway over her.

The Zetas were a gang, now a full-fledged cartel, started by an ex-military man named Arturo Guzman, who defected from the Mexican army to become a mercenary for the Gulf Cartel. His bloodlust and brutal tactics had made his paramilitary unit infamous. The use of military tactics had transformed the drug war into the fest of violence now known the world over. She needed those skills so she could murder with precision, systematically. She could never build that kind of organization here in the States, but she could parrot them, apply their brutal tactics to perfection in secret. If the thing was worth doing, then recognition was incidental, unnecessary.

She had seen the photos. Men found on the side of desert roads, headless, a goat's head sitting atop their neck where a human head should be. Severed heads being rolled into discos like bowling balls to make a point. Stacks of severed limbs and headless torsos left in piles—so badly mutilated that no person could be identified. These were the devices of the professionals.

For now, she had to settle for *her* room. Sound-proofed and fit with the same chair they used in jails for the mentally ill: a black chair with straps to stop all movement, and one strap specially made for the head that leaves the victim's neck exposed.

Transforming herself, learning these dark things: it was her ticket to something bigger. A way to leave Belle Glade and the poison of her youth behind, miles away from what was left of her family—only her Dad now: her mom had passed from lung cancer, and she had no siblings. These days, her dad stayed stone-drunk, far too old and weak to ever put his hands on her again. It was a different story when she was a young girl. Back then, he had expressed his hatred for himself and the world with his fists. He stopped when she was nineteen. She saw to that. One night, after he punched her, he pulled away in disbelief, to see the blood trickling down his side. She had stabbed him with a small knife she had hidden in her jeans. She told him if he touched her again the next one was going in this throat—it would have felt so nice to jam the blade in and see the blood rush out—but she let him live.

She walked out of his house a few months later; they hadn't spoken since.

It wasn't until she slit her first throat that she realized the black mass that lived in him had found its way into her. A gift from dear ol' dad. She had no use for booze. The need for violence, however, found a willing host— but not just any brand of violence. She had no interest in chaos and disorder. This had to be measured, a part of a craft. Something she could cultivate and control.

And then, soon, Melvin would see she could be trusted.

#

Over the same time span, Alejandro had been doing a lot of thinking about the future as well. He had a plan. One he kept close to the vest.

Chapter 33

T he second and third jobs went off without a hitch. During these hits, as promised, no one was home. The dope had numbed Hank, but there was enough juice still flowing through his brain to get a small high from the cash rolling in. They were raking in thousands of dollars, and they had done it in the space of two weeks. And to think, it had only been two months since Vince had given them the first job.

With their ill-gotten gains, Hank and Clyde said goodbye to their sad little flophouse and moved into a townhouse. At first, it unsettled Hank; it looked so much like the old place he'd shared with Lisa and Danny. But that soon faded, along with all the other ghosts of his former life. Worries. Anxieties. Those things evaporated quickly under the magic hold of the poppy.

In their new house, they had to be more discerning about who they let through the door. Clyde even hired escorts, rather than his old street girls. Gone were the days of letting anyone crash on the floor or get high in whatever room they chose. Now, if there was a knock on the door, it was a customer: another change in their lives.

Hank and Clyde had made Vince a nice chunk of change, and he rewarded them for their efforts: they got a piece of the fledgling *empire* (the word Vince used). They used a simple system: someone came to the door, knocked, placed their order, and then they texted one of Vince's underlings to meet the buyer at a public location to do the exchange. The underling would then come back and leave the cash under the flowerpot on the screened-in porch. The system worked for now, but if their customer base got too big, they would have to stop having their buyers come to the home. Or move. Either way, even if law enforcement came knocking with a warrant, they'd find an empty cupboard: none of the dope Hank and Clyde peddled was in the home. The only contraband in the house consisted of Hank and Clyde's personal stashes, which they could each flush with ease when they heard the cop-knock.

In the end, they had a product that was always in demand thanks to the War on Drugs. For the foreseeable future, they were set. No more begging. No more stealing from Home Depot. Hank still had to lie low though; there had to be a felony warrant out there from when he assaulted that rent-a-cop. Numb to everything transpiring in his life, Hank didn't spend much time worrying about an arrest warrant. The tangerine river was waiting beneath the mud to sweep away any of his anxiety: why worry? These days, every morsel of Hank, body and soul, was lost to that river.

There was a catch, however. Wasn't there always?

Vince said that they had been building up to a grand finale: one more job and then they could disappear back into their lives, though not the same ones. They worked for him now, and he would take care of them. The job was out in Belle Glade, and it was a big one. If the rumors were true, Vince said, then "the take will be around fifty grand. Maybe even more."

"Damn, you serious, Vince? That much?" Clyde asked.

"This is the big one, fellas. The last one you'll have to do. From what I've heard, no one has a clue who pulled off the other jobs."

This was a lie. Word had spread quickly. It didn't take long for things like this to echo through the drug world. But the last part was true: no one had a clue who was doing it.

"And I've been checking around, not a word."

"Well, shit, you don't have to tell me twice. We're in."

Lazily, Hank nodded along. Unbeknownst to Clyde, he had shot up before they went over. Now, they could each lock themselves away to be alone with their habit. Just them and the thing undoing them. Going over to Vince's always unnerved him, so he thought a small hit would level him out; it had done just that and more.

"Hank. Hank! What do you think, boy?" Clyde slapped Hank on the shoulder; Hank's eyelids had been half-closed as Vince and Clyde talked.

Hank came to. "Yeah. I'm in, too. Just like the last ones. In and out. No one there."

"Nice to hear, fellas. Nice to hear. Clyde, without you, those last jobs wouldn't have worked out. And I know you will pull this one off too." Unadulterated bullshit. But ego-stroking pays dividends.

"How's that new place of yours treating you?"

"Damn nice. Damn nice."

"Well after this job, you guys can get a house. And with the money that I'll keep funneling you, you'll each have your own." Vince didn't direct any of his ego-stroking at Hank. Clyde was the way to get them to do his bidding. Hank would follow suit. "And Clyde... you pulled that last job off in under ten minutes. You're getting faster, better. That's why you're ready for this one."

"I know, man, we got this. What night you want us to hit?"

"Tomorrow."

"Done."

"This one will be different, though. Clyde, you can handle it, but it will be different."

"Okay."

"Two people will be there when you hit it."

Hank had been dozing again, but that jolted him awake. "What the fuck, man? Did you say two people will be there?"

"Yes. But I said you guys can handle it."

"No. We go in when they're not there. What are we supposed to do, tie them up?"

Vince had expected this from Hank. And as he anticipated, Clyde would swoop in to temper his friend's misgivings. "Hank, will you shut the fuck up. Vince wouldn't give us the job unless it was worth doin'. Listen up. He'll have a plan for the two people in there. Right, Vince?"

"You know I always take care of you guys. The same guy that told me about the house also said there is a bedroom in the house with a deadbolt. He said he saw it on the way to the bathroom. It's simple: guns drawn, demand the

150

key, lock them in there, do your business, and get gone. And hell, maybe they won't even be there."

Hank's high had floated into the ether, gone, like a balloon ripped away by the wind. This was too much. They were thieves, not seasoned criminals. This may involve hurting people. Or worse, killing them if they go for their weapons.

Hank knew Clyde worshipped this handsome man, with his sterling white teeth, peddling them a jar of snake oil. Challenging Vince in front of Clyde was useless. Best to nod along, act like the money is enough, and then head to the house, grab his stash, and disappear. Enough was enough. He was comfortable with peddling heroin and pills so he could stay high, but one guy had already gotten shot, and this job could end with a corpse.

He was an addict, not a murderer.

In a flat voice, he spoke next. "Alright. Your guy said he saw the deadbolt."

"Yeah. This guy works for me. He is getting a cut of the take. So, he has no reason to lie."

Hank demurred again to Clyde, biding his time, waiting to get back to the car; he just needed to gin up enough energy to keep up the façade, and then leave Clyde behind.

Clyde licked his lips. "Where's the money at, in the house?"

Chapter 34

"What the fuck was that back there?" Clyde launched the question at Hank as they drove back to their place.

Which way to go? Play along, attempt to fool Clyde, then sneak out under cover of night? Or come out with it right now? Hank didn't know the right way anymore. The mud clouded his thoughts. Worst of all, it muted the voice inside his head, Lisa's voice, that wanted to keep him alive—he couldn't hear it anymore.

"Look, man, Vince doesn't give a shit what happens to us. He just wants money. You shouldn't listen to all that bullshit. He's messing with your head. He is just trying to get you to do his dirty work for him."

"God, Hank, don't you get it? We've already done a shitload of dirty work for him. We steal for him. We sell for him. And it's going to make us rich. What's one more job? Stop being such a pussy. We lock them in the room, take the cash, and get out. We'll do it in the middle of the night, just like the other jobs. Come on, man. Don't you want that money?"

He did. God, he did. Because of what came with it. "Fuck yeah, I do. But... I don't want to hurt people. We agreed to those other jobs because no one was supposed to be home. You already had to shoot the one dude. We don't even know if that guy lived."

"He did. Vince said he did."

"Oh well, if Vince said it, then it must be true. Vince the *drug dealer* would never tell a lie."

Clyde howled with laughter. "You're killing me, man. What the fuck are you getting all self-righteous about? We deal drugs, too." The redneck had a point. "You still think you're the guy you were before. You don't live in that world anymore, boy. And guess what, *that* world doesn't want you back. Trust me, I know."

"Well, whatever man, we don't know if the guy made it."

Jittery, tapping his fingers against the steering wheel, Clyde responded, "He did. We would have seen it in the news if he hadn't."

"I don't want to hurt anybody." Hank gritted his teeth as he said it.

"We won't, man. We are just going to move them into the locked room, get the shit, and then get out of there."

Throwing his hands up, Hank raised his voice: "Look man, you can get someone else to do the job with you. And I won't ask for any of the take. We can still deal together for Vince afterward and you can get a larger cut because you did the job. I don't want to do this one. It's too much."

"Fuck that. We don't do this one together, then I can't trust you. We ever get popped, then I gotta know you're willin' to go down with me. You don't do this one with me, then we are through. No more business. You can go back to your precious barbeque. Those track marks will look nice for the customers."

"Fine, man. Then I'm out." The words came out tired and flimsy, like Hank hardly believed himself.

Clyde laughed again, but this time it wasn't a bellow; it was patronizing, like he knew a secret that Hank should have figured out by now. "You think it's that easy? That you just walk back in with your tail between your legs and they hug you? Good luck. What about that warrant you got? You ready to do prison time? That's waitin' on you too. You goin' to keep living under a fake name with your family too?" Hank and Clyde lived under aliases at their townhouse. Vince had helped them get some fake IDs and social security cards. A jack of all trades, Vince believed in diversity when it came to crime: identity theft was another of his specialties. "You think they won't make you go to rehab? They will. You think they will just up and forgive you for all the shit you did? They won't. And how many theft convictions you got on your record now? You think you can just go work somewhere else? That world don't want you back. You're branded. Might as well accept it."

Maybe Clyde wasn't as dumb as he seemed. Either that, or Vince was rubbing off on him. Regardless, as he rolled it over in his mind, Hank thought, was the man currently spitting shards of dip into a plastic water bottle, wrong? Can a thieving drug addict just walk back into his old life and pick up where he left off? Not Hank, he'd have to answer for that felony warrant first. And that could result in felony probation or worse, prison. But he would come out on the other side of it, eventually, and he would be clean, rid of the poison, ready to start anew. And everyone would be ready to act like it never happened, *right*?

This wasn't the first time he tried to imagine his life free of the drugs.

Clean thoughts.

Clean body.

Focus.

A return of the things he had left behind—kissing Lisa, listening to music with Danny, playing drums. Putting the pieces of his former self back together, like gluing the shards of a broken stained-glass window back together, one fractured piece at a time, restoring its former beauty. He tried and tried to see through to a life rid of the drugs. But when he looked, he saw the sickness that would come from withdrawal, followed by the shame for the things he had done to feed his habit—oceans of it.

How could he go back?

After all the using, the stealing, the stints in jail, and now, the burglaries. They would judge him. Take one look at the dried skin, the sores, the black caverns encasing his eyes, and hate him for what he had become. Even if they took him back, they would always lord it over him—Hank the fuck-up.

The heroin erased his worries, his bad thoughts, and brought him to his mother.

Hank had found a world free from pain; how do you walk away from that?

Clyde could see that his point had struck a nerve. He offered one more thought. "Hank, we ain't robbing saints. We're robbing sinners. This is the last one, and then we sit back and collect. Get your head right, boy."

Hank felt himself being pushed again by another object in space.

Sinking back into the mud, his home.

Inertia.

Chapter 35

After a late-night run, Silvia returned home to find Alejandro out cold on the recliner. She had added an extra two miles, and now she stood in the foyer, dripping sweat, drinking bottled water, scowling at him. He snored loudly; he had passed out after polishing off a twelve-pack of Budweiser. She crossed the room and clicked the T.V. off, as Alejandro slept it off.

She stared at him in disgust. During the years of their partnership, he had never taken part in the dirty work, not once. He handled the money—kept the books, made sure to keep tally of what was socked away in the house, along with meticulous records of drugs that came in and went out. When it came to spilling blood, however, he left that to Silvia. What bothered her was the look he gave her every time she lured a hapless victim back to her sound-proof room: a look of pure revulsion—the type of look people reserved for the worst refuse of society. The way people in the gallery of a courtroom stare at a convicted murderer or a sex offender. A look that says *You are not one of us. You're sick. The planet should be rid of you.* She stared at him now, his gut mushrooming out over his beltline, and thought about what it would be like to cut his flab open, end to end, and then pull his intestines out one inch at a time. She thought of feeding him his own flesh as she cut open his throat. Her nipples hardened at the thought of having that kind of power of him. Holding his life in her hands—and then extinguishing it.

She didn't have the standing yet to kill someone that had a direct line back to Mexico. Alejandro was a low man on the totem pole, no doubt.

But he funneled the money back to Juarez and had done so for years. Half went back to the homeland, and an unnamed courier picked up the other half every two weeks; that half went on to be laundered through various businesses—restaurants, bars, retail shops, any small business that could clean cash without raising eyebrows. In that span, they had quietly made the Cartel millions, but they were still only a small cog in a gigantic wheel.

If she could get the attention of Melvin and his employer, that would change. She would have the *in* she needed. It was all she thought about during the long hours of training and exercise. She had transformed herself for this opportunity, darkened her soul for it. Surely men of their appetites would notice her soon. Surely. And once they did, then she could dispatch Alejandro with special care. With him, she would take her time.

For now, after setting the house alarm, she went to bed.

#

They waited until two in the morning to start the drive to Belle Glade. The muggy air felt as thick as smoke from a fire, almost tangible, as it came through the windows. Hank stared out at the cloudy sky; a few pinpricks of faint white light cut through the white barrier of factory smoke. Then he saw the bright white industrial lights off in the distance on the other side of the cane fields. The processing centers for the crop gave off a manmade light that felt cheap and uninspired, lacking the warm beauty of the few stars that dotted the sky this night.

Vince had given them the layout of the house. In through the front door, gather the two people living there up (Vince knew their names, but had omitted them to protect Clyde and Hank: a superficial explanation to protect his own ass, but then again, everything about Vince was superficial), and then lock them in the first room on the left—the one Vince had on good authority as having a deadbolt. They'd have to get the key out of one of the occupants, but the guns they'd be toting would get the key into their hands. Guns had a way of doing that.

The take was rumored to be as much as $50,000—their biggest score to date. Enough cash that people would ask questions, maybe even seek reprisal. But no one had a clue who had pulled off the other jobs. Hank prayed for the same luck to continue.

When they took the right onto Meridian Drive, Clyde cut the lights. They still had the windows down. Hank scanned the neighborhood, nary a soul or sound—nothing, save the black of night and the muggy air.

Clyde pulled his mask down after he parked the car. They each took a .45 into their hand. No need to stuff it in their waistband. They needed to be ready to corral the two people in the home. Only way to do that was to have the guns at the ready.

The mask muffled Clyde's voice. "Alright. Once we get them in the room, then we both stuff the bags with cash. Out in under ten. Vince said that room is foolproof, no other exit."

The adrenaline bucked away Hank's skeptical thought: How the hell did Vince know that? What did he give these guys to tell him so much?

"Once we get the bags in the car, you head back in and tell them you'll blow their heads off if they open the door. Unlock it, and hightail it out of there. I'll have the car running, just like in the Home Depot days. You ready, boy?"

Despite the adrenaline washing over him, Hank felt a pang of nostalgia for the halcyon days of stealing from Home Depot. Simple, petty theft. Frowned upon, but ultimately, shrugged off by society. What they were doing now was different, the kind of stuff that people don't forget.

Clyde slapped him on the shoulder, "I said, you ready, boy?"

Hank nodded in affirmation. He left the past to the past. This was his world now, and ten minutes from now they'd have completed their last job for Vince. After that, he would slip into the life of a mid-level dealer; he could stay high, live off-the-grid, and coast mindlessly in a world wrought by opiates, one that exiled pain.

He pulled his mask down.

He was ready.

#

Bleary-eyed, his head throbbing like it was a bass drum someone was pounding, Alejandro woke up and stumbled to the kitchen for some much-needed water. He looked up and noticed it was still pitch-black out, past midnight. He put it at three in the morning.

He gulped his water down, took a piss, and then returned to his recliner to fall back asleep. As he dozed off again, a nagging voice entered his head—Silvia's—reminding him to set the alarm.

Alejandro stumbled over, typed in the code, and then returned to the recliner. The system made the same high-pitched beep when armed and disarmed; the only difference was, when armed, it displayed a red light and when disabled, a green light.

He never bothered to look at the color of the light.

#

They ran up to the side of the red-brick home. Hank pushed his back up against the decaying brick; a row of hedges hid them from view.

Clyde nodded and pointed his head toward the front door.

They crept up the small set of stairs that led to a square stoop at the front door. The deadbolt was locked; Clyde stepped back, using the wrought iron balcony to brace himself, and then lunged his leg forward, but the door didn't budge. *Wasn't it just supposed to crash in? That's what happens in the movies,* Hank thought. He tried again, yelling out after, "Well I'll be damned." And again. "Son of a bitch." Again. "This isn't fair."

Hank's adrenaline didn't keep his anxiety from rushing to the surface. Too much noise. *If Clyde keeps this bullshit up, we are going to lose the element of surprise. If we haven't already.*

He stopped the next attempt, and told Clyde they should both try more weight.

They reared back together and kicked the door.

This time, the door gave.

#

Silvia, always a light sleeper, woke up, then heard a crash and a deep thud, something heavy falling to the hardwood floor. Then silence.

She waved it off; probably just Alejandro's fat ass falling over as he got up to go get something to eat. She closed her eyes again.

But then Silvia heard Alejandro begging someone not to do something. Not to... What? And then she heard it: *Shoot, not to shoot.*

She bolted up from her bed, and froze in pain, wincing, her lower back locked as she then tried to reach her gun from the far bedside table. The extra two miles: her muscles now protested, screamed out that they had been a mistake.

The seconds she lost due to the pain in her back proved costly. It had prevented her from grabbing her gun. When she looked up again, a man in a black mask stood in the doorway.

#

"Don't move, bitch." Hank stayed quiet, while Clyde did the talking. He wished his co-conspirator had made some attempt to disguise his voice. Clyde's southern drawl was as unique as a fingerprint in South Florida. Not many southerners in Palm Beach County. Mostly northern transplants and people from other parts of the world.

Silvia froze and put her hands up, still wincing.

"Get up, and move over here slowly."

Clyde had the gun on her. Ready to shoot if need be.

Hank was only inches behind him, with a gun to Alejandro's back. Alejandro stood with his head down, right outside of the room with the deadbolt. He swore up and down he didn't have the key; the lady in the back, it was her room, she had it, and he had said it enough times that Hank and Clyde believed him.

From over Clyde's shoulder, under the glow of lamplight, Hank saw that the woman who emerged from the covers had short, thick curly hair, the darkest he had ever seen. She was in nothing but a t-shirt and panties, her tan, muscular legs on display as she walked around the bed toward Clyde. Her walking looked labored, like she was sore.

Hank knew this didn't bode well. Clyde was incapable of functioning around an attractive woman. Continuing his monkish silence, Hank waited for Clyde to say something else.

Finally losing patience, he yelled out: "*Clyde*, what the fuck, man? Get the key."

When Clyde's head popped up, she lunged at him, quickly closing the distance.

Clyde stood a foot taller than her, so when she came at him, he brought the butt of the gun down on her head—Hank heard the crunch, and in the hazy light saw the thick, jelly-like blood that stuck to the haft, as Clyde hammered at her.

Silvia recoiled and fell to the ground, clutching her head. Black blood coated her hands.

"Alright, bitch, where is the key?"

"Do you know who you're robbing?"

Clyde moved forward as if to strike again. To Hank's shock, she didn't move an inch.

"I know that you're going to give me that key or I'm going to crack another hole in that head of yours."

"What's a redneck like you doing in south Florida? Why don't you go back home to your wife, or your sister, oh wait, there the same person aren't they?"

The next hit didn't land on Silvia's head; rather, it came across her face; the blood sprayed out on the bedcover. She spit a glob of crimson on the ground. She had yet to shed a tear. The pain was welcome.

"We can do this all night, you stubborn bitch. Or you can just tell me where that key is."

"It's up your ass."

The woman now had blood running down her chin from the last hit. Hank couldn't believe she wasn't clutching her wound or wincing from the pain. There was no indication that she was experiencing any discomfort. To the contrary, she looked happy, like a child playing their favorite game.

"The key, man. You got it?" Hank asked.

"She won't give it up."

"Have you tried the drawers?" Silvia's face changed from mischief to solemnity.

Hank caught the change out of the corner of his eye and knew they had it.

Clyde turned his back to her and went to the small nightstand by the bed. As he reached out for the drawer, Silvia shot up from the ground, as if on a spring, and jumped on Clyde's back, sinking her teeth into his neck.

Clyde shrieked.

161

"Oh my God, the bitch is biting me, do something, man. Do somethin', man. Do sumpin'."

Clyde ripped the gloves off his hands and reached back, clawing at her face. He had the nails of an ill-kempt man, long, fit to hold a bump of cocaine. He dug and dug, trying to get her to stop. Her face had red streaks on each side, as if she were crying blood. His clawing was little obstacle to her gnawing.

Hank looked back at Alejandro and then into the room where Clyde was trying to buck the deranged lady off his back. If he left the man in the hall to his own devices, he could go for a gun and then it would all be over.

Hank looked in again, Clyde was thrashing about, trying desperately to get her off, but she wouldn't let go. Hank could actually hear her gnawing on Clyde's skin. Clyde had not stopped screaming the whole time.

The neighbors, what about the neighbors? He had to do something.

He ran into the room, reared back his arm, and swung the butt of the gun as hard as he could at her head, and for the second time that night Silvia's skull emitted a crunch.

His battle-blood up, Clyde shook her off. Silvia attempted to get back up, but Clyde was on her within seconds. Blind with anger, he picked up her head and banged it against the edge of a wood table pushed against the wall. Again and again, he brought her head down, each time Hank could hear the splinter-crack of her head when it hit.

Afraid he might kill her, eventually, Hank grabbed Clyde.

This time, she didn't get back up.

#

Silvia lay still on her off-white rug; her blood had pooled into a crimson shadow around her head.

In disbelief, Hank looked down at her, wondering if Clyde had killed her. She wasn't moving.

Clyde's screechy drawl broke him from his panic, "Found it. Found it. That bitch knew we were about to get it, so she went apeshit."

Hank heard Clyde talking, but the words were faint echoes failing to materialize in his brain. He was hypnotized by the blood on the floor. Clyde grabbed him by the arm and told him to drag her to the room. Hank did as he was told without saying a word. Unable to process the violence, his brain had gone on autopilot.

As he walked down the hall, Clyde kept clutching his neck and pulling his hand back to inspect it. Blood and gristle matted his gloves.

Dragging the body, the physical labor of it, shook Hank from his trance. They still had to get out of here. Her body crumpled up the rug as Hank dragged her; the blood that spilled on the rug acted as glue, helping Hank to glide the body to the other room. Hank looked back to see that a plush trail of red lined their path to the door.

Hank also noticed that the man, the one that had been on the recliner, hadn't moved an inch. *Why?* Surely, there were more weapons in the house. Why didn't he help the woman? Based on the disparity between looks and age, Hank figured they weren't together, but there was some kind of arrangement here. And there had been ample time for him to grab something and come to her aid. But he hadn't. Maybe he didn't care what happened to her. Hank thought, if she recovered, she would be furious that her pot-bellied associate did not help her—soon he might be missing a swatch of skin on his neck too.

Clyde kept talking, but Hank ignored him for the moment. A thought occurred to him, a way to check to see if he had killed her. He knelt and felt her heart—faint, beating a dull rhythm, still alive.

Clyde's cheap drawl cut through the veil in Hank's mind, "Vampire, man, a fucking vampire. I know there's no such thing, boy, but that's what she is." The thought had occurred to Hank, hard to think of anything else when a human being leaps from the ground and latches, by the teeth, to someone's neck.

He continued. "And what if that crazy vampire has hepatitis or AIDS or something. I'm going to have to get tested. You ever seen anything like that?"

Hank ignored the question; he knew Clyde cared nothing for a reciprocal audience. This was just Clyde's internal monologue that he forced on the rest of the world.

Clyde turned the key and opened the door. He then motioned, using his gun, to the man on the ground and told him to go into the room.

This would be a night of discovery for all three men. Alejandro had yet to enter Silvia's little room of horrors. Had refused to, actually. He had neither the interest, nor the stomach, for whatever she did in here.

Now he would see.

Now he would know, forever.

#

The room was sound-proofed top to bottom, with black padding that immediately killed any echo. Lining the walls were several sterling silver carts, like a nurse pushes from room to room in a hospital, lined with various medications—small bottles with labels displaying the names of drugs Hank couldn't pronounce. Other carts were lined with all manner of tools and weapons, some looked to be antiques, with the coup de grace in the center: a beautiful miniature sword, the handle bejeweled with blue amethysts, its blade sharpened to perfection.

The men continued to stare in awe at all the nooks and crannies of this... this... well, Hank thought, there is only one way to refer to it—this kill room. As they took in the bizarre tableau, Silvia was still insensate outside the door. They weren't even pointing the gun at Alejandro any longer; each man was too distracted by the oddities that lay between these four walls.

Clyde motioned to Hank to drag her in. As he did it, Hank thought, so much for the ten-minute mark. That had sailed five minutes ago. But, for the time it seemed, none of the neighbors were wise to what was transpiring.

Using the rug again as a makeshift gurney, he moved her into the room and dropped her in the corner, her limbs folded in over her head; her body was a tangle of blood, tan skin, and dark curly hair. Hank checked again to make sure she was breathing. Soon it would be up to her roommate to get her more help.

"Alright. You get to work out there. I'll be there in a second. First, I need to have a talk with the amigo over here."

Normally, Hank would have been skeptical of such a comment. This wasn't part of the plan. Of course, by now, the plan was in shreds, along with the frayed patch of Clyde's skin, stuck to the floor in the master bedroom.

"It's important that you forget what you saw here tonight. Comprende, amigo?" Alejandro winced visibly at the sound of the gringo trying to speak Spanish.

"I understand. You and your friend were never here. You have masks anyway."

Then Clyde asked what he really wanted to know. "Who do you work for?"

Alejandro didn't hesitate. "I work for many people. And trust me, they're not people you want to know. Take the money and go. I'll handle her."

Clyde never could leave well enough alone. "Listen, you fat piece of shit, I want to know and you're going to tell me!" Clyde lunged at the crouching man with his gun drawn. "I got your attention now? Huh. Answer me. Who do you work for?" Clyde had the gun pressed to Alejandro's cheek, causing the man's fatty skin to awkwardly fold against his mouth.

"Trust me. You don't want to know."

"The day I take advice from an *illegal* is they day I'll end it. Pull the trigger myself. Tell me!"

Racist bastard, Hank thought. Even this junkie thief thought he was superior to a man from Mexico. But that was not the fight to have right now, not with the cold press of the gun against his victim's face. Hank held his tongue and watched the gun move, and then the next thing he heard was a wretched clank; there was no way that the captive could answer, as there was no room in his mouth to move his tongue—a cold piece of metal had taken its place. He backed out of the room.

#

Hank moved into the den. He stared around in amazement at the plainness of the room: the recliner, the red oriental rug, the perfectly stacked magazines on the coffee table, and then the wallpaper lining the kitchen—this home could be any grandparent's in America. Still loved. Well kept. Stuck in a decade long past.

Which room was it that had the attic access? Which one did Clyde say? He wasn't sure. Even something that simple got lost in the swamp in his head. Remembering had become so hard, like constantly having to tread water in the ocean. He stared around, confused at the sight of the tan ceilings, all taunting him and his junkie memory.

Clyde's yelling broke the hold of the mounting headache, growing precipitously as he tried to remember the right wall to break open. He ran back to the room. Clyde still had half the barrel of his .45 jammed into the man's mouth, demanding something.

"Clyde! What the hell, man? What are you doing?"

"Stay out of this. Just gettin' us some answers. I trust our man here, but it always helps to know what you're gettin' yourself into. And hell, might be a little insurance for us down the road. This fat fuck here was just about to talk before you interrupted our little dance."

Hank ran over and shoved Clyde away from the man.

"We need get out of here, man. What are you thinking?"

"I'm thinking about the future."

"There won't be any future if we don't get out of here. We need to go." Hank could see Clyde waver; he badly wanted to know who this guy and the vampire bitch answered to, but in the end, staying alive and out of prison trumped all. He demurred to Hank.

Clyde moved quickly into the den to start collecting the score. Hank followed.

#

Hank joined Clyde in the attic; the access had been in a small hallway that led to the garage.

With the other two locked securely in the kill room, they took a minute to marvel at the money lining the arc of the a-framed attic. It had been tucked under the insulation. Pulling all of the pink cotton-candy-like stuffing away had made each of them itchy, but the sight of all that green in plastic wrap made the itch disappear.

Finally, Clyde asked a question, "How in the hell are we going to get all of this out to the car?"

"I'll pull the car into their garage."

"You ever seen that much cash, boy?"

"Only in the movies."

#

It had taken the better part of an hour to load the car. The two black duffel bags were filled quickly, bursting at the seams by the time they dragged them to the car, so they stacked the cash in neat piles in the trunk.

After filling the trunk to capacity, Clyde ran back in, unlocked the door to the kill room, and then ran out of the house.

Then, they were off.

Clyde drove the speed limit and took drag after drag of his cigarette, a mischievous grin on his face.

Hank had a cigarette as well, but when he took a deep drag, causing the ember to flare up, he looked as if he had just left a funeral.

All of the blocks of money, every one of them, had twenties on the top and bottom. What if each bill was a twenty? That would be... that would be... he couldn't do the math, but he knew it flew well past that $50,000 mark. Hank put it at more like $150,000, or closer to $200,000. The kind of sum people don't forget.

He took another drag of his cigarette and stared out at the cane fields. The sun was starting to come up. Clyde turned up the radio, banged the steering wheel, and screamed that they had just pulled of the score of the century.

Chapter 36

Everett slid over a plate of meat.

"What's this? Doesn't look like pork," Lisa asked.

"Brisket. Been trying a few out in my spare time. Thinking about expanding the menu. Thought it might be nice to shake things up."

Her mouth watered at the sight of it. She hadn't eaten all day, working right through lunch to keep up with her boss's demands. For a few moments, they ate the brisket in silence.

Lately, Lisa had made a ritual of having dinner with Everett. She had to come by and pick Danny up anyway, and she worried about Everett being here on his own without Alice. She could tell Alice's death was still weighing on him, clinging to him like a shadow. She had other reasons too. She was lonely. She missed Hank. Being with Everett made her feel like her former life with Hank still had a chance of being resurrected.

Danny had already eaten, so he went out back to listen to music.

Everett finished his meal and asked a question, "So, when was the last time you actually saw him?"

"It's been months. He dropped by one night about six months ago, maybe more. We talked for a minute, he asked for money, I gave him a few bucks and then he left."

"You gave him money? You know—"

This was Everett's philosophy when it came to addiction—no lifeline. Everett was a student of the old school. No money. No support. You either get clean or you get gone.

"It was three dollars. Maybe enough to get a tallboy at the gas station. He asked to see Danny, too. I wouldn't let him. I told him he'd have to be sober to see him." She nodded after she said it to emphasize the point. She could be firm with Hank. She was no enabler.

"Alright. Just be careful. He has to know that he can't be a part of your life until he is sober. Trust me. There is nothing I wouldn't have done for some dope when I was bad off. Nothing."

Lisa understood the old-school philosophy, but Hank was out there killing himself, and the response was to do nothing? Just sit back and let fate play itself out? What if there was something she could do to make him stop? That's what she thought of the most—the guilt. That heroin would finally claim Hank for the grave and all she would be left with is guilt. Guilt of what she could have done. What she could have said. That she could have somehow saved him. "I just— I don't want him to die and have done nothing. I've lost other friends to pills. They just took them, went to sleep, and that was it." Her hands were shaking. Her composure was getting away from her. The old Lisa was surfacing, if just for a moment. She threw her fork and grabbed her hair. "Goddammit Everett, he's going to die and we're sitting here, eating fucking dinner like nothing is wrong, not doing shit about it." Disgusted, she pushed her plate away.

"This is the best thing we can do sweetie. I promise you."

"Really, 'cause it doesn't feel like everything I can do. Not even close."

"He won't quit until he is ready. That's just how it is."

"And what if that day never comes? What if he never hits bottom, huh? What the hell am I supposed to do?"

"Lisa, I—"

"Just sit here and wait for him like some sad—" Her voice caught, and she sobbed.

Everett came to her, sat down next to her. He put a hand on her shoulder and let her cry it out. Sometimes there wasn't anything to say.

When she was good and done, Lisa blew her nose and then started right back in on herself. "If I had any sense, I would just walk away. That's what any sane woman would do. High tail it right-the-fuck out that door."

Creases from age framed his kind brown eyes as he looked to her and said, "There's nothing wrong with you, Lisa. Not by a damn sight."

"Then why I can't I just walk away? Why can't I just move on?"

Those same eyes looked to her—eyes that held secrets, that had seen death, that had survived addiction—and they held sympathy for her.

"Lisa, I have something I want to tell you. I don't know if it will make you feel any better, but it's the only way I've ever been able to make sense of what you're talking about."

Then he told her something he had never told anyone before: His theory of the most powerful force in the universe. Something beyond man's understanding. Something beyond choice.

When he was finished, that is where they left it.

Chapter 37

Silvia, pressing an ice pack to her head, sat on the couch glowering at the wall. She hadn't said hardly two words since arriving back home from her surgery. When she came to in the hospital, she felt around to gauge the damage: her head was bald, smooth in some places, in others, gnarly and rugged. Woozy from the painkillers, she limped over to the mirror and recoiled at what she saw: rows of slapdash railroad tracks lining her head, with puffy, swollen peach-colored flesh looking as if it would soon swallow the ties. Her face had helter-skelter lines on each side like a cat had clawed her. All that time growing her hair out, grooming it, transforming herself into the femme fatale, all for naught. What good would that do her now? Could she even grow her hair back? She looked like a monster.

Her burner phone buzzed next to her. They had droves of the things, so many she struggled to remember to dispose of them, let alone remember the various numbers.

"We need to meet and talk." She knew Melvin's deep, hollow delivery when she heard it.

"I understand."

"How much was taken?"

"The best we can tell... two hundred thousand, give or take."

"And you're not accounting for the other two houses that were hit."

She stayed silent. This was not the time to try and correct her superior. Ultimately, Melvin and his boss had to answer for the almost $300,000 missing now.

"Do you think the drunk had anything to do with it?" That is what Melvin called Alejandro.

"As much as I wish, no. Doesn't have it in him. He's too weak to pull off something like this."

"Well, then how do we solve this problem?"

"I have a name—"

"Go on..."

"Clyde. One of them said the other's name."

She hadn't remembered this at first. It wasn't until she got home and stared at her disheveled room that the name came back to her. Looking at the fallout, she heard the name and that grating southern drawl screaming as she tore into his neck. The taste of his blood flooded back as well. A faint erotic pang stirred within her at the thought of it. Thinking of the patch of flesh against the roof of her mouth, thick yet supple, made her pulse quicken.

After a long pause, she continued, "And there's more. He talked with a southern accent, sounded like a redneck. And—" Unsteady on her feet, she stopped to cradle her head. Since her brief hospital stay, she had been on a diet of opioids. Her last pill was wearing off and she could feel the pain screaming back to the fore. Adding to her fatigue, she hadn't been able to keep anything down since she left the hospital. The doctor warned her that this might be the case for a few days. Head injuries were curious phenomena with unpredictable results. "...And I talked to Arturo, my man who got shot in the leg, and he said he remembered that one of the guys talked with a country accent. *It's got to be the same guys.* And we should be able to find them. How many people in the game here talk like a redneck? And just like a junkie, he'll walk around shooting his mouth off about what happened."

"How do you know he's a junkie?"

"He was rail-thin, and his hands shook the whole time. The other one was, too. The hit took longer than they thought it would, and the other guy started withdrawing right in front of me."

She had seen plenty of withdrawal firsthand, not from herself or Alejandro—neither of them used. She had seen it when she would ride around and check in with her people. She saw the nausea, the sweat, the shaking, and the look of desperation: they would do anything for the dope in that small plastic bag. Anything.

"Silvia... Silvia."

"Yes."

"Pay attention. Alright, so he uses. But what if he doesn't talk?"

"Then he will spend his take. Idiots always do."

"What if you can't find him?"

"We will. Trust me."

"And what do you plan to do with him, when you do?"

She took a breath, searching for the right thing to say, a harder task than usual because of the headache sounding out like a tornado siren in her head. "I'll bring him to you and the man you work for." A chance, one to show them she should be trusted. Take it, she thought. "And then I will show you what I'm capable of."

She was ready.

"And Melvin, there is another way we can identify him."

"Yeah?"

"His neck."

Chapter 38

Melvin closed the phone and re-entered the small warehouse to update his boss. This was not the opulent command post of a drug-lord: no lush couches, nor decadent chandeliers, no champagne and fine liquors in neat rows under a gilded mirror. It looked like a carpenter's shop. Odds and ends of various materials—wood, metal, copper—were strewn about, tools lining the walls. When they took the building from a man five years ago to satisfy a debt, this is how they had found it. After little thought, they decided to leave it this way. After all, the building wasn't there to impress; rather, it served an elemental purpose: it was a place for them to coordinate operations for their business in town. No drugs came through these doors. And more importantly, none of the people they took to the Portal came through these doors.

Hearing Melvin's approach, the Black-Eyed Man put his hand up to stop him from speaking. He was putting the finishing touches on a rendering that immortalized Hector's sacrifice. He had painted it before but always missed the mark. This rendering, however, was perfect, capturing the moment just as he remembered it: right as the blood rained down from his legs, his face a mixture of succor and fear; a tall, bald figure with scars crisscrossing his lead like mangled worms, looked down at him. He used his finger to smudge the crimson paint, turning the blood into a gauzy cloud.

He motioned for Melvin to come over and update him. "And..."

"She has a name and a description of the man's voice."

"And what is our would-be thief's God-given name?"

174

"Clyde."

"And what did his voice sound like?"

"He talks with a thick southern accent."

"Magnificent. You shouldn't have to shake the trees too hard to find him then."

"She said we could identify him by his neck."

"What, a tattoo or birthmark of some sort?"

"No. She said he would be missing a chunk of skin."

"And how did such a thing come to be?"

"She said she bit it out of him."

"I like Silvia more by the second."

Melvin nodded in affirmation. He was beginning to think that Silvia might have the same bloodlust as him. Maybe even mixed in with a dose of the philosophical, like his boss.

"Thieves like this Clyde don't work for themselves. We need to find out who that person is. He will have our money. And if he doesn't have it all, we'll take what he has and just up our sales this month. That, or we will increase the price."

Melvin turned to go outside to make some calls.

"And Melvin... let's bring Silvia along. It's time for her to stop toiling alone in that room of hers."

Silvia believed that she was the only one that saw the horrors in her room. She was wrong. The Black-Eyed Man and Melvin monitored every inch of the home, doing so right from a laptop here at the warehouse. Melvin had broken in and wired the place with audio and video long ago, one day when Silvia and Alejandro were not home. They had watched the robbery after-the-fact, saw that both Alejandro and Silvia were asleep when it happened. They had also seen her jump on top of one of the burglars, though they couldn't see the finer detail of her teeth rending a piece of flesh from the man's throat. Importantly, for Silvia, they saw enough of what she did that night, and what she had done in her little room, to know that she should be in league with them.

Chapter 39

Clyde and Hank walked into Vince's house. Vince welcomed them each with a hearty hug as they came through the door, congratulating them on a job well done. Clyde received the embrace with a grin, each of them giving the other loud backslaps that sounded like thunderclaps. To avoid making things awkward right from the outset, Hank accepted the hug but stood stock-still, making it look as if Vince was hugging a statue. He told them to meet him out back by the pool after he grabbed the bottle of top-shelf scotch and the high-end cigars he had stashed in the house. A celebration was in order tonight.

The job in Belle Glade was in their rearview now. Hank still feared a reprisal, but Vince and Clyde seemed to think there was nothing to fear. After all, three months had passed; if a reckoning was in the offing, it would have happened by now. Hank failed to share their optimism. Want of revenge doesn't just die off. It grows stronger with time.

"Hey, man. Don't fuck this up," Clyde hissed.

"What? I'm supposed to kiss his ass? He walked us into a nightmare over there." In the meantime, Hank, now flush with cash, had been using twice as much as usual to fend off the nightmares. Every dream was different, though there was one common thread: there was always some version of a dark-haired woman with her head cracked open. In one of the recurring nightmares, bloody white spiders spilled out of the hole in her head.

"Vince has been good to us, man. And remember when we talked on the phone, he said he's got something big for us. He called it a bonus, but one that keeps on giving. *Like a bottomless well.* That's what he said."

Of course that's what he said—Vince would say anything to get them to help him make more money. Using words to manipulate people was the man's stock and trade. But he had already said this to Clyde a hundred times before, and didn't have the energy to have the same argument again.

Slyly stepping through the sliding glass door, Vince held a bottle in one hand, and a silver tray with three unblemished glasses in the other. He set everything down on the table, then screwed the top off and poured a small amount in each glass.

"So, gentleman, once again, I've been speaking to my people: still nary a word on the street about who pulled off the job."

"We aim to please, boss." Clyde said it with that shit-eating grin of his, letting out a chuckle as his smile beamed like a beacon over to Vince.

Vince handed out the glasses.

"To you fellas, for pulling off three jobs, and getting away scot-free each time. And to your new position as collectors." Clyde snorted and hit Hank on the arm.

Feeling the momentum in his favor, Vince said, "So I've developed a different business model. One I think you two will like very much."

Hanging on every word, Clyde stared at Vince as he sat down, waiting for the big reveal. Hank feigned nonchalance.

Clyde asked, "Really, Vince?"

"That's right, fellas. You'll get a cut of everything sold in your district. We can negotiate the percentages later. Right now, let's just sit back and enjoy this high-dollar whiskey." Vince moved his glass to the center of the group, signaling a toast.

Clyde moved his glass to the center without hesitation.

Money was money. And he didn't have to risk his ass anymore going into strangers' houses. Hank moved his glass in for the toast.

Chapter 40

A head of schedule and not content to keep scrolling on Facebook, Lisa decided to head home from work early. She pulled up to the townhouse, the same one that she and Hank used to live in together; the only trace of Hank left in the place was the DCP posters still hanging in Danny's room.

It was just mid-afternoon, so she didn't expect Danny home. He would be at work with Everett at The Hickory. Odd to think that Danny was still there churning it out without Hank, and even sadder, without Alice. Occasionally, she would help out on the weekends, to be near Danny, she told herself, but she knew the real reason she wanted to be there: to be closer to the memory of what once was.

She walked up the stairs and threw her purse on the bed in the master bedroom, first thinking she'd like to continue watching the latest season of *American Horror Story* that had been scaring the bejesus out of her, then thinking that she should knock out the laundry first. She moved into Danny's room to grab up his dirty clothes, the floor a sea of crumpled black t-shirts.

Being in Danny's element, among the shirts, the records, and the posters, made her want to check in on him. She always called when he was at work; part of her had to know that Danny was okay.

She pulled out her iPhone and told Siri to call The Hickory.

"This is Everett at The Hickory."

"Hey, it's Lisa."

"Hey sweetie, what can I do for you?"

"Oh, I just wanted to check in on Danny. I don't need to talk to him. I just wanted to know he was okay."

Sounding confused, Everett said, "Lisa, Danny hasn't been in here today."

"What?"

"I didn't think anything of it. I thought maybe you guys took a day to do something together or something. Or maybe he was sick."

"He's not there? This isn't funny, Everett. Tell me right now if he's there."

"I wouldn't joke about Danny. I'm tellin' you, he's not here."

Panic and anxiety blasted through her in a violent wave, and she dropped the phone. Faintly, she could her Everett's voice, as if he was far away, over and over repeating that he'd go out and help her find him. Worried that she might puke, she put her hand over her mouth and braced her back against the wall, desperate to think her way out of this sick labyrinth. Everett was still yelling for her to get back on the phone. Finally, he said, "Stay there, I'm coming, and we'll split up and search the town for him." She hadn't heard much else of what he'd said, but she had heard one word: *town*. A laughable description of the urban sprawl that was South Florida. West Palm wasn't a town. It was a city. A city with a dense population, sandwiched between dozens and dozens of small beach towns that spanned the coast. And if Danny had gotten on the Tri-rail, that ran all the way to Miami, then there was no telling where he could be.

She had to stop; thinking the problem was intractable would solve nothing.

Her breaths came out in rapid bursts, almost no space in between them. *Calm down*, she told herself. *Calm down.*

Where would he be? Where would Danny go if he wandered off?

She grabbed her hair and pulled it in frustration. "Dammit, Danny."

God, he hadn't done this in years.

Why now? Why did he do this?

She realized there might not be a why. With Danny, you never knew. He might have just started walking for some reason—hungry, wanted to look at the pond across the street, wanted to go to the park a mile away—who knew.

She knew she needed to get out there and start looking, but she didn't want to blindly scour the town for him. She needed a direction, a target.

And she damn sure wasn't going to wait for Everett to make the drive up from Boynton. In a moment, when she gathered herself, she would call him and tell him some spots to check. No sense in them overlapping each other.

But where to start?

Her deceased mother's voice, unbeckoned, came into her head. Her mother had a phrase she always used when Lisa said she couldn't find something—her shoes, a book, her favorite hairbrush. Her mother would come up the stairs with a calm air, knowing it would take only seconds to track down the lost item. And often, it would be right there in front of Lisa. After finding it, her mother would grab the thing and say the same phrase each time.

"If it was a snake, it would have bit you."

She scanned Danny's room. The phrase from her mother reverberated in her head in a reverse echo, getting louder each time.

Then she understood where to find him: the shirts, the posters, the records.

If it was a snake, it would have bit her.

Chapter 41

After they left Vince's, Hank and Clyde headed back to the townhouse; during the drive, Hank thought about moving out and getting a place of his own. He had wanted to for months, but didn't have the scratch saved up to do it. Thanks to Vince's scheming, and he and Clyde's late-night break-in out in Belle Glade, money was no longer an issue. It wasn't long before his thoughts moved to the ample stash of heroin he kept in the cabinet under his sink. They'd be back home soon. Hank could retire into solitude and go see his mother.

Too amped up from the conversation with Vince, compounded by the fat line of cocaine he shoved up his nose, Clyde decided to go out for a drink. He cajoled Hank to come along, but Hank had no desire to go out drinking; he wanted to be alone, fix himself up, and then maybe he would listen to music.

After Clyde left in the old, battered Honda Civic they shared, Hank went to his bathroom, tied off, found his favorite vein plump, a fat blue river flowing under his skin, and expectantly squeezed down the plunger. After haphazardly throwing the implements back on his kit, and leaving it all on the bathroom floor, he went to the back porch to smoke a cigarette and listen to music.

Sitting in a cheap lawn chair, Hank stared out at the small pond behind his townhouse. The back of their house faced west, so as the sun retreated for the night, the last light it emitted—lush red, faint purple, blood orange—reflected off the pond, making the whole thing seem like a mirage.

He lit another cigarette. The sun was gone now.

His phone buzzed. He didn't bother to look at the name before picking up. "Hank?"

"Yeah."

"It's Danny."

"Danny?" Hank leaned up, trying to shake off his wooziness from the heroin. Why was Danny calling? Danny never called. Hank hadn't spoken to or seen him in months. "How you doin', bud?"

"Good. I just got a new Lamb of God t-shirt. Lisa took me to see them. I don't think she liked it, but I did. Between the Buried and Me played before them. I got one of their shirts too."

"That's great, man. Wish I could have been there." BTBAM toured with Lamb of God, and he missed it? How did he miss that? Two of his favorites on the road together and he didn't have a clue.

"Hank, can you come down here?"

"Where?"

"The Black Circle."

"Why bud?"

"I want someone to look at records with me."

"I'd like to, Danny, but I don't know if that's such a good idea. Your sister wouldn't like that."

"She's not here."

"Wait. What?" He threw his cigarette down. "Lisa's not there?"

"No. She doesn't like coming here."

He knew exactly what had happened. Danny had wandered off. Lisa must be freaking out. "I'll be there."

#

Her phone rang and rang. The fluorescent, neon glow of its light gave the car an eerie feeling, as if an alien abduction was in the offing. She looked down and saw it was Hank calling again. Why was he repeatedly calling? He usually texted. Why so many calls back-to-back?

Danny was lost. She had no time to spare for Hank's nonsense.

The system was simple: *You text to let me know you're alive so I can enjoy a modicum of peace.* That's it. That was the boundary—texting.

She flipped the phone to vibrate; if she wasn't driving, then she would have blocked Hank's calls. Stopping was out of the question.

Hank called two more times, giving the car that odd green neon glow, straight from the *X-files*. And then it stopped.

Part of her was sad when the calls stopped.

#

When Hank walked through the doors, he immediately spotted Danny in the back, headphones on, standing stock-still. The store had plush white walls matted in posters and record sleeves with no order or reason: Hank passed by Iggy Pop's image flipping the bird to the crowd, Slash with his trademark top-hat and cigarette dangling from his lip, Jack and Meg White on stage looking at each other to cue the song. The art went on and on, acting as the wallpaper for what sat beneath, among the shelves: thousands of records.

Music, a universe where time and space had no meaning.

Hank gently touched him on the shoulder and pointed down to the second headphone jack. Danny nodded. Hank plugged in as Danny started the song over. People filed by as Hank and Danny floated off into their own world.

Danny smiled.

#

The bench offered a great view of the Intracoastal, where all manner of boats—fishing boats, canoes, even giant yachts—shared space on the water. Hank remembered that Danny liked the view.

They sat down together. The time in the store had been easy; music did all the talking either of them needed. But they couldn't stay in there forever. Sooner or later, time and space had to realign.

Hank knew the question was coming. "Where have you been?"

He said the only thing he could think of that was responsive and yet not a total lie. "Around."

"You never come by the restaurant anymore."

"I'm busy, bud. And right now, Dad and I don't really see eye to eye."

Danny stared off. He wasn't one to persist. Unlike Lisa and Everett, he accepted answers at face value.

"You ever think you'll come back and start working again?"

"Don't know. Maybe."

"Well, you want to come over to the house tonight? We could keep listening to music. My sister won't care. I still have all your records." In the mad scramble to get out after things fell apart, Hank had abandoned his records, including his mom's. Too much to carry. He had planned to come back for them. He had planned to do a lot of things.

"All in... in... condition..."

"Mint condition."

"Yeah, that."

Out of the dark, dim light illuminating her pale face, Lisa walked up.

Hank had not seen her approach.

"Lisa," Danny said.

Hank turned, but could only see her silhouette: the shadow of the woman he still loved.

#

The black silhouette cut against the damp glow of the lights. He knew the figure standing in front of him, he just couldn't find the words. He worried about his appearance. Even he could tell that age had come prematurely for him, one of the costs of going to the tangerine river to commune with his mother—it sped up time. What would he look like after another two years of using? Another five? That is, if he was still around.

Sooner or later, every addict accepted the costs and started to treat the end as a foregone conclusion. Every one of them knew that the noose around their neck would continue to tighten as time marched on. They had just lost the will to cut the rope.

He looked at her, unsure of what to say.

Like old times, Danny had put his headphones on.

Lisa made the first move. "I didn't know you were going to be here."

"I called and sent you texts."

"Sorry," she said, without an ounce of contrition in her voice. She didn't feel sorry in the slightest for ignoring Hank. "I was panicking because of Danny. He hasn't done this in so long. It caught me off guard."

Without words, Hank motioned for her to take a seat next to him. She started to move towards the bench, and then she thought better of it.

Hank saw her hesitation and gritted his teeth; the veins in his neck stuck out in cords: "Well, if I make you that uncomfortable. You can just leave."

"It's not that, Hank. I just, I'm just still... this thing with Danny tonight really messed with me." True, but not the truth. "I just, I just..." Flustered, she paced back and forth.

Hank recognized the habit. It was what she had always done when she needed to confide in him and get something off her chest. Seeing an in, he motioned for her to sit again.

She shook her head. No.

Hank bit his lip in frustration.

He wanted to ask why she ignored his calls. He wanted to know if it was because she thought he needed money. But he already knew in his heart that was the answer. Would hearing it cure anything? No, it would just further open the wound, letting it spit more blood and pus.

When Lisa looked over at Danny, Hank noticed his hands shaking. His senses were heightened, and he was painfully aware of every nerve ending in his body, all screaming, all on fire, all begging for release. *Opium, wash over me.*

He hadn't shot up in hours.

But he decided to fight through the pain. This was Lisa. This was too important. He needed to hook her into staying.

"Do you ever see your mom?" he asked.

The question jarred her. In a good way, he could tell; a tinge of fascination accompanied her look of surprise. "What do you mean?"

"In your dreams, do you ever see her?"

Moving unconsciously, she sat down on the bench. Hank had never asked her something like this before. "No. She's never come to me in a dream. What are you really getting at?"

"I don't know."

"Yes, you do. You wouldn't have asked me if you didn't."

Rubbing his thighs, Hank paused for a moment and then said, "...I see my mother, sometimes. She is floating on this river. The sky is orange and red—so is the river—and we are both floating on the water. She comes to me, and we talk. We talk for what seems like forever."

"What does she say?"

"I can't ever remember."

"This comes to you in your dreams?"

Hank hesitated. "Something like that."

Lisa wasn't buying. "Is this shit you're seeing when you're high, Hank?"

Looking defeated, he nodded.

She sighed. "Is that why you keep using? I know it's not the only reason. I've read up. I know about how awful the withdrawals are. But is part of it because you want to see her? Is that what you're telling me?"

"Before this, I only had the photo. But in the dream, she's *there*: moving with me, talking to me, smiling at me."

A pang of sympathy shot through her. Even so, this was wrong. He already had the skeleton key to find his mother. In fact, he'd had it for a long time. And it wasn't heroin.

"Do you even have the picture anymore?" she asked.

He ignored the question. He didn't, and if pressed, wouldn't be able to remember the last time he did, let alone the last time he had looked at it. Another thing to fill the mausoleum of his former life.

"You're an idiot. I know your addiction is bigger than you. But you're an idiot if you think you need that shit to be with your mother. We're leaving."

She got back up, put her hand on Danny's shoulder, and motioned for him to come with her.

Realizing what was happening, Danny waved bye to Hank, keeping his eyes down as he limply moved his hand.

"Do you want me to keep texting you?"

"Do whatever you want. I don't care," Lisa said.

They couldn't leave it like this. He had no clue when he would see her again. "Well then, what should I do to be with her? At least you knew your parents. What do I have? A fucking picture. Dad has hardly ever told me anything. What should I do?"

She gave him with the patronizing look of a parent; the look of *Why can't you see that the answer is right in front of you?* A look Lisa's mother had perfected while still alive.

"The records, Hank. Your dad had her records." She paused to allow her words to resonate with him. "You're right. I've never heard him tell any stories about her. And I remember how many times you said that he has never told you much about her. *But you have her records.* And what did you do? You left them with Danny when you ran off. You chose that shit over us. And you chose the drugs over the art that could have told you everything you needed to know about her. Remember what your dad said? Do you remember? Do you?"

She screamed the questions, poking him in the chest as she repeated it again and again.

Giving in to her, he—finally—nodded yes.

"You're damn right you do. Because I remember you cried after he left the room. You had always thought they were your dad's. And then he told you the truth: they belonged to her."

Hank remembered when his dad told him. He and Lisa hadn't been together that long and losing his composure that badly in front of her had made him madly insecure. With total control, she had reached over and hugged him; and they never spoke of it again, not until right now. He also remembered the other thing his dad told him. Before he could speak about it, Lisa took the opportunity. "And he said it was the only thing of value in her place. He said they were both poor back then, him working as a cook and her trying to get by cleaning houses. But she had a great record collection. She bought each one of those albums with the scraps she had. She chose each one knowing she didn't have much money.

"Each one of them is a piece of her, Hank. Why can't you see that? You, who loves music, can't see that the art she left behind—the art you love more than anything— it's sitting right in front of you waiting to tell you who your mother was. And you're just too fucking stupid to sit down and listen." Lifting her pale, thin hand, she cradled his chin, which was stubbly, jutting out like a sharp knife. "I love you, Hank, and I think I always will, but

I'm not going to keep sitting by while you kill yourself." She offered one last thought. "Do you want to *see* her? Or do you want to *know* her?" Something in her tone signaled to him that her question was rhetorical. "That picture can't tell you what you want to know. And whatever vision or fantasy you have when you pump that shit into yourself can't tell you. Those records will help you find your way *home* to your mother. It's in the music, Hank. The answer is in the music."

Gently, she put her hand on his cheek, just for a second. And then she turned, motioned to Danny, and walked away.

Hank stayed there for a moment, staring at his quaking hands, trying to hold on to the way her palm had felt against his worn-down cheek: soft, unused, like a peach without the fuzz. And warm.

He soon lost sight of them.

Then he lost the feeling of her skin against his cheek.

Chapter 42

C lyde had come home while Hank was out with Danny and Lisa. He was right as rain. Seaworthy. Ready to check out and enjoy his high. In the beginning, Clyde's penchant was for uppers—cocaine, meth, and the like—but lately, he had changed course. Hank had convinced him that the euphoria brought by heroin was unmatched. Heroin was the wizard that wielded a magic above all others, and it could take you wherever you wanted. The feeling it gave you—the blissful numbness, erasing cares and problems in seconds—was second to none. Now that they had some money, Clyde decided he wanted to discover another world. His senses didn't need to be sharpened to a fine point all hours of the day. No, sometimes it was okay to cut the tether that latched him to reality and float off into the unknown. And that's where Clyde was right now: oblivion.

As bubbles of blood trickled out, they left a trail of crimson from the site where the needle had pierced his tattered skin. He stared at the TV; a foggy electronic ambience formed the background of the alternate world he now visited.

Lost to the dreams beckoned by the heroin, he almost didn't hear the knock at the door. Once. Twice. Then a rapid succession like a drumroll. He hadn't the will to get up. So, like anyone lost in a high, he said, "Come in."

Melvin said nothing as he entered.

Edging over to the recliner, seeing the droplets of blood flowing down the redneck's arm, Melvin stood still. Time to let *her* do the talking. That is, if there was anything to say. They knew they had their man; it only took two words (*come in*) to hear the thick drawl.

But first, a test. Let's see what she does.

Melvin stood back, giving her the lead. She felt a rush of excitement.

In the wake of her disfigurement, Silvia had eschewed the femme fatale clothes, the spandex, the too-tight dresses and the heels that accentuated her calves. Now, she wore black military-style boots, shorts, and a tight-fitting white tank top. With her new face and hair, the role of the seductress had faded in favor of the role she was born to play—the monster.

She bent down and caressed him; her hands raw and calloused from years of working on her father's farm. She had added to that scar tissue with her new pursuits; dragging and disposing of bodies with acid and lye was no easy task, and she didn't have a lackey to dig the hole. She did everything for her craft, farm to table, and her hands, as much as her soul, bore the proof.

She continued to give his cheek a steely rub, looking like a concerned mother. Eventually Clyde left the *other* world; the harsh rub of Silvia's hand, feeling like she was dragging a box grater against his cheek, rudely ferried him back to reality. He saw her, and recoiled.

"Oh, sweet baby, is it my face?"

Clyde said nothing. His high had left him abruptly. In its place, paranoia washed over him.

"Don't let my tears bother you."

Clyde clicked his eyes open and shut, thinking the stuff he got must be laced with that deadly chemical he had heard about—fenta... fenta-something. That shit must be in this batch. But no matter how many times he opened and shut the blinds, there she was: still smiling at him, still rubbing him and telling him she would do everything she could to protect him, still with scars on her cheeks that looked as if someone had clawed her with a tiller.

"Who are you?"

"That doesn't matter. I'm here to help you now, and you must come answer for your sins." *He doesn't remember me*, she thought.

She continued to soothe him as he looked about the room.

For the first time, Clyde noticed the man behind her. Clyde looked at his eyes: fixed, hollow, the eyes of a hunter. If given a thousand lives, that man would use every one of them to hurt his own kind.

He looked to Silvia again; she still caressed him, as if she was an angel, there to whisk him away from the horrors that surrounded him.

"Who are you?"

"Oh sweetie, I'm your black angel."

He didn't hear the word *black*; Clyde only heard *angel*. It gave him a modicum of comfort. The last bit of grace he would feel on this earth.

"It's time to go meet my creator. He's ready for you."

#

When Clyde came to, he blinked his eyes, trying to get his bearings. A damp glow from two overhead lights let him see some of the room; the rest of it was hidden in shadow. He saw the woman that had comforted him standing off by the door. There were some shelves behind her with various tools and jars; some of the jars appeared to have liquid and things... parts? The jars reminded him of his grandmother's house back in Georgia. She had a shed, and in it, from top to bottom, there were shelves of whatever she was pickling from her fields—green beans, peppers, carrots.

#

The Black-Eyed Man and his tribe had a similar philosophy: they preserved the pieces of their passengers as a totem, a kind of talisman. Reminders of the moments where they remade human flesh, stripping time and space of all meaning.

If Clyde wasn't so disoriented, or perhaps if he had more light to see, he would have seen the pieces of squelched flesh in sundry forms: some from the legs, some the arms, bits of a torso. No eyes. No organs. They had standards; after all, they weren't animals.

Occasionally, they would grind down a bone of the *passenger* or use a saw to cut it into a smaller piece and then wrap it in flesh before preserving it. Like Alejandro, some of his peers had received one of these talismans as a lesson against negligence and stealing.

The skin, the casing for our vessels on this earth. That is what he and Melvin prized above all else. Soon they would learn if Silvia coveted the same totem.

As a measure of her devotion, she had taken to calling the Black-Eyed Man her father. And for the first time in her misspent existence, she had found a reason to be.

They were a family now.

"Silvia, I will do the talking. When I give you the cue, comfort him. And then soon after, Melvin will get started on his work. Join in when the feeling strikes you."

They both nodded in subservience, each focused on what was to come.

#

Clyde kept scanning the room trying to find something to signal his location. He scanned and scanned, finding nothing to betray his whereabouts. What he did find came from his nose. The air was humid, boggy, the wind blowing through felt as thick as a sheet of steel, moist and heavy; it carried the smell of swamp decay. He could look and smell all he liked, but there would be nothing to guide him home. Not tonight.

"Young Clyde, I see that you keep looking about, trying to divine your location, perhaps? Allow me to help you."

The man pulled over a chair. As he shifted his weight, Clyde finally realized he was bound to the chair all over. They had strapped him to the chair, at least fifty times over, with plastic zip ties.

"Clyde, through some of our associates, it has come to our attention that you have transgressed. In a moment, I'm going to give you a chance to confess your sins."

The man sat down and adjusted himself, then turned back, seemingly to check on something. As he did, Clyde noticed the back of the man's head: a gruesome network of scars. Clyde felt his gag reflex trigger. Then he looked at the man's eyes: two matching abysses, all black.

"Ah, you noticed my eyes. Everyone does. My cross to bear, I suppose. God saw fit to make me look like a monster. And who am I to question the Almighty?" The man's eyes had rendered the droves of zip-ties holding Clyde to the chair meaningless. The two onyx orbs mummified Clyde right in place. "After all, they are a nice complement to my scars. If there were not such pressing business, I would tell you the tales of how I came to be.

192

"Now, to the matter before us. Clyde have you ever read the Bible?" The question shook Clyde from his nightmare. As a kid, Clyde's Mom took him to church every Sunday, without fail. But why did this man want to discuss *that* right now?

"I only ask because of the thick accent. I take it you grew up in the south." The man continued, taking Clyde's response for granted. "No shortage of Bible-thumpers and churches in the town where you lived, I'm sure. People ever at the ready to tell you the path to your true salvation. All speaking with that same fake enlightened tone, like they have discovered some beautiful treasure, and if only you come join in, you will be saved too." The man's face hardened. "But what if I don't want to be saved, Clyde? What if I like it here in the dark? Do you think those self-righteous zealots ever stopped to think that maybe some people don't fear Hell: that to some, it's home?" Everything the man said felt rhetorical, a planned speech that Clyde dared not interrupt. "Go ahead, answer my question about the Bible. Out with it. In all those years walking into the chapel and staring at the stained glass and praying to God and his Son he made into flesh to die for your sins, through all the hymns and all the potlucks and all the talk of helping humanity, did you ever read the Bible cover to cover?"

In truth, Clyde had never read much of anything. He was borderline illiterate, but he was adept at hiding it—well enough to have made it to tenth grade before he dropped out.

"No."

"Ahh, as I suspected. And I'm sure the same can be said for most of the people that filled the chapel with you. Why bother yourself with the good book when you can cherry-pick the lines and twist them into weapons? Weapons against the poor. Weapons against the weak. Weapons against those you despise." The man grinned. "Well, Clyde, I have read the good book from end to end. Several times, in fact. And I have to tell you, my friend, it would be a tall order to find a book more *violent* than the Bible."

A look of confusion came over Clyde's face.

"Again, just as I thought: someone who has only heard the pretty verses. The ones about self-reflection. The ones about being humble. The ones about finding your inner light. But you've never actually read the myriad pages filled with woebegone tales. Were Sodom and Gomorrah not erased in an instant with fire? Women and children all vaporized in the name of the Lord. Can you see their charred, blackened bodies, Clyde? Steam pouring out of their flesh in ribbons because their insides are boiling like water in a pot. Was John the Baptist's head not severed, bloody tendrils dangling down, and then served up on a platter? Did King Herod not order the slaughter of every child in pursuit of killing Christ? And your *Savior*, Clyde," —despite all his crimes, Clyde was a believer; it was in his DNA, like anyone that grew up in the South. Christianity, Jesus, they were a part of you whether you asked for it or not; and hearing the phrase *your Savoir* reminded him of that in a way no other words could— "Did they not whip him, and throw stones at him, before they *nailed* him up? Such violence, Clyde, what end does it serve? What is its purpose?"

The man moved his chair to Clyde's right, revealing a pile of something behind him. The other man, the one with the harsh eyes, moved into the room and rolled his sleeves up. What was in that pile? Clyde blinked and blinked, until the world dropped back into focus. Rocks, no—stones.

A pile of stones.

"And to think, if the rest of the world saw what I did here they would be aghast. Am I doing anything more violent than what appears in their good book? Because of their narrow minds, I have to carry out my *art* in shadow. I can't bear my creations to the world. Such beauty should never have to be hidden from the world."

He stopped and removed the black suit-jacket he had kept on despite the humidity. Amazingly, there were no signs on the man's shirt that he had been sweating.

"I can tell you firsthand, Clyde, that I have found a purpose for violence in this world. To what end it served in the Bible, I leave for the rest of you to sort out." The man crossed his legs; they were pencil thin and folded over each other with ease, coming together like pieces of a puzzle. "Clyde, though you haven't read it, do you know what they did to adulteresses in the Bible?" The pile of projectiles stacked just so told Clyde everything he needed to know.

"They stoned them to death. A punishment for disloyalty. But even deeper, at the heart of it, it was a punishment for dishonesty. And Clyde, you have committed an act of dishonesty, would you not agree?" Clyde nodded his head in affirmation. He had to follow this man wherever his hollow eyes wanted to take him: his only chance at survival. "And now is your chance to confess your transgression. Were you not the one that went into the house in Belle Glade and stole from us?"

"Yes."

"And who else was with you?" Clyde balked. He had known this question was coming, but it jarred him, nonetheless. "Clyde, you can answer, or my associate will make you answer. He has been waiting for an opportunity to cast those stones. He is a student of the Bible as well."

"If I tell you who went in with me, then you'll let me go?" Looking at his surroundings—the jars he now suspected contained human remains, the shed in the middle of nowhere, the walls of tools for torture—the question sounded laughable.

"Now Clyde, we are not here to bargain. What you do, you must do as an exercise in faith. You trust me, don't you, Clyde?"

Hank Grant. That was the man that was with me. He could just say it. That easy. Two words. A name.

"You should trust me, Clyde. After all, I do admire the grace with which your Savior carried himself that day. Do you think you'll have the same fortitude in just a moment?"

Rapt, Silvia looked on.

Melvin was at the ready, waiting for his cue.

With no promise of anything in return, Clyde kept Hank's name and Vince's locked away for now.

That was before the pain came.

#

Over time, the totems from the passengers took on greater and greater significance for the Black-Eyed Man and Melvin. Though the Portal allowed them to erase the meaning of time and space, when they left, time reasserted itself. And with the passage of time came the degradation of their memories.

Discussing those moments—the way the flesh tore, the way a black crusty goop of ochre settled on a wound—failed to conjure the moment full stop; it just didn't do. They needed a way to step back through time.

Hence, the totems. What some call charms.

One rub of the preserved skin and reality vanished, giving way to the scene at the Portal, whatever night or victim that may have been. Some, they kept in the jars on the shelves. Others they carried with them.

Silvia scanned the shelves of jars before Melvin started in on Clyde. She had seen this sort of thing in many movies, all there for shock value, trying to get a scare out of the audience or make them cringe in their seats. At first, she had been disappointed by it, feeling as though they were imitators of art, recreating things they had seen in films for lack of imagination. But when her new father told her its deeper meaning; that it wasn't because of some deficit of the mind, or for some wicked science experiment; instead, it was to trick time and memory. Each was a piece of magic, a way to go back in time. After he explained it, that is when she saw the singular beauty of it.

Now she looked on as if she were a culture-lover walking through an art museum. She surveyed for the smallest detail, a nick here, a gash in the skin there, the way the blood caked over the flesh. All these random pieces of human skin, all unique in their twists and fleshy bulges. Some looked crumpled, like a fallen leaf, pink and red and dried up. Others looked like a thin sheath, almost like parchment, as if you could take it out of the jar and write on it.

As she looked over, the Black-Eyed Man was standing over Clyde, stroking his hair. Clyde had proven surprisingly strong under the hail of stones. They had misjudged him. Melvin, while the Black-Eyed Man chatted with Clyde, was taking a break from the projectile-bludgeoning.

At the moment, she could only see Clyde's limbs; his legs and arms were red in many places, the spots where the flesh had sloughed away under the harsh press of the stones, but the blood was not pouring down. The blood on his arms had a sheen under the light, sheets of red glimmer. It reminded her of when she used to skin her elbows and knees when she was a child. It hurt like hell but the blood, visible and beet red, stayed put.

That was the thing about these totems: they were all blemished.

Skin without a story written on it had no purpose.

The scars, the gashes, the holes, that is where the story of what transpired that night was memorialized. She learned by looking at the countless charms lining the walls that clean flesh was no different than a blank canvas.

The memory was in the mutilation.

#

Clyde had stayed resolute through two rounds of Melvin hurling the stones at him. In the beginning, Melvin aimed for his appendages. As time wore on, Melvin started moving closer and closer to the center of the target.

"Clyde, my friend, a name is the price of your salvation. Are you ready to give it to us? Are you ready to be forgiven? Or must he continue?"

Clyde offered nothing in response.

Melvin went back to work.

#

Melvin had lost count of how many times he restacked the stones and then resumed the hail. His arm felt like jelly. He wished he could switch to his left, but he knew he would lose all control. Not an option.

His overseer had made it clear that there were to be no headshots. Also, no shots to the neck. They needed their prisoner to be able to speak; to boot, they needed his brain intact. Melvin had mostly succeeded. But the few stones that sailed wide made for devastating results.

Clyde's voice-box had been crushed. Teeth were missing. And his jaw was mangled, out of joint and out of place, bones pressing taut against his skin looking as if his maker had assembled him without the instructions. Without control of his mouth, the blood and saliva drooled out of him in a river.

He could still speak, but only in a whisper. And his voice had been reduced to mostly grunts and vowels.

The Black-Eyed Man looked back at Melvin, expressionless.

But that's not what Melvin saw; on his face, he saw disappointment.

#

"Clyde, your tenacity is admirable. But know this: we will keep you alive and breathing for as long as it takes. Our cabinet over there is filled with all manner of chemicals we can sluice through you to keep your heart pumping. And Clyde,"—he paused to lift his chin, driving his hand into the blood and mucus without hesitation— "those chemicals keep your heart beating and your lungs inflating, but they don't dull the pain. They keep the pain alive too."

The man resumed his seat and continued. "Why show this stubborn loyalty, Clyde? Is the man a relative?" Clyde shook his head no. "A friend." Again, Clyde shook his head no. He and Hank had served a need in each other's lives. Helping someone get high involves an intimacy, finding the vein, tying the band just so, ensuring that the needle is clean. Yet, if pressed, Clyde couldn't tell anyone what music Hank liked, or where he was from. The drugs demanded complete devotion from them; there wasn't room left for anything else.

"Clyde, then why continue to protect him through this agony? Just give us the names of those that helped you." Subtly, the Black-Eyed Man had started to pluralize *name*, hoping that Clyde's disorientation would trip him up, causing him to reveal who they worked for as well.

More incoherent grunts and shifts in the chair.

"Very well, Clyde, I'm going to step out of the way to allow him to continue. Soon, we will transition to more surgical pursuits. I trust you know what our wall of tools is for. I'm sure you've heard the lore surrounding this place. Those tales exist on the streets in the underworld as if they were myth." The man grabbed Clyde's chin again, setting off a blinding jolt of pain through Clyde's face, and at once making him gasp and heave up globs of bile and blood.

The man held firm to Clyde's chin through all his hacking and writhing. He waited, patiently, for Clyde to gather himself. They had all the time in the world now that they were at the Portal. Eons of it.

"Clyde, those stories are neither myth nor legend; they are all true. We have maimed. We have dismembered. We have remade people in ways that to your southern sensibilities could only be called *of the devil*. By predilection, I'm a student of anatomy. Have I mentioned that to you yet? At any rate, have you ever seen a person's eyes when you show them one of their organs, full and intact? I wouldn't risk taking a vital organ from you, though, Clyde. I wouldn't want you to give out. Then I would miss the look on your face. The moment where you realize that in this place, within these walls, time and space have no meaning."

The man dropped his chin and whipped bloody shards of Clyde onto the towel that Silvia handed him.

"So now, having that in mind, are you prepared to confess your sins?"

Before Clyde could respond, Silvia moved gracefully. And then making her hand as light as the air, she touched her father and moved past him.

"Don't you want this to end?" She caressed him as she spoke, as a mother would to her wounded child. "Tell me the name, and then you can leave this nightmare forever." Her soft voice, the lilt of it, lulled Clyde. "You will go somewhere free of the pain, but you can't go until you talk to me. Tell me, baby. That other man that was with you that night doesn't care about you. He never did. I'm the one that's here for you now."

Early on, he had just wanted to prove to himself there was still some strength left within him, some fight. But now, under the gentle weight of her words, all the fight had left him. It was time to move on.

"Baby, I can tell your ready to leave. Tell me."

"Ha... n... Ha...n...ra."

"What, baby—keep trying."

"Han... Ran...."

Unable to articulate, the grunts kept coming, mostly in vowels. But after gently asking him to repeat himself several times, she finally made it out: Hank Grant.

"And is that all, baby? Who else?"

He was already on the road to salvation. Might as well. It would all be over soon anyway. "inc... eh... vincuuh." They went through the same exercise of her lowering her ear and soothing him as he worked through the sounds. Eventually, she discerned it as *Vince*. Vince, just one name was all he could either get out or all he had.

"Thank you, baby, you did good."

"Ne... Ne... mmmm... Nehhmmm."

"What, sweetie?" She continued to pet him lithely.

With all the strength he could bring to bear, Clyde said the words clearly this time. He knew the end was fast approaching, but there was one thing he had to know before they drew the curtain. Like having to know what lay in the dark corner of the attic or behind the water heater in the basement. He had to know. "Whaat is hi... hith name?" As he said it, he looked to the Black-Eyed Man.

The man with the hollow eyes grinned, but said nothing.

Melvin did the same.

"Oh baby, names have no meaning. A name is something to hide behind."

Then, with the grace of a mother, she pulled the blade from her belt. Clyde didn't see it, neither had the Black-Eyed Man. Not even Melvin saw it.

"It's time for you to move on now."

With poise, she ran the blade across his neck, catching the veins just so, relieving them of their pressure.

The gasp. The gurgle. The sounds she had come to know like old friends.

And then, the crimson waterfall.

As he bled out, she gently picked up his hand and rubbed it across the mangled topography of her face and head.

As he was dying, Clyde realized for the first time that she was the woman from the home in Belle Glade. Without the long hair he hadn't recognized her.

She moved his hand and fingers across her scars, letting him feel every crevice, every crumple.

"You gave me my scars. And for the first time in my life, *I'm home.*"

Chapter 43

Silvia told the Black-Eyed Man and Melvin the names that Clyde had confessed, and they each took a keepsake from Clyde, then hauled his mangled corpse across the muddy, humidity-drenched grass of the Glades, so he could be given to the swamp.

Behind the Portal, the swamp ran deep, enough volume for a boat to pull up to the old dock right behind it. They stood on the dock and watched as the torn body bobbed on the surface. Soon, the frenzy would start. All manner of reptiles gliding around under the black surface would come to the top for the feeding.

The humans would wait quietly until nature finished the job.

Looking out at the vast swamp, the Black-Eyed Man reached his hand up and rubbed Silvia's scars, like a blind man running his fingers over bumps of Braille. As he rubbed, an air of approval came over his face.

They each held a piece of Clyde. A totem.

After all, the memory was in the mutilation.

PART V: The Portal

The Fifth Echo

2017: The Florida Everglades

"An odd thing, to be as fascinated with the end as I have been for most of my life. People spend too much time fearing the end, hoping that it will be postponed as long as possible. No matter how much we beg or plead, it comes, nonetheless.

"In a story, we pine for the end, the reveal, the twist. We wait with bated breath for what the narrator will unveil behind the curtain. As for life, the same cannot be said. In life, we fear the end. We are content to ignore what waits behind the curtain. And more than anything, we fear what comes after we cease to be.

"Not me. I welcome my commune with God. I—"

The captive man spoke, his breath pained, as if someone was choking him. "If you want the end to come so badly, then why don't *you* just end it."

He punctuated his sentence with a glob of blood and mucus, spat at the ground. Still strapped to a chair, being toyed with like an ensnared animal before the kill, the young man couldn't help but think how alien the man with the black eyes looked—odd, inhuman even, like he was a being not of this Earth. Through the haze of drugs they had pumped into him to keep him alive—which warped his mind, making everything seem like fantasy—he still thought how odd it was to hear a man talk like this, and even more disturbing to hear a person talk so obsessively about God and the afterlife. But as foreign as it felt to hear the speeches dripping with religion and all its curiosities, as the days slipped by and he lost all concept of time and the familiar, it started to feel expected, even normal. Like an institutionalized prisoner, he was being conditioned to accept the new laws of his surroundings. Here, lost to the Portal, listening to the deranged preacher with the black eyes was not just an aspect of being trapped within these walls: it was the very atmosphere itself.

"Fair question. The answer is simple: because once I'm on the other side, I'll have no control. I'll be in His realm. A world I have no understanding of, one where I might not have power over anything. But here, thanks to His grand experiment, I can move the pieces on the board as I wish."

The Black-Eyed Man stood up to pace the room. As he turned circles, he continued. "That is why I knew that I needed to create my masterpiece in this life, because I may not have a chance to in the next. Soon, you will become another piece of the mosaic I offer up to God. An artistic vision, once conceived, must be seen through to the end. No matter when and where that might be. Don't you agree?"

The captive offered nothing in response.

"And when I'm done—and only then—I will go meet him. Perhaps I will land in a realm beyond communication. A soundless, featureless, expanse of nothing, one where words are rendered useless, depriving me of my chance to say my piece to His face. Then again, God probably doesn't have one of *those* either. Nor will *It* have a gender, I suppose. Such things would be meaningless, trappings left for humankind to sort through.

"If an eternity in the black is the price of my art, then so be it... I will spend eternity in the dark."

The young man choked out one more question. "And what if it's not the dark waiting for you? What if it's fire?"

A harsh glint of light bounced of his black eyes as he grinned. "If bubbling skin and my eyes scratching and burning is what awaits me, then I welcome it. I welcome it all."

Chapter 44

Hank hadn't seen Clyde in weeks. He kept expecting to bump into him while he moved his things out of the townhouse. But Clyde never showed.

Originally, the plan had been for Clyde to move out and Hank would stay behind and finish out the last two months on the lease. But after more thought, Hank decided he wanted to be rid of the place, too. The memory of Clyde would always haunt it: the accent, the stale jokes, the time he vomited on the kitchen floor just after shooting up.

But Hank didn't go far. The view of the pond at sunset was one of the last things that set him at ease, aside from the drugs. Two days after seeing Lisa and Danny, he saw a place up for rent and called the company to ask about a month-to-month lease (he had no plans to put down roots). The night he saw Lisa and Danny was still on his mind. Where it stayed firmly, still to this moment as he sat behind his new townhouse, only four units down from the old one, watching the sun bleed into the horizon.

He sipped his beer, looking at the setting sun. How long had it been since he spoke to Clyde? Three weeks, at least. And Clyde's absence was riling Vince to no end. They were days away from hatching a new pill scheme, and Clyde was an integral piece of the puzzle. Vince needed Clyde back and was calling Hank umpteen times a day reminding him of that fact. Every time, Hank had the same answer: I don't know. And I'm still in if you need me—a half-hearted response if there ever was one.

Sure enough, he still planned to help Vince with his little pill scheme and with the other day to day dealing and collecting. But only long enough to make enough money to leave West Palm behind. As much as he loved the view beyond the pond, without the prospect of he and Lisa, there was nothing left here. He and his dad had been estranged for months. She was all that was left of his old life; seeing her had made him realize that he had stayed around here for her, or the *hope* of her. He could be an addict anywhere. Drugs didn't answer to geography.

But there was more to it: Clyde's disappearance had opened another fissure in his head, allowing fear to poison his thoughts. That night, as they drove away from Belle Glade, he felt that they had just signed their death warrant. A feeling that still abided within him, but one, up until Clyde went missing (*Is he missing? Is that the right word? He could just be lost and strung out somewhere*), that he had been able to cast back into the shadows. But as each day passed, and Clyde failed to surface, he feared that his premonition had been spot on: the people they stole from were coming for him with the ravenous abandon of a lynch mob. They already had Clyde and had dispensed with him. And he was next.

Yet another reason to move on.

He just needed something first. A keepsake to comfort him as he left port.

\#

He waited until late in the night, the witching hour. He knew that Everett always left one of the windows open in the back. There was an alarm system at the restaurant, but Everett only kept it there as a symbol to ward off burglars. He also had the stickers from the alarm system company plastered all over the restaurant. But Everett rarely, if ever, bothered to set it because the place was far enough removed from town.

As Hank got to the window, he could see the drunken glow of a yellow light coming from the kitchen. He tried, to no avail, to peer through the grimy window, sooty with smoke from the kitchen, to see if there was anyone moving around. The window was too matted in smoke from to see through. So he just went for it and lifted the window. At this time of night, no chance Everett was—

Hank heard the creak of the screen door right next to the window. "What the hell are you doing? Can't you see the door's unlocked?"

There was a screen door that was always left open, but it was a secondary door, masking a wooden door behind it. If Hank had looked closer, he would have noticed that the main door was cracked.

"Well, come on. Might as well come in since you saw fit to break in here in the middle of the night."

"You know, you could set the alarm, old man. Me opening the window would have triggered it."

"Not with the back door open, dumbass."

Trying to outwit Everett always left him choking on dust.

"Well..." Everett motioned with big owl-eyes and a shrug of the neck for him to come in. "Come on, man. I got some food and coffee out in here. I couldn't sleep."

Hank followed him in.

Chapter 45

The sight of pulled pork laying on the sliver table made his stomach roil. Even now that he had money, he ate like a bird. Not by choice, but because of the odd chemistry of his body. For physiological reasons he failed to grasp, the heroin stopped him up, constipation to end all constipation, a back-up only God's own plumber could fix.

Everett offered up some of the bounty he had spread out. Hank declined. He would dine on some crackers and craft beer when he got home, an appetizer to the shot of dope he had waiting in his bathroom. The mission before him was to get out of here as quickly as possible, minimizing the awkwardness to a microscopic degree.

Hank sat down and beheld the kitchen for a moment, as his father chomped down pulled pork and slurped black coffee. Comforting, he thought, that not much had changed. In truth, in the twenty-five plus years Everett had this place up and running, he had hardly changed a thing, other than adding brisket to the menu earlier this year; Hank had yet to try it because of their estrangement

Each of them dared the other to speak. Hank had nothing to say; he came for one thing and one thing only, and it wasn't to reminisce or win back Everett's favor.

He decided that, if Everett didn't speak soon, then he would just start looking for the photo. If pressed, Hank would tell him what he needed. But if Hank had his druthers, he would find it in the desk, exchange a word or two, and then head back to his place to get high.

Everett caved first. His exterior showed no signs of the sadness he felt within.

"I got bored the other day. Things were a little slow around here, so I started playing around on the internet. After a while, I found some old YouTube videos of you playing with Dead Children's Playground." Mentioning the band's name caught Hank's attention. "Some tour you guys did after the first album, what was it called?"

The question threw Hank. "The album was called Black Water and the tour was The Ghost in the Water Tour."

"What was with the *water* names? Wasn't the second album called Backwater?"

"Simon said he had some running theme he wanted to create with water. Like eventually each album would progress into a bigger body of water, he said, until we worked up to a vast dark ocean or something like that." They each laughed, remembering what a stickler Simon could be. "When I pointed out that Lisa told me that backwater was used a lot as a metaphor, like for a small town, he got frustrated because it was supposed to be the swamp-themed album. The spooky monster hidden in the backwater sort-of-thing. And then after the swamp-themed one, next he wanted to do a lake-themed one."

Hank got comfortable. Even got up and poured himself a glass of water.

"Man, watching those videos made me wish I had gotten more chances to see you guys live. Blew my mind, how fast you were playing. You remember the first set I got you?"

Hank smiled. "Of course. You got it out of the classified ads. Back when that was still a thing."

"Only paid two hundred for it. A Tama Rockstar kit from the seventies. Looked like something John Bonham would have played. Thing was silver right?"

"Yeah. And it had that real old-school dry sound to it. There weren't even heads on the bottoms of the toms. Felt like I was in Led Zeppelin or The Who or something. I loved that set. You still got it?"

"Still in storage, bud. That thing is indestructible. I take it out about once a year and dust it off for you. Just in case."

Everett filled his maw full of pork. He had never been much for table manners. "You played that thing nonstop. I had to damn-near hurt you to drag you away to eat dinner," he continued. "You remember that small house we lived in. Alice would come over and you'd be beating the hell out of those drums and she couldn't handle it. She'd just throw her arms up, grab some sweet tea out of the fridge, and tell me if I wanted to talk, I could meet her out back. In her defense, it was rough at first. You couldn't find the rhythm to save your life."

It was true. Hank remembered how hard it had been to learn an eighth note. When he would try to get his right hand to hit the hi-hat and his left hand to hit the snare, both of his hands would shoot back up in rejection. As if his body was revolting against him, telling him what he was trying was physiologically impossible, an affront to the laws of biology. But slowly, day after day, he coached his body into cooperation.

Over time, he became a real drummer. He could mimic all his favorite guys—Danny Carey, Abe Cunningham, Matt Cameron—and that's when he started inviting over friends from school that played guitar. And once word got out that he could play—*really* play—he started getting offers to play in bands, particularly metal bands. And why? Because Hank could play the double bass, the sine qua non of metal drumming. A rule Hank actually disagreed with. But, in the end, that's what people expected of a metal drummer. And Hank could do it, even back in high school.

"You ever regret not sticking with the lessons?" Everett posed the question with that longing refrain reserved for reminiscing.

"Would have helped me with Simon and Bruce."

Everett responded with a warm nod of affirmation.

Hank said, "I tried to make the lessons work. You remember. For weeks, I brought home the notebooks with the drum parts written in them. All that stuff the teacher would write down in pencil. Guy's handwriting was shit. And it would end up all smudged on the page. Most times I couldn't even read it. I just remember that before I went, I had made all this progress on my own by just playing and listening to music. And then when I tried to play the parts he had for me, it was like starting all over. Like I was stuck in wet mud or something. It made me want to quit playing." Hank tensed his jaw. "And that's when I decided that I wanted to do it on my own. I didn't want to sound like all those other robots. I wanted it to be mine, to sound like me.

"I followed the other thing in my head when I played drums. Even now, I'm not sure what it is. The muse, is what Charlie called it. He'd say, 'You have to follow the dark train of the muse's dress into the dark.'"

"Your bud's good with words."

"No doubt."

Everett paused to wipe bits from his mouth and shake out his beard, spilling the crumbs on the table. "It taught you to play with heart. I bet a hundred guys could sit back there and play and not the get the same sound out of those drums."

The first nice moment they had shared in so long. Human nature wouldn't allow it to continue, however.

"Well, at least, that's how you used to play."

And there it is. The old man can't pass up another opportunity to be self-righteous. "What's that supposed to mean?"

"You know exactly what it means, son. When's the last time you touched your drum-set? Hell, do you even know where it is?" He knew exactly where it was, or more precisely, what he did with it. He pawned it to get cash for drugs more than a year ago. A ghost he locked away in a big black chest and shoved deep into the attic amid the cobwebs and dust.

Shrinking under Everett's look, Hank demurred. A look of disappointment from a parent holds more power than an atom bomb. No contest.

"That's what I thought." Everett changed his tone to one of gentle understanding. "I know you sold it for dope, son. I've been there. By the time I left Hermitage, I hardly had anything to my name. Just my truck, a few tapes, and half a bag of clothes. I knew what happened to your drum-set. I just wanted to see if you'd tell me."

Hank noticed the tremors overtaking his hands. How long had it been?

Everett noticed it too. "How long?"

Hank didn't respond, too ashamed of talking about his addiction in the open.

"I remember the shakes, the sweats, and all those fucking sores."

Over time, Hank got better at disguising his track marks and the other sundry skin maladies that accompanied his habit. Shooting up in odd places on his body (even between his toes), hid the track marks from the outside world.

"And when I got into heroin for a while, which I couldn't handle by the way, I remember the constipation. Which was the weirdest thing. I expected the high, and the withdraw, but not that. That *shit* was weird." Everett grinned. "I guess not the best word to use there." Hank broke and grinned with him. Who can deny a good dad joke?

"You can get on the other side of this thing, son. You can change. Look at me, I haven't used in twenty-five years. My last relapse was in '93."

"Alice helped me pull myself out of that mess. And since then, not a single drug other than coffee has gone into me." Everett didn't even touch aspirin. He had given himself, whole-cloth, to the school of abstinence. And even though he had been injured during sundry construction projects around the restaurant over the years, he never touched a pain pill, too afraid of what might follow. "And you can do the same, Hank. You can get out from under this fucking boulder crushing you. I'll help you."

The self-righteousness was poison to Hank's ears. "What, liked you helped mom?"

"What's that supposed to mean?"

"You told me she had the same problems as you."

"She did."

"So why didn't you help her get clean like you? Why didn't you bring her along?"

"I told you son. She got sick. The doctors didn't know what it was, and they didn't know what to do, and she passed."

For years, Hank had accepted the story at face value, never questioning his father's motives. When he told Lisa, she remarked that it sounded like his mom might have had AIDS. It was the Eighties, and with her lifestyle... (Lisa apologized for saying it) ...and then there was the doctors not being able to identify it. All plausible. Over time, however, Everett's story began to show its cracks. And his eyes always cut to the side when Hank asked about it.

"And I told you that I don't believe you."

"Well, I don't know what else to tell you. It's the truth. She got sick and she died. She had taken care of you up until that point the best she could and when she passed, I took over and brought you here. I wanted to get us away from my old life and start our family here."

"And you've hardly ever told me anything about her. All these years, and still, no real stories. Sometimes I think you hardly even knew her."

"Hank, I've told you, she loved music—"

"Yeah, and that was it. Nothing else, the rest—"

"I told you, she liked to go explore the woods and read, but really, after work all she wanted to do was listen to records. She tried to learn to cook, but it never took." Perhaps she liked to do these things. It was plausible. Doesn't everyone like walking in the woods and reading?

"What about her family? You never told me shit about her family, except their name and that her dad worked on some rocket?"

"That's all true. And that rocket was the Saturn V, son. JFK commissioned the project and Warner Von Braun headed it up. It was a big deal. Her dad working on that was the crowning achievement of the guy's life. That rocket went to the moon." Once Google became ubiquitous, Everett found all of the information after a quick search. But that was the full breadth of it. A blurb about her dad on Wikipedia, and then the trail went cold.

"How about a story of y'all spending time with her family?"

"Buddy, they were estranged when we met, or at least that's what I thought, and then she told me that they were already dead. I never met them."

"Well then, what about one fucking story of you and mom spending time together? Just one."

"We'd listen to music, drink, that sort of thing."

"One detail. Just one. You never give any details."

"We weren't well, son. We had problems. I don't remember a lot from that time in my life. I'm sorry."

"Sometimes I think you didn't know her at all. Like y'all just hooked up and then I happened. You probably didn't give a shit about her. Just fucked her and went on your way."

"That's not true! I cared about her." *At least, I think I did. I cared about what happened to her.* "How can you not understand what we were going through? We were sick. Just like you are now. Do I really need to explain that to you, son? How it consumes your life? How it eats up every fucking thing until there's nothing left? Look at you. You're rail-thin and shaking like a leaf. Do I really need to explain why I don't remember anything about your mother and me? You know exactly why. So stop asking!"

Hank gritted his teeth. He had wanted to say so much of this for years but never had the strength. But was it strength driving him? Or anger? Resolve or hate? He didn't know anymore; and worse, he didn't care. All that remained was the will to destroy something beautiful.

"I know you didn't love her. That thing you see in people's eyes when they talk about someone they love, you don't have it when you talk about her. Your eyes are just flat. I know you didn't give a shit about my mom. You don't even have the balls to tell me how she really died."

All that he had to do now was say it.

Though he knew he wouldn't.

The lie had become their life. How do you deconstruct thirty-plus years of living? Their existence was built on fiction. It's what propped them up. Pull it away and the house will crumble into a heap of rubble and dust.

Frustration radiated from Everett. "I told you how she died. And I'm not saying it again. Stop trying to make this about me and my screw-ups. This is about you. You're sick, Hank, and you and I both know you need help." To emphasize his point, Everett pounded his fist against the table like a judge bringing down a gavel.

"I'm leaving."

"Okay, go."

"No. I'm leaving South Florida. I came here to get something and then I'm getting out of here." The picture of his mother was still at the forefront of Hank's mind. But another thought had come beckoning for attention: the tangerine river. Manifesting itself through the tremors that were roiling his hands.

"Leave? Where are you going?"

"North." The shaking was only getting worse, harder to hide.

"Well, shit, Hank, I understand that. Only way to go unless you're going down to the Keys. But where, son?" Everett's voice was as shaky as Hank's hands. Concern had replaced his earlier tone of frustration.

"I'll let you know when I get there."

"And how in the hell do you plan to pay for it?"

Raising his eyebrows, Hank looked at him, but didn't speak.

"Yeah, stupid question. Best you not tell me how you're financing this little excursion of yours."

Hank pushed his stool back from the table and walked to the office. There should still be a copy of *it* in there.

"How will you support yourself? You can't just show up in a new town and become a part of the drug game. They'll view as an outsider. Might get yourself killed, even. That is, if you even make it. Look at yourself. Hell, you look fifteen years older than the last time I saw you. If you keep using at this rate, you'll be dead in no time. Your body can only handle so much. I know, Hank. You're going to keep loading up bigger and bigger batches until you're eventually going to put one in the syringe that will make the lights go out. Please—"

"I've made up my mind."

"Does Lisa know?"

"No. And please don't tell her. We aren't speaking anymore."

Hank kept moving toward the office. Everett moved with him, on the opposite side of the table, with the panicked, solicitous look of a beggar, ready to drop to his knees and lick the crumbs from the floor.

"Please let me get you some help. We can do this together. Day by day, we can pull you out of the hole. It doesn't have to be this way."

Hank stopped. With his eyes downcast, he spoke softly, a darkness imbuing his voice, "Yes, it does. Too much has happened."

"That's not true, son. We can get you clean. And whatever it is you're talking about, you can find a way to forgive yourself."

"What, like you did? Just get some glasses and an apron and sell barbeque for a living?"

"That's right. You'll always have a place here, if you're clean."

"So that's it? Just act like I haven't done all the bad shit?"

"No son. You'll remember. But you find a way to live with it. And hopefully, a way to help other people from making the same mistakes."

"Well, I know you ran from something in Hermitage. People don't just up and leave a small town in Alabama for South Florida. I know you were running away from something." In truth, this had been Lisa's theory; it was her way of helping Hank understand the things in the world nuance hid from him.

"You can move on, son. Whatever it is that you did, you can move past it. Shit, we can move from here if you need us to. I can sell barbeque anywhere."

"You don't understand. The stuff that happened. You wouldn't understand."

"Trust me son, I understand a lot more than you know. Tell me what's going on."

Every inch of him wanted to lay the truth bare for his father to see. Expose all of its guilt and ugliness, splay it out on the table, bulbous and hissing venom: the monster of his own creation.

Then he thought of that force. The one that rivaled the atom bomb, that look of disappointment in his father's eyes. And thought better of it.

The time had come to leave, to be rid of the rot that had engulfed his life. Start over, far away from the ones he had disappointed. Miles and miles between him and whoever wanted him dead.

The time had come to shed his skin.

"I can't."

"Why not?"

"Well, I guess just like you'll never tell me the truth about mom, I can't tell you the truth about my life and what I've done."

Hank barreled into the office. He rifled through drawers, opening and shutting, opening and shutting.

After seeing papers fly and hearing wooden drawers slam in a thunderous cacophony, Everett decided to help his boy.

"I knew eventually you'd want a copy. I had some bad days now and again, and when I'd find one, I'd throw it away. We hadn't talked in so long and some days I missed you. And others, well, others I cursed you. I just couldn't handle everything that was happening, especially after losing Alice. But even as pissed as I was at you, I couldn't get rid of them all. You hid the fucking things everywhere. Dear God, I found a few taped under the chairs for the customers."

Hank shot him a look. *So where...*

"I taped two of them under the keyboard, and a few more are in a shoebox on the shelf above the computer."

Hank ripped the tape away, flipped each photo over, and beheld her for the first time since he had left Lisa and Danny. And there she was again: short, ragged hair, hips cocked to the side, a tired smile on her face. She stood in front of a small home with drab, gray wood-siding, and a small flower bed in front with plush yellow marigolds—the only things with true vibrance in the photo.

This time, when he looked at her, he didn't imagine that she was a waitress scraping by, or a schoolteacher pinching pennies to make sure her son wants for nothing. She was just his mom. And that was enough.

The photo made her real. The photo made her his mom.

If he wanted to clean up, this image would have to suffice. No more trips to that other place. No more fantasy journeys to the world the color of the poppy. The tangerine river would have to die. Was he ready for that?

He grabbed the shoebox and tossed the two errant photos in with the rest. Everett moved from the threshold of the door to clear the way for his son. Hank said nothing as he moved toward the screen door to leave.

He had his back turned to Everett now. This was it.

He couldn't let him go.

"What do I have to do to get you to stay?"

Hank, his back still turned, muttered it slowly, quietly, his voice resolute: "Tell me the truth about Mom." Hank turned, a look of singular purpose in his eyes. "Tell me the truth about my mom and I'll stay."

Everett, his bottom lip trembling, sucking in his breath to try and staunch the tears, shook his head in agreement. "I will tell you the truth. You get in the car with me and we'll drive up to Oceanside, and after we get you checked in, I will let them know that we need a minute to talk. We can head back out to the parking lot, sit in the car, and I'll tell you the whole thing. I promise."

Hank knew of Oceanside. It was a rehab facility, right on the beach. They helped you detox and get through those initial weeks of sobriety. Which, for someone as far gone as Hank, would be as much a medical battle as a mental one.

"They have doctors and nurses on staff. They will help you with the withdraws. I know you're nervous about them. The people there, they can make it easier for you. Help you wean off. I'll pay every dime, you don't have to worry about it." Hank almost wanted to say that he could pay, but thought better of it. "And I promise, as soon as we are there and you're checked in, I will tell you everything."

"Why not just tell me everything now?"

"Because you and I both know not to trust an addict."

"Once an addict, always an—"

"Not to trust an addict who is still using."

"Tell me now, or I'm leaving." Hank had to summon every ounce of his energy to say this. He was so tired. Fatigue beyond fatigue. Enough exhaustion to fill ten lifetimes. He was ready to give up. Ready to let his father carry him to the water's surface. After all, how much longer could he keep sinking deeper and deeper into the depths, where only darkness and the monsters of his mind waited? Hadn't the time come to surface and tread water? Tread like Everett, tenuously clutching sobriety at the water's surface for the rest of his life. So much of him wanted to give in, but *not all* of him. He wasn't worth saving. That was the thought that kept spotlighting in his head: *I'm not worth saving.*

"You heard me, Dad. Tell me now or I'm leaving."

"That's not the deal, Hank. You come with me, and I tell you everything."

"I'm gone." Hank cracked the screen door.

The creak of the hinge made Everett spring forward and yell out. "Hank!

217

Hank! Tell me one thing. Tell me one thing if you're so certain that I'm the one in the wrong and you know what you're doing. One thing."

Hank stopped, his back still turned to his father.

"Why did you miss Alice's funeral?"

His shoulders sank, billowing down like a parachute without wind.

Stricken with grief, Hank's shoulders trembled as he sobbed.

Everett wrapped him in a hug.

He had written the date and the time down all over the crack-house he was living in at the time, a clapboard white house near downtown West Palm. He had bought a tiny spiral notebook, one that looked like something a detective would jot notes in as a witness recounted what happened. Similar to what he had done with his mother's photo, he made note after note and spread them throughout the small house. He had even set a reminder on his phone. That same iPhone he had used to stay in touch with Lisa. It was all for naught.

Heroin takes everything.

All he had wanted to do was say goodbye to her. He missed it. And he could never get it back. "I forgot, Dad. I just forgot. I had lost track of time." With every inch of himself, he had pushed it from his mind. Denial rivaled the potency of the heroin.

"I know, son. I know."

"I don't want to be like this anymore."

"I know."

"I just don't know what to do. Things have just gotten so fucked up. I... I..." *I may have gone too far. Clyde and I might have done something that can't be taken back. Something unstoppable.*

Hank had stopped crying and his shoulders steadied.

His hands were another story. Badly needing to use, they shook erratically, and he had trouble staying still. Hard to, with the feeling that thousands of tiny needles were poking all over his flesh.

"Hank? Hank?" Hank looked ready to surrender. "Hank."

"Yeah, Dad."

"You ready?"

"Yes."

#

Hank sat at the table as Everett scurried about, putting up the food and tidying up. Out of habit, the man with the graying hair and beard, glasses dangling and bouncing precariously against his chest as he moved about, kept looking at his watch. The airing of grievances had eaten up most of the night. The first harbingers of dawn were appearing.

Looking lighter, even a shade younger, he told Hank, "I'll grab the keys to the truck and meet you out there."

Hank left through the screen door and looked at the droplets of dew gathered on the blades of grass, bloated and glistening, all encapsulating millions of tiny unknowable worlds.

#

Everett moved about his office, wondering where in the hell he set his keys last. He was one of those helpless souls that habitually misplaced his keys, wallet, debit card, and cellphone. If it was small enough to fit in his pocket and the be set down somewhere, Everett lost it. Alice had always chided him and said he should put a nail on the door jamb and hang his car keys there. And every time she had said it, he shrugged her off.

Maybe he would put that nail up now. Another way to keep her alive around here.

"Hah." Right under the manila folder with last week's invoices, among the flotsam and jetsam of paper. And, again, for no other reason but habit, he looked at the calendar and saw it.

#

"Forty-five minutes is all I need to get things started and give Alex the instructions." Alex was the new utility man Everett hired to replace Alice. He had relied on Alice with all things related to the restaurant, and he was trying to recreate that bit of magic with his new hire. As he and Hank were speaking, Alex had pulled up right on time—5:00 a.m., on the dot. The kid hadn't been late once.

"Alright. I'll go to my place and get packed up."

Everett came closer to him and whispered, firmly out of earshot from Alex, who just got out of his truck. "You don't have any dope in the house, do you?"

Hank shook his head no. "I was going to have to go score when I left here."

"Good."

Everett walked Hank to his car. Hank got in and they continued to speak through the cracked driver's side window.

"Fifteen minutes to get the fire started. I'm still teaching Alex. He's liable to screw it up if I don't help him." Everett paused and signaled his newbie to go to the smokehouse. "Kid's still just a little green around the gills. And I can't believe I forgot we have a wedding this afternoon. Huge catering order. Hundreds of people. Alex and Maria can handle it. I already got the list typed out in there for them." A laborious task for Everett, that ate up three hours yesterday. The fifty-something had no training in typing; he hen-pecked the keys one at a time. "So, fifteen minutes to start the fire and then I'm en route to your house. Alright?"

Solemnly, Hank nodded.

Everett ran over to the smokehouse. Still wavering about his decision, he opened the door to the smoke pits. It was only a few minutes, he told himself; and like Hank said, his place was bereft of drugs. Just a few minutes. It was a huge order, after all. Big enough that he might get sued for breach of contract if he didn't make sure it got fulfilled. Just a few minutes, and then he would start the arduous slog of setting Hank to rights. And maybe, just maybe, once he told Hank the truth, he would find the redemption he had hoped for all these years.

But he needed to start a fire first.

It's just a few minutes.

Chapter 46

Hank felt the cold press of the tile in his bathroom as he sat down. He had half an hour, perhaps less, to accomplish the deed. When he came into his townhouse, he had squandered precious minutes dithering about whether to cook up and plunge in the last of his stash. It wasn't much, making what he told Everett a lie by omission. He really did need to go score when he left; he just omitted that he had a small ration left in his room. When he came through the door, what his father said to him reappeared in his head: *Why did you miss Alice's funeral?* The guilt rushed back tenfold. It seized him, like thousands of dead hands contorted in rigor mortis clamping down on him. Another of his panic attacks was building, rising to a rancid boil. But he knew a way to stop it, a way to redirect his mind and trick his physiology; and the answer lay in his little black kit. That was the ticket to wash away the guilt. One last time.

His father would be furious, an inevitability that Hank accepted and then buried: another scrap of embarrassment to throw on the trash-pile of shameful incidents. One more instance of disappointment wouldn't alter the course of human events.

He opened his black kit and went to work.

He heated up his spoon, and watched the tiny bubbles form and mushroom, resembling the billows of ocean foam he had seen gather on the beach. It wasn't long before the syringe was brimming, bloated with the narcotic that had come to define his life.

No need to hide this one from the world, he thought. He would soon be at the colony with the other lepers. An open track mark, still seeping blood, would bother no one.

He waited and watched as his vein grew, plumping up with blood. Checking the clock on his phone, he realized that Everett would be there any minute. He exhaled, gritted his teeth, and pressed down the plunger. He stared in muted disgust as a gout of blood sucked into the cylinder, looking like a fat drop of ink in water, and then disappeared back into his body. Instantly, he felt a warm rush flood his veins; his jaw muscles relaxed, releasing his teeth from the grinding and gritting they so often did; his arms went slack, and soon his mind would drift to the other world where his mother floated.

Before he left to see her, he looked over to the needle, still pricked into his arm, dangling there like a giant tick.

#

The world in his head had taken on a cast of the familiar to him, instilling a sense of peace and comfort every time he came back. Not like the sensation of returning to his own home: more like the feeling of going out to the country to your grandmother's house. Familiar enough to lay his head down at night without fear of a visit from an intruder or a ghost, but still presenting hints of mystery, fostering a curiosity about what happened in the months when you're absent.

The trip always started the same way: he would float backwards up the river, against the current, an impossible thing, but such a thing didn't seem to matter in this opiate-fantasy world. And then after an indeterminate amount of time, his mother would float up next to him. She, with the current. They would turn their heads, meet eyes, and then after beholding each other—Hank taking long enough to tell himself that *Yes, this is really happening*—they would talk. About what, Hank could never recall when he came out of the trance. What he did remember was her boy-short blonde hair, the cut and glint of her emerald-green eyes, and her pale skin.

Every time he went, he coached himself to remember something she said. One morsel to bring back home. Figure out some way to store it in his brain, like those mnemonics that his teachers used to make him memorize. Even so, he couldn't ever remember the things she said afterward.

On this, his last trip to the world of unreality where his mother's spirit lived, he planned to ask which album, in the stash that Everett grabbed, was her favorite. Before doing it, he planned to grab a stone, a stick, a leaf, some piece of refuse floating down the river and, when she said it, he would look at his makeshift memory totem, and repeat it a million times, creating a tether between the content of her words and the object. That way he could cheat the barrier between the worlds and finally bring a piece of his mother back to *this* world.

As with the other times, he floated into place, and before long, she came up, right by his side, wearing the same thing she had on in the photo. The river streamed around her, pristine and green, clear as glass all the way to the brown and black stones that lined its bottom. Hazy orange light reflected off the surface, surrounding his mother in a ghostly corona. Dead leaves and water-logged branches lazily floated by to parts unknown. Suddenly, a voice in his head reminded him to pick up a piece of the river's debris; he quickly found a branch as wide as his wrist and gripped it tight. Relief shot through him. Maybe he would really be able to remember this time.

He asked the question with ease; his voice had an underpinning of grace, a trait normally foreign to Hank, but one that came to him in abundance in this tangerine-colored world. Maybe here you could be what you wanted to be.

She smiled at him.

But when she answered, nothing came out.

He asked again. *Which one was your favorite?*

In response, her mouth moved, but no sound came out. She had no voice.

He tried again. He saw her tiny teeth, and the black hole of her maw, moving up and down, offering no sound.

He looked up at the orange sky, which now had an artery of red running through it, in frustration. And instead of moving on, like a scientist repeating an experiment over and over, no matter the cost, nor the evidence to the contrary, he screamed the question again. And again. Grace had left him.

Yelling made no difference. The same result carried.

Finally losing steam, he turned away from her for a moment, debating whether to surrender. He quickly scuttled the idea of leaving and turned back to ask her again.

When he did, his thoughts and his voice left him.

Who was on the bank of the river?

#

Sensing his distraction, April's spirit stopped resisting the soft current and was pushed downriver. Too enthralled by the new sight in this world that had heretofore played host to only he and his mother, he gave no protest when his mother floated away.

He redirected his body to the bank of the river. Time and the laws of physics meant nothing here. Judging by the distance, the bank was a half-mile away, but he closed the distance in seconds.

On his knees, orange-tinged water dripping from him, feeling the smooth river rocks pressing against his skin, he looked up to say hello.

She spoke first. "Hola, mi'jo."

It was Alice. She was alive.

#

After the initial shock of seeing her, and then hearing her speak, and even more mind-bending, seeing that she looked decades younger than in the months before she died, he finally took his seat next to her on a felled tree.

"Alice, you look..."

"I know, my skin is back. I wish I had a mirror. I just keep touching and touching it."

"I can't believe it. I've missed you so much."

"Me too, mi'jo."

"So has Dad. He can hardly function without you."

"I know." She said it with an endearing laugh. "What has been going on with you? How have things been?"

In better times, this would be the part where he caught her up on the band—the next tour, the next album, how their fanbase was growing; then she would ask him about Lisa and marriage. *Pretty girls like her don't wait around forever.* She had said it to him so many times it was tattooed on the wires of his brain.

These were bad times, however. No tales of hope. No tales of evolution and the blossoming of new life. Only tales of deconstruction. Of decay. Of heroin turning Hank's heart and mind away from everything and everyone he had ever loved. That, in her absence, even before her death, he had started down a path that led him into a darkness that he could never have before fathomed. And now he was trapped there. A creature of the black, eyeless and lost, blindly feeling of the walls trying to find a curve or a bend pointing the way home.

Turning down, his eyes found the moss-covered stones lining the bank of the river. The blood-orange sky gave the moss an odd hue, as if the tips of the moss were on fire, almost like embers.

With the loving glow of a grandmother, she saved him from his thoughts. "Mi'jo, talk to me." Her words were welcoming, imbued with the same sense of warmth as they had been when she was alive. Like the savior she had worshipped so fervently in life, Alice telegraphed that all those that were weary could find rest with her.

"I'm lost, Alice."

"That happens to us all, Hank."

"I've done some horrible things."

"Nothing that can't be forgiven. Christ forgives all those that ask for help. Remember what he said, Hank. *Come to me, you weary, and I will give you rest.* All you have to do is surrender."

In all his time unmoored from the things that he loved, and in all the hours he had whiled away in this tangerine-fantasy world, until now, he had never once thought of asking God for help. Everett was devout, as was Alice. But religion had never offered any solace for Hank. The whole thing felt like a legend, a campfire story that people used to keep children in line. A way to control adults too. Sin and ask for forgiveness, and you will be set free. Sin and remain unrepentant and then you will know an eternity of agony—where neither friend, nor family, can save you. It all felt mythical to Hank, of another time.

But now, coming from Alice's lips (or the spirit of Alice or the ghost of her in his head or whatever the hell *it* was) he felt a nucleus of comfort spring up within him. Her talk of God's forgiveness calmed him, and he hadn't the foggiest why.

"Surrender. And ask for forgiveness."

"I'm trying to. I'm going with my dad to get better. I just needed to come here one more time to see *her*." Out of the corner of his eye, the red artery he had noticed earlier had branched out into a system of veins, almost like the tangerine sky was being infected.

Abandoning her warm tone, Alice said, "This is no place for you."

"It's the only place where I can see her."

"What about the picture?"

On the defensive, his voice cracking, Hank pleaded: "It's lifeless. Just a picture. *Here*, she is alive. She talks to me." Distracted again by the sky, Hank looked up: the veins were hemorrhaging blood; the sky was turning red.

"And what about the things of hers your father gave you? Is that not a way to speak to her? Do those things not help you know her?"

Hank had never told Alice about having some of his mother's effects. The photo, she knew about, and Everett had grabbed some other bric-a-brac before he left the house in Hermitage (a keychain, a magnet, an unused cookbook of hers), but Hank had never talked to Alice about the records. He had only told Lisa about that; Danny had heard some of them, but he was none the wiser because they were just mixed in with Hank's collection. Maybe Everett had told her. Or maybe she knew because the rules of reality didn't apply here.

"Yes. But it's not the same. I want to be able to talk to her."

"You think I don't know that pain? After what happened to my family, I would give anything to talk to them. But do you think they would want me to kill myself to do it? Do you think they would want me to shove that poison in my body just for a few words with them?"

Hank shook his head in response; he knew the answer.

"The way through to her is the music, mi'jo."

"Lisa said the same thing to me."

"Lisa's a smart girl. Go to her. Get yourself better. This is no place for you.

Your mother would not want you here. She wouldn't want you doing this to yourself."

"But I only have the photo. She only exists in my head."

"Does she, though? Do I only exist in your mind? After all, this is all"—she held her arms aloft and surveyed the tangerine world with big eyes— "in your mind. But your mother and I, we are also locked away somewhere else. A place where we can never be taken from you."

She stood and placed herself in front of him, bending her knees and squatting like a catcher. And with an unworldly grace, she held out her hand—palm flat, fingers outstretched—and placed it over his heart and smiled.

"No one can ever take us from you, Hank. Leave this place."

"I'm so sorry I didn't come to your funeral."

"Funerals are for the living, mi'jo. It's no bother."

She wrapped him in a hug and Hank wept as he buried his head in her meaty shoulder.

As she pulled away from him, he wiped the tears from his eyes, which felt real; he could taste the salt, feel the moisture.

The sky was now blood-red.

Alice continued to speak, but her words failed to find purchase with Hank. He was distracted by another figure in the distance—tall, clad in black, darting back and forth, and then disappearing, only to materialize again in another spot. At first, he saw him by the treeline, then in an instant, the man appeared shin-deep in the river. But just as soon as he stood in the water, he vaporized and then reappeared on the smooth river stones lining the bank. Fear dug its rusty hooks into him.

Appear.

Disappear.

And right before he would vanish, Hank heard white noise in his head, and then the man's image would splinter into blurry lines and zigzags; other times, the man's image splotched into a pool of rainbows, the thing that happens when a person presses their thumb against the screen of a laptop. Over and over, as Alice spoke, he heard the white noise, accompanied by the sound of a blade scraping metal, and then the man would dismember in a fit of colorful static, and within moments, appear in another place. Then, suddenly, the tall man dropped from the red sky and landed sturdily on the bank. The man started to approach behind Alice.

"I'm right where I want to be now. With my family, we meet at the table. Talking and talking by candlelight."

"There is someone behind you. We need to leave." Alice seemed to totally ignore the panic in his voice.

"No. There's no one else here. Just us."

"No, Alice. I'm telling you. There is a man walking up behind you right now. And he has something in his hand."

Alice turned to look. "There is nothing there, Hank."

"What? You don't see him. How can you not see him?"

Terrified, Hank turned her around to look; the man was only a few feet away from them now.

As the man dropped to his knees behind Alice, Hank heard a clicking sound over the static; the man gnashed his teeth. Again and again.

"Who are you?" All he got in response was the same thing: Click. Click. Click.

The man, his head even with Alice's, took his right hand and pulled her shoulder-length hair—restored to the former beauty it carried in her youth—away, leaving her olive neck exposed. The click of his teeth continued. Gnash. Gnash. Gnash.

Hank looked into the man's eyes and saw nothing but black: two circles of oblivion where human eyes should be. Next, he saw the scars covering the man's head, scars that looked like tree branches, barren of leaves. The scars, bulbous and puckered, ate up almost every piece of flesh on the man's head.

Hank asked again: *Who are you? Why are you here?*

Gnash. Gnash. Gnash.

By the time the Black-Eyed Man raised what he had in his hand, it was too late for Hank to do anything. He screamed in horror as the man, still clanking his teeth, ripped the blade across Alice's neck.

A plume of black-red spray hit him; he looked down at his shirt; it looked like someone had poured crimson paint through a wire sifter down on him.

And worse, her blood covered his face, his eyes, and invaded his mouth. Against his will, his taste buds absorbed the substance. Where he expected a copper taste, like licking a penny, instead he found the flavorless taste of, of, *water?*

He felt for the drops of her blood that had splattered his face. He brushed his hand against his cheek and put his fingers in his mouth to taste: same thing, *water.*

He looked up: the man was gone, so was Alice.

Suddenly, he felt another spray.

And another.

Then, in an instant, the world of the poppy dropped away.

He was back in his bathroom, his kit to his right, unzipped and burping up its contents—syringes, yellow tubing, antiseptic wipes. Nothing unusual. But when he looked up, he saw something that hollowed him out: the monster with black eyes and scars had followed him back from the other world.

Chapter 47

The spray Hank felt, what he had thought was Alice's blood, was water from his own sink. The Black-Eyed Man had been flicking water on him to bring him back from his dream world.

"Hank Grant." *How does he know my name?* "Pleased to make your acquaintance. Your friend Clyde told us all about you."

Hank noticed another man standing at the threshold of the door. The man had a close-cropped beard and rock-hard jaws.

The two men felt familiar to Hank, but he couldn't quite place them.

"I think we can both agree that poor Clyde wasn't long for this world. That flimsy constitution he had, weak-willed to his core. But even as pathetic as he was, he still submitted to the chance to serve a higher purpose." Still trying to get his bearings, Hank kept blinking his eyes. Enough heroin was still coursing through him to make the world slightly blurry.

"Who are you?"

"A messenger of God."

"Stop fucking with me. What's your name?" Hank's eyes hung lazily as he spoke; his head wobbled back and forth like a loose newel post.

"You can call me whatever you want, Hank. Names are of no consequence to me. Actions are what really matter." Hank's vision had sharpened enough for him to see the light shimmering off the scars on the man's head. Unbeckoned, he pictured a gaggle of snakes slithering across the man's scalp, interweaving, trying to become one.

Hank shook his head to rid his mind of what he assumed was a drug-induced hallucination. But he kept seeing a crown of snakes.

Despite his mounting fear, Hank's words came out sluggish: "What do you want?"

"What I'm doing. And *why* I'm doing it will come later. We will take you to a place where you can escape your junkie trappings. To a place where the shame of your habit loses all meaning. But before we show you our world, you're going to help us."

The heroin had made Hank's mouth dry as desert sand; he choked out a question. "How?"

"As forthcoming as your cowardly friend Clyde was, he found it within himself to hold back the man you work for."

Even though he was still reeling from being ripped away from his high, and trying to make sense of the monster staring down at him, Hank still had enough sense not to give up names—not yet, anyway. That was the way of the underworld. Names were currency. Hank needed to save what he knew about Vince for the right moment. It might be the only play he had to save his own life. "I have nothing to say to you."

"Oh, you will though, Hank. You will. Soon, you will have such helpful things to say. And surely you won't be as ignoble as Clyde in his last moments. The shrieking and mewling, unbecoming no matter the station of the person issuing those pitiful sounds. I told him it was all for a purpose. Yet he persisted with the begging, and the clawing, and the weeping. I'd wager that you're made of sturdier cells." He lithely brushed Hank's cheek as he continued speaking. "You will talk to us, Hank. Or we can find out how you sound when put to the test. What kind of noises do you think you'll make right before you die?"

The man's words pulverized the remaining bits of heroin in Hank, sobering him up. A voice in Hank's head hollowly whispered to him that, in the end, what he knew about Vince probably wouldn't matter. That for the man with the snakes on his head, it wasn't really about getting information. It was about hurting Hank. Watching as he squealed and begged for his life.

The man broke from the conversation to mutter something to his second. The other man, who resembled a mercenary, left the bathroom momentarily to chat with someone in the other room, a female; Hank could tell by the voice.

In the meantime, Hank, now firmly planted back in this world, remembered that his father was on the way. Maybe he would get here in time to call the police. *Or* he would get here just in time to be outnumbered and attacked.

The other man didn't return.

"Hank did I mention what I saw just after Clyde's death?" Hank shook his head. "In the twilight, just after Clyde's passing, I saw his wraith and spoke to it." Hank didn't know the word and the man could tell. "His *ghost*, son. I see that like Clyde, you are dull of intellect. That explains why you willingly kept company with such a festering imbecile."

The man spat on the floor in frustration, muttering to himself about people's stupidity, about the brunt of mankind's resistance to feeding their imagination. People like Hank and Clyde's refusal to pursue ways to bend space and time.

"You see, even in spirit-form, he looked just as he did right after we killed him."

With large eyes brimming with dread, Hank stared at the man.

"After we opened his throat and bled him, I took his eyes and his tongue, even his teeth for good measure. You see, Hank, I collect things, artifacts to help remember our subjects. We call them passengers, Hank. And the places we take them... transcend beauty." He opened his hand for Hank to see what was in it: a dried-up tongue next to three stained teeth.

Where were Clyde's eyes?

"It seems the merciful Almighty decided that Clyde had no need for his eyes or his tongue in the hereafter. Because there was Clyde's wraith right in front of me: without eyes and teeth, gnashing his gums up and down, still weeping."

#

In the haze of the early morning dawn, Melvin and Silvia moved Hank quickly outside and loaded his limp body into the trunk. From what they could tell, not a soul was stirring. The timing had been just right. No early morning walkers or joggers. No groggy-eyed retiree aimlessly following their trinket of a dog down the sidewalk. And Hank offered no resistance. Prior to leaving the cold tile of the bathroom floor, Melvin had force-fed his new captive a strong sedative. Initially, Hank flailed his bedrugged arms, pitifully trying to fend off his captor. To no avail, of course. Melvin was pure muscle through and through, as if he were cut from granite.

After putting Hank in the trunk, Melvin and Silvia reentered Hank's townhouse. And there *he* sat waiting for them in a reading chair, legs crossed, with the air of a diplomat or a sophisticate that jumped at the opportunity to speak of fine wines and rare books. "Silvia, you will stay here and stage the scene. Make it look as if our junkie friend skipped town. Leave enough undisturbed to make it look like he left in haste."

The Black-Eyed Man continued to unveil the plan: what they would do once they got back to The Portal, the supplies they needed, and who they would be bringing.

In awe, like a disciple at a tent revival lapping up every word that spilled from the preacher's mouth, Silvia nodded. Never once did she question the directive. Nor would she have dreamed of doing so.

"When you finish, meet us out at the Portal.'

The Black-Eyed Man kissed her on the forehead, stopping for a moment to admire her—a loving father fawning over his daughter. She stared back at him with the manic loyalty of a disciple beholding their savior. Running his hands over the bumpy terrain of her scars, he smiled at her, then glided out the front door. Melvin followed in his wake.

Chapter 48

Everett skittered around the smokehouse, trying to keep count of how many butts he had already put on. The customers now expected around a thousand people at the wedding—two hundred more than they told him originally. Shortly after Hank left, they had called to increase the order. Normally this would have been no bother, but today was different. Everett had precious minutes to get this done before his son lost his nerve and disappeared back into the city's underbelly.

Now, making haste, they had started another fire in one of the other brick pits. He put the remaining meat from the cart on the grill as Alex fed both smokers with embers that had burned down from logs of hickory. Everett stepped back to make a count of the shoulders and thought, *This should do.*

"That enough you think, boss?" Alex asked.

"Yeah. Wait a few hours before you bring the ribs out. They don't need near as long. When you're done, remember, wrap everything in plastic wrap, foil them, and then fill as many coolers as it takes."

"That will really hold the heat in and keep them fresh?"

"Trust me."

Everett ran back into the restaurant to check on the prep of the sides. Scrambling and scrambling, trying to get it all done, he had given little thought to what he was going to say to Hank. He moved about the kitchen, harum-scarum, more in everybody's way than anything else.

Taking stock of the room, Everett could see that Maria and her small crew had it covered. Maria lacked Alice's sharp wit in conversation, but each of them had a mother's gift of intuition. "Go to him, Everett. We have this."

Everett kept moving about the kitchen, ignoring her.

"Everett! Go to him. *Go!*"

"I'll be back as soon as I can. Watch Alex. He's still learning. Have him get the grill going as soon as he gets out to the venue. If anyone tries to take the meat inside and heat it up on a gas grill or in a fucking microwave, then tell them they're fired."

"Go."

He ran out the screen door, causing it to snap back furiously. He hadn't even thought to take off his apron.

Fighting early morning traffic—there was an art festival in downtown Boynton, causing cars to back up from the shore to interstate 95—Everett raced over to Hank's townhouse. The drive finally gave him some time to think about how to present the truth to Hank. While he ran around getting things ready for the wedding, the frenzy of it all had distracted him from the monstrous task ahead. Perhaps it would feel better once he unshouldered it. As if Atlas finally got to end his punishment and put down the sky, free to rest for what remained of eternity.

He would just start talking. Start at the beginning. Pull one stick away. And then another. Remove a rock. Then a branch. Keep picking away at the makeshift dam he had erected to keep the truth from spilling over. Keep picking at that son of a bitch until it finally gave way and the water burst through.

Booth would be the villain. April would be the victim. And Everett, Everett would be the penitent.

There were no heroes in Everett's tale.

Chapter 49

Carrying black trash bags with her, trying to stage the scene like her father had asked her, she opened all four drawers of the dresser, which was set back in the closet: two had nothing in them, and the other two were chock full of black t-shirts, all with band names, none she had heard of—names like Cave In and Sumac. She packed all the shirts into the bags, then took stock of what she had done, nodded, and thought—this will do.

Standing up to exit the closet, a movement caught her eye, her reflection from a mirror hung on the open closet door. Her hair had started to grow back. At first, she had been shaving it, navigating around the scar tissue with a razor, being careful not to nick or scrape the ropes of flesh lining the skin of her cranium. Enrapt by her image in the mirror, she moved her head about, beholding the rolling hills and dimples of every scar—the bulbs and puckers, the asymmetry of it all. The doctors told her that they had stitched things up the best they could; the presiding physician said that he had even declined to let the resident do it because of the exorbitant number of stiches required. The days following the surgery were hazy; he said they did their level best to fix the damage, but there would always be some residual scarring on her face and head. However, she could use a potent cream they prescribed to patients with pronounced mutilation of the skin. The cream would curb the inflammation and mitigate the size of the scars. If she was lucky, they would shrink enough to allow her to grow her hair out—use her dark locks to hide what lay beneath. *Pitiful,* she thought. *I would never.* The first thing she did as she left the hospital was throw the small tube of cream in the trash can.

She smiled at herself. She liked the monster she saw staring back.

Growing up, she had always been overweight and insecure. And itchy—she had always felt itchy in her clothes. Like she needed to scratch them right off, scratch them right into threadbare tatters.

Now when she looked in the mirror, she felt no shame.

The monster could be beautiful; the monster was a transport to other worlds. Worlds were laws, physics, and the whims of God—that Almighty always pointing down at them and judging—had no control.

She owed God nothing.

Through *ruin* she could find her salvation.

Through *ruin* she could find peace.

His words swam back through her head like a lullaby as she looked at her scars in the mirror. A beautiful monster was she: That's what her new father had—

She heard a knocking sound. Turning from the mirror, she listened, waiting to see if it came again.

Then, more knocking.

"Hank. Hank you ready?"

#

Steeling his resolve before he left the car, Everett assured himself that everything would be okay. In the end, this was the right thing to do. Results be damned; it was time for Hank to know what happened to his mother. It was like Hank said: the time had come for Everett to follow the muse into the dark.

He walked up to the stoop, noticing that the door was slightly cracked.

He knocked and leaned his head in to yell out, "Hank. Hank you ready?"

Everett walked into the kitchen off to the left, passing the stairs on his right and noticed that several of the drawers in the kitchen were open. With his back to the stairs, he moved around the kitchen.

"Hank, bud. Let's go." Must be up in the bathroom. *Oh God.* He cursed himself for being so naïve.

Everett turned to run up the stairs, to confront Hank.

237

As he spun around, the first thing he felt was the tip of a knife against his throat.

#

"Who are you?" Silvia kept the knife nestled just below his Adam's apple.

"I'm... I'm Hank's dad." Acutely aware of the fine point against his throat, Everett whispered his response. He saw the patchwork of scars lining her head. It made him think of a car accident; one where the person wasn't wearing a seatbelt and got ejected.

"Why are you here?"

Before he could answer, she pressed the tip of the knife into this throat, enough to draw a pinprick of blood.

Everett saw her eyes alight on the blood as it seeped out in tiny rivulets. He saw the mad intensity in her eyes, looking like... pleasure; she took pleasure from the sight of the blood trickling down his neck.

"I'm here to help him. Whatever he owes you, I can pay it. I will clear his debt. I can pay you or your—" She pushed him up against the refrigerator and moved the knife in deeper.

Down to the cell, Everett felt his tissue shred and tear away. He had never been more aware of his body—its functions, its casing, its desire to continue pulsing with life.

She eased the knife back and forth, needling the tissue that encased his throat.

"Is money all you think we want?" She hissed as the question flew from her mouth.

Everett felt his heart jackhammering in his chest; sweat poured into his eyes, but the sting was nothing compared to his panic. "I don't know what you want." He thought of Hank. Had this woman hurt him? Or worse, had she already killed him?

The knife went in further, causing sharp, hot pain to shoot up his neck, briefly blacking out his vision. Space was running out. How much further could it go before the pipes burst? And he couldn't help but think this short moment of agony was mere preamble. What would it feel like when she sliced him open? Like his neck was on fire? Even if it did, that feeling of inferno wouldn't last long. Because after a few moments, when enough of his blood flooded out, he wouldn't feel much of anything.

"You're right. Your son did steal from us. And like everyone else, we work for other people. We will have to make good on that money. But we know we will never get it back from you or him. 'Cause it's too much."

Everett whispered. He didn't want to talk to loud for fear of accidentally driving the knife deeper while his throat moved back and forth. "Trust me." Somehow, she moved the knife further in without opening a vein. "Trust me. I can settle his debt. I have money stowed away. Thousands I've saved from my business." Transfixed by the trickle of blood on his neck, she wasn't making eye contact with him.

"We'll be happy to take your money. But that's not all we're going to take."

"I'll give you whatev—"

She ripped the knife out; thicker tendrils of blood leaked down from the small wound on Everett's neck. Quickly, she raised her arm, brought the hilt down again and again, bludgeoning the top of his head. Everett didn't have time to react.

Involuntarily, the pain made him grit his teeth; the blows blotted out his vision. He reached out for her and found only air.

She brought the butt of the knife down again, hard, like a carnival-goer violently bringing down the mallet, pounding the puck to the bell at the top.

Blinded now, Everett's limbs flailed about, pinwheeling like someone trying not to fall of a beam. He felt warm liquid on his face, and the taste of salt and metal on his tongue.

Again, the knife pounded his head.

Then, he was lost in black.

Chapter 50

Odd, she thought. Everett was always in the kitchen when she dropped Danny off. Always. She had tried to track down Maria to ask her where he was, but hadn't been able to find her either. Perhaps she had been out back in the smoke house; Lisa hadn't had time to investigate; she needed to get to work. It would be a marathon of a day: quarterly reports were due, and the bank that loaned them money for big projects required the reports to keep lending to the company. An all-day affair for Lisa, that usually ended with her still in the office well after sunset, eyes bulging and bloodshot, hair askance, still quietly grinding it out at the computer.

Maybe she could get done early today to avoid being alone. She could skip lunch. Coffee was her primary sustenance when she did these reports. Actual food was ancillary. All she needed to power through was the caffeine and solitude.

#

Lunch had come and gone; a spent granola bar wrapper lay ripped open on her desk, spilling crumbs on the surface. Steam rose from her fifth (sixth?) cup of coffee. The trips to the bathroom were coming in quicker and quicker succession. She was in the home stretch, however. Almost there.

She saw that it was a little past three in the afternoon.

Another hour of work, and she would be finished. Go pick up Danny and then figure out what they would have for dinner. Danny always wanted Tex Mex. If Danny had his druthers, he would live off cheese dip and salsa, endlessly dipping his way into a cheesy-tomato oblivion. They ate it, at minimum, two times a week, and it always shredded Lisa's stomach. Maybe she could convince him to go for Chinese tonight.

The thought of convincing Danny to pivot made her stop scrolling the grid for a moment. Sometimes trying to redirect Danny sent him into a tantrum. During it, he never screamed, nor did he get violent, but he would storm off, leave the room without a word and shut himself away with his music for the rest of the night.

Hank had been so good at keeping Danny level. With unusual grace, Hank could calmly look at Danny, tell him about his favorite thing at the restaurant and Danny would instantly change his mind. In those moments, there was no trace of the Hank that had anxiety problems, random bouts of panic that seized him and blotted out his senses. That Hank, if for just a moment, departed, and in his place came Danny's talisman: the person above all others that could bring Danny's mind into harmony.

She shook herself from her thoughts and returned to her hallowed spreadsheet. Five o'clock was fast approaching, and she just about had it wrapped up.

And that's when she saw it: a data input error that threw off an entire column of work.

No early dinner with Danny. It was going to take a few hours to set the spreadsheet to rights.

#

When she looked up again, she noticed her coffee cup was empty—only a few dregs floating in a light brownish liquid—and she saw that it was almost eight. She had spent the better part of the last four hours trying to reverse the mistake. After she cussed herself for the slip, which she traced back to the week where she last saw Hank, she entrenched herself in the pattern of the grid and set about traveling back in time to cure her misstep.

Almost there, she thought. And, finally, *done*. The universe had been rebalanced. The error of the column was no more. Out of habit, she finished the last tepid sip of coffee. No sense in wasting it. As she always did after an arduous project, she leaned back in her chair to behold her labor. Months of work spread out in symmetrical boxes, all holding the keys to keeping the business flowing. She scrolled and scrolled, filling herself up with positive reinforcement: the grandeur of knowing the business would be screwed without her. No one had her eye for detail.

She checked her phone, saw the time, and started to gather her things.

Purse in hand, she reached for the light switch in her office.

#

After starting a podcast, she backed out of her parking spot. She hadn't made it far before she decided that listening to people vent about Trump's latest bit of lunacy only spiked her anxiety. She pulled off the to the side of the lot, at the corner of the strip mall where the office was located, and thumbed through her phone until she found an episode of *Astonishing Legends*.

Before she even set her phone down, however, a notification flashed the latest imbecilic remark tweeted by none other than President Trump. She read the incendiary tweet, a humdinger about violent illegal immigrants. *The dickhead can't help himself*, she thought. A boy disguised as a miserable, orange-faced man. Desensitized to his madness, she could only summon mock disgust. "What an assh—"

A steady tap on her window broke her concentration and made her go quiet. It was a man.

He had his head turned, seemingly to talk to somebody, looking in the direction of a black SUV. There, next to the black car, she saw the silhouette of another man, though she couldn't see any of his features.

Something was off here, she thought. *And why was he still wearing sunglasses?* Her instincts hadn't quite sounded the alarm yet. But she had already decided there was no way in hell she was getting out of her car.

The man next to her spoke back to the person off in the distance, his words muffled by the closed window. She failed to make out what they were saying to one another.

She started her car. He tapped again. Triggering a burst of anxiety that made her chest feel like it was seconds from splitting open.

Enough of this shit. This was the age of cellphones; these guys could call for help. With a shaky hand, she reached down to put the car into—

Suddenly, the man next to her window screamed, and this time she understood him. "He's dying. My friend is dying. He's a diabetic and he is out of insulin."

Dying. Did he just say his friend is dying? She kept her foot planted on the brake, the window still up. "What?"

"His insulin. He thought he had more in his kit. He was mistaken. Look." Still with his head turned at an odd angle, his face masked by darkness, the man's finger shot out in a frantic jolt and pointed toward the black car. He was holding what looked to be a black flashlight in his other hand. "Look at him, he's shaking!"

She craned her neck to look at the convulsing man off in the distance. Soon after, the man collapsed in a heap.

"Oh God. Please help us. He's seizing. Please help us!"

Listening to her heart, instead of her head—still screaming at her to get gone—she yelled through the window, "I'll call an ambulance." In case he couldn't hear her clearly, she held her phone up to show him what she meant.

Something still felt off. But she'd never forgive herself if the man off in the distance was really dying and she could have done something. She reached down to start dialing 911.

"There's no time. We have to get him to a hospital *now.* I'd do it myself if I could, but our car isn't working. Please. He is going to die. You could save him. Please!"

She stopped her fingers before they touched the screen. *His tone.* It didn't match the moment—a mediocre actor trying to ape genuine panic. This thought dislodged another, causing her to ask, "Why haven't you called an ambulance? Don't you have a phone?"

In a swift movement, he pulled a mag light from his jacket pocket, and used the handle-end to bust out her passenger window. She screamed and recoiled against the driver's side door as the shards of glass sprayed out in a violent hail.

Then, he clicked on a flashlight and held it up to his face.

The man was grinning. She couldn't fucking believe it. But that's what was happening. His smile was as wide as a canyon—the widest she had ever seen—revealing giant white teeth that looked like polished piano keys. He removed his glasses before he spoke, and what she saw when he did, silenced her. She told herself it couldn't be possible: his eyes were the night. The night was *inside* of him.

"Well, you got me there *Lisa*. Our little ruse wasn't well conceived, I suppose. Truth is, we were just a little restless. We thought a little theater might be gratifying."

How does he know my name?

"You're a good person, Lisa. I saw you weighing the options. You were actually considering helping us. Most people would have driven right off. I can see why he loves you. This will be perfect. The thing I have been waiting for."

Lisa was crumpled into a ball against the driver's side door, wishing to hell that she had put the car into drive and sped out of here. But maybe it wasn't too late.

Fighting through the panic crashing through her like a tsunami, she shot her hand down to the gearshift and moved her foot to the brake.

Quick to react, the Black-Eyed Man reached down and clicked the unlock button. Simultaneously, Melvin, now by the car, ripped the driver's side door open and fished her out with a deranged grace. Lisa's legs and arms lashed out in a furious gaggle as she tried to free herself, but he hit her twice with the hilt of his Maglite.

Her neck went slack as she sank into a black sea.

Chapter 51

Melvin had taken the vial containing the liquid sedative with him, forcing Silvia to use the butt-end of her knife to keep Everett out. Nor did she have a car with a trunk to hide her misdeed. Currently, Everett was laid out in her back seat, a trickle of blood, looking like a red strike of lightning, drying on his face. She followed the speed limit on her way out to Belle Glade.

The Black-Eyed Man had recited a long list to her, giving her a large swath of the responsibility. They needed more tools out at the Portal, some for amusement, others for necessity. However, for this mission, the tools were a secondary concern: Melvin and her father needed money too, and Silvia and Alejandro's war-chest at the new house was once again busting at the gills with the enterprise's ill-gotten gains. Silvia had lied to Everett—they had paid *some* of the debt owed to their shadowy employers, but not all of it. More was owed, and though she knew next to nothing about their employer's identities, these were not the type of people that forgave debts.

His instructions to her had been clear: get enough to pay back their employers—$150,000, the balance remaining from what Hank and the recently deceased Clyde had stolen—and enough for her and Melvin to leave town for a week or so while he made the trip to set things to rights: $10,000 apiece.

She kept thinking about all of this, as she drove out to Belle Glade. Another thought was dogging her too: she had left her phone in the other car, the one Melvin and the Black-Eyed Man drove off in, leaving her with no means to communicate with them and let them know about Hank's father popping up. *Would they want her to bring him out to the Portal too?* She would just have to call and find out as soon as she got home.

All of this could be overcome. Just a few bumps in the road, nothing more.

They would pay back what they owed to the Cartel and be free of the threat of death. And they could disappear the father, just as they planned to do with the son.

There was no need to worry, she kept telling herself.

#

True to form, Alejandro was passed out in the recliner. She kicked him awake, causing him to spill the half-drank beer that teetered in his hand.

"Get up. We have a guest. I need you to watch him while I bring the cash down. Think you can handle that?"

Alejandro offered nothing in response. That feeling of festering hatred was a two-way street. He only spoke to her if he had to. A dark, calculating part of him understood the business of drug trafficking; it was basic economics. A supplier fulfilling a need as old as the Bible. He really did understand when someone said *it was just business.* But Silvia's twisted brand of violence was beyond him. She didn't do it to send a message, and it had nothing to do with prolonging the enterprise: she killed people because she enjoyed it. *Foul creature*, was all he could think when he looked at her now. *Foul creature*, indeed.

"Come on, fat ass. Come help me move him into the house."

He cussed her in his head as he sauntered out to the driveway. The heat was near hellfire; he immediately started sweating out the beer he had just drunk. Alejandro opened the back door of the black car and looked in: he saw a man with limp arms and legs all piled up, splotches of dried blood on his cheek and forehead.

"What'd you do to him?"

"Shut up and pull from your end and I'll push. Once we get him out, we'll drag him around to the back door. Got it? Or do I need to draw you a picture?"

Alejandro grabbed the man without responding.

Silvia scanned the area for prying eyes. Neighbors on both sides were at work and there hadn't been a single car drive by.

"I'm going to get the duffel bags out of the garage. Do not leave him, you understand? Not for any reason."

"I got it. I got it, bitch."

She recoiled at the word *bitch.* "I'm going to make you into art one day, Alejandro."

"Stop talking crazy, and get to work. No need to speak your spells to me. I'm sure the weirdo with the black eyes and his follower are expecting you. You think because they're letting you run around with them that you're safe? You're lying to yourself."

"Insult *him* again and I will open you up."

In response, Alejandro pulled a Ruger .380 from the waistband of his jeans. To avoid a further escalation of hostilities, he didn't point it right at her, but exposed the gun to make himself clear.

Silvia still had a gun wedged in her pants, nestled against her back. She reached behind her, gripped its handle, but then thought better of it.

In the end, the pudgy drunk was right.

"One day I'm going to remake you."

"Take your crazy talk into the den and get to work."

With that, Silvia went to the garage to get tools; Alejandro moved to the fridge and cracked another beer; and Everett sat unconscious, propped up by an ugly set of kitchen cabinets.

#

Minutes passed. Alejandro sipped to the steady thumps as Silvia walked above them, and then up and down the ladder, gathering the cash. The cabinets blocked Alejandro and Everett from Silvia's view. Alejandro had failed to notice that Everett's foot was moving back and forth in short, choppy motions, a dysfunctional pendulum.

Everett had come back to the world of the living.

In a pained whisper, his throat feeling as if he had eaten a chunk of drywall, he spoke. "Who are you?" The stocky man next to him gave no indication he heard him. He tried again, louder. "Who are you?" Everett tried to focus through the walloping pound of his headache. The kitchen looked straight out of the eighties: white linoleum floors, blue tiled counters, and a couple of hanging houseplants bookending the sink. The space was clean, too. He had expected that she'd take him somewhere dark and dingy, like a ratty warehouse or a moldy basement. Not a kitchen from the not-so-distant past in which you could eat off the floor.

Alejandro jumped at the sound of Everett's voice, almost spilling his beer. He turned to his right but didn't speak.

"Not going to talk to me. I get it. You also not going to tell her that I'm awake?" Everett kept his voice low. Why hadn't the man turned to her immediately and said their prisoner was awake? Dissension in the ranks. Maybe this was an opportunity.

"Is my son here?"

Looking confused and a little drunk, Alejandro turned to him.

Everett could tell the man hadn't the foggiest about the answer to his question. "My son. They took him. He's here, right? In the back somewhere?" Large brown eyes stared back at Everett; he saw kindness in there. You had to look to find it, but it was there, buried deep. Something about this man struck Everett as odd, given the context. He seemed more like a dad than an underling in the drug world—clean golf shirt, baggy jeans, beer gut, and a slightly grumpy disposition. He felt out of place. That could be of use.

Alejandro shook his head *no.*

"Do you know where he is? Please tell me."

Stoically, Alejandro turned away from him and continued to nurse his beer.

Everett offered more questions to no avail. He said his son was sick. That he needed help. That he, Everett, wouldn't say anything to the police. And he could be trusted because he used to live on the wrong side of the law. He hated cops just as much as they did. Please, please, please...

Alejandro's mien stayed the same, the wet slurp of a beer his only response.

"You must not have kids. If you did, then you'd know what I'm going through. No one with a daughter or son could be this cold." Everett noticed the man wince as if he had been bitten by an insect—a sign he took offense. Maybe he was making headway.

#

The man Silvia had kidnapped kept nudging him for answers. Alejandro was doing his level best to ignore him, but the man's words about fatherhood grated. A heavy shadow of shame had overtaken him. He knew he was being manipulated, but he was helpless to ignore the magnetic pull of the accusations.

"I have two children." When he spoke, he could feel the suffocating weight of the shame in his chest, shortening his breaths, making his voice deeper and burdened. "They don't live here with me. I don't get to speak with them much."

"Why not?" The man looked to Everett, gauging whether or not he should tell him the truth: that like Everett, in a way, he was a captive. That well-to-do men had come to his home, offering him an opportunity to make money in America. That he would go there to help manage what they called a conglomerate. That when he said no because he didn't want to leave his family, those same men threatened his family. They said they would watch over his family while he was gone. That *they would watch their every move.* And then they sent a local police officer to make sure he accepted the offer. That officer also said he'd keep close watch over his family. That cop said, *You're welcome to live here with your family of course. Just as you're welcome to die here with them.* And that was it. Alejandro went to the states.

"I talk with them when I can. It's hard. They live very far away." Despite the beer, his words came out clear, but they were anchored down by grief, sounding like a dirge.

Alejandro had burner phones, scores of them, that he hid from Silvia and all the others involved in their drug business. When Silvia was out of the house—which was more and more often recently, now that she had her new friends, her *cult*—he called his wife back home. She also used burner phones, and they would speak briefly and if possible, if his son and daughter weren't outside playing, they would come over and speak with him about their latest obsession. During their last talk, his son had discovered the beautiful simplicity of skipping rocks across a small river that ran through their land. Alejandro told him how to hold the rock just so to get the best result. And his daughter, older than his son, spoke of a book written by a British woman, with a boy that was a wizard with a mean aunt and uncle. He could listen to his little girl talk all day about anything or nothing.

When had this man last spoken to his son? Alejandro thought. But that's not what he asked him. "How many children do you have?"

"Hank is my only child."

"No others?"

Smiling, the man said, "Not that I know of."

Alejandro softened at the sight of the man's grin. "Your son must have really stepped into some shit if her and those other men took him."

"Other men? What other men?" Alejandro balked. He had slipped; he shouldn't have mentioned the other men, even obliquely like he did.

"Is there anything you wouldn't do if someone took your children? You would do anything to get them back. Wouldn't you?"

Without hesitation, Alejandro said, "Of course."

"Then, father to father, help me get my son back."

Chapter 52

The Black-Eyed Man and Melvin spoke little on the way to the Portal. Prior to loading him into the trunk, they had wrapped extra straps and zip-ties around the man to ensure that he stayed ensnared. Hank was twined and trussed like a piece of dinner meat.

As the car moved down the highway, behind them, a neon glow illuminated the way-back of the SUV, accompanied by a buzzing vibration that came in timed waves, as if set by a metronome. The Black-Eyed Man nodded for Melvin to pull over on the side of the haggard, long-forgotten highway. It wasn't like Melvin to make such an error, but, alas, he was human.

Wearing a mask of equanimity, Melvin pulled the car over; then went and searched the woman in the backseat again. "She's clean."

"And her love?"

Melvin shut the door and walked around to the rear, quickly popping the back hatch open. The man watched silently as Melvin rifled through the young man's pockets. In short order, he found the source of the alien green light: a small cellphone (of the flip-phone variety) he had missed during the initial search.

Melvin threw it into the dense woods near the highway.

The journey resumed.

Lost in the deep haze of an intravenous sedative, Lisa lay insensate under a thick blanket.

Only the metal and leather of a seat separated Lisa from Hank: Hank was in the cargo area behind the last seat and Lisa was unconscious just in front of him on the backseat.

PART VI

The Final Echo

Chapter 53

"In a moment, you're going to go meet God. I want you to tell Him something."

The man with the black eyes once again pulled up Hank's blood-soaked chin to make sure he was paying attention. "God's gift to man is free will. The Grand Experiment. He never interferes with any of our actions. But what He or She, or It, fails to see is that people like me are the product of free will. And I am a poison."

He stopped to towel off the blood that had transferred from his passenger's chin to his hand. The man bound to the chair, Hank Grant, had no unblemished skin left—his body was a mosaic of bruises, gashes, ripped skin, and blood. And holes: there were holes in his forearm and foot from the drill. In the end, he had had no choice but to submit and listen to this ugly creature unspool his black philosophy.

"You tell Him that one day, I'll be there to collect my apology for what His Grand Experiment allowed to happen to my mother." He paused to look down and gather his breath. Then he turned to Hank, as if responding to an accusation. "*See.* I feel. I feel it every day. The sight and the pain of seeing my mother defiled and then dismembered like an animal. I saw every second of it. His Grand Experiment played out right before my eyes."

For a moment, the Black-Eyed Man stopped, perhaps stricken by an image of his dead mother, in pieces.

"Have I told you that my mother was a devout Christian? When I was young, we gathered together in the morning to pray as a family. She even carried a rosary. Not because she was Catholic, but because she said it made her feel comfortable. I suppose it was the charm that kept away the dark spirits from her. We all have those don't we, Hank? For a child, it's their favorite stuffed animal that they clutch tight to their chest to ward off the evil monster under the bed or the masked man hiding in the closet. Adults have them too: little charms and superstitions they carry to protect them from darkness. Some as silly as turning the car around when a black cat crosses the road. But for most adults, the ultimate shield is religion. They use it to comfort themselves against all this supposed *evil* in the world. That's what my mother did. She held that rosary tight and prayed and prayed. Every day. She was one of *Its* most loyal followers. And yet she ended up bloodied and torn apart all the same. So, when you get *up* there, or down there, or if you wake up in some far-flung realm, you tell Him that he has failed. And I'm going to spend my remaining breaths making Him regret creating me. You tell Him that, young Hank."

With grace, the man rubbed the back of Hank's head with his left hand, as he pressed the serrated edge of a blade against Hank's neck with the right.

This was the end.

Lisa. He would never get a chance to make things right with her. A chance to say he was sorry for the hell he had put her through. Loyal to a fault, she had stuck with him through so much of his bullshit—the lies, the stealing, and the shame. At minimum, she deserved to hear him atone and say two simple words without qualification—*I'm sorry.* Maybe he would get that chance in whatever waited for him in the hereafter. And if such a thing existed, he certainly had no intention of delivering this man's message. But maybe Lisa could still meet him there one day. Just maybe.

And Danny. It would have been nice to sit down with him and listen to one more record. Maybe for the first time, Hank would've had the courage to select one of his mother's records—Pink Floyd's *Wish You Were Here* or the one that looked the most worn, possibly her favorite by the looks of the wear and tear, Fleetwood Mac's *Rumors*—and they could sit and listen without any thought of the time or the day or the next errand to run. Just sit and listen and be transported away.

Everett. His father had finally been ready to tell him the truth. Ready to help Hank be rid of the poison that was killing him. What had he found when he went to Hank's townhouse? Surely, he had found his kit lying unkempt on the floor of the bathroom, the sharp disappointment he must have felt at the sight of it. *Was he still searching for me? Would he continue to?* Be one of those parents that gets interviewed by the news or a documentary team, sitting in an old, tattered house teeming with stacks of papers, notepads, and the other detritus of a life-long search for their lost child. What would become of his father?

The man had not stopped talking. "Soon, young Hank, I'm going to spill every drop of blood from your body, right down to the last teaspoon. But not yet, Hank. Not yet. First, we have something to show you."

He moved in front of Hank. "First we need to show you what you're going to be a part of before you leave us."

He motioned for Melvin to go get her.

Chapter 54

They had kept Lisa out in the car for three days, having her subsist on water and crackers. To prevent her from suffocating in the sweltering humidity put off by the bog, they had left the windows cracked. Even so, the time in the car had dehydrated her badly. Already thin, she looked downright skeletal now, her dried skin clinging and stretched over her bones. Melvin grabbed her body up; she slumped over his shoulder. He noticed that she was lighter than when he put her in the car three nights ago.

Melvin stepped back into the Portal with her lolling over his shoulder like a felled deer.

The Black-Eyed Man kept his eyes trained on Hank, wanting to soak up every drop of his captive's surprise at the sight of his love captured: here now to be taught how to bend time and space.

Melvin dropped Lisa to the ground. The impact forced a cough from her, and she sluggishly writhed on the ground, unaware of her new surroundings.

Hank stared at her crumpled form in utter disbelief. He was hallucinating. They had pumped narcotics in him non-stop to keep him alive and withdraw-free, and in the process they must have scrambled his brain, short-circuiting it, making it spit out nightmarish images. This couldn't be real. Lisa wasn't involved in the underside of his life—she knew nothing of it. How had they known to grab her? How did they even know she and Hank knew each other?

It's not possible.

"We will show you a thing beyond the mortal beauty of this world, Hank.

Something far, far beyond it."

#

Hissing from the pain, Hank kept blinking and blinking his bruised and swollen eyes—like someone trying to wake up from a bad dream—as Melvin moved her into place. He tied her down to a chair directly across from Hank, so they could look at each other, face to face. Lisa hadn't yet made a sound. But she would soon enough, he thought.

While Melvin trussed her limp body to the chair, the Black-Eyed Man busied himself over at the shelves, looking at the totems they had kept from other passengers. To call them pieces of the dead would have offended him. They were more than that—they were *art*. He looked at his handiwork on the shelves, a cemetery of sorts. Some preserved in jars, others through an odd form of taxidermy they had developed. The stuffed specimens weren't put into jars; those pieces were hung on the walls, left out to fight the humid air of the swamp. He turned to look at his creations: each piece was a remnant of a person. Each was unique. Each was remade into something that could still be identified as human flesh and gristle, but as to where it used to be on a person, that question could no longer be answered. These transformed pieces of passengers were spaced out and displayed like a hunter preserved animals in a lodge, a small house of memories for he and Melvin. Where they went to worship and remember.

They didn't label the jars. There was no need to put the former person's name on it; names were of no use. The transport back through time was all that mattered.

The young man's mumbling distracted him: "This isn't happening." He was looking directly at the girl. "You're not here. This isn't happening."

Under his limitless black eyes, his wide mouth stretched into an awful grin.

The woman, Lisa, had still not woken. They had kept her on a steady diet of sedatives the last few days. They didn't want her causing problems. But, in order to accomplish their goal, they had kept her hydrated, having to resort to an IV, when she wouldn't wake up from her narco-coma. Yesterday, Melvin had started to wean her off the regimen to get her ready to become a passenger. Soon, if she didn't wake up on her own, they would inject her with a stimulant that would set off a flood of anxiety and panic to jolt her awake. Heart aflutter, she would scream out and then they could watch as her fear mounted and mounted while she beheld her new environment.

Bound.

Trapped.

In a world apart from reality.

He stepped outside briefly, to flip the switch on a small generator. Normally, he would have had Melvin perform the grunt work, but his right hand was busy setting the stage and needn't be bothered. After turning on the power source, he returned to the light switches, which were mounted on a moldy piece of plywood by the entrance. With each flick, a row of a hundred or so bright yellow lights, almost like Christmas lights, came on; each row came closer and closer to Hank and Lisa. Soon the whole room was saturated in a dim yellow glow, as if the stars had fallen to earth, finding shelter in this tiny, corrugated room.

For the Black-Eyed Man, the lights signaled the dissolution of time and space.

They lit the path to eternity.

Chapter 55

Darkness was gone, but the light was worse. Human remains were displayed on the walls to the right and left, and the shelves lining the back wall were teeming with dusky jars that contained unidentifiable scraps of people. With the lights glowing, Hank could finally see what was in those jars and he found himself unexpectedly mesmerized by all the little horrors. He couldn't place a single thing. Not once did he think, there is an arm, there is a hand, that is a heart, but they were human relics, that much he could tell. Amalgams of bone, flesh, and sinew, recreations of what once was. The longer he looked, the sicker he got. And the things on the walls were just as sickening—he could feel the bile stewing in his stomach, begging for release. Preserved remains hung from the walls like deranged trophies. Except, Hank knew now, these things were more than trophies to these sick men. They were sacred. Objects of worship. And this was their church.

Next, he noticed the weapons lining a wall of pegboard, like he had seen in so many garages. Some of the pegs held normal power tools—drills, a handsaw, a nail-gun—alongside typical household implements—hammer, saw, Phillips head screwdriver. On others, he saw tools he couldn't place, ones not of this time—chains and spikes and crude, worn metal. His body already bore gouges, gashes, and cuts from many of these tools. Up until now, Hank hadn't been able to see their full arsenal, Melvin had been returning these objects to the shadows, only to emerge with some other instrument of pain. He no longer worried what they would do to him; now he worried for

Lisa.

Melvin, having finished binding Lisa to the chair, straightened and walked over to his prophet.

Hank could read his lips with the help of the faint glow coming off the lights: *Where is she?*

Who was she? Was it that lady that was with them at the townhouse? The woman he had seen that had had scars on her cheeks?

Lisa's head began to bob up and down, moving in a drunken swirl. At first, her hair obscured her eyes, leaving her face hidden in shadow. As she came to, she blew the wet, matted tendrils of dark hair out of her face.

Overcome with shame, Hank wished he could make her disappear. His eye sockets itched from the dried blood that had settled in the curves. He now saw the world through splotches of red, as if someone had taken a red laminate insert from one of the cheap stage lights he and the guys used when he was still playing in DCP, and slid it over his vision. His world was decorated in red birthmarks. But through the red, it looked like Lisa was trying to say something.

#

"Ha... nnnk." His name crawled out of her dry throat in pieces. She swallowed a few times to try to wet her parched throat, blinked her eyes, and then took a closer look at him. "Oh my God, Hank, *baby*." Her face crumpled up in grief. "My God. What have they done to you?"

She surveyed his body, now a map of dried blood, plush bruises, and ripped skin.

They had tortured him.

"Oh baby, look at you." Sensing the two men weren't too far behind her, she kept her voice low.

All she could do was sob. She heaved at the sight of the love of her life, beaten and torn.

"I'm so sorry. This is all my fault. All mine. I'm so—"

"Baby, I know." The grief could wait. Right now, she wanted to survive. They needed to find a way out. "Where are we?"

"I don't know."

Wincing from the cruel pounding in her head, she said, "How long have you been here?"

"I think four days, five maybe. I can't tell. They haven't given me anything to eat or drink. They just keep pumping shit into me. How long have you been out here?"

"Two, maybe three days." Every word hurt. In addition to the splitting-crack of her headache, which felt like someone was using a power-drill to split her skull open, her body felt as though it had aged decades—every muscle and joint ached magnificently. She felt like a stripped car left to rust and die in the sun.

"How can you tell?"

"The man, the one with hair, kept coming out and giving me pills. It didn't take long to knock me out. But before I went back down, I saw the sun come up twice, I think."

"How did they get you?"

"I was leaving work. They knew where I worked. How did they—"

"Finally, we have you both awake."

Chapter 56

The bald man with the scars had interrupted Lisa. His associate, the man with the beard, stepped outside. While he did, the nameless man with the black eyes walked over and positioned himself where they both could see him. All Hank kept thinking was that he just didn't want anything to happen to Lisa.

"I know you're both wondering how you each got here. Don't worry. We will get to that. First, Hank here must give us what we need, and then we will move on to what really matters. Hank, I'll ask again: who were you working for?"

The man repeated the question again and again. He stroked Lisa's hair as if she were his pet—his plaything. To no avail, Lisa flinched and tried to move away.

Jaw clenched, veins popping out of his forehead like mad worms, Hank said, "Take your fucking hand off her."

The man ignored Hank's comment. Then, with the soothing tone of a concerned parent, he said, "Hank, you owe that man nothing. Where is he now? He's not here to save you. So out with it. Who were you working for?"

Lisa stayed silent as Hank considered the man's offer. He had held that piece of information back because it was the only reason for them to keep him alive. It certainly had nothing to do with misguided loyalty to Vince or Clyde. In the end, he knew it was his only bargaining chip. And he realized now that maybe he could use it to serve a better purpose.

Hank pointed his head at Lisa. "If I tell you, then she leaves. You have to let her go." It was impossible to tell what he was thinking behind those black eyes.

The man sighed. "Why would I do such a thing?"

Hank pleaded, "She had nothing to do with what we did."

"That's irrelevant now, Hank."

Over Lisa's shoulder, Hank saw the other man reenter the room. He stayed on the other side of the shed, waiting, something in his hand.

"Your man, whoever he is, will have to answer to us. That is the order of things, Hank. So, I ask you again: who sent you?"

The other man appeared behind Lisa before Hank could respond. Worse, he saw the glint of the large knife in the man's hand.

"Tell us, Hank."

Panicking, Hank screamed, "Just let her go, and I will tell you."

The man once again ignored Hank's plea. "Can you imagine anything more beautiful? Is there anything more divine on this planet?" Under the sick halo cast by the yellow lights, the Black-Eyed Man offered the questions to the room, addressing no one in particular.

With the desperate screams of a drowning man, Hank kept on: "She had nothing to do with what we did. You can let her go."

"She now has a purpose with us. It didn't take much looking through your phone to see that you love her. The things you wrote were a little saccharine for my taste; you should learn the beauty in subtlety, young man." The Black-Eyed Man seemed to divine the thought racing through Hank's head. "Once Clyde fulfilled his purpose, we followed you, then cloned your phone when you left it in your car. It took several tries, but even as attached as humanity is to their screens these days, sooner or later, we all break free of our devices, whether we intend to or not. Sad, really, everyone is now a junkie in their own right, getting bloated on all those images of what *could be*, rather than stepping outside to see what already *is*. All junkies, just like you Hank. All weighed down to those new-age anchors that diminish us at every turn. Promising us convenience in exchange for robbing us of our creativity."

Moving aside the black tentacles of Lisa's dirt-greased hair, he started to drag his nails up and down her neck. Hank could see the goosepimples form on her throat as she trembled under his touch.

"Though, those little devices do have an upside. They leave a digital tattoo of all our movements. We made short work of tracking you down. All with the help of an app that we bought legitimately." He laughed at the irony. "We also low-jacked your car for good measure."

The man with the coal-black eyes kneeled down next to Lisa, still gracefully stroking her neck.

Hank envisioned a menacing kid, petting the neck of its tiny pet bird. Softly at first. Gently. And then, sneering at the beauty of the bird, wanting to test the limits of its fragility and helplessness, snapping the bird's neck—he could almost see its head leaning to the side, lifeless.

Like the visions of Lisa's neck, lolling to the side, that flooded his head.

The other man, the enforcer, moved closer to Hank. Again, he saw the glint as the yellow lights hit the blade. He saw the grooves of the knife, and, unbeckoned, he thought of what those jagged indentations could do to human flesh.

With an evangelical tone, he said: "Oh, what an age we live in. We've sacrificed privacy for convenience. Those messages on your phone, Hank, especially the ones you saved, showed us the bedrock of your heart. And what could be more beautiful than a person forced to watch the person they love gashed and mutilated, all the while powerless to change the course of fate? *Don't you understand, Hank?* It is love laid bare. The closest thing to divinity on earth."

Abruptly, the Black-Eyed Man moved to the side.

"It will be a moment outside of time, where seconds feel like an eternity. Soaked in your desperation to change what's happening, but you can't, because my free will stops yours from saving the creature you love most in this world. The haunt on your face as Melvin splits open her throat: that will be my totem."

He raised his arms aloft, shaking them with the fervor of a preacher at a tent revival: "Can't you see the beauty in it, Hank? Can't you see it?"

Hank noticed some energy had flowed back into Lisa—she looked angry.

Hank figured it was the man spewing his bullshit philosophy that had sparked her back to life. Lisa had never had much patience for bullshit. She asked, "Well, how *did* you find me?" She knew that Hank always saved her in his phone under some ridiculous pet name. Zena, Warrior Princess had been one of the many gems over the years.

"Why, Lisa, with the internet, no one is a stranger. Post after post about every minute facet of life, all out there for the world to see. As if they let you right into their home. Once Clyde informed on Hank here, we were always going to find him. And with all that information out there at the touch of a button, finding you was just as inevitable. Facebook, Instagram, Twitter, all full of breadcrumbs that span from the superhighway right to the very roads that led us to your home. Your name wasn't in his phone, but, in the end, it made no difference." He seemed to feed off the energy of explaining his philosophy; he paced. "Social media: everyone's life exposed for mankind to see. Picture after picture. You open your home to us. We are in your kitchen, your den, your bedroom. We are with you *always*, millions of unknown eyes staring at your life on a screen."

Then, suddenly, he stopped pacing and stood right in front of her. "You see, Lisa, privacy is a ghost of the past.

"Once we put together the pieces of each of your lives on social media—Hank's posts first, which led us in turn to you, Lisa—we went to the places where you live and then the places where you work. Lisa, you had a nasty habit of leaving your phone in your car when you dropped your brother off at the restaurant. So we cloned it and then tracked it. And again, because we leave no stone unturned, we put a GPS tracker on your car as well. We know all your habits. All your movements. We were with you, Lisa. Always."

The other man (Melvin, Hank thought. He could have sworn he had heard the deranged man call him Melvin) moved closer. There was no space left now between Melvin and Lisa.

"This was inevitable. Don't be ashamed. We were always going to find you and yours. We make it our practice to stay on the cusp of technology." The man pivoted. "The Hickory. Nice place. Hector used to work there, did he not?"

Lisa said what Hank was thinking: "So you were the ones that took Hector?"

"Hector, like Hank here, transgressed and was duly punished."

The sound of Hector's name knocked loose a memory: Everett talking to a tall, bald man, with scars covering his head, who had just left the restaurant. Everett, before he could stop himself, had said the man bothered him. That he had never really seen or met anyone like him. Rambling on, Everett had said the man seemed, almost, well... alien. Hank had bumped into *this* man on his way into the restaurant. How had he not remembered until now? The obvious answer was the drugs they had given him. And at this point, the realization changed nothing.

"And what about Hector's kids? What is your answer for that? You seem to have a readymade bullshit explanation for everything you're doing. How do you explain orphaning children?" Lisa said.

"That, I leave to God. I, after all, was orphaned too. God knows me, just as He knows you and everyone else plodding the Earth. Except I want Him to remember me above others. I want to shame our Maker."

For a moment, her fear left her. Anger replaced it.

Her face roiling with anger, Lisa sneered and said, "You're a coward." She seemed to have had made peace with a simple fact: they were never going to leave alive, so she might as well fight. She didn't have to die in supplication. "All this talk of a higher purpose is your bullshit way of covering up the fact that you're an errand boy for the mob or cartel or whoever pays your bills. You're just a bitch-boy for some drug dealer. And that asshole probably calls himself a *businessman*, just like you call yourself an *artist*. All bullshit to hide what you really are."

Surprised at her pluck, he stepped back. "And what is that?"

"Take your pick: weak, insecure, scared. Dragging the rest of the world through therapy with you. Making others suffer while you try to prove something to *yourself* or your *mommy* or your *daddy* or in your fucked-up head, *God*. But, at the end of the day, you're all the same. You're just a scared little boy with a grudge."

"I'm sorry you se—"

"You're not sorry. But I hope you will be. If there is a God, I hope She makes you beg before She sends you to Hell." With her head, she motioned to the shelf, acknowledging all the victims that had come before her. "I hope all the people you've killed are waiting there in the rafters, ready to watch you scream for help as you melt." Lisa looked at the man with unalloyed contempt. Hank thought that if she wasn't bound, she would have driven a knife into the man's chest without a second's remorse.

Rather than looking hurt or shamed by Lisa's remarks, he looked curious. "You hedged, Lisa. You said *if* there is a God waiting on the other side. Do you believe in God?"

"I don't."

"When we are done, you will. You'll wish and wish to go meet Him and for it all to end. Minutes, seconds, all those pesky intervals of time, they have no bearing here. Those moments, where you're crying out to be released from your anguish, they will exist apart from time. That is what we do here. We stretch the pain into an eternity. Time will be stripped of its meaning as Hank here watches you writhe and claw, begging for the end. Once I've gotten what I need, then—and only then—will we release you to God. And I assure you He is up there, Lisa... But by then, I won't have to convince you."

The tent-revival preacher zeal left him. He grew grim and solemn, his features downcast, as if in mourning.

"Now Hank: the name, please."

As if trading roles, the other man grabbed Lisa's neck, but his fingers stretched clear across her throat, clenching it, steading his prey.

"At least, Hank, give us his address."

Despite the man's hand around her throat, Lisa managed to say, "You don't have to give them anything, Hank."

"Oh, you see, but you do, Hank. How is your father, Everett, these days? A little worse for wear, I imagine? How is the restaurant?"

Hank hadn't expected to hear his father's name. After the initial shock from the sound of it wore off, shame and guilt sluiced through him in a flood:

his dad would see his open black drug-kit up in the bathroom and think Hank had gotten high, then ran away. That's the last thing he would remember about his son: going to his house to help him and then his boy disappearing. His thoughts shot to what his dad was doing right now. Was he still looking for him? How many days had it been, four, five? Was he roaming the alleys and the hideouts beneath the overpasses, asking if anyone had seen his boy? Or was he sitting in the kitchen of his restaurant alone, paralyzed by disappointment for the son that once again betrayed him?

Then much blacker thoughts weaved a spindly web through Hank's mind: What if these men went after his father? What if they tortured him? What if they killed him?

The Black-Eyed Man let that linger; he wanted to let Hank stew on hearing his father's name. Let it sink in that his father would never be safe as long as he and Melvin trod the Earth. The Black-Eyed Man gestured, and he and Melvin stepped over to the other side of the Portal, near the door.

Lisa tried to get Hank's attention, but Hank failed to notice. His mind was still in a tailspin, worrying about what would become of his father.

The bald man turned. "Now, are you both ready to begin?"

In a flash, Melvin stepped forward, knife brandished, and swiftly ran the blade down Lisa's left arm. She cried out in terror and pain.

Shell-shocked, Hank watched as the skin of her upper arm splayed back, peeling away like the rind of an orange. Then came the blood, moving down her arm in a lazy creek, thick and maroon under the sallow lights. Hank watched as she tried to fight off the pain. Her initial screams had been replaced by a keening moan, an attempt to steady her breathing and her shaking body. The wretched sound—low and ghostly, eerily like the sound of the upright bass on thirties' jazz records—kept coming out of her in waves, while she fought to compose herself. Hank knew why she was doing it. Lisa didn't want to show these men any weakness. She didn't want to give them the satisfaction. Watching her struggle, his heart blackened with hate for these men. But, well and truly, it made him hate himself even more.

"We will watch over Everett for you, Hank, though I can't promise that no harm will come to him. And Lisa, we will keep a watchful eye on your half-witted brother. It's never been my practice to prey on the disabled. I suppose that should be far outside of my bailiwick. Though, when it comes to my art, I abhor boundaries. Art should never be constrained. Perhaps even Danny would like to leave time and space."

Hank saw Lisa's resolve melt away in an instant. Danny had always been her most vulnerable spot. Despite his utter fatigue, seeing her deflate at the sound of Danny's name triggered his last reserves of anger. He tensed his gaunt arms against his bindings; he moved his legs, struggling to break free from the plastic zip-ties that held him in place. As he writhed and contorted his body, a sanatorium patient trying to break out of a straitjacket, he screamed and moaned and cussed and offloaded every last bit of the rancid stew that had been boiling in him ever since they brought in the love of his life and tied her up. And it was all his goddamn fault. His fucking fault.

Finally, when he had nothing left, he took stock of what his fit had accomplished. All he had done was further gouge the scores of wounds covering his body and what was worse, during his bout of mania, he had reopened many of the holes—the ones they had drilled into him—that dotted his arms and legs.

All there was left to do now was bleed and cry.

Sobbing, he said, "Please stop. Don't cut her again."

"My free will and his" —the man nodded towards Melvin— "supersede yours. Melvin will open her up in ways beyond imagination. And don't you fear: we have a slew of drugs handy to prevent her from passing out from the shock. That small cut of flesh is only the beginning. We've only scratched the surface. By the end, she'll come to know God. And by then, you'll have come to hate that coward just as much as I do."

#

Lisa looked at Hank, trying to find the will to speak—her throat felt as though someone had rubbed sandpaper against it. The threat against Danny had drained the fight out of her. In its place, despair had taken root. Hearing her brother's name brought home the futility of their situation in a way nothing else could. She realized there was nothing to be gained by interacting with these small men. And practically speaking, there was nothing to be gained by fighting against the ties that bound her to the chair.

I am going to die out here.

She allowed that simple sentence to run through her head for the first time. What surprised her was that it didn't bring the hollow chill that she thought it would; instead, it let her know what she wanted to think about as she left port.

She wanted to peacefully look at Hank, to try to remember him as he *had been*. She wanted to reach backward in time and remember their relationship; in her last moments, she would live as if it were years before and they were happy, in the days long before drugs toxified and blistered their bond. She didn't want to see the wan man with the black crescents under his eyes. She wanted to see *her* Hank. The tall, dark-haired, awkward nerd she had fallen in love with. The one she had to softly coax out of his anxiety attacks. The one that stood by her without objection, that had accepted her brother with patience and grace, showing the quiet loyalty she had always wanted from a man. A person that she believed she could look at years down the road, after all the stuff of life—status, competing with neighbors, getting ahead at work—ceased to matter. Once the storm had settled, she would reach out her liver-spotted hand and he would reach out his, and without a word or a look, they would hold hands. A silent way of letting her know he was still there and that he was still with her. That was Lisa's idea of love, more than anything else: love is quiet gestures of loyalty.

When she at last spoke, her tone was faint. "Hank? Hank?" He turned his head. His eyes were bloated with tears. "Will you just keep looking at me? We don't have to speak to them anymore. We can pretend they're not here. Don't give them the name. They'll just kill us anyway. Let's just act as if they're not here." She sucked back the snot and tears. "Hank, just don't stop looking at me, baby." Hank's face softened. And as he nodded, she was able to see him as he *had been*. No cuts. No bruises. No drugs. *Her Hank.*

For a moment, here at the eye of the storm, Lisa had found a measure of peace. "I don't want to be alone when it happens. Promise me?"

"I promise."

At the sound of these words, the Black-Eyed Man smiled. "Do you

271

understand now, Hank? When it happens, the look on your face, it will be love in its purest form, bared for the world to see. The closest an emotion will ever get to being *tangible* on this Earth. I want that moment for myself. Can't you understand that?"

Enrapt in his own gospel, the man with the hollow eyes continued to speak, raising his arms to the heavens.

Lisa kept her eyes locked on Hank's, ignoring the horror that now entombed them.

Hank made good on his promise. When Melvin drove the knife into Lisa's stomach, Hank never stopped looking into her pale green eyes.

Chapter 57

Everett's question hung in Alejandro's mind. *Father to father, will you help me?*

The conversation about his children had triggered something in him. For years now, he had subdued the thought of his family, pushing it down deep into the dark, ignoring the pain that emanated from his heart every time he thought of his family back in Mexico. He only summoned memories of them when he was at his lowest. Lately, though, he had taken the governor off his thoughts. He thought of them as much and as often as he could. Even pulling out old pictures that he had stowed away in the chest of drawers in his room. He was tired of pretending he didn't miss them. He was tired of sharing a house with that sadist. He was tired of missing the precious years of his son and daughter's growth; he had already missed so much. The first lost tooth. Teaching them how to read. Their first crush. He was tired well beyond his years, sick of it all. Maybe the time had come to journey back home.

Things were already in motion back in his hometown. Maybe this was his chance.

"Please. All I want is my son back." Everett's whisper interrupted his thoughts. "I don't know your name. And I don't know hers. Just untie me and I'll run out the back door."

And go where? Alejandro thought. *She'd have you back here in minutes.* Belle Glade is South Florida's version of a small backwater—isolated and in the middle of nowhere. If the man tried to run back to West Palm, Silvia would track him down easily. And that's assuming he could even get off the property without her knowing.

Images of his wife and children continued to move through his head. Alejandro held on to them, making them stay visible in the window of his mind. He needed them to give him the strength to fight.

Leaning in closer, Everett pleaded with him. Desperate tremors rattled his voice. "Please, man. Father to father. I can't fail him again. I can't. Please. I'll do whatever you want after."

"I want nothing from you 'mano. I understand the power of a father's love."

"Then help me."

I don't know if I have the strength, Alejandro thought. If he went through with this, then he and his family would be on the run for the rest of their lives. They would have to assume aliases, then sneak across the border in New Mexico. The coyote had already been paid, and his wife already had bags packed, just in case the day came. They had hatched the plan in snippets over the last three years. Cobbling it together, piece by piece, speaking to one another on scores of different burner phones. And from what Alejandro could tell, no one here, nor anyone back in his homeland, had caught on. And thank God for that: if those merciless bastards back home had learned of his scheming, they might have killed his wife and children just to make a point.

This might be his only chance. He made up his mind.

"Listen 'mano, here's what we will—"

"You fat motherfucker, are you talking to him?" Even as she insulted him, Silvia was careful not to use his name. They couldn't let their captive know their identities. She stood there, shoulders hunched forward, covered in sweat, eyes bloodshot to hell, full of hate. Clenching her hands into fists, she said, "What in the hell makes you think you can talk to him? You know the rules, you fat fuck. We never talk to them." Her body was a concentrated mortar shell, anxious for the pressure of release.

Alejandro remained silent.

"Answer me. Or I'll make you answer."

Alejandro's eyes alighted on her, not with anger, but with calm resignation. "The man wanted some water, bruja. You got a problem with that?"

"You had to sit on the floor with him to answer a question? You needed to be right beside him to respond to him?"

"No, I had to sit on the floor with him to stand guard. Like you asked, remember? Now if you don't mind, I'm going to get up and get him some water. And you better get back to counting and stacking—sounds like you and your band of freaks really fucked up this time."

Alejandro stood up to get the water, moving to the cabinets that hung down from the ceiling. As he moved to the sink, out of the corner of his eye, he kept checking on Everett.

Silvia moved as if she would return to her labors, but then, changing direction, she walked over to where Everett slumped against the cabinets. She kneeled in front of him and began to rub his head; the same thing she had seen done to Clyde, petting and grooming him, preparing him for slaughter.

Alejandro knew what she was doing.

When he turned, Alejandro saw the glint of afternoon sunlight reflected in the knife she held. She had it out, but hidden behind her back where Everett couldn't see it.

My family, was all he thought when he saw her knife. I want to see *my family.*

Alejandro had watched, firsthand, as she grew into a monster. All the men she brought to the old stash house and then killed in her little room. Some of them because that man with the scars and black eyes ordered her to, and some of them just because she wanted to. She tortured them and then hacked them up. Worse, sometimes she made him help carry the bags. One time when he refused, she pulled her knife and nicked a tag of flesh off his face. Which was quickly overshadowed by the searing pain of her slicing open his forearm. He still had the scar on his arm—a thin angry stream of puckered tissue that ran from his elbow to his wrist. She had branded him that day, causing his hate for her to grow tenfold.

He had wanted to see his family again someday, so he helped her. What else was he to do? Captive, he had witnessed her transformation up close.

He had stood by and kept his mouth closed as the veil of black overlapped her, making the black cast of her shadow and her soul indistinguishable.

What kind of man would your children think you are if you let this man be slaughtered? A man that wants nothing more than to save his son.

Who was he?

Ilk of the Cartel? Was he content to be a quiet instrument of those evil men, who manipulated and killed without thought, disappearing person after person, tearing apart family after family, all in the name of the business?

Who was he?

Those evil men had forced him into servitude. The same men that contracted with the man with the black eyes—a horrible man. He and his sidekick had maimed and killed, time and time again, and there was no end in sight. And this was the same organization that forced him to sit by idly as Silvia sliced throat after throat in her bid to make it to the top of the syndicate.

Who was he?

Was he their pawn? A puppet?

Or was he a man that wanted to look his son and daughter in the eye without a shred of shame?

It wasn't too late to be an example for his boy and girl.

The time had come for Alejandro Mercado to shed his skin.

Silvia moved the knife to Everett's throat and placed its sharp point right on the same spot she had back at the townhouse. She started needling at the black blood that had clotted and dried over the wound, releasing a lazy meridian down his throat.

The captive shrank back, screaming, begging for his life and the life of his son. In supplication, he asked, again and again, his son's whereabouts. He meant them no harm. He had a past, he said. He knew what it was like to live outside of the law. He was no snitch. He just wanted to find Hank and take him home and get him clean.

The man just wanted to take his son home.

It was time to go *home*.

Alejandro pulled out his own knife, which lately he kept in a small sheath on his hip—the leather case hidden in his pants and the hilt of the knife under his shirt. He tiptoed up behind her; she was still crouching down in front of Everett.

He exhaled, pictured his family, then thrust the tip of his blade into Silvia's neck with all the force he could muster. It came out the other side, matted in blood and gristle. Without hesitating, he pulled the knife out. Red gushes poured from both sides of her neck. Leaving no room for error, he steadied her left shoulder, then dragged the knife across her throat, slicing a half-crescent that connected the twin wounds.

Slowly, as if pumped full of a sedative, she stood up and turned toward Alejandro. Horror and revulsion seized his body when he saw the ruin of her throat. Up until now, he had never committed an act of violence this grisly in his entire life. He had helped cover up things after the fact, but had never actually done the deed.

Trying to calm himself, he summoned images of his family into his head. They spun in his mind a beautiful kaleidoscope, reminding him why he had mangled her—it was the only way back to his family. He had to do it. He had to.

She continued to stumble around. The wound opened wider as she moved, a grinning black maw eager to keep spilling its contents. In a futile attempt to stop the torrent, she dropped her knife and put her hands on her throat. Streams of crimson flowed through her fingers like water through cracks in a dam.

With an odd mixture of relief and disgust animating his face, Everett watched her, shifting his body, best he could, to avoid the blood.

Alejandro briefly thought about stabbing her again, but then let go of the idea. She had already lost too much blood. She was finished.

Silvia fell to her knees and looked to Alejandro, wanting desperately to curse him for his cowardice, for stabbing her while she wasn't looking. She gasped and gasped, trying to summon the words. All that came out of her blood-clogged pipes was a wet, crunchy gurgle. It sounded like she had a pint of riverbed mud and gravel in her throat. With every attempt to speak, a gout of dark fluid fell from her mouth. Her too-tight white tank top was a splatter-print of red and black.

She kept on like this for seconds that felt like hours. Choking and hacking. Kneeling in a bath of her own blood. At one point, she took one of her hands away from her throat, trying to reach out for her knife, mere inches away. In slow motion, her benumbed hand flopped in that direction, then went limp. Lifeless, it hung against her side like a dead eel.

In her last moments, her face was not one of weakness, nor of helplessness. She didn't cast her eyes about looking for someone or something to save her.

It wasn't in her to be vulnerable, not even in death, Alejandro thought.

Unrepentant, her eyes brimmed with rage—pure and overflowing, funneled straight up from her rotten heart.

Alejandro walked over to her, after he noticed her bleeding had slowed down. He bent down and looked her in the eyes, offering his final words to her in a low growl: "Your victims are there waiting for you in Hell. They will be with you in the dark."

In response, an amulet of blood seeped out of her mutilated throat. Her body, bereft of its animating force, nothing more than a gore-strewn bag of bones, fell forward to the floor with a concussive thud.

At first, he didn't believe it. He had seen dead people before, much more than he ever cared to remember, in fact. Their eyes had been hollow. Blank.

Not Silvia's.

Even after her death, Silvia's eyes showcased the thing that had come to define her.

Silvia's eyes still held on to her hate.

Chapter 58

In shock, Everett looked at the woman's lifeless body. Her throat was torn into shards, a thick maroon pool surrounded her.

Shaking, he pulled his gaze away, and asked the stocky Hispanic man an obvious question: "What are you going do with her?"

"That is for me to worry about, 'mano. But don't worry, no one will be able to trace it. As much as I hated her and the people we work for, I did learn some things from them."

Everett understood. No one would ever find her body. Burial at sea. Given to the swamp to feed the wildlife. Buried in the corner of some abandoned farmland. One way or another, her body would disappear from the sight of the world. Once it was done, she would never be found.

Alejandro turned to use his knife to cut the plastic ties that bound Everett. He then stepped over to the sink to clean the gore from the knife and wash his hands.

As the man washed off, Everett rubbed his wrists, welcoming the warm feeling of blood flowing through his veins. He stood; in the sink the water had a pinkish hue as it twirled diluted blood to the drain. Taking a moment to appraise his own body, he noticed the flecks of her blood on his shoes and legs. He grabbed a rag next to the sink, wet it, and attempted to clean the stains off. The man didn't seem to mind.

His senses realigned. Adrenaline righted his back and sharpened his thoughts. There was only one thing now: finding Hank. "Where is he?"

For now, Alejandro dodged the question, opting to let this man, a fellow father, get a glimpse of what he was getting himself into. "The men that took him are sadists. They love making people feel pain. That puta"—even now, Alejandro was too cautious to use her name— "and those two freaks call it *art*. I've heard them talk about it. They try to dress their violence up in all these fancy words. But they're just murderers."

"I just want to know where my son is."

"Listen, 'mano," Alejandro turned to face him. "If you go out there, then you need to be ready to kill. They will show you no mercy. And if they capture you, then you will be another one of their experiments. The things they do to people, it is ungodly. I'm telling you, if they grab you and you have the chance, kill yourself and your son before they start in on you."

Everett accepted the advice without comment.

Rather than ask the location again, he decided on a different approach. "Who are the men that took him?"

"One of them seems like an ex-military type. No place to take in society, so he went back to what he does best."

Everett looked to the bloodied corpse on the floor. "What was her role in this whole thing?"

"She started out as a dealer, and then got savvy enough to stay off the street and let other people take the risk. She had a small network running out of Del Ray. Her guys went down all the time for low-level sales. But never her. And she always replaced those that either died or got locked up. She had money coming in hand over fist. They noticed her talents and recruited her."

"Talents?"

"The people that worked for her rarely crossed her, and no one ever tried to rob them. That's because she made an example of the ones that did. Early on, she only took fingers or crippled people. She also did things like scar up their face, so people would know. She liked *living* symbols so other people would know not to fuck with her business. Later on, after *they* took notice of her, that is when she started killing. Once she got the taste for it, she never stopped." Alejandro dried his hands with a paper towel and motioned with his head for Everett to follow him so he could change shirts. During the short walk to the room, Everett offered up his name—even though he pretty much assumed this man already knew it—and in response, the man said Everett could call him Fernando. Everett figured it was probably a fake name, but he didn't care. He kept listening as his new friend laid out the sordid history of their cell. "She started killing men on the side, for pleasure, 'mano, because she liked it. She'd meet them out at bars and clubs, and they'd be back here lazy eyed and sweaty, thinking they were going to get laid. And then she'd take them into her room. She soundproofed the damn thing so no one could hear what she put them through, but I saw some of them after she was done with them. I will never forget what I saw. *Never.*"

God, What had Hank gotten himself into?

"The man, the military one, came by one day while I was counting the month's take. He never said much, but he would always walk around the whole joint before he talked to me, like he was a cop sweeping the place or something. He saw the extra deadbolts on the door and demanded to see what was behind it. He thought maybe we were skimming or doing business on the side and hiding it in there. Silvia didn't hesitate for a second, she let him in the room. He grinned when he saw her room. He *grinned,* 'mano." Alejandro slipped his shirt over his head. "After that, I was low man on the totem pole. I still can't believe she never tried to kill me. I know she thought about it. All I know is that she never thought I'd get the drop on her." There was no pride in the man's face as he spoke of outwitting her. Everett could tell he had taken no pleasure it what happened. He had done it because it was the only way back to his family. He wasn't like her. He didn't rejoice in watching another's vulnerability before death. "Anyway, they will come looking for her soon."

This man seemed so down-to-earth. Without ambition. The type of person that could grow up in a small town, knowing the same people all his life, doing the same thing day after day and still be content. How the hell did he end up tangled in this mess?

The man packed the cash in the bag as he spoke, then moved the bags Silvia had already packed into a stack near the front door. He was planning an escape. All the while, as he provisioned himself to flee, the man never paid any mind to the corpse over in the kitchen. Everett could tell this man had no remorse for killing her. None. Whatever had transpired between the two had blackened this man's view so much that he no longer saw her as another human. She was a monster. And you don't reason with a monster. You don't rehabilitate it. You put it down.

"I know you don't know me. And maybe you don't care. But I'm a good man. I've only worked for these assholes because they threatened my family. And that's why I did what I did." *Fernando* looked to Silvia's body. "To get back to my family. You understand?"

Everett nodded.

"But understand this, too: the men I work for do the things they do in the name of business. Yes, they do awful things to send a message, but it's all in the name of keeping the money flowing in. The man that has your son is not like them." He stopped moving and looked intently at Everett. "He kills because it fulfills him. It's a need for him. You understand?"

Everett wished to God he didn't; but he did know the type of man he was about to confront.

"Once you see his eyes, you'll know what I mean."

"His eyes?"

"They're black. Both of them. All black."

All black. Everett's mind raced back to the tall bald man with the scars and dark eyes that had been looking for Hector.

"He and his little follower take everyone out to the swamp, so no one—"

Everett interrupted. "Do you know where they take them?"

"I've been there only once. I followed them, but they never knew about it." With the pained look of a person confronting dark memories, the man rubbed his black stubble. "And the things I saw in there, they were of the devil. Pieces of people displayed like collector's items. I threw up on the spot."

Without pause, Everett asked, "How do I get there?" The man's warnings had failed to register with Everett. He had to get to Hank.

"Here's how you find him."

Chapter 59

Everett drove down the highway in a beat-up Honda Accord gifted to him by the stocky man from Mexico; it had been stashed in a detached garage out behind the house in Belle Glade. He was driving south, toward the center of the state and the glades. The man had laid it all out for him using real maps (apparently, the Google car had yet to make it out to this particular piece of nowhere); he had showed Everett the route he had taken the one time he was there. The Everglades were further south, most a part of the national park system. The site where they took people was on a piece of private land. Fernando had stayed hidden behind a copse of trees roughly a mile away, necessary because the land was flat for miles, until *they* left the shed—the thing they called the Portal.

Then the man recounted the *why* of following Silvia out there. As leverage, he said, just in case he ever needed to negotiate himself or his family out of trouble. He had been in the game long enough to know that secrets were currency. Their employers back in Mexico didn't know the full scale of what the others did out by the swamp. So perhaps having the information could help him bargain himself or his family out of a bad situation. Thus, he followed her, staying well behind in case she saw his car. That day, when he reached the glades, he had tracked them by the tire prints and, deeper in, by the felled grass. Eventually, this led him to the Portal.

A place he now wished he could wipe from his memory.

When he saw the terrain, he knew there was no way he could drive up unnoticed; he would be totally exposed. So he pulled off into the brush, hid the car, and waited. Hours and hours later, he saw their black SUV leave, kicking up dust as it blew past him, while he hid in the brush; then he went to investigate the rusty structure. His voice faltered at this part, and he had to grab his mouth to keep from vomiting.

It was then that he suggested that Everett approach by boat.

After Fernando left the shed, he had walked around to the back, and saw a small tributary that led back to a bigger stretch of the swamp, which, in turn would take him to a small Glades version of a marina. He showed Everett the system of backwaters and tiny stretches of swamp, all looking like tiny blood-veins sprawled across the map, that finally found its way to the southern Everglades. It'd be at least an hour to the marina by boat, maybe more, depending on the water. No doubt, the swamp was unpredictable; one felled tree could upend the boat. One wrong turn would take you into an entirely different system within the giant swamp. He'd need a special boat, and he'd have to paddle by oar for some stretches, but that was the only way to get there undetected with certainty. The only way.

An image of an airboat had flashed through Everett's mind. It had been years, but there had been a time when he was younger that he could drive one. Back before you needed a special license to fish or drive such a boat. A dirt-stained, overall clad man that owned a ramshackle marina (if you blinked, you'd miss it) had taught him how to drive it. He'd also charged him next to nothing to rent one. Everett used to like to fish from them in the swamp. But that had been years ago.

Everett appreciated the information more than the man would ever know. But all he could think was, *How in the hell am I going to get a boat? Steal it?* That's when the man, after rummaging through is closet and grabbing something, had handed Everett a black bag, the size of a carry on. "Go buy an airboat off one of the country boys at the marina. They won't say no to that much cash." While the man kept talking, Everett had opened the bag. It contained a small pile of cash, a large knife, a burner phone, and most importantly, a black handgun. Then Fernando said if he was able to separate them, to use the knife first, that way he wouldn't alert the other.

Before he left, he asked Fernando if, somehow, he and Hank survived, would the men in Mexico come for them? "No. But they will come for me. The man with the dead eyes and his boy toy haven't finished paying their debt. The Cartel doesn't come for the thief necessarily, they come for the contractor. You see, when money is stolen from the syndicate, those contractors that were responsible for collecting and safe transport don't just pay back the same amount. They have to pay triple: the price of their negligence. That's why Silvia was cleaning out the attic. They were going to have to pretty much send the whole stash to make things right. But that money is never going to make it to Mexico. That money is my severance package." Fernando had laughed heartily. then slapped Everett on his back, telling him Godspeed.

Everett asked him where he was going.

He smiled and said one word. "Home."

Now, Everett drove and drove. Judging by the map, the marina was two hours away.

#

He made short work of buying the boat. The man at the marina, his face and forearms smudged with oil and dirt, gawked at the sight of the two stacks of bills. After giving Everett a hasty tutorial on how to drive the thing, he pushed the boat away from the dock.

From there, Everett entered the rambling network of water. Despite his best efforts, he lost all sense of location. Everything looked the same, an unending expanse of lily pads, felled trees, sawgrass, and muggy bogs with gators' heads cropping up just above the water's surface. At times, the swamp forced him to choose between a right or a left, judging as best as he could by the map to make his way to the proverbial X the man drew on it. All the while his body radiated with the anxiety of not knowing what was happening to his son. Or worse, not knowing what had already happened to him.

And Everett wasn't alone out here in the swamp. Impending doom was riding shotgun, smiling at him with rotten, black teeth.

To his surprise, within the first ten or so hours, he passed a broken-down shed just off the bank on a skinny run of the swamp. He panicked and lay down in the boat, fearing he had already been spotted. Aping the cops and soldiers he had seen in movies, he slipped onto the bank, army-crawled over the terrain, laden with soggy mud and felled tall grass, and then put his back against the shed. He never thought to look for a car—the absence of it should have been a dead giveaway that no one was there. Heart pounding, he popped out in the threshold of the door, gun drawn, and yelled at a stack of rusted metal and moss-bitten wood. Shrugging his shoulders, he returned to the boat, cried, and then continued.

#

He slept in a small cul-de-sac the first night. The moon gave off enough light that he could have read if he had had a book. He ate three bags of chips for dinner; the only food he'd brought. Well, except the box of mini donuts he bought at the marina too. He wouldn't last long in this heat, eating only junk food. On the brighter side, he'd had the foresight to buy a case of water from the bait shop owned by the man that sold him the boat.

#

The next day held much of the same.

Lost again in the maze. Dehydrated and exhausted.

To boot, the wound on his throat kept itching as it began healing. Flies kept alighting on it too. Batting them away had become one of his past-times. And to cap it all off, the phone Fernando had given him had died. So much for calling for help.

He tried to use the map to make sense of the bends and unpredictable turns. Dead end after dead end. Under the unforgiving heat of the sun, it all blended together, an unending labyrinth of green and brown. Being a stranger to the glades, Everett couldn't distinguish its nuances. Most frustrating to him, he could see where he needed to end up, but the twists and turns of the water kept taking him further away from the X.

Impending doom grinned at him from the passenger seat. Then it gave Everett the middle finger.

Late in the afternoon, he saw another decrepit structure that could be *it*. He rode his adrenaline high right up to the structure, looked in and again, he was disappointed.

This time, he didn't even get out of the boat. He looked for a car—there was none to be found—then he angled the boat so he could see inside. This one didn't even have any scrap; it was empty. Sad and forgotten, left to deteriorate under the hard press of the humidity.

Tired and hungry, he let the boat edge up into the long grass topped with foxtails, in front of the empty shed. The sun had started to recede. He noticed he had only a few bottles of water left, a bag of chips, and a half of a donut.

To no avail, he tried not to think of what they were doing to Hank. The man had said *human remains*. At the time, his mind had shielded him from the reality of the words. Now it sank in.

The dark thoughts made him sob. One after another the visions came, each worse than the last, multiplying the horror and causing him to heave. He rocked back and forth, trying to rattle the pictures out of his mind.

Night came.

Reeling from the despair that had augured deep into him, he decided to stay put. Maybe he would finally choose the right vein of the mire tomorrow.

Just before he drifted off to sleep, he noticed that decrepit fucker, doom, was laughing at him, saying in a cheap Southern drawl from between blackened teeth: *Good luck getting it right tomorrow ol' buddy. I'm sure Hank's just fine.*

#

Another day lost in the maze. More tears. More sweat. And a world-class sunburn that left blisters popping up all over his body like inverted dunes and his lips as cracked and dry as desert hardpan. Delirium had set in too. Well, truth be told, it had already reached its claws into him yesterday. That sense of doom he felt as he left the marina had taken human form; it was sitting right next to him now as he maneuvered the boat: a cynical, quick-witted junkie with black teeth, wearing a brown-stained tank top and tattered blue pants, letting his bare sore-ridden feet rest on the dash.

At this rate, Everett wasn't going to be able to last much longer out here.

But then, finally, when evening came, the lazy purple-pink light of dusk lit the way to a small building with a tin roof. In that same grating drawl, the junkie next to him whispered that it was just a mirage, a hallucination induced by dehydration. *Good luck, ol' buddy. Good luck.* As he looked at the structure, hope and adrenaline began to sluice through his veins and Everett told that shoeless hanger-on to shut the fuck up.

He had long since cut the large fan mounted on the back of the boat. Fighting off his bone-deep fatigue, he paddled up to the back of the small structure. It was slow going; his arms felt like wet noodles. The steady whir of a generator masked any noise he made. In front of the small building, there was nothing but short grass for acres.

Though the area surrounding the structure was dark, Everett could see light through the cracks. As he approached the bank, he saw that the inside was lit up like a Christmas tree, filled to the brim with yellow lights.

He floated closer and drew to a stop, using a waist-high embankment with a large tree as cover.

Now what? Wait?

Try and separate them. As with so much of the advice Everett had received during his more than five decades on the planet, easier said than done.

He surveyed the small building, trying to see if there was more than one way in. The thing reminded him of the ramshackle sheds that housed broken down tractors and hollowed out cars back in his hometown. After scanning the place, he was convinced there was a single entrance. He took a moment to come up with a plan.

Ideas were in short supply. Not fear, anxiety, and stress though—he had those in spades. He was standing at the small prow of the wind boat, refusing to look back at his black-toothed passenger. That thing was all his mind's worst fears personified, the doomsayer that he knew in his heart wasn't real, but that his addled mind had conjured up in the wake of overwhelming stress and dehydration. He had to come up with something. Hank's life depended on it.

His mind jumped to the heroes of his youth. Nostalgically, he thought of all the old westerns he watched when he was growing up. Like John Wayne or Clint Eastwood, he could just walk in and let the saloon doors seesaw back and forth behind him—and start shooting before his nemeses could even draw their six-shooters.

Over the hum of the generator, he heard a shriek: female, no doubt, someone wracked in horrible pain. He heard the woman give off a flurry of guttural sounds; her body's response to the agony that besieged it. Though he never heard her beg for mercy. No cries to her captor to stop the abuse among the screams. The sound cut right through him.

Horror and terror reached into him with iron hands, squeezing his heart and stomach to the point of bursting. He recognized the voice that emitted those haunting wails—it was Lisa.

And then he heard his son's voice, begging for them to stop.

He reached for the small black bag at his feet and removed its contents. Under the setting sun, the knife looked almost gray as he surveyed it and placed it back in its leather sheath; he stuffed the blade into his pocket. Then he double-checked to make sure the gun was loaded. It was a semi-automatic, more advanced than the revolvers in the westerns of old, so he could just keep pulling the trigger until he ran out of bullets.

In his mind's eye, he ran through it. He would burst in and shoot the one closest to him first. Two bullets for him, then shift to the next one. No hesitation. And then he would stand over them and finish the job: one to the head for each. Suffering under the delusional touch of exhaustion, he saw it playing out smoothly, unfolding in only seconds. In the end, he knew better. It would be messy. Bloody and ugly.

Then he remembered. *Separate them.*

The Christmas lights.

Chapter 60

Gun in hand, he scurried up the bank and bear-crawled to the orange generator. He found the kill switch.

Everett said a short prayer as he reached for it. In the moment, under immense pressure, it felt natural. The decades sloughed away, and he was a boy again, sitting in the chapel of United Methodist in downtown Hermitage. As he said the prayer, he saw the rich maroon carpet that lined the whole church. And he saw the giant stained-glass windows that loomed over the congregation. As a boy, he could gaze up and move his head back and forth slowly, watching the light change colors as he changed the angle of his view. Sometimes, he would spin his eyes in circles to make the images on the windows turn like a kaleidoscope. He had always thought that something as beautiful as those windows had to have some connection to God. No human was capable of creating something that beautiful on their own.

Just before he touched the metal switch, that's what he saw inside his mind: a kaleidoscope of Christ, spinning, lit by the crisp Alabama sunlight.

Christ in colors.

He pulled the lever.

\#

The bright sheen of the white lights disappeared in a flicker. Specs of red still burned on Hank's retinas when he closed his eyes.

The Black-Eyed Man looked to the ceiling, jerking his head back and forth. He didn't even look at Melvin when he spoke. His frustration was evident. "Go, Melvin. See what ails our generator."

Intently, Melvin shot out the door.

For a moment, the horror had stopped. Hank's pained gaze was drawn back to Lisa, whose screams had died down to a low, steady moan. The hilt of Melvin's knife protruded from her belly like an ugly tumor. With the command of a surgeon, Melvin had stabbed her twice, each stroke carried out with careful precision. Maybe he was trying to avoid the major organs. Maybe he wanted to keep her alive to prolong the torture. He didn't know. The wounds were deep, however; if he had made a mistake, off a millimeter in either direction, then she would bleed out in this hellhole.

Their eyes met. For a moment, it was like they weren't trapped here, as if they had been transported to the precipice of eternity, where they could be alone and forgotten. Despite her agony, Lisa's mouth cracked into a small grin.

She was still with him, and he with her. Nothing else mattered.

#

Melvin slowed his pace and took a quick survey of the land around him. Whenever he entered a new setting, he always searched for things that could make him vulnerable. The sun had set, but there was still enough of an afterglow that he could make out his surroundings. He felt a wave of relief: no one else but him, his boss, and the two hapless passengers they were about to dispatch into the great beyond.

Turning his back to the small vein of water that led up to the back of the shed, he bent over and clicked the generator back on.

When the knife went into his back—scraping past his spine as it separated his flesh and sinew—it felt cold, though the sensation didn't last long. What followed was interminable heat, like someone had lit a brushfire inside of him.

#

Everett saw the same vision of the church of his childhood, the one he had seen only moments before. Said the same prayer. And before he leapt up over the edge of the bank, saw the same thing: Kaleidoscope Jesus.

At first, Everett crept over the wet, muddy ground on his tiptoes, looking like a drunk fox. He would never make it to the tall man before he got back up. He sped up to a run, to close the distance in time.

As he ran, he heard the generator roar on and saw the lights of the shed spring back to life. Following a split-second cry from his instincts, he decided against the gun—too worried the man inside the shed would hear the blast—and tucked it into his waistband. Without a clue what he was doing, he freed the knife from its small sheath. He raised it over his head with both hands and drove it as hard as he could into the crouched man's lower back, like he was driving a shovel into the ground. He felt it catch on the man's spine, as if he had nicked the root of a tree, before something gave way and it sank deep into the man's body.

The man cried out in pain, but the hum of the generator was louder.

In shock, trying to think through his next move, Everett tried to wrench the knife free. As he twisted the heft, trying to dislodge it from the man's back, his opponent spun around and drove his own knife into Everett's gut, then twisted—right then left, right then left. Everett hadn't seen him grab the serrated tactical knife from a holder on his ankle. He had seen, however, that a black rectangle fell from the man's pocket—a phone—and in his haste to puncture Everett, he had stomped on it—driving it down in a puddle and cracking the screen.

Both men staggered, each using the other for balance. Despite the jolt of shock from the wound, Everett held tight to his knife. It had come free in his hand when the man spun to stab him. Face to face now, Everett recognized the beard and the eyes: the man from the restaurant, who had stood off behind his boss, waiting and watching.

For the moment, the adrenaline masked the pain of his wound and Everett hoisted him up by the shoulders. The man tried to raise the knife to stab Everett again, but his hand moved like it was on a delay, the labored motions of a person stranded in below-freezing weather. Everett saw the knife was slipping from his hand—clumsy fingers fumbled over the handle.

Seizing on his adversary's weakness, Everett thrust his knife forward again, deep into the pit between his stomach and chest. A bulb of blood burst from his mouth and ran down his chin like melted red sealing wax.

Hands shaking, Everett held the knife in place, but soon realized that the weapon was the only thing keeping *his* body upright. He drew the blade out—a wet plunging sound followed with it, and the man fell to the ground.

Everett moved around him and vomited a hail of bile and blood, his right hand tightly clutched around the knife's handle, and his left keeping the bric-a-brac of his torso from spilling out.

#

Unable to move or feel his limbs, Melvin lay still on the blood-drenched ground.

He thought of the gun he had left sitting on the side shelf, among some of the tools he had used to hurt people. The gun that could have saved him. His last thought: *Too late now.*

Melvin.

Man from nowhere.

Child of nothing.

Bound for Hell.

Chapter 61

A few blessed moments of silence had given way to more of the Black-Eyed Man's nonsense.

"When Melvin comes back in, we will continue. I hope by now that both of you see the purpose in what we're doing. If nothing else, I know that you, Hank, an artist yourself, can see the beauty in what I aim to accomplish. That's all this is: my need to create something beautiful outside of myself. A living legacy. Perhaps you realize that now."

Through the marks of red that tattooed his eyes, Hank continued to steal looks at Lisa, trying hard not to look at the knife jutting from her gut.

The man droned on.

Hank had long since stopped trying to make sense of this man's misguided edicts. Whatever this man answered to—God, the deranged voice in his head, the Cosmos—had failed to make him capable of responding to the dictates of human reason. His philosophy was *his* and his alone: mired in contradictions, lacking a singular purpose, and possessing a twisted harmony only he understood. The greater meaning of his craft, if such a thing existed, wasn't for Hank to understand.

That, or the man was just plumb-fucking crazy.

Hank had finally realized that the *why* behind this man wasn't for him to know. The *why* belonged to the *It* way up there hidden behind the moon and the stars.

"Now, enough with the suspense... Where is—" He turned to find his right hand. It wasn't like Melvin to dawdle. The lights were on, and he could hear the generator running again, so why hadn't Melvin come back?

Under the bright cloud of lights dangling from the ceiling, he moved toward the door.

#

Twilight had faded. Now the sky was a starless black. The only light for miles was the yellow haze that bled through the myriad cracks lining the metal structure.

Pain colored every aspect of Everett's world. He knew he needed to get in there, but he had spent the last moments trying to coach himself to remove the knife from his body. He had settled on a ripping-off-the-band-aid approach: in one quick motion, pull it straight free. But every time he rested his hand on the hilt to start, starbursts of pain exploded through his midsection.

After several moments, he eased the blade out, little bits at a time, as if he were unscrewing it from himself. Blood didn't spray out when the knife was free of him, but it came nevertheless, an oozing stream that gained volume with each passing second.

Hobbling slowly, doing his damnedest to keep his vital pieces from falling onto the wet mud, Everett moved to the door. He prayed that the other man inside, the one with the awful eyes, didn't have a gun. He wouldn't be able to close the space in time if the tall man had a pistol.

At the threshold of the door, he took a breath and pressed his guts back into his skin. Moonlight allowed him to see the rich trail of blood extending back to where he had left Melvin for dead. The sight of it made him feel empty and scared. But this was no time to despair. That could come later, if at all.

Hank and Lisa's screams from earlier rang out again in his mind, a doomsday bell to remind him why he was there, sharpening his instincts, helping him remember he had a gun. Using the corrugated metal as a ballast, he leaned back and took the gun from his waistband. He tossed the blood-splattered knife off into the brush.

With yet another prayer to Kaleidoscope Jesus, he pushed off the jamb to go inside.

Plush black eyes stopped him in his tracks.

Face to face for the first time since that day at the Hickory.

"His father?" A blend of subdued surprise and mourning, the words floated out in a low moan. The monster was weaponless and totally exposed. Everett had the advantage.

Before the man said another word, Everett squeezed off two rounds. Dark blood came out of the man's torso like freshly tapped oil. His hands clutched his stomach as he stumbled backwards into the Portal. Still holding himself together, Everett went inside.

Relief briefly blotted out his pain, as Everett watched the man fall in a heap, grasping and feeling of his wounds. Every time the man flinched or drew breath, a squirt of blood burped out of his gut.

His black eyes said nothing of his shock and surprise at what had just happened. His mouth, however, was held taut in fear and amazement; he was clearly scared, but there was more to the clench of his jaw—the man was in utter disbelief. Even without the benefit of being able to read the man's eyes, the rest of his face said it all: this wasn't the way this was supposed to happen.

Everett turned to Hank, still trying to keep his insides from falling out.

He saw his son: black holes spread in random constellations across his body, his face was a puffy mass of swollen flesh, and his left leg looked like it had been mangled in a bear trap. Everett struggled to remember if it was the same leg that had been injured in the car wreck. He believed that it wasn't. Which meant that both of Hank's legs were shot now. He'd probably never be able to play again. Something that didn't matter a whole helluva lot right now, but the thought came, nonetheless.

He saw Lisa, the long handle of a knife sticking out from her belly and flaps of skin on her forearm splayed open like the pages of a book.

Even so, he smiled: they were both still alive.

The tears came later, once he got close enough to behold the true measure of the pain his son and Lisa had endured.

They had survived Hell.

#

Struggling to stay upright, Everett swayed as he reached out to his son. He still had one hand firmly clutched to his torso, fearing what would happen if he let go, as if removing his hand meant immediate death. Hank's face was scratched and gnarled, covered in open gashes and wounds. For the moment, however, the wounds and the refuse staining his son's eyes, as horrible as they looked, didn't matter.

All that mattered was his son was alive.

"Dad. I can't believe—"

"I know."

"How did you..." Everett's presence, at least temporarily, had revitalized Hank's speech. He sounded like himself again.

"Doesn't matter. I found you, that's all that—" Everett's legs faltered and he tumbled to the ground. The blood loss was taking a toll, making him feel weightless.

What he wouldn't give to have the power to mend himself back together so his son wouldn't have to see him vulnerable and weak like this—every father's worst fear. It should be something a son can never quite imagine: their dad's mortality.

"Everett, we need you to cut us free and then we can help you," Lisa said.

Everett continued to roll on the ground in mind-blinding pain. Thoughts had ceased. Agony was all that remained.

"Everett, please. We need you."

"Dad. Dad... Dad!" That word had unique power. He still remembered the first time he heard Hank say it clearly. Hank was only three years old, and the doctor had already told Everett that Hank might be experiencing a speech delay. But the doc assured him he would talk when he was ready; some babies just started later than others. Everything up until that point had been gibberish and indecipherable vowel-moans. They were out in the half-acre or so of grass behind the Hickory. The smokehouse, back in the early days, had been much smaller, a cinderblock structure that had been built on the cheap. At the time, Alice had been inside, yelling at some of the new prep cooks, and Everett was busy checking the temps on the butts to make sure they could cover that night's catering order. Hank was out back bouncing around, moving in zigzags, searching the property for every wildflower he could find. When he was satisfied with the lot he had clumped together in his hand, he ran up to Everett and tapped his hand; Everett opened it wide. Hank dropped the smudged flowers into his palm and said a magical word: Daaa-ddy.

"Dad!" That word, and all its beautiful forms, still carried power. And all these years later it was still enough to get him moving, despite the gaping hole in his center.

He propped himself up on his knees. Wobbly, and sweating buckets, he coughed and hacked out a chunk of bloody gristle from his mouth. He then swiveled his head slowly, searching for his knife, then remembered he had discarded it outside. Looking to his left, Everett saw the gallery of taxidermied flesh on the wall, all manner of twisted shapes and forms. He used one of these hellish trophies as a handle to pull himself up, wincing and grunting the whole way. Then he told them to hold on, as he stumbled, like a drunk deep into a bender, back outside to retrieve the knife. In a series of sloshing steps, he returned to Hank and started to cut the zip-ties. He was making poor work of it. "Dad. Dad. Just do the ones on my arms, so I can cut the rest." He did as he was told.

Soon Hank was free.

Everett fell back onto the ground in a tumble as soon as he saw Hank's arms moving around. Though it took many agonizing seconds to accomplish, he shimmied his body up against the wall of the shed, resting his back against it. Using both of his hands to batten down his wound, he was careful to keep clocking the Black-Eyed Man on the opposite side, also leaning against the wall, still close to the door. The man seemed like he was finished, but it was hard to be sure.

With a limp like he was dragging a dead tree branch, Hank crossed to Lisa, wincing, trying to ignore the pain; he pressed forward and cut the rest of the ties.

Once she was free, he kissed her on the forehead and hugged her head to his chest, being careful not to touch the handle that stuck almost straight out.

"Baby, what are we going to do about the knife?" Hank asked.

Everett heard it and grunted out, "Leave it in. You have to leave it in." Everett was no doctor, and truth be told, he was calling on his knowledge from years of watching action movies. And right now, maybe he was wishing he had done the same. Though, in the end, he knew his wound was different. The man had ripped the blade side to side, ensuring the hole was beyond suture. Lisa's wound looked to be the result of a single stab. Leaving it might be just the thing to keep her alive.

They both heard Everett. After quickly looking at him, Lisa looked back at Hank and said, "Leave it in."

"I told you that Melvin and I were students of anatomy. We are precise in all endeavors, young Hank. Did you think we aimed to kill her with the first stroke?" Despite his wounds, the Black-Eyed Man's words still carried vitality. But it was evident he couldn't move.

"Stay in the chair for now. I need to help Dad."

Hank turned to his father, surrounded by ounces of dark blood. Everett's eyes kept darting over to Hank's torturer on the opposite side of the shed. "Go search him first."

Hank followed his father's order without question. He hobbled over to the man, who slumped only a few feet away. Everett kept his eye on his son.

"Ahh... young Hank, nice for us to be so close again." Slow and measured, the voice was oily. "I don't have any weapons. Take my word for it." Scarlet drops leaked out of the Black-Eyed Man's smile. "What do we have if we can't trust one another?"

Ignoring him, Hank put his weight on his right leg and lowered himself to pat down his former captor's pockets. He ran his hands down the legs of his pants and even reached behind him and felt around his lower back for good measure. Nothing. The man was defenseless.

Hank limped back over. "Dad, we need to get you help." Hank put his hands on top of his father's and pressed down with him. "Do you have a phone?"

Everett thought of the burner phone Alejandro had given to him. Useless now. "It's on the boat, dead."

"What about that guy out there?" Hank's head nodded towards the door. "He has a phone. I saw him using it. I can go—"

Everett remembered another stroke of bad lack. "No, son, no... his phone is fucked, trust me." He pictured it in a brown puddle of swamp water, its screen cracked. "Besides, even if you called, I wouldn't make it to the hospital, son. Take them forever to find this place. Y'all are better off driving out of here." Everett had accepted what was coming. He hoped that, soon, Hank would too.

"Don't talk like that. Lisa and I can help you to your car—"

"God, look at you, Hank. Your leg is banged to shit. You can't carry me, and neither can she, for God's sake."

Every word hurt, but he knew he had to continue. This would be his last chance to tell Hank the truth.

For the time being, Lisa turned one of the metal chairs toward Everett and Hank and eased herself into it. She was right next to Hank, within arm's reach. Scratching at the hilt of the knife as if it were a bug bite, she looked at them. Hank sat down to be near his father, placing his back against the wall so they could be eye to eye.

"This is it for me, son, and I'm okay with that. I spent the first half of my life chasin' the devil and I was damn lucky to make it this far." The pain abided with every breath, every word. "You're a good kid, Hank. Always have been. You were sensitive as a boy—cried a lot—and got picked on by some of the other kids." Between labored breaths, Everett kept on. "Alice was always trying to get me to toughen you up. Sometimes, you needed to, but others... it was just fine. From sensitivity came compassion; you always had a good mind for others."

"Dad, I ... uh—"

He could see the guilt welling up in his son's eyes. "I've been there, son. I know you've done some bad things."

"But it's not just these guys we robbed, it's—"

"I know more than you think. I went looking for you and I stumbled on some of the people you robbed. The woman with the scars on her face..."

Hank looked dumbfounded. For a moment, Everett felt Hank's hands lighten, releasing some pressure, and with it came more blood. Everett saw Hank notice the red flow out of the corner of his eye; he quickly placed his hands back on top of Everett's; the pressure returned, setting off a fresh blast of pain. Taking a moment, he did his best to navigate the shock, then said, "I went back to your place. When I got there, this lady was there looking for you. Walked right into her hands. God, she was awful." Everett stopped talking but his mind kept running. He saw the blood spurt from her throat again. And he saw the look of unalloyed hate that had been in her eyes as she died. She died in a fit of rage—overcome with anger, leaving the world clawing and spitting.

That's not how he would go. He would go in peace.

"She took me to their stash house—a man there helped me. Told me how much you took and that you... had robbed the Cartel."

"Dad. I—"

Accepting this was it had lent a steadiness to Everett's voice. It wasn't his normal tone, but it certainly wasn't the shaky last words of an old man either. "Save it, bud. From one sinner to another, you can make it past this shit. I know you've done bad, Hank, but I also know this: I'm willing to bet my last few seconds on Earth that you haven't hurt a single soul outside of the drug world." Hank softened a bit in the face and shoulders, letting Everett know he was right. "They chose to be a part of the game, just like you. The rules are different once you're a player in that world."

Everett had said too much.

With his hands and his son's still pressed to his middle, he tilted to the side to hack up some blood and bile. He had to blink twice to make sure he was really seeing what lay on the dirt. He was no student of biology, but he could have sworn that a chunk of his lung was now matted to the dirt floor. Messy tendrils of vomit clung to his chin.

Everett didn't have much longer—and Hank and Lisa needed to get a hospital. It was time to stop being scared of his ultimate responsibility. He had to tell his son the naked truth. "You don't have to let your sins define you, Hank. You can walk away from it, son. Don't let the shadows of what you did drag you down into the dark. If you do, then you'll be..." A fit of coughing halted Everett's words. "You're a good kid. I know *who* you are. I saw it in you from the moment I looked at you in your mom's house."

Hank's face crumpled in confusion. "...Mom's house?"

Everett sucked in a ragged breath and accepted that this was it: the moment he had been dreading for more than three decades.

Time to let the old ghosts go free.

"Back in Hermitage, it was the first place I saw you. Picked you right up and just stared at you. I still don't know how long she had left you there, but it didn't seem to faze you any. Your eyes were as bright as the sun. You were all smiles. I grabbed you up and we took off." Everett's voice still had a steadiness that belied his condition.

"Where was she?" Everett could see Hank needed to hear the words—whatever their shape or cast—from his father.

"She was already dead. Shot by a piece of shit drug dealer me and my band of idiots had just robbed. Booth Sheridan was the guy's name. Biggest dealer in Hermitage County, we went in there to take everything. I told you I understand the mess you're in better than you think." Groaning, Everett moved to adjust himself, so he could breathe easier as he talked. He felt more blood pour out and dampen his legs. He decided it best not to look down. "None of my guys made it out."

"What about Mom?" The words shot out of Hank.

"She was there, sitting on the couch when we came in."

"What was she doing there?" Hank sounded like a frightened kid.

"Drugs, son. She needed drugs." Everett allowed a small moment for the sting to settle. "Before I left to come to you, I was with her."

Small tears dotted Hank's swollen face, almost invisible among the dried blood and bruises. "Did y'all talk at all? Did she say anything to you?"

"Yes. She told me I was your father. Up until then, I had no idea."

"Wait. What?"

Everett winced, not from the pain this time, but from the innocent hurt in his boy's voice. "I'm sorry, bud. I didn't know. She and I weren't really together. We met at a party one night and... We both had a lot of problems. But you came out of it, the best thing that ever happened to me."

"You really didn't know her at all."

"I'm so sorry, son. I didn't know what to do. What happened between us... just happened, I never had time to get to know her. But that's why I grabbed you those records. I thought it might be a way for you to, I don't know..."

"Find her through the music."

Lisa looked at Hank with approval and a wan smile.

"Exactly. I wish I had known her, Hank. I really do." Looking shellshocked, Hank drew his hands back. His mouth hung open and even though his eyes were swollen near-shut, Everett could see the truth had frozen them in place. Then, suddenly, Hank looked focused. Imbued with a singular purpose.

Hank asked a simple question. "How did she die?"

Everett gritted his teeth. "Booth wasn't dead. He aimed for me... got her instead."

"Where did the bullet hit her?"

"Hank, you don't want to—"

"Where did it hit her?" Everett saw Hank's gaunt arms go taut as copper coils. Some of the black scabs dotting his arms cracked open from the strain, crying black teardrops.

"In the head, son. In the head."

"What... what were her last words?"

Slowly and awkwardly, Lisa reached out and put her hand on his shoulder. She didn't speak. Sometimes being there is all that you can do.

"After she told me I was your dad, she told me to get over to her house and protect you. She told me that I needed to be a father now." Everett still heard her voice in his head as he repeated her words. Facing her mortality had erased everything but April's maternal instinct, and that is what she held onto in her final moments—being a mother to her son in any way she could. Telling Everett the truth, telling him to get to his son and shield him from harm, that was her final act. "And then, well, then she died." Everett thought Hank might say something, but he remained silent.

"I grabbed the bag of cash, got my sorry self to her house, and I found you." A smile broke across Everett's face. "I looked down and saw you, with those blue eyes... and I just... everything in my world was so ugly, and you were beautiful, not a scratch on you. I looked at you and I wanted to hold onto that beauty as long as I could. You were everything my life wasn't. You gave me a reason to live, Hank."

Everett paused and smiled at his son, hoping to God that Hank didn't hate him, hoping that his son, in time, could find a way to forgive him.

"I grabbed you up, and with the money I'd taken, we blew town." Everett gasped, still clutching his bloody stomach. "I knew that it was me, my decision, that caused your mother to die. She didn't deserve what she got. I'm sorry, Hank. I'm just so sorry."

Everett was mumbling now, apologizing through the tears and blood, begging his only child for absolution.

Hank's eyes, the same blue that hypnotized Everett all those years ago, showed that he was confused and scared. What should he say? What did he feel?

Finally, after long, punishing seconds where he refused to look at Everett, Hank turned to him. Everett saw recognition had dawned in his boy's eyes, carrying with it a sense of doom. This was their last moment together.

Hank reached out and put his hand on his dad's shoulder, just as Lisa had done for him a moment ago.

A simple touch. Perhaps that's all you can do when a person you love sits broken before you. There were no words.

All that was right.

All that was left.

Was simply *being there.*

Everett felt Hank's touch; his body flooded with relief. Hank may not be ready to forgive him, but he still loved him. He could carry that much with him when he laid down to die.

"We need to get you out of here, Dad." This time, Everett didn't respond. "Dad. I'm not leaving you here to die in this place."

"Where it happens makes no difference, son. It's going to happen no matter where I am."

"No. You're coming with us."

"You need every bit of energy you've got to get you and Lisa to a hospital. Besides, son, I wouldn't even make it to the car. Y'all need to go. Lisa's got to get help." None of them looked at the knife again. They all knew where it was lodged.

"Dad... I..." This time, it was Hank that wept.

"I know, bud."

"These guys I'm into it for—they will hunt us down. They will never—"

"You'll need to leave south Florida, but they shouldn't be coming for you." Not comprehending, Hank looked at his father.

"The man that helped me find you, he said that they will come for him. 'Cause it was him and Black-Eyes over there on the hook for the debt. You see, don't you? The bosses, the *real* ones, don't know about the robbery." Everett saw relief in Hank's eyes. "Soon enough they will know a shitload of cash missing. But they will include the loss from what you stole with the money that just got taken by the guy that helped me. It's like new snow covering your tracks. But just to be—"

"Dad, stop talking. Your body can't handle it."

Somehow, Everett's lungs once again found purchase. "You still get out of Florida. Just to be safe." Instinctually, Everett looked to the Black-Eyed Man, curious if he'd heard his warning. The man was motionless. A sad sack of flesh.

Hank was still with him. His revelation had failed to break his son's loyalty. Everett's recognition of this simple fact gave him the courage to commit his last act as a father: he clasped Hank's left forearm, and cradled it in his hand. Even through the dried blood, scratches, and tattoos, some of Hank's track marks were still visible. Lightly, Everett brushed the scars with his finger and looked at him.

"Your mother and I gave this *thing* to you. But this isn't who you are, Hank. *I know who you are.*" Everett looked at Lisa, pale, smeared with dirt, her opened forearm still seeping. The smallest flinch had been causing her face to contort in a rictus of anguish; he had even heard her grinding her teeth into dust, maybe to distract herself, maybe because she couldn't help it. "She knows who you are. She loves the good part of you. Don't take that from her."

For a brief second, Lisa smiled, her pale skin and green eyes as luminescent as the yellow Christmas lights hanging above.

"You promise me you'll get clean, one way or another. You promise me."

"I promise."

"Now, give me a moment here to say goodbye to my future daughter-in-law."

With the awkward mechanics of a geriatric, Hank heaved himself up onto unsteady legs and hobbled a few feet away—closer to the door, and closer to his dying torturer.

Grimacing, and lowering her hands from her stomach, afraid to touch the butt of the knife, Lisa stood up and moved close to Everett. Every movement was hell.

"You remember what I told you that night in the kitchen? Not about Booth's house. There was more, remember?"

"Of course."

"Tell him what I told you. It should come from you." Everett offered no further explanation as to why. "He's lost in the dark without you. And if he needs to be angry at me down the road, you let him. If he needs to hate me—"

"Stop. You don't need to—"

"I'm sorry for what my boy put you through."

Quivering like a cymbal, Everett raised his free hand up to Lisa. He regretted that he wouldn't get to see her come through the restaurant as his daughter-in-law, maybe with a disheveled grandson or daughter in tow. Those would have been nice years, watching Hank and Lisa buy a home, raise a family. "I'm sorry, darling. I'm so sorry that you got caught up in all this."

Tears welled in her eyes. "You're a good man, Everett Grant."

She kissed his hand. And then she said goodbye.

"Hey. Take these," Everett said.

Lisa paused.

Everett used his free hand to clumsily bring the thin lanyard that held his brown-framed glasses over his head. He handed them over to her. "A little something for you and Hank to remember me by."

Chapter 62

S he had decided, as she exited—as slow and awkward as that would be—not to say a word to the Black-Eyed Man, no matter what. She refused to let him goad her into any response. The only benediction she had for him was one of hate; but she wouldn't speak such poison. She would survive and forget him, because that was the way to hurt him the most—to forget. To kill his legacy.

Hank staggered over to his father.

"Time for you to go."

He knew there was no swaying his father. And truthfully, in his state, he doubted whether he could get his dad off the ground.

Hank knew there was an SUV out there. He just needed to get the keys off the dead man outside.

Hank kept his eyes on his father's face; he didn't want to look down at the black and red hole cored out of his torso. Everett's face showed no fear, no vulnerability; it showed a man that had made peace with the inevitability of the end.

Nauseous, Hank bent down, blinking against the white star flashes that popped up from the pain, and wrapped his arms around his father. How long they stayed like that, he would never be able to tell. He held the man that had always been there for him; it was as if time and space evaporated. He would recall the moment countless times later in life, as he sat and thought about his father and the improbable journey his dad took to save him.

Hank straightened up and walked stiffly toward the open door, putting all his weight on his right leg. He didn't see Lisa; she must have already slipped outside into the night.

At the door, Hank turned to his father, one last goodb— "I see you're off now, young Hank." The man had not even tried to engage Lisa. Hank was not so lucky. "A pity that we couldn't consummate the art we began together."

Under the lights, Hank saw sweat dripping off the man's ropey scars, beads of it running through the spaces between the pulpy flesh like water through the tributaries of the glades. His voice was still sludgy, and it still had that unexpected lilt of a sophisticate overlayed on top, but he was sweating and wheezing and coughing and best of all—he was fucking dying. "You're sick." Hank spat the words like so much acid.

"Aren't we all?"

"No. Not like you. Whatever is in you, it's a sickness."

"I've never been trapped by my mortal coil, unlike so many others. I stole and killed and remade people into whatever I wanted them to be. I never feared my fellow man and I never feared God's retribution. I lived free. How many of you have ever dared to live free?"

He took one last look at the man's blank eyes, not out of want, but out of morbid fascination. Hank knew he would never again view something so other-worldly on a fellow human.

"Fare-thee-well, young Hank. I will be waiting for you out in the black."

Hank turned from the Black-Eyed Man without a response. He looked back at his father one last time.

Through the tears and the snot and the dried blood, he said, "Bye, Dad. I love you." The softness of his tone surprised him. He had sounded like he did when he was a kid.

"I love you too, son." Hank hung his head and took another step. "Hank!" He turned back to his dad. "You won't be out there lost in the dark. Alice and I will be waiting at the restaurant, at the table in the back. Dinner will be ready. We'll be waiting for you, bud."

Hank smiled at his father, and then he limped out, using the door frame to steady himself. Melvin's body lay a few feet from the wall of the shed.

He saw that Lisa had made it to the car; she stood, leaning against it, waiting by the passenger door. He would have to find the strength to hoist her up into the seat.

Putting any extra weight on his injured leg was out of the question. He hopped toward the embankment and began to look for a walking stick. As a kid, when Everett would take him to Big Cypress National Park, he would always leave the trail and beckon Hank to come along.

"To hike, son, you always need a good walking stick. It should come about up to your shoulder." Then he would leave the path, find them each one, stopping to break off any excess, and then hand it over to Hank. Hank thought of that now—a walking stick—he desperately needed one if he was going to keep moving. Soon enough, he found one and broke off the twigs jutting from the side of the branch.

He shimmied himself down to the airboat, using the walking stick as a dragging anchor, and lowered himself into the boat. He grabbed the map, used the sturdy lip at the top of the branch to gain purchase, and then he pulled himself up—pain sliced through him with every inch he gained—and he limped his way back to the car.

"I can't stop thinking about taking the knife out. I feel it every time I move. God, Hank. I never thought something could feel so awful." Lisa's voice was laced with sadness when she spoke, a lament for a time when her body had been intact. Her skin was as pale as the wan moonlight hanging over the water. Her eyelids heavy as stones. Hank thought it would be a miracle if she made it to the hospital conscious.

They both screamed and grunted, as he awkwardly helped her get into the car. Afterward, he had to lean back against the car to catch his breath. In those seconds, while he steadied his hitching breath, he worried over Lisa's state and his ability to actually drive them back to civilization. Birth pangs of withdraw were setting in as well, right alongside the dehydration. He was no longer receiving the wean of suboxone or methadone or whatever they had been sluicing into him to keep withdraw at bay. The hallucinations and the vomiting would come for him later. There to embrace him again with their sallow, gangrenous arms.

If he passed out or got too sick to drive, they would need help.

In that moment, fate took pity on him and conjured back up something his father said to him: *His phone is fucked, trust me.* But Hank wondered now if his father had been in the best state to judge that.

With the labored walk of old man using a cane, Hank returned to the edge of the Portal, fighting the urge to look in on his father, and, using the stick for support, and gritting his teeth to endure yet another titanic round of agony while he bent over, he rifled through the dead man's pockets. He grabbed the keys, grateful that his hands seemed not to have suffered any nerve damage. Then, spotting a glint of moonlight reflecting of an object close by, he shuffled over—still bent over—and picked up the phone. The screen was indeed cracked, but the phone still worked. Hank saw that it needed a thumbprint verification to open. Avoiding looking into the empty eyes, with a shaky arm, he hoisted up the man's hand, steadied his wrist, and pressed his dead thumb down on the spider-webbed screen.

It opened.

The phone had service and though it was slow, it eventually connected to the internet. After a quick search, Hank had directions to a small hospital. They were about forty minutes out.

He planned to call 911 as soon as they hit the highway. Tell them a mile marker or landmark or something, the name of the hospital, the direction they were heading, and a description of the car. He would also warn them, in case they didn't make it, to look for a wrecked or pulled-over SUV.

Finally making it back to the car, where Lisa waited—her eyes closed, her breathing shallow—Hank asked, "You ready?"

"God, yes."

Chapter 63

When the car roared to life, Everett gasped a sigh of relief.

Time to let go.

The damnable thing about it was, though he kept bleeding and bleeding, his body held on. When would the moment come? He had already lost count of the times he thought he was right on the precipice. But his heart still kept beating, blood still kept circulating. Air into the lungs. Thoughts into the mind.

Not quite how he had pictured it: dying in a shed filled with human horrors, next to a forgotten swamp, with the embodiment of evil bleeding out on the other side of the room.

The Black-Eyed Man had been talking to him, his voice faint. At first, Everett ignored him, but as he continued to speak, Everett thought, *What the hell? Not like I have much longer, anyway.*

Using the wall for support, Everett shuffled along it until he was within earshot of the man. Along the way, he noticed *his* blood loss had slowed.

After he had settled closer, the man asked a familiar question, one Everett had heard a million times.

"Do you believe in God, Everett Grant?"

"As a matter of fact, I do."

"Much as I suspected. You have the look of a Godly man. There is a peace that people of God carry in their face, a serenity that suffuses their mien, whether they realize it or not."

Cockeyed, Everett looked back to the man—this monster that had been an agent of misery, destroying countless lives, inflicting bloodshed that would echo for years—unsure how to respond to all the ten-dollar words. Then, he asked his own question: "Can a man like you believe in God?"

The Black-Eyed Man grinned, exposing his giant white teeth, coated in a membranous red veil. "A man like me does awful things because of God."

"You mean because of the devil."

"No, you see, to me, God and the devil are one in the same. Unlike you, I just believe in all aspects of Him, the good and the bad. I suppose, too, that I just thought He'd never make good on His promise of damnation for evil acts." The man turned his head, meeting Everett eye to eye. Everett gazed into the two back holes. "No father can ever truly forsake his son, can he, Everett?"

He continued to speak, embarking on the philosophical brain dump of a man that knew the end was in the offing. His voice weakened with each word. He didn't have long. "I used to look out into the night and wonder if God would speak to me. Or maybe He would let *her* speak to me. The starless nights were the ones I cherished the most. Nothing but black, stretching as far as I could see. I'd sit with my legs dangling off the side of the brick building I lived in and look out into the endless black."

"Why didn't you like the stars?" Everett felt a flash of disgust at himself for engaging. But he was actually curious about the answer.

"They distracted me. If I stared at them, then I couldn't focus on the echoes. There were two times, just two, where I heard a voice. It came in waves, carried on the wind. I kept going back and listening, hoping to hear what had become of my mother. I wanted to know which world she now called home. But the selfish son of a bitch wouldn't let her tell me. He kept *her* to Himself. *God is a hoarder.* Piling up all of life's mysteries like treasure, and hiding them from us." He hissed these last words. Like Silvia, even on the edge of death, this man couldn't divorce himself from his anger.

Anger was one of the only things he had left.

That, and a grudge against his Creator. Moments ago, blood had been pouring out of the Black-Eyed Man in dollops, but Everett could see that the stream had stopped flowing; his heart was still beating, but the pressure in his veins was fading.

But even as the shadow of death enveloped him, he continued his speech, never showing a second's remorse for the torture he had meted out.

No regrets. No elegies for days gone by. All that was left was the grudge.

Everett was shocked that this man, after all the evil shit he had done, still felt he was owed something. "So, what did the voice say to you?"

"Both times, I asked the Black where my mother was, and all I heard back was one word: Safe."

Everett's faith allowed him to give the man the benefit of the doubt. He believed that God spoke to those willing to listen. And, truthfully, he didn't think twice when the man said God spoke to him. Where Everett found fault was the man's intransigence; his stubbornness; his lack of humility; his inability to see the gift God had laid at his feet. God's voice had travelled on the wind, against the backdrop of a starless night, and tried to comfort this man with a single word. But the man couldn't see the beauty in the benediction God sent him. Instead, he only saw the void left by his mother's death. He had sacrificed his whole existence to that void, leaving nothing but two hollow eyes, a black heart, and a mind as dark as the far reaches of the universe—no stars, no planets, no life, and no light—only the absence of it.

"I cursed Him as a liar. And ordered Him to tell me where she was. Nothing happened. Nothing changed. Night after night, I just stared out and all I saw was black. He... He... took her—"

He tried to speak again, lips moving, mouthing the words, but no sound came out. Blood spurted from his mouth, staining his chin and his neck in a scarlet bib. He kept trying, but nothing came.

His back slid against the wall as his upper half keeled over to the floor; a popping noise echoed when his face collided with the dirt floor. A dark island of red formed a boundary around him.

The Black-Eyed Man disappeared into eternity.

Chapter 64

Everett did his level best to hold the slimy ropes of his intestines within his skin, having to again use one of the sick wall ornaments to pull himself up. Dizziness sent his world flying off-kilter. He closed his eyes and stood still. Eventually, things fell back into place. Girding himself for his final steps, he sauntered to the door in a slow, deliberate shuffle. Before stepping out into the night, he looked back at the Black-Eyed Man's lifeless body—thanking God his eyelids had curtained those eyes. As he did, something occurred to him, an elemental question he had never asked the man.

Everett had never asked him his name.

#

The Black-Eyed Man's passing marked the last death inside the Portal. Time and space had realigned.

Chapter 65

Hank did the driving; his left leg dangled off the driver's seat, limp and worn. He kept checking to make sure Lisa was still conscious. For now, the mission was to get her to a hospital, which distracted him from ill thoughts of leaving his father to die. But those ghosts would come to greet him in the quiet of night. Of that, he was certain.

They were on a small, beaten-up highway. In about ten miles or so, judging by the digital map on the dead man's phone, it connected up to a larger highway that led to civilization, and if the information was right, a rural hospital. Hank had already called 911, reporting their circumstances. He felt like he was going to make it, but now even if something went wrong, the paramedics should be able to find them. How he would explain why he had this phone or this car, or their severe injuries, he had no clue.

In the meantime, too, withdraw had crept in. At this moment, it was only shakes and stomach pain. He'd have been sweating non-stop too if he hadn't been so dehydrated. Later, it would be vomiting, world-class nausea, hallucinations, and for another round of fun, maybe even seizures. He'd be at a hospital by then, though. Maybe they could prevent him from having to slide full-scale into the mad carnival of detox.

Since he started to drive, Lisa hadn't said a word. From what Hank could tell, she was spending her time trying to catch her breath. Her breathing was smoother now, less taxed, but still fast and short. She had her back pinned against the seat, doing her best not to move in the slightest, lest she upset the knife still buried in her.

Hank looked at her several times, trying without words to offer comfort. But she was looking out the window, eyes growing heavy.

Shame and disgust overwhelmed him every time he looked at the open wound on her arm and the knife—it was impossible not to see that fucking thing.

This was all his fault.

#

Lisa could feel herself fading. She couldn't seem to get a full breath into her lungs. Every time, she came up short. Fast and shallow, oxygen deprivation making her dizzy, making her float off. The pain was still there too. But it was becoming fuzzy and faint, taking on a sense of unreality.

Days from now, lying in a hospital bed, with all manner of tubes sprawling out of her arms like tendrils and with a jarring symphony of beeps and alarms constantly sounding around her, she would think back on what she had said to Hank in the car. It was the last thing she remembered doing before slipping off into the black. At the time, even through the dream-like fog induced by her injuries and her fatigue, she had remembered Everett's dying wish to her. *Tell him what I told you that night. It should come from you.*

A sense of urgency had gripped her. Because when she floated off, she might not wake back up. This could be it; she could be dying, at least that's what she had thought at the time.

She had always liked Everett, and if these were to be her last words, well, then there were far worse ways to spend your final seconds.

Through cracked lips, she spoke in a near-whisper. Her tone was weak—and in the hospital, as she thought back on it, her voice had the careworn lull her grandmother would take on when discussing the latest horrors on the local news—she had told Hank his dad's theory of the most powerful force in the universe.

"Listen to me, Hank." Hank looked at her, seemingly comforted by the sound of her voice. "Just listen to me." She tried to stay stock-still as she spoke. Hank's sharp blue eyes were small under the swelling. He kept swiveling his head to her and then turning to look back at the road. Each time he did it, a wave of nausea crashed through her. "Hank. Stop moving.

317

Just look forward." He straightened up and looked ahead. She picked a point right at the side of his ocean blue eye and held it to hopefully mute the fire in her belly long enough to say what she had to say. Doing her best to repeat Everett's words verbatim, she told Hank Everett's story.

Here were his words that had lived on in Lisa's head, best she could remember:

"When I was younger, a tornado ripped through Hermitage. Killed twenty-two people, which was a big deal for a town of about only two thousand. Just came through one night and wiped out an entire neighborhood. Then jumped Highway 17 and kicked trailers around like they were board game pieces. The day after—I was old enough to ride my bike by then—I rode around looking at the damage. I had never seen anything like it. Wood and metal piled up as far as I could see. Like God had a tantrum and just decided to demolish His project and start over. After that, for a long time, I thought I had seen the strongest force in the universe.

"It wasn't until I started going to AA when we got down here, that I learned there was something much stronger out there. I'd listen to people's stories about what their addiction did to all the people they loved. Their mothers, their fathers, their kids, their girlfriends, boyfriends, spouses. Some of them would say that their wife or husband just got fed up and left. That's what I expected. I figured that everyone in their right mind would leave a drunk, dope-fiend like me behind in the dust. Who would stick around with someone like that? Who the hell would stand by someone that time after time will choose the dope over their loved ones? But here were all these people who were still married, still together. Hell, some of their significant others would come with them to the meetings. Proud of their spouse. Loyal beyond all reason.

"And that's when I finally realized it: Mother Nature only destroys what is already doomed anyway. People, houses, trees, all things renting time here on Earth before inevitably returning to it. But as strong as she is, Mother Nature can't compete with the thing, or force, or essence— whatever the hell you want to call it—that makes you love someone. Because it doesn't come from this Earth or even this life; it is something that none of us really understand.

"Some of those people that got fed up may never have loved their addict spouse. But the ones that did, and still decided to leave, fooled themselves into thinking they can outsmart the strongest force in the universe.

"That's why you're here, Lisa. You can't stop what you can't choose."

Chapter 66

The small pond reminded Everett of the one hidden in the woods behind his house when he was a boy, where he and his friend Billy would go skip rocks, and later on, sneak a cigarette or two. Using the damp grass and foxtails as a makeshift bed, he laid down to look at the stars. He could taste and smell the brackish water coming off the damp mud.

At first, he saw the man's eyes, forever black, speaking of an eternity of nothingness. But the image soon faded, overtaken by the thing that had salvaged Everett's soul.

Time faded.

He was back in April's house; it was 1985, and he bobbed Hank up and down in his arms and stared into his pure blue eyes.

Then Everett Grant stepped into eternity.

END

Made in the USA
Columbia, SC
10 March 2023

13495799R00195